THE WOMAN OF COLOUR

broadview editions
series editor: L.W. Conolly

West Indian Creole Woman with her Black Servant, c. 1780 (oil on canvas) by Agostino Brunias, (1728-96) ©Yale Center for British Art, Paul Mellon Collection, USA. Used by permission.

THE WOMAN OF COLOUR
A Tale

Anonymous

edited by Lyndon J. Dominique

broadview editions

Library and Archives Canada Cataloguing in Publication

The woman of colour / Anonymous ; edited by Lyndon J. Dominique.

(Broadview editions)
Includes bibliographical references.
ISBN 978-1-55111-176-6

I. Dominique, Lyndon Janson, 1972-   II. Series.

PR3991.A1W64 2007   823'.7   C2007-903458-6

Broadview Editions

The Broadview Editions series represents the ever-changing canon of literature in English by bringing together texts long regarded as classics with valuable lesser-known works.

Advisory editor for this volume: Michel Pharand

Broadview Press is an independent, international publishing house, incorporated in 1985. Broadview believes in shared ownership, both with its employees and with the general public; since the year 2000 Broadview shares have traded publicly on the Toronto Venture Exchange under the symbol BDP.

We welcome comments and suggestions regarding any aspect of our publications—please feel free to contact us at the addresses below or at broadview@broadviewpress.com.

North America
Post Office Box 1243, Peterborough, Ontario, Canada K9J 7H5
3576 California Road, Post Office Box 1015, Orchard Park, NY, USA 14127
Tel: (705) 743-8990; Fax: (705) 743-8353;
email: customerservice@broadviewpress.com

UK, Ireland, and continental Europe
NBN International, Estover Road, Plymouth PL6 7PY UK
Tel: 44 (0) 1752 202300   Fax: 44 (0) 1752 202330
email: enquiries@nbninternational.com

Australia and New Zealand
UNIREPS, University of New South Wales
Sydney, NSW, 2052 Australia
Tel: 61 2 9664 0999; Fax: 61 2 9664 5420
email: info.press@unsw.edu.au

www.broadviewpress.com

This book is printed on paper containing 100% post-consumer fibre.

Typesetting and assembly: True to Type Inc., Claremont, Canada.

PRINTED IN CANADA

For people of all colours, everywhere.

Contents

Acknowledgements

I would like to thank the British Library, whose copy of the first edition of *The Woman of Colour* was used to check this edition. Generous summer research grants from Princeton and Georgetown Universities allowed me to begin and complete this work. I must also thank my undergraduate and graduate students in "Crossing Boundaries in Eighteenth-Century Prose Fiction" and "Critical Race Studies and Eighteenth-Century British Literature" at Georgetown for many stimulating discussions about this novel. The Earl of Mansfield kindly allowed me to use the detail of Dido Elizabeth Belle's portrait taken from the painting in the collection of the Earl of Mansfield, Scone Palace. The excerpt from Jane Austen's *Fragment of a Novel* (Appendix C2) is reprinted by kind permission of Oxford University Press. My excellent colleagues Dennis Todd, Kathy Temple, Angelyn Mitchell, Louise Bernard, Scott Heath, Mark McMorris, Patricia O'Connor, Kelley Wickham-Crowley, Gay Cima, Michael Ragussis, and John Glavin have offered tremendously helpful research suggestions along the way, as did Claudia L. Johnson and Jonathan Lamb at the very beginning and Emily M. Belcher at the very end. The editorial team at Broadview Press—Leonard Conolly, Marjorie Mather, Julia Gaunce, and Michel Pharand— were a pleasure to work with. Immense thanks for all your sound advice and suggestions concerning this project. I gained invaluable support from Julian Snr., Julian Joseph, Jan, and Sandra Pierre, Juanita Beau-Pierre, Frankie, Karen and Kai John-Lewis, Timothy, Fumi and Andre Alexander, Emmanuel Fevrier, Jean and Vernon Nembhard, Louise, Enord and Valdora Leatham, Carla, Chantel and Charisma Nash, Andrina Dominique, Leroy Dominique, Simon Regis, Alonzo Brown, Roderick McGuire, Tammy Brown, Danielle Elliot, Rufina Prevost, Elizabeth Velez, Terry Carter, Corey Daniels, and the Dominique, Pierre, Nembhard, Merryfield, Charles, John-Lewis, and Regis families. This book is also dedicated to my mother and father, Rita and Victor Dominique, whose unconditional love and support made my work on *The Woman of Colour* both easy and rewarding.

Introduction

Spectral and Literal Black Heroines in Eighteenth Century British Literature

Two of the most unexplored lines of critical inquiry in contemporary studies of British literature have to be the roles that black heroines play, and the influence they collectively wield, in long prose fiction written during the long eighteenth century.[1] These women usually fall into two distinct categories. First, minor black heroines such as Savannah in Amelia Opie's *Adeline Mowbray* (1805) or Anana in Sophia Lee's *The Recess* (1785) perform acts of heroism designed to support the white female explicitly acknowledged as the lead character in the novel's title or plot. For the rarer, second type of black heroine the reverse is true: a black woman is explicitly acknowledged in a novel's title or plot as the major character supported by a white female cast. Yet, in one notable instance, this reversal does not appear to enhance the status of eighteenth-century prose fiction's most celebrated black heroine.

Imoinda may be the leading lady in Aphra Behn's seminal work *Oroonoko* (1688), but her heroic impact is certainly diminished by the fact that she appears "only flickeringly"[2] in the

---

1 Felicity Nussbaum's *Limits of the Human: Fictions of Anomaly, Race and Gender in the Long Eighteenth Century* (Cambridge: Cambridge UP, 2003) offers the most recent analysis of the influence of black women and men from this period. Nussbaum's book is preceded and complimented by other important examinations of race and gender both inside and outside eighteenth century studies, notably Roxann Wheeler's *The Complexion of Race: Categories of Difference in Eighteenth-Century British Culture* (Philadelphia: U of Pennsylvania P, 2000), Kim Hall's *Things of Darkness: Economies of Race and Gender in Early Modern England* (Ithaca: Cornell UP, 1995), Jennifer Devere Brody's *Impossible Purities: Blackness, Femininity and Victorian Culture* (Durham: Duke UP, 1998), and Dwight A. McBride's *Impossible Witnesses: Truth, Abolition and Slave Testimony* (New York: NYU Press, 2001).

2 Joyce Green Macdonald, "The Disappearing African Woman: Imoinda in *Oroonoko* After Behn" *English Literary History* 66 (1999) 76. Macdonald's charge has since been countered by Joseph M. Ortiz who claims "Imoinda's vagueness is strategic" in "Arms and the Woman: Narrative, Imperialism and Virgilian *Memoria* in Aphra Behn's *Oroonoko*," *Studies in the Novel* 34 (2002) 121.

novella, while outside of it, her character has been largely ignored during 300 years of criticism that have privileged Behn's heroic roles as first professional woman writer and literary abolitionist.[1] Little wonder then that the period's other prose fiction black heroines are such a critically unexplored group; if the most influential one cannot appear more forcefully within her own text, we assume that the others must not only be more scarce, but make even less of an impression, in theirs.

Critical race work done in an earlier field of British literary studies, however, allows us to refute this assumption. Kim Hall and other early modern race critics believe that black female characters have a definite literary impact even when they are textually absent. Hall has, long since, urged early modernists to engage in the process of "reading what isn't there,"[2] a process which produces readings that are resistant to the dominant culture's view of black women. For instance, by historically contextualizing a jest Lancelot Gobbo makes about a Moorish woman in *The Merchant of Venice*, Hall shows how this critically "unnoticed black woman" can be read as a figure of power who subverts Shakespeare's comedic use of her body and, instead, projects a "fertility as dangerous and ultimately disruptive of the desired homology between Christianity and economic vitality."[3] Similarly, Lynda Boose describes black women in early modern texts as "unrepresentable" because the British male writers who dominated literary production were fearful of a black woman "whose signifying capacity as a mother threatens nothing less than the wholesale negation of white patriarchal authority."[4] From Boose and Hall, then, we learn to read "unrepresentable" or "unnoticed" examples of black fertility in British texts as threats to dominant systems of representation controlled by white men. While offering a way to assess the significance of even the most trivial black female representation, this early modern premise also allows us to begin constructing a reading of Imoinda

---

1 Ortiz agrees with this assessment and his essay is an attempt to re-establish "the centrality of the figure of Imoinda (who, to some extent, has also been confined to the margins of critical attention)." Ibid. 121.

2 "Reading What Isn't There: 'Black' Studies in Early Modern England," *Stanford Humanities Review* 3 (1993) 23-33.

3 Ibid. 30.

4 Lynda E. Boose, "'The Getting of a Lawful Race': Racial discourse in early modern England and the unrepresentable black woman," Chapter 2 of *Women, "Race" & Writing in the Early Modern Period*, ed. Margo Hendricks and Patricia Parker (London: Routledge, 1994) 46.

and the influence this "flickering" black doyenne of eighteenth-century prose fiction commands in British culture.

It was, perhaps, the fleeting image of her as a "big" (with child) black woman in Behn's text that threatened Thomas Southerne—frightened him even—and influenced him to change her heavily-pregnant, black African body into a nominally-pregnant white one in his extremely popular stage adaptation of *Oroonoko*.[1] By blanching Behn's heroine and de-emphasizing her pregnancy, Southerne begins nullifying the threatening influence of a fertile black heroine in a process that Joyce Green Macdonald has, somewhat erroneously, called the "disappearing African woman." Macdonald correctly describes Southerne's play as the first of many in which British men rewrite *Oroonoko*,[2] each time erasing the central role Behn's black Imoinda played in the original story with a white replacement whose presence suppresses the threat of "conflict—racial conflict, as well as the gender conflict between white men and white women played out through the bodies of black women."[3] But these successive acts of erasure do not require that the *African* woman disappear, as Macdonald's title contends; it is, specifically, the *fertile black African* woman who must vanish. British rewritings of *Oroonoko* show that while this type of black woman had limited appeal for writers of literature, the nominally-pregnant white woman *becomes* the pre-eminent and visually acceptable African woman of color with mass appeal in the eighteenth century.[4]

The slue of white, nominally-pregnant Imoindas in dramatic

1 See Macdonald's "Disappearing African Woman" and Nussbaum's "Black Women: Why Imoinda Turns White" (*Limits of the Human*, Chapter 6) for more discussion of Imoinda's change from a black to a white woman. I consider Imoinda's pregnancy nominal because none of the frontispieces or stage directions to *Oroonoko* plays present the "big" (with child) body that Behn describes in her novella.

2 John Hawkesworth (1759), Francis Gentleman (1760), John Ferriar (1786), and an anonymous author (1760) all wrote versions of *Oroonoko* with white Imoindas.

3 Macdonald, "The Disappearing African Woman," *ELH* 66, 81-82.

4 Srinivas Aravamudan writes that, "Southerne's Imoinda, though white, still possesses some 'ethnic' qualities carried over from Behn's novella, making her an 'Indian' and a 'Heathen'." See *Tropicopolitans* (Durham and London: Duke UP, 2000) 57. Curiously, he does not consider the African origin of these 'ethnic qualities' despite the West African roots of Behn's original heroine. I contend that the ethnic qualities carried over from Behn's novella to Southerne's play are all mere signifiers of the original heroine's geographic connection to Africa.

versions of *Oroonoko* gives the impression that only British male writers were interested in a particular type of popular African heroine.[1] Women writers were, too. At the end of the period, Claire de Duras writes *Ourika* (1823) and introduces to French society a black Senegalese woman whose characterization undergoes as deliberate a process of racial and reproductive muting as Southerne's Imoinda. Originally a novella, *Ourika* was poised to receive as popular a response on the French stage as *Oroonoko* did in England because Duras completely contains the threat of a fertile black African woman's body on display when she shrouds Ourika's once "fashionably beautiful figure"[2] in a nun's habit. Ourika's deliberate transformation from a fertile African woman to a spiritual yet barren one allowed French audiences to identify with Duras' racially and sexually sanitized black heroine without fear or conflict and with the same, if not more, enthusiasm than British audiences had for Southerne's white African, Imoinda.[3]

Clearly, eighteenth-century African women influenced European audiences, but not in the same way as their early modern forebears. Viewed alongside Boose's and Hall's "unnoticed" and "unrepresentable" black heroines, Southerne and Duras' popular African heroines reveal that black women, who had the power to threaten dominant systems of representation in the early modern period, lose that power once muted representations of white and

---

1 This poem confirms that Imoinda's white "complexion" was used to sanitize what this observer saw as a salacious character which Henry Neville's *Isle of Pines* (1668) had already connected to a black woman: "Soft Imoinda's tender Air despise; / Beware the force of her designing Eyes: / She sells her Vertue, and complexion buys. / Who thinks her chaste, perchance may be mistook, / Her innocence is only in her look." "Against the Luxury of the Town in Eating and Drinking. A Satyr," in *Reflections, Moral, Comical, Satyrical, &c. on the Vices and Folies of the Age* (London: Printed 1707) 7-8.
2 Claire de Duras, *Ourika, an English Translation* by John Fowles (New York: MLA, 1994) 10. In the "Introduction" to this edition, Joan DeJean notes that there were four dramatic versions of *Ourika* within a few years of the original text (viii).
3 Women were enthusiastic about both texts. See *Oroonoko*, ed. Maximillian E. Novak and David Stuart Rodes (Lincoln: U of Nebraska P, 1976). My ideas build on Novak and Rodes' assumption that Southerne's skill at "pathetic tragedy" made *Oroonoko* "attractive to the ladies in the audience" (xvi). I suggest that Southerne's manipulation of the racial and sexual dynamics that Behn's text establishes has as much to do with the reasons why *Oroonoko* came to be known as "the Favourite of the Ladies" (xvi).

black African women appear in popular eighteenth-century texts. In other words, when blackness and fertility are deliberately sanitized, the African woman appeals to, rather than threatens, the dominant white culture.

However, Felicity Nussbaum's review of late eighteenth-century frontispieces to dramatic *Oroonoko*s complicates this conclusion. She finds a distinct strain of exoticism in the visual depictions of white Imoindas, which leads her to conclude that "Behn's Imoinda lingers over Southerne's altered version and other performances throughout the period. Black women in the eighteenth century are not so much *absent* as they are a spectral *presence* that links desire with fear, dread, physical defect, and monstrosity."[1] By exploring how black women are a "spectral *presence*" haunting both dramatic *Oroonoko*s and a dominant white culture that deliberately excludes them, Nussbaum harks back to Boose, Hall, and Macdonald and builds on their "unnoticed," "unrepresentable," and "disappearing" readings of literary black women with the knowledge that the popular, appealing African heroine still retains elements of the original black woman's power to threaten the dominant white culture. Indeed, Nussbaum's work exposes the fact that the popular African heroine's appeal to the British depended on the repression of the threats that the original Imoinda embodied—threats that ultimately re-surface in the exoticized depictions of white Imoindas at the century's end.[2]

This knowledge about the black woman's 'spectral presence' has the potential to expand current thinking about the black female influence at the height of the British abolition movement during the last half of the long eighteenth century. Countless historians tell us that there were more black men than black women in England at this time, men who arrived in Britain as sailors on merchant ships, as soldiers who fought for the British in the American Wars of Independence, or as domestics brought over to work for absentee colonial masters.[3] Black men were more visible not only on the streets of port cities like London and Bristol but

---

1 Nussbaum, *Limits of the Human*, 188.
2 Further examples of the way people of color influence the British psyche can be found in Appendix E.
3 For discussions of black people in Britain, see Peter Fryer, *Staying Power: The History of Black People in Britain* (New Jersey: Highlands Press, 1984); Folarin Shyllon, *Black People in Britain* (London; New York: Oxford UP, 1977); Norma Myers, *Reconstructing the Black British Past 1780-1830* (London; Portland, OR: Frank Cass, 1996); Gretchen Gerzina, *Black London: Life Before Emancipation* (Rutgers: Rutgers UP, 1995).

as the figures over which the political debates and iconography of British slavery depended: it was James Sommersett whose plight Granville Sharpe championed in England, giving rise to the Mansfield Judgement of 1772;[1] it was a kneeling black man that Josiah Wedgwood emblazoned on his slave medallions; it was Ottobah Cugoano's polemic that offered the slave's most direct criticism of slavery.[2]

Little was done to counter this masculine imbalance. Although famous images showing slaves lining the interiors of slave ships like *The Brooks* (1788) clearly depicted women in the middle passage, Moira Ferguson has shown that white British women writers initially usurped the discourse of slavery in order to shed light on their own gender oppression, and only offered focused resolutions about the treatment of women slaves "toward the end of the campaign."[3] The greater preponderance of black men in British culture and antislavery iconography coupled with the fact that antislavery rhetoric lay in the hands of white male politicians and female activists un-attuned to, or indifferent about, the specifics of gender and slavery, altogether illustrate the pronounced relegation of the black woman to the fringes of eighteenth-century racial representation. Yet, with Nussbaum in mind, we must ask in what ways this spectral black female's presence on the fringes haunts the abolitionist representations promoted by white activists. Are black women deliberately excised from the forefront of abolitionist representation because black men are more appealing symbols? If so, what can be said about the repressed desires and fears of the white activists who enforce this exclusion?

Questions like these will certainly add to our understanding of the ways black women influence the white British cultural imag-

---

1 Concerning the Mansfield Judgement, it is worth pointing out that, "All Mansfield said was that a master could not by force compel a slave to go out of England. Black slavery still existed there. Long after the Somersett case advertisements for the sale of black slaves continued to appear in English newspapers." *Staying Power,* 125-26.

2 Published in 1787, *Thoughts and Sentiments on the Evil and Wicked Traffic of the Slavery and Commerce of the Human Species* was "Humbly Submitted to the Inhabitants of Great Britain by Ottobah Cugoano, a Native of Africa." For more about Cugoano and his work see Vincent Carretta's introduction to *Thoughts and Sentiments* (Middlesex, England: Penguin, 1999).

3 Moira Ferguson *Subject to Others: British Women Writers and Colonial Slavery 1670-1834* (London and New York: Routledge, 1992) 4.

ination. But a 'spectral' approach still leaves one pressing and important question wholly unanswered: who were these women *really*? A rich array of living subjects from the period provides a tentative answer to this question. The eighteenth-century black woman is seen dancing a jig with a white working-class man in an illustration from Tom and Jerry's routs around London; she is Elizabeth Rosina Clemens, servant to the famously parsimonious painter Joseph Nollekens; she is reported as Silvia Woodcock, whose murder led to the execution of her husband, William, in 1789; she is Black Moll, the proprietor of a well known London bordello; she is Dido Elizabeth Belle, the black grand-niece of Lord Chief Justice Mansfield whose enigmatic portrait graces the cover of this edition.[1] Far from wholly spectral then, the black woman's presence in the eighteenth century is *literal* and *pervasive*; she's written-about, caricatured, painted, commented-on and sympathized-with at all societal levels. But she's never known. Even though her literal presence makes numerous impressions in the white cultural imagination, the fleeting, ephemeral nature of these impressions do not successfully inform her "real" identity.

If critics rely too heavily on spectral impressions, contemporary race studies risks unnecessarily reproducing what Ziggi Alexander calls a "sketchy picture"[2] of the lives and influence of black women in pre-twentieth century British culture—limited because it tells only half a tale. To know the black woman further, to understand her influence in more detail, we need primary source material that represents her interiority. But, as Alexander notes, "black women have not been considered suitable subjects for study, even when a great deal of evidence is readily available"; contemporary race "studies have concentrated on the activities of

---

1   See Fryer, *Staying Power*, 75-77; Nussbaum, *Limits of the Human*, 162-69; and Gerzina, *Black London*, 68-89 for discussions of these and other eighteenth-century black women in England. Pierce Egan's *Life in London, or Days and Nights of Jerry Hawthorne and his elegant friend Corinthian Tom* (New York: D. Appleton & Company, 1904) p. 227, contains the print of the dancing black woman. For Sylvia Woodcock (a mulatto East Indian) see *The British Tribunal for 1789. Containing the Most Remarkable Trials for Street and Highway Robberies, Murder etc. from the Notes of a Student who Attends the Different Judicial Courts* (London: J.S. Barr, 1790). For Dido Elizabeth Belle see Gene Adams, "A Black Girl at Kenwood; An Account of the Protégée of the First Lord Mansfield," *Camden History Review* 12 (1984) 10-14.

2   Ziggi Alexander "Let it lie Upon the table: The Status of Black Women's Biography in the UK," *Gender and History* 2 (1990) 24.

men," and British academics are indifferent to the fact that a "greater knowledge of [black] women's lives would provide a fascinating insight into the race, gender and class politics of their time."[1] To alter this imbalance, Alexander discusses Mary Seacole's *Wonderful Adventures* (1857) as a Crimean War nurse and businesswoman, and explores the celebrated life of this nineteenth-century black heroine largely ignored by the academic community until the republication of her narrative in the 1980s. She implies that Seacole's existence is just as relevant "to the totality of the international African experience, continental and diaspora particularly in the Americas"[2] as Marcus Garvey, the man usually associated with pan-Africanism.

With its substantive case for excavating and critically acknowledging a black woman's "literal" influence, Alexander's essay provides a jolt to eighteenth century studies. The "spectral presence" discussed by Nussbaum is helpful but insufficient; it must be supplemented with more "literal" evidence from the period so that we obtain the most complete understanding of the life and influence of the eighteenth-century black woman. *The Woman of Colour* allows this work to begin. It presents the literal life of a black woman in Britain at a time when such characters are merely spectral presences in British literature; it informs, clarifies and compliments the "spectral" impression that currently dominates discussions of eighteenth-century black women; it provides a missing link in the narrative history of black heroines from Imoinda to Ourika; it allows us to gain some insight into the race and gender politics of the time as black women might have experienced them; and, finally, it answers Alexander's call for contemporary critics to champion black female narratives which have been left to "lie upon the table" as openly ignored as Mary Prince's petition for freedom was by Parliament in 1829.[3] This rare black woman's narrative deserves to be seen, not only because it is the first long prose fiction in British literature to prominently feature a racially-conscious mulatto heroine,[4] but also because, conceivably, a woman of color could have written it.

---

1 Ibid.
2 Ibid. 23.
3 Ibid. 29.
4 It is important to note that women of color who are not racially conscious appear in British literature well before 1808. My thanks to Laura J. Rosenthal for bringing to my attention the *Genuine Memoirs of the Late Celebrated Jane D****s* (1761), a text which provides a brief sketch of

The Woman of Colour: Term and Title

It is, at once, an astonishing fact and an egregious error that a long prose fiction about a black woman has been largely ignored for almost 200 years.[1] Thankfully, this was not its original fate. Published in 1808, *The Woman of Colour* received enough notice to attract three reviews in contemporary journals,[2] something that separates it from *Mansfield Park* (1814), a text which, Claudia Johnson tells us, was never critically reviewed by Austen's contemporaries,[3] yet is highly revered today for its subtext about slavery, colonialism, and empire. *The Woman of Colour* received only muted praise from critics. But the fact remains that contemporaries had read it and reviewers were commenting on it in the leading literary journals, thus making the reading public aware of it. *The Woman of Colour*, as novel

---

the eponymous heroine's black father and white mother but makes no further use or mention of her race. Jane and Mrs. Llwhuddwhydd from *The Dramatic History of Master Edward, Miss Ann, Mrs. Llwhuddwhydd and Others. The Extraordinaries of These Times. Collected from Zaphaniel's Original Papers* (1743) are, thus, examples of the fact that women of color have long been a presence in eighteenth-century British literature, in texts where their racial identities have been signified but never expounded upon with the sustained force that we find in *The Woman of Colour*.

1   To my knowledge, E.M. McClelland was the first to, briefly, bring the novel to the attention of contemporary critics in *Comparative Studies in Society & History* 9 (1967) 355-56. Thereafter, *Impossible Purities*, Chapter 1 discusses it. Further efforts to increase awareness about it are crucial, since Felicity Nussbaum notes that "there are very few accounts of black women traveling from the East or West Indies, Africa or the South Pacific, real or imagined, to eighteenth century England" (*Limits*, 162). Additionally, Sara Salih believes that "Mary Prince's *History* is the first narrative of the life of a black woman to be published in England" (London: Penguin, 2000), vii; while Joan DeJean states that Ourika is "the first black heroine in a novel set in Europe" (*Ourika*, xi). Obviously, claims such as these need to be re-evaluated in light of *The Woman of Colour*.

2   See Appendix F.

3   Jane Austen, *Mansfield Park*, ed. Claudia Johnson (New York: Norton, 1998) xi.

or review, was definitely positioned to be seen, if not read, by many.[1]

It is, perhaps, more astonishing that this tale managed to gain critical attention at all considering it was published in a year that was, quite literally, bursting at the seams with new long prose fictions. In the tremendously useful analysis accompanying his *Bibliographical Survey*, Peter Garside has already shown that 1808 was an anomalous year in the history of English publishing since it was the only one within the thirty year period from 1800-1829 in which more than one hundred works of long fiction were published.[2] This means that despite an over-saturation, something must have made this text stand out from the many others eligible for critical attention. The question is, what?

The title provides one crucial answer.[3] After all, *The Woman of Colour* appears two years after Charles Fox, William Wilberforce and Lord Milbanke headed a summer of heated debates about abolition in the Lords and the Commons,[4] and one year after Britain officially abolished its involvement in the Atlantic slave trade. When the 1807 abolition bill came into effect, *The Woman of Colour* must have been well underway, if not completely finished in manuscript form prior to its publication at Samuel Hamilton's new printing press in Surrey. With its evocation of a racial character from the slave colonies, *The Woman of Colour* was topical, allowing publishers Black, Parry and Kingsbury to capitalize on the public's interest in British abolition.[5]

---

1   Peter Garside and his team of research associates state that, "8 out of 19 possible Circulating Libraries and 1 out of 5 possible Subscription Libraries" list *The Woman of Colour* in catalogues that they consulted which range geographically from London to Dublin between 1814 and 1834 (P. D. Garside, J. E. Belanger, and S. A. Ragaz, *British Fiction, 1800–1829: A Database of Production, Circulation & Reception*, designer A. A. Mandal <http://www.british-fiction.cf.ac.uk> [May 24 2006]: DBF Record No. 1808A019/Libraries).

2   A year-by-year chart outlining this information can be found in *The English Novel, 1770-1829: A Bibliographical Survey of Prose Fiction Published in the British Isles. Vol. II 1800-1829*, eds. Peter Garside, James Raven, and Rainer Schowerling (Oxford: Oxford UP, 2000), 73.

3   Ibid. 49-63 provides a helpful discussion about the importance of titles during this period.

4   For more on the abolition debates see *Substance of the Debates on a Resolution for Abolishing the Slave Trade* (London: Dawson's, 1968).

5   Both the publishers and the printer of *The Woman of Colour* were experienced in the book trade but relatively new commercial entities. Trade

But as revealing as the connection between publication date, title, and abolition seems, it can also be misleading. For the informed, contemporary reader, knowledgeable about people of color, the title actually announces that the tale is probably not about a traditional slave at all, and only tangentially about slavery and abolition. Where we today refer to 'people of color' as individuals of all races other than Caucasian, eighteenth-century Britons often understood this term to refer to specific groups of *free* people in the Americas—the *gens de couleur* in Haiti, free mixed-race and Negro North Americans, and mixed-race freedmen and women in Caribbean outposts such as Jamaica, the island where Olivia Fairfield, *The Woman of Colour*'s heroine, originates.[1]

As both Caribbean term and novel title, *The Woman of Colour* was unusual not simply because it announced a free black heroine at a time when they were scarce, but also because it distinguishes this heroine from other contemporary Caribbean heroes in popular British literature. "West Indian" was commonly used to refer to white colonials like Peregrine Lovel, "the young West Indian of fortune" in James Townley's farce *High Life Below Stairs* (1759), Mr. Belcour from Richard Cumberland's sentimental comedy *The West Indian* (1771), or Helena Wells' eponymous heroine *Constantia Neville, or The West Indian* (1800). These texts involve plots in which white colonials born and raised in the Caribbean are ultimately integrated into white British society after they have either shirked off their vulgar Caribbean excesses, as Lovel and Belcour do, or they have shown that they never had any to begin with, as Neville frequently points out. In these texts Britons see that white West Indians have the capacity to be just like them.

---

records indicate that Samuel Hamilton filed for bankruptcy in 1803 but opened a new press in Surrey in 1808. Booksellers Black and Parry added Kingsbury to the business in 1807 and traded under this arrangement until 1812.

1 Writing about Santo Domingo, Thomas Clarkson uses the term 'People of Colour' to include "Free Negroes, and all such as have the smallest mixture of negro-blood; many of whom are as white as any of the native West Indians" (*The True State of the Case Respecting the Insurrection at St. Domingo* (Ipswich: Printed by J. Bush, 1792) 4. However, the Jamaican historian, Bryan Edwards, excludes free Negroes in his definition of the term, limiting it exclusively to "people of mixed complexion" (see Appendix D). Politically, Olivia embodies more of Clarkson's view of the term than Edwards' since she is a mixed-race Jamaican woman who, as I will show, advocates for the freedom of black people of all colors.

"West Indian" is, of course, closely aligned and often used interchangeably with the term "Creole," and for good reason: both were colonial natives. The infamous Edward Long refers to "The native white men, or Creoles, of Jamaica"[1] as the "permanent natives" "who never have quitted the Island"[2] until they traveled to England to study, live lavishly, or reunite with family like the hero in Sir John Hill's *The Adventures of George Edwards, A Creole* (1751). But Creole Jamaicans were not only natives by birth. *The Secret History of the Life and Adventures of the Celebrated Polly Haycock* (1748) is written "By a Creole" who blends native "Creolians"[3] with nouveau-riche Jamaicans, like Polly, who were not born in the colony but primarily lived and made their wealth there. Race adds another level of complexity to the Creole term. Long mentions "Creole Blacks"[4] in his *History of Jamaica* (1773), implying that "Creole" meant anyone of any race who was born or socialized in a West Indian colony. Contemporary literary texts take this view a step further by emphasizing the racial indistinctiveness of the term. The heroine of Lucy Peacock's short story, "The Creole" (1786), is the daughter of an English merchant and a deceased Creole mother whose racial lineage is never openly discussed but perhaps inferred by her daughter's exoticized name, Zemira, and noticeably "dark"[5] complexion. Moreover, the hero in Samuel Arnold's gothic novel, *The Creole* (1796), is the son of Elmira, "a native of Circassia" who Selim, the emperor of Morocco and the Creole's father, "had purchased as a slave in Jamaica, where he had resided a considerable time."[6]

In popular British literature, then, "West Indians" are usually white and endowed with the potential to be integrated into British society, but 'Creoles' increasingly come to be seen as anything but British, white, or assimilable. This distinction caused much racial anxiety among white colonial women as Deidre

1 Edward Long, *The History of Jamaica. Or, General Survey of the Antient and Modern State of That Island: with Reflections on its Situation, Settlements, Inhabitants, Climate, Products, Commerce, Laws, and Government. In Three Volumes* (London: T. Lowndes, 1774) Vol. II. II. xiii. 261.

2 Ibid., 262.

3 *The Fortunate Transport, or The Secret History of the life and adventures of the celebrated Polly Haycock, the lady of the gold watch. By a Creole* (London. Printed for T. Taylor, 1748) 43.

4 *History of Jamaica*, II.xiii.262.

5 Lucy Peacock, "The Creole," taken from *The Rambles of Fancy; or, Moral and Interesting Tales* (London: Printed by T. Bensley, for the Author, 1786) 112. See Appendix A for the full text.

6 *The Creole, or The Haunted Island* (London: C. Whittingham, 1796) 2.

Coleman has addressed in detail.[1] Already prized in colonial societies starved of British women, white West Indian women resented creoleness as an affront to their beauty, Britishness, and whiteness. One literary mother, identified as a "vain and fashionable woman," writes that her daughter Louisa's "skin is *lamentable*; still as *brown* as a *Creolian*";[2] and in *Constantia Neville*, the heroine labels Felicia and Ned Carleton 'Afric-Creolian,' a racially inflected term designed to distinguish them from the white *West Indian* heroine in the title who culturally aligns herself with England. It is, however, the only extant account of a performance of Margaret Cheer's 1781 play, *West Indian Lady's Arrival in London*, that best illustrates the reason white West Indians resented being creolized. Cheer's white heroine is called a "West Indian Lady" in the title; yet the plot calls for this character to speak extensively in Jamaican dialect. The spectacle of a white woman publicly performing speech commonly associated with inferior Creole blacks so enraged the Jamaican whites who saw the play that Cheer was forced to publish an apologetic explanation for the character in the *Jamaican Gazette*.[3] Jamaican

1 See her essay "Janet Schaw and the Complexions of Empire," *Eighteenth-Century Studies* 36 (2003). Also see Appendix C1 for Musgrave's description of the manner in which the "distinction" between "creole young ladies" and girls of color is "kept up" in a British school.

2 Letter XIV "On the Acquirements of Girls in the Knowledge of Music, Needlework, Drawing, Dancing &c.—Thoughts on the Education of the Heart in preference to the Shewy Accomplishments," in *Letters Addressed to Two Young Married Ladies, on the Most Interesting Subjects* (Dublin: Printed for James and William Porter, and for John Cash, 1782) 208-10. Indeed, Edward Long describes the extreme lengths white Caribbean women went to 'secure' their whiteness when he writes, "The Creole white ladies, till lately, adopted the practice so far, as never to venture a journey, without securing their complexions with a brace of handkerchiefs; one of which being tied over the forehead, the other under the nose, and covering the lower part of the face, formed a compleat helmet." *The History of Jamaica* Vol. II. III. iii. 413.

3 Her letter appears in Richardson Wright's *Revels In Jamaica 1682-1838* (New York: Dodd, Mead, 1937) 155. The stigma of speaking in a Creole dialect is reflected further by this contemporary observer: "yet I must own myself most deplorably Ignorant, as to many of the *American* Languages, particularly those that are spoke in some of the more Inland Parts of that vast Continent... especially that beautiful pybald, black and white Lingo pallarber'd in its greatest purity by the *Creolians* of *Jamaica*" (John Armstrong, "To Omichron *Lick-Devil, esq. Printer in London"), in *Miscellanies. In Two Volumes* (London, 1770) 34-35. Also see Appendix D3 for Moreton's derision of Creole dialect.

whites obviously resented any display of Creole traits in complexion, lineage, or speech which implied that their women were more Negroid than white.

The Woman of Colour sets itself and its heroine apart from these white women who are anxious about the Caribbean terms that threaten to align them with Negroes. Olivia never identifies herself as a Creole or simply a West Indian. As the illegitimate issue of Mr. Fairfield, a white English planter, and Marcia, his African slave, she calls herself a "mulatto West Indian" (92) and blatantly draws attention to her African heritage with an openness that white Caribbean women rigorously avoid. This identification might have been a necessity rather than a choice, however, for Alexander tells us, "few mulattoes were ever in a position to disregard their African ancestry"[1] presumably because they were not light enough to pass as white. But by making racial identity an explicit part of its marketing strategy, the title displays certainty in, and full confidence about, both the novel's Caribbean backdrop and its heroine's African roots; this despite the fact that Jamaica and Jamaican mulattoes such as Olivia were usually stigmatized rather than venerated because the country's large mixed-race population stood as a constant reminder of its lax sexual mores. Of course, mulattoes were not the only ones stigmatized in this way; *Between Black and White*, Gad Heuman's examination of Jamaican people of color in the early nineteenth century, includes quadroons and octoroons among this group.[2] Thus, *The Woman of Colour* markets the interests of a wide swath of disparaged colored women—those whom Felicity Nussbaum calls the other women of empire and Jennifer DeVere Brody calls "mulattaroons."[3]

This generalization, however, should not detract from the text's specific use of Olivia's mulattoness. Her hybridity represents much more than the outcome of a union between a white slave master and his black female slave; it also announces another identity that results independently of such unions. One half of

---

1 "Let it Lie Upon the Table," 24.

2 *Between Black and White: Race, Politics, and the Free Coloreds in Jamaica 1792-1865* (Westport, Connecticut: Greenwood Press, 1981). Heuman's book offers a solid account of the political activities of people of color in Jamaica both pre- and post-emancipation.

3 *Torrid Zones: Maternity, Sexuality, and Empire in 18th Century English Narratives* (Baltimore: Johns Hopkins UP, 1995) 1. *Impossible Purities* (16).

this identity appears when Olivia calls herself "more than *half* an English woman," (111) an expression of female subjectivity that arises more from the instruction of her English governess, Mrs. Milbanke, than her English father. The other half appears in the pronounced yet muted African features that publicly confirm Olivia is 'more than half an African woman' like her deceased mother, Marcia. These overtly gendered, racial and cultural influences reveal that Olivia is a "mulatto West Indian" of *maternal descent*—one who manages to combine the cultural and racial excesses of her female lineage in a way that produces a well-balanced, rather than conflicted, identity. With her Africanized body on full display in England, Olivia subverts the societal stigmas and expectations of inferiority leveled at it by performing the identity she has learned from her governess—the one that Britons would least expect a black Caribbean woman to know well: English femininity. The result is a balanced double consciousness: Olivia embodies an "African-British" subjectivity which, in print, looks oxymoronic, but when performed makes perfect sense. Combining racial awareness with cultural entitlement, Olivia, like Mary Seacole after her, is a free black colonial subject who has as legitimate a claim to the privileges of citizenship routinely bestowed on whites in the newly constituted United Kingdom.[1]

Therein lies one of the fundamental conflicts at the heart of this novel.

The Woman of Colour: *Text*

Although Jamaican people of color could, biologically, lay claim to whiteness, they were systematically denied legal access to the fundamental privileges enjoyed by colonial whites. As Kathleen Wilson points out,

> Jamaican law created a bifurcated system that divided the numerous castes into four classes: whites, who alone had access to English common law and its most sacred plank, trial by jury; free people of color having special privileges granted by private acts; free people of color not possessing such privileges; and slaves.[2]

---

1 The 1800 Act of Union created the United Kingdom of Great Britain and Ireland.
2 Kathleen Wilson, *The Island Race: Englishness, Empire and Gender in the Eighteenth Century* (London: Routledge, 2003) 148.

Unlike many illegitimate offspring, Olivia carries her father's surname and a "nearly sixty thousand pound" (60) dowry, money presumably raised from the profits of Mr. Fairfield's Jamaican estate. These facts suggest that Olivia is one of Wilson's "free people of color having special privileges granted by private acts." The novel's main plot, however, shows how conflicted such "special privileges" are, and how egregious "private acts" can be, even in a father who is racially enlightened enough to hope "that a more liberal, a more distinguishing spirit" (58) present in his native country will help his daughter to a better life after his death.

Due to a special condition in her father's will, Olivia must travel to England where Augustus Merton, her Caucasian first-cousin who is described as the "image" (59) of her father, must agree to marry her and change his surname to 'Fairfield' in order to receive the 60,000 pound dowry. If Augustus refuses this lucrative arranged marriage, the money goes to his elder brother and sister-in-law, George and Letitia Merton, thereby forcing Olivia into a dependency on them for her maintenance. Thus, forty years before *Jane Eyre* (1847), *The Woman of Colour* plots a transatlantic marriage arranged by the will of an ostensibly benevolent white paternalist that disempowers the dark-skinned colonial woman, subjecting her to what seems to be a life of perpetual, legally-sanctioned, white male domination from the colony to the metropolis. However oppressive it, at first, seems, Mr. Fairfield's will may actually be laudatory when we consider that Jamaican law prevented people of color from owning personal property worth more than 2,000 pounds.[1] Forcing Olivia to be economically dependent on her male first cousins could be Mr. Fairfield's posthumous attempt to ensure that his daughter's wealth is protected by people who should have more than a mercenary interest in her welfare. And yet, as protective as this sounds, readers cannot ignore the will's uncomfortable demand that Olivia marry and reproduce with a man described as the "image" of her father—clearly evoking a crime of incest only once

---

1 This amount is recorded in Act 28, clause IX of 1761, "to prevent the inconveniences arising from exorbitant grants and devises made by white persons to negroes, and the issue of negroes; and to restrain and limit such grants and devises." *The Laws of Jamaica: Comprehending All The Acts In Force Passed Between the Thirty-Second Year of the Reign of King Charles The Second, and the Thirty-Third Year of the Reign of King George The Third.* Vol. II, The Second Edition (St. Jago de la Vega, Jamaica: Printed by Alexander Aikman, 1802).

removed from the plantation. With the valence of incest surrounding it, the benignity of Mr. Fairfield's will becomes suspicious, a suspicion made even more pronounced when Olivia expresses her own concerns to Mrs. Honeywood, a fellow traveler to England: "My father acted from the best of motives. If he erred, madam; if the *sequel* should *prove* that he has erred, give him credit, I conjure you, for the best intentions." (58)

The benevolent yet erring will of a father whose "private acts" disempower and abuse Olivia because they only offer the dubious 'special privileges' of arranged marriage and financial dependency parallels the behavior of a Jamaican paternalistic society which granted rights to people of color that were almost but not entirely equal to whites, and thus, only halfheartedly ensured their protection. Free black people like Elizabeth Ann Miller could petition influential whites or colonial assemblies for privileges reserved for whites only,[1] but even if they got them they were still constantly faced with the threat of having those rights revoked.[2] To stave off such egregious practices, people of color agitated politically for full rights of equality with whites. But in trying to safeguard their own interests they often ignored or trampled on the rights of Negro slaves.[3] Thus, caught between the racial categories black and white, people of color also teetered between the categories enslaved yet free, oppressors yet oppressed.

The Woman of Colour deliberately skews its representation of a person of color caught within these binaries because it is interested more in promoting Olivia as a woman enslaved and oppressed by white men rather than their equal as suppressors of freedom and oppressors of Negro slaves. The title emphasizes Olivia's hybridity and femininity; the plot, the consequences surrounding her enslavement to her father's will; and the text frequently underscores the prejudice she experiences in an ostensibly enlightened British society. Altogether, the novel deliberately compounds Olivia's helplessness and vulnerability

---

1 See Appendix G1.
2 Indeed, beginning in 1801, Miller spent six years trying to secure freedom for her children who were born free but had been trepanned back into slavery. See Jerome S. Handler's *The Unappropriated People: Freedmen in the Slave Society of Barbados* (Baltimore, MD; London, UK: Johns Hopkins UP, 1974) 60.
3 See Appendix D1 for Edwards' description of the way people of color treated Negro slaves.

as a young woman of color in an alien white society because there are political advantages to making her subjection wholly over-determined.

Although she is completely subject to the will of white men, and so essentially unguarded against the villainy of white women, like Letitia Merton and her friend, Miss Danby, who plot against her, Olivia is, nevertheless, called upon to act in ways that subvert her disempowered vulnerability as soon as she enters English society. She describes her first breakfast with the Mertons in this letter to Mrs. Milbanke:

A servant ... entered with a large plate of rice. Mrs. Merton half raised her head, saying—"set it there," pointing towards the part of the table where I sat.

"What is this?" asked Mr. Merton. "Oh, I thought that Miss Fairfield—I understood that people of your—I thought that you almost *lived* upon rice," said Mrs. Merton, "And so I ordered some to be got,—for my own part, I never tasted it in my life, I believe!" ... this was evidently meant to mortify your Olivia; it was blending *her* with the poor negro slaves of the West Indies! It was meant to show her, that, in Mrs. Merton's idea there was no distinction between us ... I could not be wounded at being classed with my brethren!"... I, perfectly unabashed and mistress of myself, pretended to take the mischievous officiousness, or impertinence (which you will), of Mrs. Merton in a literal sense; and, turning towards her, said, "I thank you for studying my palate, but I assure you there is no occasion; I eat just as you do, I believe: and though in Jamaica, our poor slaves (*my brothers and sisters*, smiling) are kept upon rice as their chief food, yet they would be glad to exchange it for a little of your nice wheaten bread here;" taking a piece of baked bread in my hand. (77–78)

Two different types of acting occur in this "rice scene." Letitia pretends to be the hospitable 'host' catering to Olivia's taste but really making a concerted effort to "mortify" her by "blending *her* with the poor negro slaves of the West Indies." Olivia also acts. Playing the part of the gracious "guest," she pretends to take Letitia's "impertinence ... in a literal sense" and forcefully turns the intended insult into a threatening revelation. Her "smiling" use of the words "brethren," and "*brothers and sisters*," diachronically confirms what the Mertons assembled at a breakfast table in Bristol cannot but acknowledge and the Bertrams assembled "in the evening circle"[1] at Mansfield Park would rather avoid discussing: the disempowered heroines seated in the company of nouveau riche families in *The Woman of Colour* and *Mansfield Park* are, indeed, spiritually and fraternally blended with West Indian slaves. Not in the same way, of course. Fanny Price's connection to slaves and slavery is implicit whereas Olivia's is not, a fact that explicitly underscores the way white and black women of empire politically diverge.

Despite her implied connection to slaves, Fanny is hardly their advocate when she brings up the topic of the "slave-trade" "in the evening circle." She "cannot act"[2] as critically or decisively against Sir Thomas Bertram's will with respect to his Antiguan plantations as she does later in the novel with respect to his will that she marry Mr. Crawford. In the passage above, however, Olivia explicitly conflates her own "palate" with those of slaves and she actively performs both her own and slaves' combined desire for better treatment from whites with the loaded gesture of "taking a piece of baked bread in [her] hand." This simple act succeeds in challenging not merely Mrs. Merton's prejudiced inhospitality but also questions the inhospitable practices by which her slave-holding father managed his plantations. In a performance that can never take place at Mansfield Park, Olivia, exhibiting none of Fanny's shyness about acting, acts decisively to connect her own appetite for equitable treatment as a victimized woman in England with that of Negro slaves in the colonies.

Olivia's polite yet aggressive behavior as a guest at the Merton breakfast table illustrates how vigorously *The Woman of Colour* politicizes the domestic sphere, a space to which colonial black women had long been denied access. As a political actor in England, Olivia's behavior must be read in conjunction with those acts performed by women of color such as Elizabeth Ann Miller and Mary Seacole who, respectively, crossed the Atlantic to secure the freedom of children and to nurse Britons fighting in the Crimean War. With these courageous acts, real and fictional women of color subtly transform traditional female roles of 'mother,' 'nurse,' and 'guest' in England into politicized identities that forcefully demand racial equity. Collectively, these women reveal the *literal* presence of a domestic black female activism in late eighteenth and nineteenth century Britain, one that compli-

---

1   *Mansfield Park*, 136.
2   Ibid., 102.

ments Heuman's historical focus on the legal activism led largely by men of color in Jamaica.[1]

This domestic black female activism extends even to the literal 'body' of the novel itself. Only a few years before *The Woman of Colour* was published, Lady Maria Nugent, wife to the Governor of Jamaica, writes in the *Journal of her Residence in Jamaica from 1801-1805*: "According to usual custom, when I went to my bedroom, I was surrounded by all the mulatto ladies the neighbourhood afforded."[2] Phillip Wright explains that "usual custom" meant receiving "coloured ladies apart from the rest of the company" since "it is very doubtful whether a coloured person ever sat down [to a state dinner, for instance] with Mrs. Nugent."[3] Prominent white women like Nugent would not break with local tradition by publicly associating with any women of color in Jamaica.[4] Yet, in an attempt to expunge the stigma that Nugent's *Journal* conveys, *The Woman of Colour* allows English women to associate with a representative "mulatto lady" in the privacy of their bedrooms so that they may shed their public disdain for such women once they realize how virtuous and unthreatening they can be.

The author deliberately uses the tool of racial muting to make Olivia more appealing and less threatening to white Britons. Her complexion is as "olive" (53) as her name implies, a clear attempt to mute the stigmas surrounding her blackness by equating her color with Mediterranean whites in the same way that Patrick Healy, the first black president of Georgetown University, was informally known as 'the Spaniard' when he walked those venerable halls.[5] However, this deliberate act of racial muting stops short of severing Olivia's connection to stigmatized blackness. In a remarkable scene of reeducation, Olivia uses her own body to teach Letitia's son, George Merton, to rethink the prejudice he

---

1   *Between Black and White*, Gad Heuman's excellent history about people of color in Jamaica, focuses largely on men.
2   Mary Nugent, *The Journal of her Residence in Jamaica from 1801-1805*, ed. Philip Wright (Mona, Jamaica: UWI Press, 2002) 69.
3   Ibid., xxix.
4   Nugent's refusal to publicly associate with women of color contrasts with Teresia Constantia Phillips who, Kathleen Wilson argues, buoyed her reputation in the colonies by openly surrounding herself with people of color. See "The Black Widow: Gender, Race and Performance in England and Jamaica," Chapter 4 of *The Island Race* 129-68.
5   My sincere thanks to Hoya extraordinaire, John Glavin, for this revealing piece of Georgetown lore.

expresses towards Dido, Olivia's Negro maid. At this point, the
mulatto heroine in *The Woman of Colour* is clearly championing
racial equality for *all* people of African descent, not just the
appealing light-skinned ones. As such, we must call Olivia by the
name that Srinivas Aravamudan uses "for the colonized subject
who exists both as fictive construct of colonial tropology *and*
actual resident of tropical space, object of representation *and*
agent of resistance:"[1] she is a "tropicopolitan"—a literal, subver-
sive, and political threat sent to expose the dominant system of
prejudice in England and to undermine it by associating with,
and re-educating, Britons. Her qualifications for such a task can
be found in the erudition of the biblical and literary allusions that
fill her tale.

But who would be interested in writing an extensive examination of this powerful black woman? Garside and Schowerling's
Bibliographical Survey (69-70, 265) has confidently disproved the
authorship of E.M. Foster, the woman inferred as the author
from the series of titles included on the original frontispiece.[2]
They also indicate that this list of earlier novels was a strategy
used to boost sales of long fiction by giving the impression that
an established author was responsible for work actually written
by an unknown one. A few details suggest that this unknown
writer was female. First, the fictional "Editor" (100) of the text is
acknowledged as a woman. This detail would be of little significance except for the fact that fifty percent of the novels published
in 1808 are by known or implied female authors,[3] making it
entirely plausible that a woman wrote this novel as a man.
Second, turn of the century women writers such as Mary Hays
(*The Victim of Prejudice*, 1799) and Amelia Opie (*Adeline
Mowbray*) show an interest in heroines like Olivia who are besot-
ted by prejudice in England. These women writers, however, are
clearly more interested in using terms like "prejudice" and black
characters like "Savannah" to contextualize the gender oppression experienced by their white heroines. Moreover, despite all
their efforts, when black women appear in the work of writers like
Opie and Edgeworth they are not displayed with the elaboration
or depth of August Von Kotzebue's Ada, Heinrich Von Kleist's

---

1 *Tropicopolitans*, 4.
2 These titles are listed on the original 1808 title page contained in this
   edition.
3 Peter Garside believes that women writers dominated the novel genre at
   the turn of the 19th century (*Bibliographical Survey*, 74-75).

Toni Bertrand, and J.B. Piquenard's Zoflora,[1] all of whom appeared within a decade or so of *The Woman of Colour*. Weighing the facts that this text was probably written by a woman but not a British one—rather, one who had significant ties to the colonies as well as in-depth knowledge of British society—it seems most plausible to propose that a woman of color wrote *The Woman of Colour*.[2] The racial specificity of the title alone indicates that the author lived or spent considerable time in the Caribbean and wanted to replicate a woman of color's identity with a rigor that went beyond the conception or interest of the vast majority of white women from this region. At the turn of the century there was already a well-established practice of 'Rhoda Swartzs'[3] being sent to school in England by their white West Indian fathers. Hester Thrale complains of this class of people, describing herself as being "really haunted by *black shadows*. Men of colour in the rank of gentleman; a black Lady, cover'd with finery, in the Pit at the Opera, and tawny children playing in the Squares...with their nurses."[4] A dearth of primary source material about such observably wealthy people of color cannot hide the fact that out the estimated 14,000 to 20,000 people of African descent living in London during the late eighteenth century, *one* might have been an anonymously published

---

1   The heroines in *The Negro Slaves* (1796), *The Betrothal in Santo Domingo* (1811) and *Zoflora, or the Generous Negro Girl* (1804). These female characters show that male writers on the European Continent recognized the significance of a central black heroine; however, I have ruled out the possibility that *The Woman of Colour*'s author was a continental European since there is no indication that the novel is written in translation. Furthermore, none of the texts above were originally published in English.

2   Faced with a similar problem of unknown authorship, Michele Burnham astutely observes that "it is finally not because of who its author may or may not have been that this novel is important ... *The Female American* articulated for readers ... an often radical vision of race and gender." *The Female American* (Peterborough, ON: Broadview, 2001) 23-24. The same holds true for *The Woman of Colour*.

3   I am referring here to the well-known heiress of color in William Makepeace Thackeray's *Vanity Fair* (1847-8).

4   See Appendix E2. Hester Thrale's alarm is shared by *Humphrey Clinker*'s Mr. Melford who, in a letter to Sir Watkin Phillips, describes himself as "extremely diverted" to see a mix of people at a ball which "was opened by a Scotch Lord, with a mulatto heiress from St. Christopher's" (Boston: Houghton Mifflin, 1968) 46.

author, and that *one* might have been a Caribbean "black Lady."[1] 1808 would have been the most opportune time for such a woman to publish since, as I mentioned earlier, this unprecedented year in the production of long prose fiction coincided with cultural interest in all things abolition. Ultimately, amidst all this speculation, Olivia's story actually contains more than an oblique parallel with a contemporary Jamaican woman of color's lived experience.

In 1806, Andrew Wright, a prosperous white English planter from Jamaica, died in England leaving a very curious demand in his will.[2] To his two illegitimate daughters of color, Ann and Rebecca, (who, it seems, were in England at the time), he bequeaths considerable wealth both to them and their future issue. But to obtain this wealth, Wright emphatically demands that these daughters marry in England. If they do not, Ann and Rebecca entirely forfeit their entitlements in the will. A clause this extreme seems more than incidentally designed to ensure that these young women married white Englishmen. Yet Ann, the eldest daughter, seems to have maneuvered around this by marrying Francis Maitland, a free man of color, *in England* only a few months after her father's death.[3] Two years later, *The Woman of Colour* appears on the boards of Samuel Hamilton's printing press in Weybridge, not twenty miles from the Mitcham area where Wright allegedly died and within thirty miles of his last recorded address at Great Tower Street, London. It is entirely plausible that someone in this area knew of the Wright will and wrote the tale to popularize the way it wrongs the marital choice of a free colonial woman of color. Indeed, Ann Wright could have been that person. *The Woman of Colour* could be her response to the will of her benevolent yet erring father. Without direct proof, however, this idea is merely an intriguing speculation. But even

---

1   See Appendix B for an example of a Grenadian "Mulatto Woman" poet published prior to 1808.

2   His brief obituary appears in *The Times* of 1 March 1806: "On Tuesday, the 18th instant, after a long and painful illness in Great Tower Street, Andrew Wright, Esq. of St. Elizabeth's Jamaica." See Appendix G2 for relevant portions of Andrew Wright's will.

3   Antony Maitland's *Wrights of St Elizabeth's Family* 30 March 2004 <http://www.antonymaitland.com/wright01.htm> and *Jamaican Maitland Family* 9 June 2005 <http://www.antonymaitland.com/jammaitl. htm> provided this extremely helpful genealogical information. Ann's marriage is recorded on 29 July 1806.

without proof, *The Woman of Colour* is a stronger candidate than Behn's *Oroonoko* to be called the first novel in British literature to be based on the literal experiences of a real woman of African descent even if we're not entirely sure it was written by one.

Black Pride, British Prejudice, and Women of Color in England

Whoever wrote this long fiction, she (or he) clearly wanted to convey two important points: race is a socially constructed discourse, and fiction should be a means of deconstructing it especially when it relates to gender. For there are women of *many* colors in *The Woman of Colour*: from the "olive" Olivia and her "black" Negro maid, Dido, to the "transparent" Angelina and the "alabaster" Letitia Merton, not to mention the presumably suntanned East Indian Nabob, Lady Ingot, and the geriatric Miss Singleton, whose "natural complexion is not far removed from ... Olivia's." (87) Collectively, this focus on women and race is designed to expose and undo two societal prejudices in England: one that demeans all black women, and another that exalts all white ones.

Of the two black women of color, Dido is the novel's sole Negro character. Her name—referring to the first queen of Carthage in Roman mythology—appears to mark her as one of those blacks both in fiction and in real life who were given exaggerated names that made a mockery of their positions as slaves.[1] Yet the author actually subverts this humiliation by establishing a number of crucial links between this original 'North African queen' and Olivia whom Dido refers to with the novel title, "queen of Indee." (57) Although she displays the unswerving fidelity to a benevolent superior that Maria Edgeworth famously illustrated in *The Grateful Negro*, Dido's gratitude is much more discriminating. "Mrs. Merton's maid treats me, as if me was her slave," she tells Olivia, "and Dido was never slave but to her dear own Missee, and she was proud of that!" (100) Clearly, Dido understands her present state of freedom in England when she twice uses "was" to refer to her prior enslavement. She also understands that as an English resident, deference does not

---

1 Such exaggerated names led Thomas Pringle to write, "It is a common practice with the colonists to give ridiculous names of this description to their slaves; being, in fact, one of the numberless modes of expressing the habitual contempt with which they regard the negro race." *The History of Mary Prince*, ed. Sara Salih (London: Penguin, 2000) 29.

immediately devolve to all white people irrespective of class as it would have done in the colonies.[1] Dido's simple objection shows that she is as active in questioning the terms of freedom in England for people of African descent, albeit without the syntactical refinement that comes naturally to the educated Olivia.

Dido and Olivia's experiences as black women of color in England are also linked by subtleties like the "large gold earrings" (68) that Dido wears in anticipation of her arrival in England. Before that, they "had been carefully laid in cotton during the voyage" from Jamaica but Dido pulls them out and puts them on as soon as the ship is about to lay "anchor in Kingroad," Bristol. Surely we are expected to ask why they appear at this time. Representing more than a love of finery, the gaudy yet timely appearance of Dido's gold earrings has parallels with Olivia's 'sixty thousand pound' dowry since they both represent the material armor that these 'queens' of color use to defend themselves and project their importance as soon as they come within the environs of a slave-port society which, they instinctively know, will not value either of them for their black beauty. Experience proves that they were right to be on their guards. When she is called "blacky" and "wowsky" and "squabby" and "guashy," Dido "feels a sense of injury" more acute than the mortifying hostility Olivia experiences at the Merton breakfast table, "and all because she has a skin not quite so white ... me don't mind that though, do we, my dear Missee?" (99-100) This is not the first time that Dido mixes up her pronouns but it is one of the most revealing; her confusion of *me* and *we* subtly connects her own fight against racism with Olivia's. Dialect and scale of wealth may separate Dido from Olivia in terms of class, yet the author's skillful use of syntax and imagery allows us to recognize their united experiences and subversions of prejudice as black women of color in England.

The marriage plot is, undoubtedly, the most important device that the author uses to prove that black women of color are connected despite pronounced differences in class and complexion. When Olivia eventually marries and rents a house at New Park, "Dido is delighted" because the new residence reestablishes both her and Olivia's rank in England: "it is like the 'dear Fairfield estate'" she remarks, "and she entered into all the mysteries of

---

1 Racial deference was a fact of life for all classes of people of color, as Bryan Edwards points out: "the lowest and most worthless white will behave with insolence to the best educated free man of colour" (see Appendix D1).

housekeeping, and bears about the insignia of her office, in the bunch of keys at her side, and the *important* expression of her face." (105) Both women are socially elevated by this move; they become the top females—wife and housekeeper—in an English upper-middle, merchant-class household. For Olivia, however, this transition from ex-heiress to new wife has, implied within it, evidence of a class demotion that would be familiar to Dido as well as a significant number of English women. At the beginning of the eighteenth century, Mary Astell's *Some Reflections Upon Marriage* claimed that "all women are born slaves" since they are all forced into marriage, which she defines as "the perfect condition of Slavery"; like a slave, a married woman became "subject to the inconstant, uncertain, unknown, arbitrary will of men."[1] Of all the types of women 'enslaved' by marriage, the heiress experienced conditions of loss most approximating a slave if she was legally divested of all her property, her name and individuality under a marriage contract. A married mulatto heiress, whose very complexion and father's will both contain within them the taint of enslavement, reinforces, much more bluntly, Astell's connection between marriage and slavery.[2]

Another major 'heiress of color' text, *The Female American* (1767), has a heroine who not only confronts but tries to stave off the threat of marital enslavement.[3] In her efforts to avoid it, Unca, (a superior markswoman), creates as a condition of marriage a bow and arrow challenge that she is highly unlikely to lose: she claims that she will only marry a man who is capable of out-shooting her. The challenge is obviously a defense mechanism that allows Unca the freedom to avoid marriage and maintain her independence—a power which reaches its climax when she, single-handedly, converts an Indian tribe to Christianity. In the end, however, custom rather than passion forces this powerful woman into a marriage with her Caucasian cousin, perhaps

---

1 *Some Reflections Upon Marriage with Additions. The Fourth Edition, 1730* (New York: Source Book Press, 1970) 107.
2 Minor, marriageable heiresses of color who appear in British literature do not usually address this issue with as much depth. See Appendices C4 and C5.
3 There are significant parallels between Olivia and Unca: both are mixed race heiresses unconstrained by the limits of domesticity; both are racial outcasts within English society; both are romantically pursued by white men; both combine rigorous obedience to a father's will with an equal dedication to religion.

indicating an authorial anxiety about a need to control the influence of independent women of color.

The Woman of Colour works to stave off the threat of marital enslavement more completely than *The Female American*. After the disastrous fallout of her marriage, another Caucasian heir courts Olivia; yet she rejects this sincere marriage proposal, preferring instead to call herself a "widow." We can, of course, read this as a mark of the author's own prejudice—a refusal to disconcert readers with the uncomfortable image of an interracial marriage, an approach adopted later in Maria Edgeworth's *Harrington* (1817) and Sir Walter Scott's *Ivanhoe* (1819). Yet unlike these Jewish texts,[1] the author's refusal to provide a Caribbean woman of color with a white husband who resembles her slaveholding father must be read alongside the history of enslavement and liberation within which the text obviously grounds itself. I interpret this decision as the author's conscious political statement about women and blacks having the freedom to empower themselves outside the oppressive institutions of marriage and slavery, a point I develop in this introduction's conclusion.

For the present, the author evidently takes pains to alleviate the prejudices leveled at black women of all classes and colors by allowing Dido's and Olivia's joint experiences and subversions of prejudice a central place in this narrative. She (or he) also, quite skillfully, undermines representations of white women of color with subtle deconstructions of their usually exalted complexions. For instance, the highly educated peer, Lady Ingot, and the spinster, Miss Singleton, may ostensibly convey progressive ideas about female education and independence, but their sunburned complexions also indicate that their characters are not the typically beautiful white women readers should admire; the whitened perfection of Letitia's "alabaster" (73) skin also evokes the cold imperviousness of her villainous character; and even the "transparent" (102) glow of Olivia's nemesis, Angelina, contains within it the implication that she is a ghostly and dead representation of ideal white femininity, not a living one. Eschewing polemics, the author subtly undermines the most salutary white and demeaning black characterizations in *The Woman of Colour*, a mark of the text's strategic activism.

---

1 For more on the Jewish elements in these texts see Michael Ragussis' *Figures of Conversion: "The Jewish Question" and English National Identity* (Durham: Duke UP, 1995), 57-88, 89-129.

The Woman of Colour, A Tale and Traditions of Prose Fiction

The Woman of Colour is a protest novel that does a skillful job of critiquing British prejudices without alienating British readers. It is part of at least two protest traditions: the black West Indian one that Sara Salih and Lise Winer et al. discuss respectively in the introductions to Mary Prince's History (1831) and Adolphus, A Tale (1853);[1] and a white British one that involves female authored political novels like Adeline Mowbray and The Victim of Prejudice which specifically confront gender prejudice in England. These protest traditions converge at the end of Olivia's narrative, where an extra-textual "Dialogue between the Editor and a Friend" accounts for her protest in explicit detail. The Friend, having read Olivia's complete letters, complains that "there is no moral to the work" since the Editor has "not rewarded Olivia even with the usual meed of virtue—a husband." "What do you propose from the publication of the foregoing tale?" the Friend asks the Editor, "I do not see the drift of your labours." The Editor replies,

> if these pages should teach ... one sceptical European to look with compassionate eye towards the despised native of Africa— then, whether Olivia Fairfield's be a real or an imaginary character, I shall not regret that I have edited the Letters of a Woman of Colour. (189)

Bypassing the question of verisimilitude, the Editor underscores Olivia's epistemological function. Like Mary Hays and Amelia Opie's heroines, Olivia deliberately resists the teleology of the marriage plot (famously rendered in the last chapter of Jane Eyre) that demands a virtuous woman's narrative end harmoniously with marriage. Instead, The Woman of Colour and these other female-

---

1 Lise Winer et al. states that protest novels, "focused primarily on making points about racism and slavery, and protest literature tends to have luridly violent villains, handsome and brave heroes, and heroines whose virtue is surpassed only by their helplessness" Adolphus, A Tale & The Slave Son (Jamaica: UWI Press, 2003) 1. Sara Salih writes that "Mary Prince's History is ... a piece of propaganda, a protest designed to convince the English reader that the iniquities in the colonies continued even though an Act of Parliament ending the slave trade had been passed in 1807" (xxx). In this introduction, I have argued that The Woman of Colour agrees with, but historically pre-dates, both of these definitions of "protest literature."

authored political novels of the long eighteenth century conclude with dissonance in which beleaguered but fiercely independent women teach "compassionate" English readers greater lessons about the racial, sexual and gender prejudices that virtuous women unjustly experience and seek to combat in England.

And yet, despite this affinity in combating prejudice, *The Victim of Prejudice, Adeline Mowbray* and *The Woman of Colour* differ in one important respect. Rather than being a naively misguided advocate for the female cause like Adeline Mowbray, or a completely embattled one as Mary Raymond appears to be at the end of her text, Olivia avoids succumbing to the overwhelming societal prejudices that ultimately destroy both of these white women. At the end of her narrative, Olivia flourishes as a self-proclaimed 'widow' who returns to Jamaica to "again zealously engage [her]self in ameliorating the situation, in instructing the minds—in mending the morals of our poor blacks," (188) aided in this work by her father's wealth. The fact that Olivia's text does not end with *marriage* then needs to be offset by the certainty that it does end with *freedom*—from her father's will, English society, financial constraint, marriage, and motherhood—*freedom to be active*. Having successfully challenged prejudice in England, Olivia has the potential to become an independent advocate for societal reform, equity, and emancipation in Jamaica. This makes *The Woman of Colour* an important addition to the tradition of black Atlantic writing by women like Mary Prince and Harriet Jacobs whose *Incidents in the Life of a Slave Girl*, Ann duCille has argued, deliberately manipulates the conventional marriage plot in order to make a more pointed statement about the importance of freedom for black people.[1] By underscoring duCille's argument, the Editor puts Olivia squarely at the forefront of the ongoing fight against slavery, and suggests that this long prose fiction about the liberation of a free, privileged black woman should be as much a part of the abolitionist literary canon as any contemporary male or female slave narrative.

Additionally, *The Woman of Colour* must also be considered an equal part of two canons of long prose fiction: "the West Indian novel" which George Lamming defined as "the novel written by the West Indian about the West Indian reality,"[2] and the modern British novel commonly associated with the publication of Samuel

---

1 Ann duCille, *The Coupling Convention: Sex, Text and Tradition in Black Women's Fiction* (New York: Oxford UP, 1993) 4-5.
2 *The Pleasures of Exile* (Ann Arbor: U of Michigan P, 1999) 38.

Richardson's *Pamela, or Virtue Rewarded* (1740). Because it is an epistolary narrative comprised of letters written by a woman of color in England to her English governess in Jamaica, *Pamela* is *The Woman of Colour*'s obvious forebear; but the West Indian connection also makes Olivia's tale part of another, largely ignored, epistolary tradition. Exotic epistolary narratives appeared intermittently throughout the century, usually written by Britons ventriloquizing the voice of a colonial visitor to England who sends letters back to *his* home-country describing the habits, customs, and culture of English society.[1] I deliver my pronoun with deliberate emphasis here because most of the known examples involve men such as the Indian king, the Polynesian, Omai, and the Hottentot of Distinction.[2] Male voices also dominate. Elizabeth Hamilton's *Letters of a Hindoo Rajah* (1796). *The Woman of Colour* could be a rare female addition to this male tradition of exotic epistolarity—another elaborate hoax designed to make readers see England anew through the rarely utilized eyes of a West Indian heiress.

Yet, by utilizing the exotic epistolary genre, flagrantly flirting with the verisimilitude of the heroine, and championing her right to be free, *The Woman of Colour*'s author also challenges wholly fictional works of long prose that uncritically accept dependence in marriage as the only alternative for rich women—works like Fanny Burney's *Cecilia, or Memoirs of an Heiress* (1782) which romanticize marital enslavement. Burney's plot also involves a conflict between a daughter's freewill and her duty to marry according to the dictates of her father's will; however, Cecilia and Olivia differ in the way they resolve this conflict. Cecilia defies

---

1   A contemporary reviewer of Elizabeth Hamilton's *Letters of a Hindoo Rajah* (ed. P. Perkins and S. Russell; Peterborough, ON: Broadview, 1999) writes: "There is no better vehicle for local satire than that of presenting remarks on the manners, laws, and customs of a nation, through the supposed medium of a foreigner, whose different view of things, as tinctured by the particular ideas and associations to which his mind has been habituated, often affords an excellent scope for raillery" (309).

2   See *Tatler* 171, 13 May 1710 and especially *Spectator* No. 50, 27 April 1711, for the Indian King Sa Ga Yean Qua Rash Tow's "lost" manuscript; *An Heroic Epistle, from Omiah, to the Queen of Otaheite; being his remarks on the English nation. With notes by the Editor* (London: T. Evans, 1775); *The Ranelean Religion Displayed in a Letter From a Hottentot of Distinction, Now in London, To his Friend at the Cape of Good Hope. Containing the Reasons assign'd by the Raneleans for abolishing Christianity, together with a true copy of their New Liturgy* (London: W. Webb, 1750).

her father's will and sacrifices both her surname and inheritance in order to marry Mr. Delville; she willingly enslaves herself to the man she loves, but in the process, trades independence for the precarious marital dependence that Mary Astell exposed. By contrast, Olivia "pant[s] for independence!" (144) after her marriage ends, and *The Woman of Colour* allows her to achieve it as a self-proclaimed 'widow for life.' In this status, Olivia not only refuses to succumb to the dependence, protection or anonymity of marriage, she also gets to control her own destiny within a marriage market that, under Mr. Fairfield and the Mertons, has already shown itself to be governed by the wills of white Englishmen that are precarious, and flawed, and negligent. A widow's independent control of her own destiny is a viable alternative to "all dhe sweet liberty ov wedlock"[1] that Burney's British heroine and others like her romantically promote.

Olivia's most crucial triumph as an independent widow occurs at the end of her narrative when she decides to leave England and return home. Edward Long believed "it is impossible but that a well-educated Mulatta must lead a very unpleasant kind of a life here [in Jamaica]; and justly may apply to her reputed father what Iphicrates said of his, 'After all your pains, you have made me no better than a slave; on the other hand, my mother did every thing in her power to render me free.'"[2] *The Woman of Colour* turns this defeatist statement on its head with a tale about a "Mulatta's" liberation from her father's will through the racially-aware and culturally-entitled character she manages to channel from her deceased black, and distant white, mother figures. "Whether Olivia Fairfield's be a *real* or an *imaginary* character, I shall not regret that I have edited the *Letters of a Woman of Colour*" (189) since the marvelous concluding image of her about to leave England via the slave port of Bristol—a free, wealthy, independent, racially-aware, politically-active woman, poised to "revisit Jamaica" to "again zealously engage ... in ameliorating the situation ... of our poor blacks," (188)—reminds us, as we commemorate the two-hundredth anniversary of the abolition of the British slave trade, that eighteenth and nineteenth century black

---

1 *Forty Years' Correspondence Between Geniusses Ov Boath Sexes, and James Elphinston; In Six Pocket-Vollumes: Foar Ov Oridginal Letters, Two' Ov Poetry.* Vollume II (London: W. Ritchardson, J. Deighton, R. Cheyn, and P. Hil, 1791) Letter cxvii, 6.

2 See Appendix D2.

women were formidable weapons, deliberately "conveyed over the water at the instigation of political contrivance" (59) to play a literal part in the fight against prejudice in England and slavery in the larger British colonial world.

A Chronology of Women of Color in Drama and Long Prose Fiction

Year *Title* / Author / **Woman of Color**

1605 *The History of the Renowned Don Quixote de la Mancha*
Miguel de Cervantes Saavedra / **Lela Zoraida** (moor)

The Masque of Blacknesse / Ben Jonson / **Ethiopian Nymphs**

1608 *The Masque of Beauty* / Ben Jonson / **Ethiopian Nymphs**

1613 *El Celoso Extremeño (The Jealous Husband)* from *Novellas Ejemplares* / Miguel de Cervantes Saavedra / **Guiomar**

1652 *The English Moor* / Richard Brome / **Millicent and Phillis** (both disguised as black moors)

1668 *The Isle of Pines* / Henry Neville / **Philippa**

1671 *An Evening's Love, or, The Mock Astrologer* / John Dryden / **Jacinta** (disguises herself as a mulatta in IV.i)

1675 *Calisto; or, The Chaste Nymph* / John Crown / **Three African women** (singers)

1688 *Oroonoko: or, The Royal Slave. A True History* / Aphra Behn / **Imoinda, Onahal**

1696 *The Adventure of the Black Lady* / Aphra Behn / **Bellamora**

1707 *Injured Love; or, The Cruel Husband* / Nahum Tate / **Zanche** (a moor)

1719 *Pure Love: a novel: being a History of the Princess Zulima, the beautiful daughter of the Sultan of Egypt* (trans. of *Zulima, ou, L'amour pur*) (1694) / Eustache Le Noble / **Zulima**

1720 *The Life of Bavia; or, The Jamaica Lady* / William Pittis / **Holmesia** (a Creole), **Quomina** (a Negro)

1727 *The English Hermit; or, Unparalleled Sufferings and Surprising Adventures of Mr. Phillip Quarll* / Peter Longueville / **Antiope, Diana, Elizabeth, Juno**

Year	*Title* / Author / **Woman of Color**

1730   *Histoire de Fleur d'Epine* (trans. *History of May-Flower. A Circassian Tale*) (1796) / Anthony Hamilton / **Negress** (Mother Long Tooth)

1740   "The History of of Prince Kader-Bilah" in *Chinese Tales: or The Wonderful Adventures of the Mandarin Fum-Hoam* / Thomas-Simon Gueullette / **Mergian Banou**

1743   *The Dramatic History of Master Edward, Miss Ann, Mrs. Llwhuddwhydd and Others* / George Alexander Stevens / **Mrs. Llwhuddwhydd** (nee Justice) (quadroon)

1754   *Tquassuow and Knonmquaiha. A Hottentot Story* / George Colman, the Elder / **Knonmquaiha**

1759   *High Life Below Stairs* / James Townley / **Cloe**

1761   *Genuine Memoirs of the Late Celebrated Jane D****s* / Anonymous / **Jane Douglas**

1767   *Love in the City* / Isaac Bickerstaffe / **Quasheba**

        The Female American / Unca Eliza Winkfield (pseudonym) / **Unca, Alluca,** (both Native American), **Unca Eliza** (Native American / British)

1775   *The Norwich Tragedy; or Unnatural Ingratitude, being an Account of Sir Peter Symonds* / Anonymous / **Blackamore maid**

        Die Mohrinn zu Hamburg / Ernst Lorenz Rathelf / **Cadige**

1783   *The Recess* / Sophia Lee / **Anana**

1786   *The Creole* / Lucy Peacock / **Zemira**

1787   *Adventures of Jonathan Corncob, A Loyal American Refugee* / Anonymous / **Mr. Winter's incestuous women of color**

        Inkle and Yarico / George Colman, the Younger / **Yarico, Wowski** (American Indian women)

1789   *The Princess of Zanfara; A Dramatic Poem* / William Hutchinson / **Jaqueena** (The Princess of Zanfara, who takes the name Laura)

1790   *The New Cosmetic, or, The Triumph of Beauty* / Samuel
Jackson Pratt / **Louisa** (a sunburned Englishwoman),
Hannah Bananah (a Creole)

1791   *Memoirs of a Scots Heiress* / Mrs. Charles Mathews /
Miranda Vanderparcke (mulatto)

1792   *Man As He Ia* / Robert Bage / **Flowney**

    Slavery: or, The Times / Anna Maria Mackenzie / **Omra**

1793   *The Irishman in London; or, The Happy African* / William
Macready / **Cubba**

1795   *Babay. A True Story of a Good Negro Woman* / Anonymous
/ **Babay**

1796   *The Negro Slaves* / August von Kotzebue / **Lilli, Ada,
Negro Woman**

    *Rambles Farther: A Continuation of Rural Walks: in Dia-
logues. Intended for the Use of Young Persons* / Charlotte
Turner Smith / **Ella** (Creole), **Mimbah** (Negro)

1797   *Edmund and Eleonora: or, Memoirs of the Houses of Summerfield and Gretton* / Edmund Marshall / **Alicia Seldon**

    Walsingham / Mary Robinson / **Lady Ethiop**

1798   *Henry Willoughby* / Anonymous / **Galla** (in Vol. II)

    "Thou Shalt Not Steal": The School For Ingratitude / Fisher
/ **Quasheba**

1799   *The Negro Slaves* / Archibald McClaren / **Sela**

    Douglas: or The Highlander / Robert Bissett / **Mrs.
Dulman**

1800   *Letters of a Solitary Wanderer* / Charlotte Turner Smith /
Three unnamed young women of color (who are
Henrietta's "sisters by the half blood") Vol. I

    Obi; or, Three Fingered Jack / John Fawcett / **Obi Woman,
Quashee's Wife, Sam's Wife**

    *Obi; or, The History of Three Fingered Jack. In a Series of
Letters from a Resident in Jamaica to his Friend in England*
/ William Earle / **Amri**

Constantia Neville; or, The West Indian / Helena Whitford / **Felicia Carleton** (an Afric-Creolian)

1801   The Grateful Negro / Maria Edgeworth / **Clara, Esther, Hector's wife**

Die Mohrinn / Karl Friedrich Wilhelm Ziegler / **Toni**

1802   *Family Quarrels* / Thomas Dibdin / **Lady Selina Sugar-cane** (a Creole), **Betty Lilly** (Negro)

1804   *Zoflora, or, The Generous Negro Girl* / Jean Baptiste Pique-nard / **Zoflora**

1805   *Adeline Mowbray; or, The Mother and Daughter* / Amelia Opie / **Savannah** (mulatto)

1808   *The Woman of Colour* / Anonymous / **Olivia Fairfield, Dido, Marcia**

The Africans; or, War, Love and Duty / George Colman, the Younger / **Darina, Berissa, Sutta**

The African / Anonymous (however, an anonymous American reviewer writes, "we had understood the author was a lady, and that the materials on which it was founded, were collected from *facts*—But its want of success disappointed our hopes, mortified the author, and injured the American drama." *The Emerald, or Miscellany of Literature* 1, 11 (1808) 124) / **Zulima**

1811   *Die Verlobung in St. Domingo (The Betrothal in Santo Domingo)* / Heinrich von Kleist / **Toni Bertrand** (mestiza), **Babekan** (mulatto), **Negress with yellow fever**

1814   *The Wanderer* / Frances Burney / **Juliet Granville** (begins the novel disguised as a black woman)

1816   *The Slave* / Thomas Morton / **Zelinda** (a quadroon)

1817   *Fragment of a Novel (Sanditon)* / Jane Austen / **Miss Lambe** (half mulatto)

1823   *Ourika* / Claire de Duras / **Ourika**

1827   *Hamel, The Obeah Man* / Anonymous / **Michal** (quadroon)

Year	Title / Author / **Woman of Color**

1842 *The Quadroons* / Lydia Maria Child / **Rosalie, Xarifa**

1847 *Vanity Fair* / William Makepeace Thackeray / **Rhoda Swartz**

1850 *Olive* / Dinah Craik / **Celia** (quadroon), **Christal Manners** (octoroon)

1853 Clotel; or, The President's Daughter / William Wells Brown / **Currer, Clotel, Althesa, Salome, Mary**

'The Woman of Colour' (manuscript of a play submitted to the Lord Chamberlain, London; set in America) / Captain Williams / **Florida Brandon, Marion**

Adolphus, a Tale / Anonymous / **Mrs. Romelia** (coloured, of African descent), **Antonia Romelia** (coloured, of African descent), **Agilai** (a black African), **Agilai's daughter / Adolphus's mother** [not named] (mulatto), **Selina** (Negro), **Black woman** (on the road)

1854 *The Slave Son* / Marcella Fanny Wilkins / **"young lady of colour"** [not named] (in the introduction), **Laurine** (mulatto), **La Catalina, Madelaine** (Negro), **Talima** (a black African princess), **Coraly** (Negro)

1855 *Busha's Mistress, or Catherine the Fugitive* / Anonymous / **Catherine**

1856 *The Quadroon* / Thomas Mayne Reid / **Aurore** (quadroon), **Chloe** (a mulatto), **little Chloe** (a yellow girl), **Eugénie Besançon** (a Creole)

1859 *The Octoroon* / Dion Boucicault / **Zoe, Grace, Dido, Minnie**

1861 *Louisa Picquet: The Octoroon* / Louisa Picquet & Hiram Mattison / **Louisa Picquet**

A Note on the Text

In preparing this edition of *The Woman of Colour*, I have relied on a copy of the first edition held in the British Library in London. I silently corrected the very few typographical errors in the first edition. The author's idiosyncratic punctuation (frequent use of the hyphen, exclamation and question marks within, rather than at the end, of sentences) has been retained. During the course of the tale, Olivia uses "key phrases" in quotation marks, the great majority of which I have been able to trace. I have indicated actual and possible sources for these 'key phrases' in the footnotes. While my footnotes and appendices are not meant to be exhaustive, they are designed to familiarize the reader with historical, religious, cultural, and literary sources from the period, some of which might have, and others that actually, informed and influenced the author. The fictional Editor also makes two interjections in packets two and five; following the original text, I have put these interjections in brackets within the body of the narrative. I have also followed the spelling and punctuation of the original documents in all of materials included in this book.

THE

WOMAN OF COLOUR,

A TALE.

"He finds his brother guilty of a skin not colour'd like his own," COWPER.[1]

**BY THE AUTHOR OF "LIGHT AND SHADE," "THE AUNT
AND THE NIECE," "EBERSFIELD ABBEY," &c.**[2]

IN TWO VOLUMES.

VOL. I.

LONDON:

PRINTED FOR BLACK, PARRY, AND KINGSBURY,[3]
**BOOKSELLERS TO THE HONOURABLE EAST INDIA COMPANY,
LEADENHALL-STREET.**

—

1808

---

1 The William Cowper epigraph is from *The Task* (1784), Book II, "The
Time Piece": "He finds his fellow guilty of a skin / Not colour'd like his
own; and, having power / To enforce the wrong, for such a worthy cause
/ Dooms and devotes him as his lawful prey" (12-15).

[over]

2   The list of titles assumes E.M. Foster's authorship; however, Peter
    Garside et al.'s work on the English novel refutes this claim as well as
    other writers mistakenly recorded as *The Woman of Colour*'s author. See
    *The English Novel 1770-1829: A Bibliographical Survey of Prose Fiction
    Published in the British Isles. Vol. II 1800-1829* ed. Peter Garside, James
    Raven, and Rainer Schowerling (Oxford: OUP, 2000) 69-70.

3   With some isolated exceptions, James Black, Henry Parry, and John
    Kingsbury operated under this business relationship most consistently
    between 1808 and 1812.

THE WOMAN OF COLOUR

PACKET[1] THE FIRST
OLIVIA FAIRFIELD TO MRS. MILBANKE

At Sea, on board the **.**
180—

[handwritten margin note: ✳ Bemoaning the prejudiced state of the world to Mrs M]

LAUNCHED on a new world, what can have power to console me for leaving the scenes of my infancy, and the friend of my youth? Nothing but the consciousness of acting in obedience to the commands of my departed father. Oh, dearest Mrs. Milbanke! your poor girl is every minute wishing for your friendly guidance, your maternal counsel, your sober judgement!—Every day, as it takes me farther from Jamaica, as it brings me nearer to England, heightens my fears of the future, and makes my presaging heart sink within itself! You charged me to confide to you its every throb; and till it ceases to beat, it will turn with the warmest affection to my earliest and best friend; my governess, my instructress!—and I cannot help asking why am I sent from her? why was it necessary for Olivia Fairfield to tempt the untried deep, and untried friends?—But I check these useless interrogatories, these vain regrets, by recollecting that it was the will of *him* who always studied the happiness of his child. *but . . . .*

My dear father, doatingly fond as he was of his Olivia, saw her situation in a point of view which distressed his feeling heart. The illegitimate offspring of his *slave* could never be considered in the light of equality by the English planters. Such is their prejudice, such is the wretched state of degradation to which my unhappy fellow-creatures are sunk in the western hemisphere. *We* are considered, my dear Mrs. Milbanke, as an inferior race, but little removed from the brutes, because the Almighty Maker of all-created beings has tinged our skins with jet instead of ivory!—I say *our*, for though the jet has been faded to the olive in my own complexion, yet I am not ashamed to acknowledge my affinity with the swarthiest negro that was ever brought from Guinea's coast!—All, all are brethren, children of one common Parent! The soul of my mother, though shrouded in a sable covering, broke through the gloom of night, and shone celestial in her

[handwritten margin note: he recognizes Olivia's situation — he could not legally make her his "heir" be of social moves, but he wants to arrange a marriage for her that grants her the same privileges.]

1 Packet has a double meaning, referring not only to the collection of letters but also the mailboat used to carry them to Jamaica.

sparkling eyes!—Sprung from a race of native kings and heroes, with folded hands, and tearful eyes, she saw herself torn from all the endearing ties of affinity, and relative intercourse! A gloomy, yet a proud sorrow, filled her indignant breast; and when exhibited on the shores of my native island, the symmetry and majesty of her form, the inflexible haughtiness of her manner, attracted the attention of Mr. Fairfield. He purchased the youthful Marcia; *Olivia's mother* his kindness, his familiarity, his humanity, soon gained him an interest in her grateful heart! She loved her master! She had not learnt the art of concealing her sentiments, she knew not that she was doing wrong in indulging them, and she yielded herself to her passion, and fell the victim of gratitude![1]—But as her understanding became enlightened, and her manners improved, she was eager for information; my father yielded it to her from the rich stores of his own capacious mind; and while he poured into her attentive and docile ear, those truths for which the soul of Marcia panted, he made her start with horror at the crime of which she had been innocently guilty: and the *new* Christian pointed her finger at *him*, who, educated under the influence of the Gospel, lived in direct opposition to its laws!

My father felt the justice of the reproof; for though his offence was considered as a venial error by all with whom he lived, yet his conscience was not so easily appeased. He knew that the difference of climate, or of colour, made no difference in the crime; and that if the seducer of innocence was always guilty, the case must be greatly aggravated where benefits and kindnesses were the weapons employed against untutored ignorance and native simplicity. Marcia was not "almost but altogether a Christian!"[2]—with the knowledge of her crime she abjured a continuance in it; with tears and sighs she confessed her love for her betrayer, at the same time that she deplored her fall from virtue! The scholar taught her master—The wild and uncivilized

---

1   Olivia's claim that Marcia "fell the victim of gratitude" develops Maria Edgeworth's relatively uncomplicated representation of this emotion in *The Grateful Negro*. Where gratitude unquestionably ennobles Edgeworth's enslaved Caesar, *The Woman of Colour*'s author clearly evokes Marcia's victimized exploitation from the same emotion.

2   A phrase used in numerous secular and spiritual instances but particularly resonant with John Wesley, the eighteenth century preacher and founder of the Methodist church, who in 1741 published "Almost a Christian. A Sermon" which, by 1766, was in its eleventh edition and still being remarked upon 'by a member of the established church' in 1792.

African taught a lesson of noble self-denial and self-conquest to the enlightened and educated European.

Mr. Fairfield dared not combat a resolution which appeared to him to be almost a command of Heaven. He loved Marcia with fervour; but the pride of the man, the quick feeling of the European, the prejudices which he had imbibed in common with his countrymen, forbade his making this affectionate and heroic girl his wife. Marcia's was a strong soul, but it inhabited a weak tenement of clay. In giving birth to me she paid the debt of nature and went down to that grave, where the captive is made free!

You will ask me why I recapitulate these events? events which are so well known to you. It is that I love to dwell on the character of my mother; it is that here I see the distributions of Providence are equally bestowed, and that it is culture not capacity, which the negro wants! It was from my father that I adopted this opinion of my mother— I caught the enthusiasm of his manner and learned to venerate the memory of this sable heroine (for a heroine I *must* call her) from the time that my mind has been enabled to distinguish between vice and virtue!

My father saw the sensibility of my disposition; he saw that it was daily wounded, at witnessing the wrongs of my fellow-beings; his wishes, and his principles, would have led him to reform abuses, but his health was daily declining, and he could not give the tone of morals to an island; he could not adopt a line of conduct which would draw on him the odium of all his countrymen: he contented himself, therefore, with seeing that slaves on his estate were well kept and fed, and treated with humanity,— but their minds were suffered to remain in the dormant state in which he found them![1]

I see the generous intention of my father's will; I see that he meant at once to secure to his child a proper protector in a husband, and to place her far from scenes which were daily hurting her sensibility and the pride of human nature!—But, ah! respected Mrs. Milbanke! in guarding against these evils may he not have opened the way to those which are still more dangerous for your poor Olivia?

I sometimes think, that had my dear parent left me a decent

---

1 Another ideological stab at the policy of benevolent paternalism famously espoused in Edgeworth's *The Grateful Negro*. Neither Mr. Edwards nor Mr. Fairfield tries to improve their slaves intellectually. By pointing this out, Olivia is directly critiquing the extent of her father's benevolence.

competence, I could have placed myself in some tranquil nook of my native island, and have been happily and usefully employed in meliorating the sorrows of the poor slaves who came within my reach, and in pouring into their bruised souls the sweet consolations of religious hope!— But my father willed it otherwise—Lie still, then, rebellious and repining heart!

Mrs. Milbanke, I yet behold your tearful eye—I yet hear your fond adieu— I yet feel your fervent embrace! The recollection is almost insupportable; for the present, I lay down my pen!

IN CONTINUATION

WAS my mind in any other state, I could be much amused and entertained by the novel customs of a ship's company, and the novel situation (to me) of a sea voyage. How wonderful is the construction of this vessel, which is now ploughing its way on the ocean! but how much more wonderful that Almighty Pilot, which steers it in safety through the horrors of the deep!

Mrs. Honeywood is all that your skill in physiognomy predicted. Separated from my beloved Mrs. Milbanke, I question if I could have met with a preferable *Compagnon du Voyage*. I fear that her native country will not restore her health; but I dare not hint an idea of the sort to her watchful and attentive son. Honeywood possesses all the enthusiasm of your Olivia; and when I hear his sanguine hopes of his mother's recovery, and his visionary schemes of long years of happiness to be enjoyed in her highly-prized society, I sigh with prophetic sadness, and, looking on the colour of my robes, I remember such was the fallacy of my own wishes!

Mrs. Honeywood seems perfectly acquainted with the particulars of my father's will, and frequently and studiously refers to my intended marriage with my cousin. If you will not accuse me of vanity, my dearest madam, I should be almost tempted to fancy, that she sometimes wished to remind her son of this; and yet there is nothing to fear for him. An unportioned girl of *my* colour, can never be a dangerous object; but in the habits of intimacy which our present situation naturally produces, confidence usurps the place of common-place politeness, and I insensibly talk to Honeywood as I should do to a brother. Had his familiarity any thing of boldness in it, was there any thing assuming in his manners, my sensitive heart would shrink, and I should then feel as reserved and constrained as I now do the reverse.

IN CONTINUATION

YOU bid me tell you every thing that should occur; and, in the absence of events and incidents, I must give you conversations and reflections, even at the hazard of appearing in the character of an egotist. I am just returned to my own little cabin, after a pretty long *tête-à-tête* with Mrs. Honeywood; I call it a *tête-à-tête* for though my faithful Dido formed the third of the party, yet her half-broken language did not bear a principal share in the conversation; but, as you well know, she *will* be heard on all occasions when she deems it right to speak. Honeywood had retired to study; he usually passes a great portion of the morning amongst his books: and that he reads with advantage and improvement, a more superficial observer than your Olivia would soon discover. He possesses a discriminating judgement, and a fine taste; and, without attempting at wit or humour, he never fails to please when he wishes it.

But to return to my proposed detail:—I was seated with my drawing implements before me, finishing a little sketch which I had taken from the Fairfield Plantation a few days before I quitted it; Mrs. Honeywood sat opposite to me, knitting; while Dido, ever officiously happy and busy about her "Missee," was standing behind the sofa (which she had drawn towards the table), and very assiduously watching for the colours I wanted, and rubbing them on the slab, pretending to be occupied, in order to retain her station; and at intervals I felt her removing and replacing the combs of my hair, and smoothing it gently down with her hands, then looking over my shoulder, marking the progress of my pencil, and exclaiming, "Ah, my goody Heaven! if my dear Missee be not making the own good Massee's plantation, and all of dis little bit of brush, and dis bit of paper!"

Mrs. Honeywood lifted her head; looking at us through her spectacles, "I would give something to be able to take dat brush and dat bit of paper, Dido," said she, laughingly imitating her, "and paint your lady and yourself, as you are now placed before my eyes."

Dido grinned, while Mrs. Honeywood still looking at me, said,—

"I never view you on that seat, with Dido standing in her place of attendance, without figuring you in my imagination as some great princess going over to her betrothed lord."

"Iss, iss,[1] my Missee be de queen of Indee, going over to marry wid de prince in England," said Dido, nodding very significantly.

---

1 Yes, yes.

"Such alliances do not very often turn out happily," said I, sighing.

"And how should they?" asked Mrs. Honeywood; "A total ignorance of persons can indeed be, in some measure, set aside by the painter, but the manners, the customs of different countries are so widely different, and there ought to be so many corresponding traits of character, to form any thing like comfort in the connubial state, that it is my wonder when any one of these matches turns out merely tolerable."

"You are looking grave, Miss Fairfield."

"Indeed, my dear madam, I am; and have I not cause? My manners, my pursuits, my whole deportment, may be strange and disagreeable to him whom I have pledged myself to receive as a husband! and further,—oh, madam!—my *person* may disgust him!"

"No, not so, Miss Fairfield: your sensitive mind, and delicate imagination, lead you to see things in too strong a light."

"No light can be too strong to convey to me a knowledge of that wretchedness which would be my portion, were I to be beheld with disgust and abhorrence by the man whom I have sworn to receive as my husband!"

"Sworn, my dear girl?"

"Yes, madam, sworn!"

"You astonish me!—and could Mr. Fairfield, could your father extort such an oath, such a blind submission from you?—you, whose understanding he must have seen superior to the generality of your sex,—you, whose judgement could only have elected where it had approved!"

"My father acted from the best of motives. If he erred, madam; if the *sequel* should *prove* that he has erred, give him credit, I conjure you, for the best intentions; his whole soul recoiled at the idea of leaving me in Jamaica, or of uniting me to any of the planters there: for to them he knew that his money would be the only bait. In England, in his native country, he deemed, that a more liberal, a more distinguishing spirit had gone abroad;"—(dear Mrs. Milbanke, I thought a sceptical expression overspread the marked countenance of Mrs. Honeywood)—"a connexion with his own family, with the son of a dearly beloved sister, was what his most sanguine hopes rested on for the security of his Olivia's happiness!"

"Your father knew this nephew?"

"No, madam, only by report; and that that report was very liberal in praise of his accomplishments and virtues, I need not say, when my father resolved to hazard the happiness of his child to his care. Mr. Merton, the husband of my deceased aunt, is, as you may have heard, a wealthy merchant, and has maintained a character of strict honour and probity. Mrs. Merton died within the last two years; she always spoke highly of her husband, and expressed the most fervent fondness for her son, Augustus, whom she frequently styled, in her letters to Jamaica, the 'image of her dear brother.' It was easy to perceive that Augustus was the mother's favourite; and I fancy, that my father surmised that the elder young man ranked highest in Mr. Merton's esteem. Indeed, my dear madam, I must be tiring you with my details, and I frequently think, that I can talk as coolly, and with as little *mauvaise honte* of this intended alliance as if I was a mere *state machine!*—conveyed over the water at the instigation of political contrivance; yet believe me, my dear madam, I have a sense of my sex's more exclusive feeling delicacy. My heart revolts, it shrinks within me, as every day draws me nearer to the scene of my trial; and the anxiety with which I, at some moments await the period, is frequently changed into a desolating revulsion of every feeling, when I recollect that I must appear in so very humiliating a situation when I reach England!"

"No, not humiliating," said Mrs. Honeywood, "for every generous mind will feel for the peculiarity of it, and exert every art to win you to self-confidence. You have great powers of exertion, Miss Fairfield; your father knew the strength of your mind; he knew that it could bear itself up in circumstances which would overwhelm half the female world!"

"You are good to embolden me, madam," said I, "my trust is in *Him* who has promised to strengthen the weak-hearted. I hope the name of Fairfield shall never be disgraced by me."

"I am *sure* it will not," said Mrs. Honeywood, "but your ingenuousness invites my curiosity; on *your* side I perfectly understand the terms. You have promised to accept Mr. Augustus Merton as your husband. Has a similar promise been received on the gentleman's part? not that I mean to infer, that there could be so undiscerning an Englishman found, as to refuse the offered hand of Miss Fairfield!"

"Do not say *offered*, dear Mrs. Honeywood; it sounds so—so very forward!" She smiled— "Ah, my dear madam, I *know* you pity me!"

"From the bottom of my heart!" said she with fervour.

"Pittee, no pittee," said Dido; "beauty lady—great deal monies—going marry fine gentleman as soon as she be come to

England town;—me don't pittee dear Missee one bit—one bit!" But Dido covered my hand with tears, and kissed it a hundred times, while she said, she did not "pittee Missee one bit—one bit." Her manner affected me; she saw it, and, letting her hands fall on each side of her, she stole out of the cabin. I tried to assume cheerfulness: "I bear with me a dower of nearly sixty thousand pounds," said I, "which is to become the property of my cousin Augustus Merton on his becoming my husband, and taking the name of Fairfield, within one month after my arrival in England."

Mrs. Honeywood seemed to look at me with the most painful and quickened attention; "but if," said she, "he should, that is, I mean"—

"I know what you mean," said I, smiling; "if Augustus refuses to accept these terms, the whole fortune devolves to his brother, and my maintenance exclusively devolves on him also!"

"Strange and unheard of clause!" said Mrs. Honeywood, rising hastily from her seat, and turning to the window, her back towards me.

"You must see it, as I see it, dear Mrs. Honeywood!" said I, going to her, and taking her hand; "even though *you* do not see poor Olivia with her *father's eyes*, *he* thought that no one *could* refuse *his* girl!"

"And no one *could*, who *knew* her!" said Mrs. Honeywood, straining me affectionately to her bosom. "Sweetest Miss Fairfield, may your happiness be equal to your virtues! may your cousin properly appreciate your worth!"

"Thank you,—thank you!" returned I, with a voice almost too full for utterance. I then quitted this warm-hearted woman, and hastened to relieve myself, in my usual method, writing to you.

IN CONTINUATION

I HAVE frequently thought, my dearest friend, that few young men would have resolution to refuse sixty thousand pounds; for the wife would be a very trifling embargo to most of our gay West Indians,—I can speak of the world only as I have seen it.—Mrs. Milbanke, I do not wish to be uncharitable or harsh in my judgement; but did we not every day see matches made in Jamaica, for which gold was the only inducement? And why do I encourage my overweening expectations—why do I expect my cousin to be different from the rest of his sex? Conscious of my own inferior powers of attraction, to what can I impute his acceptance of my hand? Hope will sometimes whisper, that gratitude will ensure kindness—but the cold feeling which alone springs from a grateful principle—could my warm heart be satisfied with that?—Vain, weak Olivia! go to thy mirror, and ask what is it thou canst expect more?

IN CONTINUATION

WEAK and impotent beings that we are, we know not what we wish, nor what we hope.—I retired last night to my cabin in a frame of mind which I should vainly seek to describe. The conversation which I had with Mrs. Honeywood, had made a forcible impression on my mind. I fancied that I was hastening to England, to be immolated at the shrine of avarice; all the bright prospects of my youth seemed blighted; I was friendless —fatherless—forlorn—journeying towards a land of strangers, who would despise and insult me. Bitter tears coursed each other down my cheeks; I wrung my hands in agony together—my heart sank within me—I had no resolution—no confidence left—I believed myself the most forlorn of human creatures, and I thought that a cessation of being, would be a cessation of misery. Ah! my dear friend, I am proving to you what you have long known, that your Olivia is no heroine! I was awakened from this agonizing trance to the tumultuous waves, which hove the ship with boisterous violence; the wind rattled in the shrouds, and increased in violence with each moment, while at intervals it was drowned by the long and reverberating peals of deep-toned thunder, and my cabin was as frequently illuminated by vivid lightning. There was a noise of bustle and alarm on the deck, and the voice of the sailors was distinguished amidst the horrors of the storm. Dido, shaking with affright and terror, burst into my cabin,—

"Oh, Missee, we be going down—we be going sink in the very, very deep sea!"

Alas! I thought so likewise; and in this hour of *real* danger I prayed for a deliverance from *that* death which I believed I could have fearlessly met, nay, had almost *courted*, the preceding hour. This taught me how very short a progress I had made in self-knowledge, and while Dido rolled herself up and made a sort of pillow at my feet, I tried to collect my thoughts, and to lift up my soul to him who "walketh on the wings of the wind,"[1] and to beseech him to give me a patient and contented spirit. The

1 Psalm 104: 3.

tempest still raged with redoubled violence; a soft tap at my door roused Dido:—"Me be here" was answered by the voice of Honeywood.

"I could not be easy," said he, "without asking after your lady."

"Oh it be very bad terrible storm, sir; me be much fear'd we must go down to the bottom."

"Oh no, not so," said Honeywood, in the most soothing voice; "assure Miss Fairfield, my good Dido, that there is nothing to fear. Tell her I am now come from the deck, where I have been the last two hours; the captain assures me, the storm is abating, and I am now returning to my hammock: pray don't distress Miss Fairfield: I beseech you do not heighten her alarm!"

I heard every word, you find, my dear madam; and so friendly were they, so truly benevolent, and the manner, too, in which they were spoken, that I felt the utmost gratitude for his attention. The interest which he had expressed for me was grateful to my self-love, whilst my fears were allayed by his assurances of our safety. The storm did abate, and your Olivia is snatched from the horrors of the deep. I trust I shall not be forgetful of the mercy of that Being who has been graciously pleased to preserve my life!

IN CONTINUATION

"THEY that go down to the sea in ships, and occupy their business in great waters, these men see the mercies of the Lord and his wonders in the deep!"[1]

These words have been in my thoughts the whole of this day. The storm still rages in my mind's eye. How fearful, how tremendous—Surely, if "by night an atheist half believes a God,"[2] he must *hear* him, he must *see* him, in the scene I have so recently witnessed, and a *doubt* could never more find entrance in his soul!

Honeywood eagerly advanced to me as I made my appearance at breakfast and renewed his inquiries. I felt confused: this confusion seemed infectious; for, as I tried to express my thanks to him for the friendly interest he had evinced for me, he suddenly let go the hand which he had taken, coloured, sighed, and let me take my place in silence. Mrs. Honeywood at this moment appeared, and broke a silence which had succeeded, as if by a mutual inclination, to our first civilities. The first topic was, of course, the recent storm, and the sickly countenance and dim-

---

1 Psalm 107: 23-24.
2 Edward Young, *The Complaint, or Night Thoughts on Life, Death and Immortality* (1742), "Night the Fifth."

med eye of the poor invalid, proved that a wakeful night was much to be dreaded for her. She congratulated me on my safety, and said,—

"You were very courageous in not quitting your cabin. Fear, in general, renders us all sociable; and I expected every moment to have seen you come to me. I could not pacify Charles till he had gone to you; but I question whether you were much comforted by *his* assurances of your safety, as he is a fresh-water sailor."

I answered that I was; and Mrs. Honeywood, pursuing the subject, said,—"For myself, I had not much to regret in leaving a world to which an attenuated thread alone holds me!" Her countenance had that patient serenity on it, which gave it an expression which nearly comes up to my idea of celestial, and, though apparently talking to me, I imagined that she meant more particularly to address her son.

"Youth, beauty, talent, virtue, and riches, to be consigned at once to the o'erwhelming wave, would, indeed, be a sad contemplation," said she, "and even where death has long been anticipated, the thoughts of resigning life, by any other than the common lot of humanity, is appalling. If it please the Almighty to let me reach my native shores, I think I can summon fortitude to meet the stroke as a Christian!"

"My dearest mother, rive not my heart!" said Honeywood.

"Charles, you are not philosopher" said Mrs. Honeywood, attempting to smile, as she held out her hand to him; he took it,— never shall I forget with what an expression of love and reverence he held it to his lips in silence, then pressed it to his breast.

"If philosophy is to steel my heart against such feelings as these," said he, wiping off the starting tear with the back of his hand, "my mother, who shall teach it me? But Heaven, in its mercy, will long preserve to me a parent for whom alone I would wish to live!"

"When I am laid in the peaceful tomb, my Charles, your heart shall seek another being, whose life shall be sweetened, as mine long has been, by your cares and attentions. Your mother will be changed for the closer—the yet more endearing tie of wife. With a companion of your own age, whose pursuits are similar to your own, whose mind has been cultivated, and whose principles are good, you are formed, my son, to partake with *such* a woman the very *acmé* of human happiness."

The eyes of Honeywood sought mine, for a moment, with an expression which I cannot define; then hastily pressing his hand on his forehead, as if in pain, he rose from his seat, and said—

"Never, never! my dearest madam; you unman me quite!" and left the cabin.

"'Tis always thus," said Mrs. Honeywood; "nothing that I can say will open the dear boy's eyes to my danger; and, with his impetuous, his ardent feelings, I dread for him the shock of an event for which he *will not* be prepared! Talk to him, for me, my good Miss Fairfield; you have great influence over him; he will listen to you: tell him that he must make up his mind to resign his parent!"

"Alas!" sighed I, "I am ill qualified for such an office,—I that continue to mourn the loss of the best of fathers!—*My* loss is certain, my dear madam; Mr. Honeywood's is only in prospective—*I* feel the sad reality—*he* shudders at the supposition—how then shall *I* teach *him* that fortitude which I cannot practise myself? The loss of a parent can never be supplied to a child!— My father was my guide, my counsellor, my friend; he was the impulse of my life; he was the guide of my every action; almost the director of my thoughts! When I lost my father, I lost every thing which could make life desirable; and when poor Honeywood shall lose you, he will then know the wretchedness of my situation!"

IN CONTINUATION

WHERE there is any thing to conciliate regard or esteem, how soon do we get attached! I already feel as if I had been known to Mrs. Honeywood all my life, and I regret that when I lose sight of her, and of her amiable son, on our landing, it must be among the chance events of the future, whether we may ever meet again.

I sat for two hours of the last evening on the deck watching the mildly radiant moon, and the thousand sparkling rays which were caused by her shadow on the tranquil ocean; no longer heaving with tumultuous waves as on the preceding night, but peaceful as the translucent lake. Honeywood attached himself to my side, his mother was apprehensive of the night air, and remained in the cabin—

"How still is the water!" said Honeywood; "how bright the lustre of that celestial orb! what a contrast is this scene to that which I last night witnessed in this place!"

"And how doubly are we interested in the beauty of this night from that very contrast which you have remarked!" said I.—"So it is in life, we recover from the dreadful shock of some fearful calamity, to those placid and calm sensations, which such a contemplation as this is calculated to produce: we remember what we have suffered, and we are doubly grateful to Him who has enabled us to endure afflictions, and caused the storm to pass over our heads!"

"You can extract good from every evil," said Honeywood, "morality from every passing occurrence—you can find sermons in stones, and God in every thing!"[1]—He spoke this with enthusiasm. "Indeed, Miss Fairfield, I know of no one like you—you will shame our English ladies—or rather, you are going where your virtues will not be known or appreciated!"

"How am I to understand you?" asked I, willing to take the compliment that my *moralizing* disposition has extorted as *applicable*; "how then shall I account for the latter part of your speech without accusing *you* of vanity? Does Mr. Honeywood imagine that *he* only has discernment to discover those *great* and *extraordinary* virtues which I possess?"

"By no means," said he, answering gravely to my tone of raillery—"by no means; but the superficial characters of our modern females, their frivolous pursuits, their worse than childish conversation—oh! you will be soon sickened of them; and, if I do not mistake *your* disposition, the sensitive plant will then recoil, and never expand itself again, till drawn out by an assimilating look, or spark of sentiment!"

"Oh, what a fearful prospect!" said I, still affecting to trifle—"Am I then so *very* fastidious a being, Mr. Honeywood? Believe me, I look not for perfection in an imperfect state; my own faults are great and manifold and, I trust, I can behold those of my fellow-mortals with charity, and make allowances in proportion!"

"That you can do *all*, and *more* than this, I am well satisfied," said Honeywood; "but if your heart is not interested, I mean if no kindred emotion—that is—I believe," said he, "like many others who set out in discussing a subject, I have confused myself, and want somebody to explain my own meaning."

He then reverted to his mother's health, a topic which never fails to interest.

"When I consider," said he, "that her illness may be in some measure traced to a three years' residence in your warm climate

---

1 Here, Honeywood manipulates part of Duke Senior's speech in Shakespeare's *As You Like It*: "And this our life exempt from public haunt / Find tongues in trees, books in the running brooks, / Sermons in stones and good in everything" (II.i). Honeywood's use of "God" in place of "good" emphasizes the anonymous author's need to construct Olivia not merely as a moral woman but an overtly religious one.

(for though the latent seeds of the disease might have been in her constitution, yet it was there that they first burst forth), and that she undertook the voyage merely on my account, in order to gather up the wreck of a shattered fortune for my use, I know not how to estimate the sacrifice; and that affection which I feel for her, tells me that the independence which she has secured to me, has been too dearly earned for me to enjoy it, if bought with the price of her health, perhaps her life!"—He paused a moment as if to recover the power of articulation—

"On the other hand," said he, "I remember the anxiety with which this dear parent passed the lingering days previous to her setting out for the West Indies. I was brought up to the prospect of inheriting a large fortune, and was then too old to enter into either of the professions with advantage to myself.— She had seen enough of the world to know that a proud and a sensitive spirit struggling with adversity, was a most pitiable situation. My mother has had her share of sorrows—My father was not able to appreciate her worth or her uncomplaining fortitude—'tis a sad story, my dear Miss Fairfield, one day you may perhaps hear it— for I cannot, I will not think," said he, taking my hand, "that our acquaintance shall cease with this voyage!"

"I hope not," said I.

"Say it shall not," said he, with earnestness.

"We can speak with certainty of nothing," said I, "and you must remember, that from the moment when I set my foot on your land of liberty, I yield up my independence—my uncle's family are then to be the disposers of my future fate; and, though they can never teach my heart to forego its nature, or my mind its principles, yet in all irrelevant points, and in all local opinions, I must resolve to yield myself to their guidance!"

"If *such* be your determination; if you thus at once resolve to give up the liberty of action—farewell for *ever* when we separate!" said Honeywood with some asperity: "*we* shall never be allowed to prosecute our acquaintance with our interesting companion!"

"And why should you think so? why should you suppose that the family of Mr. Merton were illiberal or unjust?"

"I judge by myself—a fair standard you will allow," said he: "and I know that if I was in the place of these Mertons (you observe, my dear friend, he was too delicate to refer to Augustus only) I should be a monopolizer of the time, the conversation, even the looks of Miss Fairfield!" He reddened as he spoke these words; he probably thought he had said too much—I *felt* that he *had*, however—and sought Mrs. Honeywood.

IN CONTINUATION

I AM not without my sex's vanity, dearest Mrs. Milbanke, perhaps indeed I have a larger portion of it than the generality, from the knowledge that I owe nothing to the score of my personal attractions; yet I must be blind if I did not perceive that Honeywood beholds me with a more than common degree of partiality. Were I a romantic *beauty*, in the *noble compassion* of my nature I should say that it would give me pleasure, on *his* account, when our voyage was ended—but I am not so *far* gone as this. I know that the charms of mind divested of a prepossessing exterior, can only captivate the judgement, not mislead the heart; and that a preference originating in reason, will be referable to reason for its extinction.

Honeywood is certainly a very estimable young man; I like his conversation extremely; and without feeling any thing more for him than I should for an amiable brother, I confess that I shall be much mortified if Augustus Merton is not a little like him in sentiment and principle. In this case, although you may laugh at me for such an idea, yet I really think the miniature of Augustus has been serviceable to me. When I have felt a more than common interest for Honeywood, I have retired to my cabin, and spent some moments in contemplating the inanimate resemblance of him to whom I am affianced. I never behold the picture without emotion—the likeness to my dear father is so very striking, although the countenance is much handsomer, and there is a speaking sensibility in the eye which rivets my attention; for *there* I fondly imagine I behold all that I seek for of mind and sentiment in my destined husband—and yet perhaps, my dear madam, I do but flatter myself, as the artist has flattered his employer.

IN CONTINUATION

IT is the sweet bard of Avon, I believe who so well expresses an idea which runs in my head, but which my treacherous memory cannot clothe in his happy words. It is the dreadful pause between the expectation and the accomplishment of an apprehended event.[1] Your better memory will recollect the lines from my remote reference, and you will know the inference I draw. A few days more, and we shall reach England.—Ah! the hopes and the fears of this beating heart.

---

1 The "bard of Avon" is, undoubtedly, William Shakespeare, but the reference is very oblique. It is, perhaps, Helena's claim in *All's Well That Ends Well*: "Oft expectation fails and most oft there / Where most it promises, and oft it hits / Where hope is coldest and despair most fits" (II.i.150-52).

That period will surely fix the fiat of my destiny.—I shall have your prayers—I shall offer my own;—and shall I not be encompassed by the guardian spirit of my father? —Oh! if it be permitted from the realms of bliss, to look down on these terrestrial abodes, the thought of a father's taking cognizance of the actions of his child, must infuse new courage into her soul!

IN CONTINUATION

WE are already in the Bristol Channel,[1] and in a few hours shall expect to anchor in Kingroad. As Mrs. Honeywood heard this intelligence from our captain, a bright beam of pleasure illuminated her faded countenance. Dido rubbed her hands, and skipped about the cabin in ecstasy; and, as if she expected to do *instantaneous* execution, she had, within five minutes, put her large gold rings into her ears, which had been carefully laid in cotton during the voyage. I felt the blood forsake my cheeks, my legs trembled, and, standing at the moment, I was obliged to catch the arm of Mrs. Honeywood's chair, to keep me from falling. Honeywood saw my emotion, he rose hastily, and, placing me a chair, quitted the cabin.

IN CONTINUATION

WE are anchored, my beloved friend; already have the eyes of your Olivia rested on the shores of England! We are impatient of delay; and Honeywood has adjusted matters for us to row to shore this evening. The boat is already in view.

Adieu, my dearest Mrs. Milbanke.

IN CONTINUATION

Bush Tavern,[2] Bristol.

I MOMENTARILY expect Mr. Merton; figure to yourself the nature of my present feeling. I write in order to divert my mind; for, to dwell on my own thoughts during this period of suspense, is agony. We came to this place last evening. Mrs. Honeywood, her son, and servant, myself, and Dido. What an evening it was! Surely nothing was ever so serenely beautiful; surely, nothing was

---

1 Located on the west coast of England, Bristol was a port city second only to Liverpool in trading goods associated with the slave trade.
2 A well-known and bustling tavern on Corn Street in Bristol. It was demolished in 1854.

ever more romantically picturesque, than the wooded cliffs, and the boldly gigantic rocks, on either side the river, as we swiftly glided along its surface! The moon shone with unclouded brightness; the air was soft and mellow; the nightingales warbled from amidst their leafy coverts; and, at intervals, a French horn and a clarionet breathed forth their shrill tones, softening as they issued from the tremendous heights above our heads; while the soft dashing of the oars, and the sparkling play of the waters in the moonbeam, made up this scene of enchantment. Spite of the conflicting emotions of my mind, I was wrapt in enthusiastic admiration. Mrs. Honeywood enjoyed the scene; while her son fixed his eyes alternately on me and on the water, with an expression of melancholy resignation in his countenance.

When we got nearer to the large and mercantile city of Bristol,—when I could distinguish the "busy hum of men,"[1] and could discern the traits of active life which even at the still hour of evening are to be seen on the quay's of this place, my heart seemed to be thrown back upon itself, and I felt that I was entering into a world of strangers. All resolution—all self-confidence was banished with this idea. I leant back in the boat, and sobbed with apprehensive sorrow. Mrs. Honeywood did not observe my emotion, and if her son did, he knew that at such moments as these the voice of consolation cannot be heard.

Honeywood carefully assisted us in landing; a hackney-coach was in waiting: for Mrs. Honeywood, long disused as she has been to any exercise, was incapable of walking the shortest distance. In less than ten minutes, we were set down at this bustling tavern, where the noise, the closeness, and the gloom of the apartments, exceed any thing that I could have imagined. We chilly beings, however, were soon seated around a cheerful fire. Dido walked off with Mrs. Honeywood's maid, in great admiration and surprise at every thing which met her eye; and in the tone and voice of affection, which a fond parent would have used towards a favourite child, Mrs. Honeywood took my hand in hers, and congratulated me on my safe arrival in England.

How grateful is the expression of kindness to the human ear!—"Alas!" thought I, "how do I know if this is not the last time when I shall call forth the sympathetic regard of another?"

As I made this reflection, I lifted her hand to my lips, and while I held it there, I almost bathed it in my tears.

---

1 John Milton, *L'Allegro* (1645): "Towered cities please us then, / And the busy hum of men."

At this moment, the master of the inn entered the room, and, respectfully addressing himself to Honeywood, inquired if either lady's name was Fairfield: on being directed towards me, he presented me a letter which he held in his hand.

"This, madam, was left with me by Mr. Merton himself, and he has made daily inquiries concerning the arrival of the ★★★ every day for the last fortnight."

My hand trembled so, that I let the letter drop from between my fingers. Honeywood picked it up, but he was infected by my tremour as he returned it to me. The landlord retired, and I read the following words:

"TO MISS FAIRFIELD."

"My dearest Miss Fairfield! We are waiting your arrival in England with the greatest anxiety; and that you may experience the least possible inconvenience at landing in a strange country, understanding that the ★★★★, in which your passage was taken, is bound for the port of Bristol, Augustus and myself have taken a house at Clifton; and Mrs. George Morton, the wife of my eldest son, has kindly accompanied us from London, in order, if possible, to do away every feeling of embarrassment in your situation. On your landing be kind enough to send a messenger to me, No.—Gloucester-row, Clifton, and half an hour will bring to you, your affectionate relatives.

"I have the honour to be, dearest madam, your obliged friend, and uncle,

"GEORGE MERTON."

A faint sickishness seemed to overcome me as I read this letter: I mechanically threw it into Mrs. Honeywood's lap, and hid my face with both my hands. Mrs. Honeywood perused it, and returning it to me, said,—

"It is a very proper and considerate letter: and much as I must grieve that our separation is so near, yet I am pleased to observe the affectionate solicitude which Mr. Merton evinces towards you!"

"Our separation is near, certainly," said Honeywood; "but surely, madam, Miss Fairfield need not instantaneously make her arrival known to the Mertons; they may be abridged of her company a few short hours, just while she recovers from the fatigue of the voyage. Consider, from henceforth she will be *always* with them, while *we*—"

He stopped.—"Miss Fairfield must judge for herself," said Mrs. Honeywood with some gravity in her manner: "I will most readily be her chaperon, while she stays here, and shall be but too much gratified in her society. But—"

"But it would be extremely improper," said I, hastily interrupting her, "to let my uncle remain in ignorance of my arrival after to-morrow morning. This night, my dear madam," said I, "shall be passed here, and under your protection and vainly shall I endeavour to express my sense of your more than maternal care and attention."

Ah, dearest Mrs. Milbanke! —an elegant chariot stops at the door. I am summoned,—how—how shall I support this trying interview!

IN CONTINUATION

Gloucester-row, Clifton.

You used to like my description of persons and characters as they struck my eye; and I the more readily indulge my pen in being minute. Yes! I will write what I think, my dear madam, even at hazard of being thought severe; for you will not accuse your Olivia of ill-natured severity, and to no other will my remarks be open. You perceive that I have *outlived* yesterday, that I can even be a trifler to day, and from these facts your warm heart will augur all that is good. I will try to be methodical. I reached the dining-room we occupied before my visitors; Mrs. Honeywood and her son offered to withdraw. I could not speak, but I motioned to Honeywood, and grasped the arm of his mother to detain her. Dido officiously threw open the door, and as my fearful eyes met hers, I could perceive a triumphant and consequential toss, which always designates her manner when she is particularly pleased.

"How fleet is a glance of the mind!" says our own dear Cowper:[1]—*immediately*, there entered a very fashionable and showy looking young woman, leaning on the arm of a tall man, of a good though stiff figure. I was conscious that a *third* person followed them but I dared not look *beyond*. Mrs. Honeywood most kindly acted as mistress of ceremonies, and announced the trembling, agitated Olivia, as Miss Fairfield, while Mr. Merton said, as he advanced towards me,—"My dear niece, let me introduce you to Mrs. George Merton."

I believe I held out my hand, and that lady was *very near* taking it in hers; but I fancy its *colour* disgusted her, for she recoiled a

---

1 William Cowper, "Verses Supposed to be written by Alexander Selkirk during his solitary abode in the Island of Juan Fernandez" (1782).

few paces with a blended curtesy and shrug, and simpering, threw herself on a sofa. My uncle seemed to have no prejudices; he held me to his breast, and pressed his lips on my cheek; he then led his son to me, but again my eyes sought the carpet, though I was conscious of the trembling hand which held mine, he stammered out some words of pleasure and happiness. Honeywood was then introduced by his mother; the languid drawl of the fine lady, Mrs. Merton, detained him in conversation. Mr. Merton paid me the utmost attention, and, in part, relieved me from my embarrassment. I looked up, and for the first time *saw* Augustus Merton:—*he* seemed to have been examining me with scrutinizing attention.—Alas! I fear it was but a melancholy contemplation in a double sense; for I thought I distinguished a suppressed sigh, as he hastily addressed himself to Honeywood!

No, my dear friend! the painter did not flatter! Were I to draw a model of manly beauty and grace, I would desire Augustus Merton to sit for the likeness. And yet, I do not know, that his face is so regularly handsome; but there is an expression in his eye of tender melancholy, which is irresistibly interesting; and his smile has more sweetness, if possible, than had my father's! The likeness to him is very strong, and his voice has the very tones which used to bless my ear! Can I, then, fail to listen, when Augustus speaks? His manners are elegant, without being studied or coxcomical. As yet he has not talked much, but I suspect the singular situation in which we are placed has been the cause of this taciturnity; for I have now and then observed an arch turn of humour, not quite free from sarcasm, when he has addressed himself to Mrs. Merton, but more of this hereafter.

I am not likely to lose my *senses* and *fall in love*, as it is called; but I freely confess to you, my dear Mrs. Milbanke, that I think my cousin is a singularly prepossessing young man,—most probably his opinion of your Olivia is quite the reverse. But to proceed.—

After half an hour's conversation, in which Mrs. Merton and my uncle were the chief speakers, the latter proposed our departure, expressing his sense of obligation to Mrs. Honeywood in high terms of politeness. I could only throw myself into the arms of this kind friend, whom, in all human probability, I shall never see again. My heart was too full for utterance, but she felt and understood its beatings. I tore myself from her, and giving my hand to Honeywood, I indistinctly murmured farewel; he pressed it to his lips, his "God bless you!" was fervently audible, and it drew forth the affected smile of Mrs. Merton, as she preceded us down the stairs with a languid careless step, which could not have been exceeded by the most die-away lady in the whole island of Jamaica.

My uncle was leading me; but, as if fearful that there should be any failure of attention, he said, "Augustus, assist Mrs. Merton." The son was obedient, and the lady's—"I do very well, I thank you," was said in a tone of restrained mortification.

Mrs. Merton would be thought pretty by any person who looks for feature only. She is very fair, and very fat; her eyes are the lightest blue, her cheeks exhibit a most beautiful (but I am apt to believe not a natural) carmine; her hair is flaxen; her teeth are dazzlingly white; her hand and arm would rival alabaster. Yet with all these concomitants to beauty, she fails to interest or to please your Olivia. And you must allow, my dear friend, that I am not usually difficult; and you remember that I have frequently told you, that I had not a greater pleasure, than in studying the countenance of a beautiful woman of your country. Whence, then, is this change of sentiment, you will say, in regard to Mrs. Merton?—Ah! whence is it, indeed! for I am but too well inclined to behold my uncle's family with partiality.

I do not think this lady seems endowed with a more than common portion of feeling; this may be her misfortune, and not her fault: or rather, I should say, that too much feeling is to be considered as a misfortune to the possessor; therefore, on this score, I should be invidious and unchristian-like, to judge harshly of Mrs. Merton: but there is such a splenetic tendency in every word she utters, such a look of *design*, accompanied with so much self-importance, and so large a portion of conceit and affectation, with such frivolous conversation, that I seem hardly to consider her as a rational being; though she is a wholly inoffensive one to me, for I can never be hurt by the manners of a person whom I do not respect; and that *she* considers *me* as but *one* remove from the brute creation, is very evident.

So here, perhaps, we meet on equal terms. Mrs. Merton was a city-heiress, with a large fortune, which she thinks entitles her to a large portion of respect and attention;—and my good uncle administers it unceasingly. Perhaps he thinks it necessary to be doubly assiduous from seeing the carelessness of Augustus, who, without being rude (which I suspect is not in his nature), seems perfectly indifferent to all the imposing claims of his fair sister-in-law.

Mr. Merton appears about sixty years of age; he wears his own thin and grey hair, nicely dressed and powdered; his person is tall, but not graceful, for there is a stiffness in it which he cannot shake off, though he tries to divest himself of it by an invariable politeness and attention. His dress is plain, but remarkably neat; and his polished shoes, and silk stockings, are always in print. He treats me with the most studied regard,—"My dear niece,—my dearest Miss Fairfield,—and my beloved ward,"—are the appellations which he distinguishes me by,—and could I suspect myself of so speedily inspiring regard, I should judge that he already felt for me a paternal affection; but while he addresses me in this style, to Mrs. Merton he is, on the other hand, as kind and as tender:—"My dear madam, my good daughter," and such pleasing expressions, are dealt in equal, if not larger portions to her; as, perhaps, he guesses that *this* lady would not be very well pleased to have a *rival* even in *his* favour. My uncle's conversation is formal and precise: he tries to be what is called a lady's man, but does not *quite* know the way to set about it. Subjects on which he talks to them, are not, I can easily perceive, those on which he is most conversant. I suspect, that he devoted too many years to the compting-house, to make him an agreeable trifler. Yet his principles appear honest and upright, and I dare say he is a man who has passed through the world, maintaining a strict character for probity and integrity as a merchant. As I have said before, I have seen too little of Augustus, to judge of his talents, or his qualities. Ah! my dear friend, a prepossessing exterior has oft been known to veil a deformed mind! Yet, surely, this cannot be the case here;—and if it were—if I were to make the fatal discovery, what should I gain, when a month,—a short month, will probably unite me to him for life: probably, I say, for it is optional to Augustus. You know, my dear Mrs. Milbanke, he has the *liberty* of refusing me, and when, at times, I perceive an abstraction of manner, when I see the melancholy expressions which overspreads his countenance, I am ready to spring from my seat, to fall on my knees before him, and to beseech him, not to make a sacrifice of his own and of my happiness; till called to order, by an address of his father, an application for his opinion, or a reference to his judgment, the smile plays round his mouth, and his whole countenance is illumined by an expression of sweetness and placidity which makes me a sceptic to my preconceived opinion.

IN CONTINUATION
    IF I may judge by the servants, carriages, &c. which I see, Mr. Merton and his son both live in a style of princely magnificence.

There is something, I think, not very far removed from ostentation in the manner of Mr. Merton; he loves to talk of thousands and tens of thousands, in the indifferent careless way with which another would speak of pence. Persons who have risen to importance by their own means, often fall into this failing. I have frequently remarked it among some of our wealthy planters. I must proceed with my history when an opportunity offers, therefore you will have a packet of mutilated scraps.

IN CONTINUATION

THE first day was passed by my uncle in inquiries concerning the Fairfield estate, its situation, its produce, and other topics on which he thought I was conversant. I felt the kindness of his intention, and gave him all the information which I thought might entertain him: insensibly I lost the timidity of my manner, and became unrestrained and at ease. I am naturally of a communicative, and, I hope, of a cheerful temper; I felt that I could gain nothing by silence and seeming stupidity. I knew that my first appearance could not have been very prepossessing, and by gently sliding into my natural character, I should show my new relatives what they might expect; and, I confess, to be thought favourably of by them (ah! why should I deny it? by Augustus in particular) is a wish very near my heart. Mr. Merton, all politesse and attention, seemed much pleased by my remarks. Mrs. Merton affected to take no interest or share in the conversation, but played, by turns, with her little boy, about three years of age, and her pug dog: it would be difficult to say which was the greatest pet, if the partiality of grand-papa did not obviously turn the scale on the side of the child, who would really be a most lovely creature if mamma did not so entirely spoil him. All this is to be understood in parenthesis. Augustus said little: he seemed distrait and embarrassed in his manner, yet he occasionally roused himself; and more than once, when I bore honest testimony to the virtues of my father, which a reference to his estates, and their management, naturally produced from me, he seemed affected by my manner, and looked at me with an expression of solicitude which made my heart flutter, and my cheeks glow.

IN CONTINUATION

I CAN see that there is not a being in creation for whom Mrs. Merton had a stronger portion of contempt, than for myself: if her husband is of her disposition, how dreadful would be a state of dependence on such a pair! And yet, if Augustus Merton refuses her offered hand, such must be the situation of your poor Olivia!—Perhaps this city lady, whose ideas are all centred in self, and in money, as the grand minister to all her capricious indulgences—perhaps this lady might have no objection to become the *protectress* of a poor *girl of colour*, or to *receive* an acquisition of *fortune* at the same time; and for this reason she may be acting politically, by trying to infect Augustus with a portion of that distaste and antipathy which she invariably evinces towards me; thinking that she may thus induce him to forego his claim to *me* and to *my* fortune—but a generous mind would not thus be warped—Mrs. Merton foils herself. The very means she employs to humble and mortify me, excites the attention and the respectful consideration of Augustus. This inactive lady cannot leave her bed very soon of a morning. I had some time waited a summons to breakfast, when at last I ventured down stairs; Dido having assured me that Mr. Augustus's man had dressed his master more than two hours: however, there was no sign of breakfast below, and I returned to my own room, and wrote the foregoing page before the bell had sounded; but, in returning to my apartment, the door of a room being a-jar, my eyes caught the figure of Augustus Merton. His arms were folded, his head almost rested on his breast, and he looked the very image of melancholy despondence.—Alas! was *I*, then, the cause of these sorrowful reflections? was he meditating on the *sacrifice* he was so *soon* required to make?—A sacrifice, perhaps, of the cherished affections of his heart—a sacrifice of his happiness!—Oh, Mrs. Milbanke, how fraught with misery is the idea!

IN CONTINUATION

IN an elegant morning dishabille,[1] Mrs. Merton reclined on an ottoman: she just made the morning salutation as I entered, and then relapsed again into the intent and important study (as it appeared) of "Bell's Belle Assembly, or Gallery of Fashion:"[2] a modern periodical publication, where the ladies have coloured specimens of the costume and habits in which they are to array themselves every month. Mr. Merton was reading the newspapers, but he laid them down on seeing me; advanced—took my hand—made particular inquiries after my health—drew a chair

---

1 The state of being carelessly or partially dressed.
2 Nikolaus Heideloff's *Gallery of Fashion*, a luxurious fashion magazine published between 1794 and 1803.

for me—and placed himself next me. The urn steamed before her, but the fashionable fair did not notice it, till gently reminded by Mr. Merton with,—"Shall I assist you in putting some water in the tea-pot, Mrs. Merton?"

"Oh, by all means," said she, yawning, "and make the tea also; for it is a terrible bore!"

"I see you are engaged in an interesting study," said Mr. Merton; "you ladies employ every opportunity in rendering yourselves, if possible, more irresistible than you were formed by nature!" And the old gentleman very accommodatingly took the tea-chest in his hand.

"You must suffer *me* to do this, sir," said I; "I like the office; it is one which I have been accustomed to; and you see I am perfectly disengaged."

"I yield it with pleasure into abler hands," said Mr. Merton, bowing gallantly as he resigned it to me.

Augustus now came in, and paid his compliments in a cheerful, unconstrained manner. "So soon put in employ, Miss Fairfield?" said he.

"Oh yes, the *lady* is of an *active* turn I find," said Mrs. Merton, still meditating on the coloured print which she held in her hand.

A servant now entered with a large plate of boiled rice. Mrs. Merton half raised her head, saying—"Set it there," pointing towards the part of the table where I sat.

"What is this?" asked Mr. Merton.

"Oh, I thought that Miss Fairfield—I understood that people of your—I thought that you almost *lived* upon rice," said Mrs. Merton, "and so I ordered some to be got,—for my own part, I never tasted it in my life, I believe!"

Mrs. Milbanke, this was evidently meant to mortify your Olivia; it was blending *her* with the poor negro slaves of the West Indies! It was meant to show her, that, in Mrs. Merton's idea, there was no distinction between us—you will believe that *I could not* be wounded at being classed with my brethren!

Augustus coloured, and looked indignantly towards Mrs. Merton: his father tried to palliate, by saying, if I would give him leave, he would help himself to a little of it; while I, perfectly unabashed, and mistress of myself, pretended to take the mischievous officiousness, or impertinence (which you will), of Mrs. Merton in a literal sense; and, turning towards her, said,—"I thank you for studying my palate, but I assure you there is no occasion; I eat just as you do, I believe: and though, in Jamaica, our poor slaves (*my brothers and sisters*, smiling) are kept upon rice as their chief food, yet they would be glad to exchange it for a little of your nice wheaten bread here;" taking a piece of baked bread in my hand.

The lady looked rather awkward, I thought, but she was doubly diligent in the study of the fashions; while Augustus offered me the butter, and my father's smile played round his mouth.

I am confident, that at *this* moment his countenance expressed approbation of your Olivia. Presently, little George came running into the room, and, without noticing the opened arms of his grandfather, he ran to his mother— "Oh. Mamma! mamma! look at poor George's face—that nasty black woman has been kissing me, and dirtying my face all over!"

"Hush, hush!" said Mrs. Merton, *pretending* to silence the child on *my* account, while the pleased expression of her countenance could not be misconstrued.

"No, I don't mean *her*," said George pointing at me, "but one much, *much* dirtier—so *very* dirty, you can't think, mamma!— Nasty woman, to dirty my face!"

"You must go to your room, George, if you do not hold your tongue directly!"

"Pray do not check him, Mrs. Merton," said I; "there is something bewitchingly charming in infantine simplicity.—How artless is this little fellow! his lips utter the sentiments of his heart—and those alone!—My love, you will soon lose that beautiful character of your mind, ingenuousness; for it is a sad and melancholy truth, that as we grow older, we grow acquainted with dissimulation."

"It is too true, indeed!" said Mr. Merton.

Augustus sighed deeply.

"Come hither, my little fellow," said I, "and I promise *I* will not kiss you!"

"Why, I should not so much mind if *you* were to kiss me," said he; "for your lips are red, and besides, your face is not so very, *very* dirty."

"Go to Miss Fairfield, George," said Augustus.

"With all my heart, uncle!" said he.

I took him on my lap, and holding his hand in mine, I said,— "You see the difference in our hands?"

"Yes, I do, indeed," said he, shaking his head. "Mine looks *clean* and *yours* looks *not* so very dirty."

"I am glad it does not look so *very* dirty," said I; "but you will be surprised when I tell you that mine is quite as clean as your own, and that the black woman's below, is as clean as either of them."

"Oh now, what nonsense you are telling me!" said he, lifting up both his hands in astonishment.

"No," returned I, "it is very good sense: do you know who made you?"

"My grand-papa said God," answered he.

"Oh, if you mean *that*, he is very backward in his *catechism*," said Mrs. Merton: "I am sure *I* could not pretend to *teach* it to him."

"So I should imagine, if you think Miss Fairfield put the first question of it to him," said Augustus, rather sarcastically.

"The same God that made *you* made me," continued I—"the poor black woman —the whole world—and every creature in it! A great part of this world is peopled by creatures with skins as black as Dido's, and as yellow as mine. God chose it should be so, and we cannot make *our* skins white, any more than you can make yours black."

"Oh! But *I* can make mine black if I choose it," said he, "by rubbing myself with coals."

"And so can I make mine white by rubbing myself with *chalk*," said I; "but both the coal and the chalk would be soon rubbed off again."

"And won't *yours* and *hers* rub off?" said he.

"Try," said I, giving him the corner of my handkerchief; and to work the little fellow went with all his might.

"George, you are very rude and troublesome to Miss Fairfield," said Mr. Merton.

"Not in the least," said I; "it is right that he should *prove* the truth of what I have been telling him, he will then believe me another time."

"Yes, that I shall," said he, sighing and resigning his employment, as if it had wearied him.

"What do you sigh for, George?" asked Augustus.

"I could wish," said he, looking at me, "that God had made you white, ma'am, because you are so *very* good-natured; but I will kiss *you*, if you like."

"Thank you for the wish, my dear child, and for the favour conferred upon me," said I, pressing his cherub lips to mine. "I am not a little proud of this as I consider it a conquest over prejudice!"

"*Your* arguments are irresistible, you find, Miss Fairfleld," said my uncle, smiling.

"Prejudices imbibed in the nursery are frequently attached to the being of ripened years," said Augustus; "and to eradicate them as they appear, is a labour well worth the endeavour of the judicious preceptor."

"Suppose I proceed a little further," said I, "for at present I have gained but half a victory.—So you still dislike my poor Dido, George?"

"She is *very* dirty," said he, again shaking his head; but colouring, he said, "I mean *very black*."

"She is a *poor negro*, you know," said Mrs. Merton, in a most sneering and contemptuous tone.

"But she is the most faithful of creatures, George," said I, not deigning to answer his mother, "and I love her dearly!"

"Do *you* love her dearly?" said he, looking up in my face, with a very scrutinizing expression. "Only think grand-papa, only think uncle, Miss Fairfield says she loves the blackamoor dearly!"

"I dare say she has reason to estimate her," said Mr. Merton.

"Indeed I have, sir, as your grandson shall hear:—She was born upon my papa's estate," said I, addressing my attentive little hearer; "her father and her mother were slaves, or, as *you* would call them, servants to him."

"But these black slaves are no better than horses over there," said George, interrupting me; "for I heard the coachman telling one of the grooms so, in the servants' hall, last night."

"You should not go into the servants' hall, George," said his grandfather.

"I only went to ask about your black mare, sir," said the little fellow "you know you told me yourself that she was lame!"

There was no resisting this sweet and simple apology.

"Well, do not interrupt Miss Fairfield, when she is so good as to talk to you," said Mr. Merton, smiling significantly at Augustus; for Mrs. Merton now appeared to think the conversation as great a *bore* as making *tea*, and, walking to the further part of the room, she was patting her pug dog, and humming a tune at the same time.

"Those black slaves are, by some cruel masters, obliged to work like horses," said I; "but God Almighty created them *men*, equal with their masters, if they had the same advantages, and the same blessings of education."

"But what *right* have their naughty masters got to make them slave like horses? for I'm *sure* they can't like it— I shouldn't like to work like mamma's coach-horses, and stand shivering for hours in the wet and cold, as they do."

"There will be no end of this conversation, if we come to the *right* and the *wrong*," said I.

"It is beginning to wear an interesting form, I think," said Mr. Merton. "George, we shall have your sentiments on the abolition presently."

"Miss *Fairfield's rather!*" said Mrs. Merton.

"Mine will, I hope, be immediately understood; the feelings of humanity, the principles of my religion, would lead me, as a Christian, I trust, to pray for the extermination of this disgraceful traffic, while *kindred claims* (for such I must term them) would likewise impel me to be anxious for the emancipation of *my* more immediate brethren!"

"Born, as you were, in the West Indies, your father a planter, I should have imagined that you would have entertained quite the contrary side of the question," said Mrs. Merton, who now thought she had found a subject on which to attack me.

I slightly answered, "You did *not know* my father, madam!"

But I could not pursue my story with George; something swelled at my throat and I was obliged to leave the room, though little George took my promised vindication of Dido upon trust, and running after me said—"Miss Fairfield, if you are going to Dido, let me go with you."

I fear I shall tire you, my friend, by this prolix narration, but I was willing to give you a complete surfeit of Mrs. Merton, even though I may frequently be under the necessity of repeating the dose.

IN CONTINUATION

HOW many pages have I written without having mentioned the dear Honeywoods; but they have not been forgotten; their kindness and sympathetic attention will often force the unbidden tear to roll over my cheek, when I am retired to my own apartment, and to rumination. Mrs. Honeywood promised to write to me, and I impatiently wait the fulfillment of it;—but, alas! my fearfully foreboding heart tells me that we shall never meet again in this world! And thus may I be said to have lost my two only friends!—for, ah! what a wide expanse of ocean now lies between Mrs. Milbanke and her ever affectionate

OLIVIA FAIRFIELD!

IN CONTINUATION

ARE my letters to be constantly filled with sarcastic observations on Mrs. Merton? I must speak of what I see, and while she is my exclusive female companion, I fear I shall have but too many opportunities of noticing the—what shall I call it—give her behaviour a name, dearest Mrs. Milbanke—I would not willingly be too harsh; I *ought* not be so, for I suspect that the respectful attention which Augustus pays me, is from his witnessing the uniform negligence or insolence of this woman.—I mark the deep flush which crimsons his countenance, when a new instance of either kind falls under his notice, and the dexterity with which he contrives to evince his disapprobation without being personal to his sister, and the generous consideration which bids him respect my feelings—whilst his even-handed father goes on smoothly, looking to the right and the left by turns, now complimenting and now smiling, temporizing and glossing over, and never swerving from the rule which he has laid down for his conduct. And yet I think, that could I dive to the bottom of his complaisant heart, I should discover that I ranked pretty high in his favour. I walk with him arm in arm over the beautiful downs near this place; a favour which I shrewdly suspect Mrs. Merton never conferred upon him; for with regard to the *use* which she has made of them during the few days I have been here, a casual observer might have been led to inquire, whether she *had* any legs; for she certainly seems to derive no manner of assistance from them!—*You* taught me activity, both mental and bodily, my beloved friend; and nothing more frequently excited my surprise, and I may add, disgust, than the languid affectation and supine manners of some of our West Indians; but I never saw any one of them who could in the least compare with Mrs. Merton, who seems to have attained the very height of *inaction*. In our walks we are sometimes joined by Augustus, and to give you my reason for imputing his general conduct to his dislike of Mrs. Merton's behaviour to me, he is then thoughtfully silent, and leaves his father to keep up the ball of conversation without interruption on his part.— Ah, my dear madam! my heart flutters while I make this observation even to myself—a thoughtful, an abstracted companion, to one of my open—my communicative turn of mind—no confidence, no reciprocal interchange of opinions and sentiments!— What a blank!—what a chasm does existence appear, taken in this view!—It is in the mercy of my heavenly Father that I look for support through the trials which await me, and how thankful am I to my dear Father for *implanting*, and to you for nourishing, in my mind a strong sense of a superintending Providence. If I was at this moment destitute of religion, I should be the most pitiable of human beings; for, indeed, my dearest friend, there are so many conflicting emotions in this poor bosom—I am transplanted into a scene so perfectly new—Mrs. Merton's manners are so different from any person's with whom the *petted Olivia* ever associated—and then, the *short* period which is allotted me by my father's will, ere I am to change my situation—with no friend into whose ear I can pour the presaging fears with which, at times, my heart is fraught—the delicacy of my situation—the seeming impossibility of my learning the *real* sentiments of Augustus—if, I say, it was not for my firm faith in God, how could I support myself? And, amidst every unpleasantry by which I am surrounded, it is an inexpressible source of satisfaction, to be in a country where the rites of religion are duly and properly performed. Our great distance from a place of worship, when at the Fairfield estate, was, you know, frequently lamented by us all. In England the "sound of the church-going bell"[1] will always reach the ear on the morning of the Sabbath, and I trust that your Olivia shall never be unmindful of the pious summons.

IN CONTINUATION

YOU have frequently remarked, that I walk in a manner peculiar to myself. *You* have termed it majestic and graceful; I have been fearful that it carried something of a proud expression: but I believe it is very difficult to alter the natural gait, and I am too much above the common size, with regard to height, to walk like the generality of my sex. There must surely, however, be something very particular in my air; for I find I am an object of general curiousity, and many a gentleman follows to repass me, and to be mortified at his folly when he has caught a view of my mulatto countenance. I laugh at this, and tell Mr. Merton to observe them, while he most gallantly, retains all the fine things that he hears (or fancies he hears) on my shape and person, and very injudiciously has retailed them before his daughter-in-law, whose form being *any* thing but elegant or graceful, you may conceive that the old gentleman soon found out that he had been "all in the wrong;" especially, when, after hearing a remark of the kind, Mrs. Merton turned round with great *nonchalance* to me, saying,—

"Pray, Miss Fairfield, did you ever learn to tread the stage?"

"I am now learning, madam," returned I (but without any pet-

---

1 William Cowper, "Verses Supposed to be written by Alexander Selkirk during his solitary abode in the Island of Juan Fernandez" (1782).

tishness of manner, if I know myself), "to tread on the great stage of the world, and, I fear, I shall find it very difficult to play my part as I could wish."

"It is the peculiar province of real merit, to be diffident of its powers," said Augustus.—

"Even while its superiority is acknowledged by an admiring multitude," said his father.

"A tragedy-queen would suit you vastly, I should think," said Mrs. Merton, pursing up her lip.

"I should prefer comedy, both in real and artificial scenes," said I.

"But you have nothing comic about you," rejoined she.

"'Except temper and inclination,' said I. "I bless God, that till I had the misfortune of losing my dear parent, I was always one of the 'laughter-loving crew.'"

"How mistaken have I been in your character!"

"So I think," said Augustus, drily.

I never know when to lay down my pen, when addressing my earliest friend, but I must break off, as it is high time to attend to the toilette; for tonight I am going to the ball with Mrs. Merton, and Dido is almost out of patience with her "Missee."

IN CONTINUATION

YOU will expect an account of the first English ball which I have ever seen, and I will not tell you that I thought it an unpleasant one, for my partner was Augustus Merton. I never saw him so agreeable, so animated, or so attentive before; he gave me confidence in myself, his gaiety inspired mine, and, I believe, I danced with more than my usual spirit. I wore a black sarsnet, made in the mode, of course, and had no ornaments but a large string of corals round my neck. I could observe that I was an object of pretty general curiosity, as I entered the room. In such a place as this, the wealth of the Mertons makes them generally known. *My* colour, you know, renders *me* remarkable, and, no doubt, the Clifton world are well acquainted with the particulars of my father's will, and, seeing me leaning on the arm of Augustus, gave it general publicity; for Mrs. Merton, on stepping from the carriage, seized the arm of the old gentleman, and I was, consequently, thrown upon the protection of his son. But Augustus came forwards with the utmost promptitude; and this readiness on his part, gave me resolution to acquit myself in as unconstrained a manner as I could have wished. I could even listen, with much entertainment, to the remarks which escaped him from time to time, and became, in my turn, communicative.

Surely, my dearest Mrs. Milbanke, it is the fashion to be very affected, or very rude: there seems, in the generality of the people that I see here, to be no medium between these extremes. Some of the ladies, so mincing, so simpering, so lisping, and others so bold, so loud, so confident; all the shame-facedness of the sex, which was once thought a charm by the wisest of men, seems entirely exploded: and the men—also believe me—they walked up in pairs, hanging one on another's arm, and, with a stare of effrontery, eyed your Olivia, as if they had been admitted purposely to see the *untamed savage* at a shilling a piece! While Augustus, was engaged in conversation at a little distance, I heard one of these *animals* say to another—

"Come, let's have a stare at *Gusty's* black princess!"

And with the greatest *sang froid* they *slouched* (for it could not be called walking) up to me; one of them placed his glass most leisurely to his eye, then shrugging his shoulders, as he looked, he said—

"*Pauvre diable!* how I pity him!—a *hundred* thousand wouldn't be enough for the cursed sacrifice!—*Allons Alex.* Let's 'keep moving.' I've had enough—no more—I thank you—quite satisfied, 'pon honour."

Then, touching the shoulder of Mrs. Merton, he said,—

"Ah, *ma bella* Merton, is this you?—What! you sport a *native* to-night, I find."

"I do, *en vérité*," said she, smiling, and appearing thoroughly to understand his knowing wink.

"In *native* elegance unrivalled!" said a gentleman, who stood at his elbow, and had, some minutes before, been attentively surveying me. "More grace, more expression, more characteristic dignity, I never yet beheld in one female figure!"

Mrs. Milbanke, *you* will not accuse me of any foolish vanity in retailing these hyperbolical compliments on myself.

"Monkland is ever in the sublime," said my *quizzing* beau. "Dear Monkland, now *do* fall desperately in love with this sable goddess, and strive to wrest the palm of victory from the enviable Augustus Merton!"

"No," said he, "I love Merton too well to envy him his happiness; but I will get introduced to Miss Fairfield immediately, for I must know if she is really what her countenance bespeaks."

"Exactly, believe me!" said Mrs. Merton.

Mr. Monkland, however, did not, or would not, hear; he was

instantly introduced to me by Augustus.—Perhaps I was flattered by having overheard his favourable opinion of me; we entered into conversation, and I found him a pleasant though an eccentric and visionary being; he made sarcastic observations on every body he saw, and seemed to wield his talent for satire with no light hand. I was introduced to several more of both sexes whose names I have forgotten, for common characters passing indiscriminately, leave no impression on the mind or the memory; but as I was standing in the dance; I was somewhat surprised to see Mrs. Merton led to the top of it by a gentleman, who footing it off with her at the moment when my eyes caught them, so forcible was the contrast, that I could scarcely refrain from laughter—Indeed I have a great taste for the ridiculous, and here I am likely to have it *improved,—improved* is a bad word for *such* a taste my dear governess will say, but she has been used to see the spontaneous effusions of her pupil's mind—so it shall pass. I have described the person of Mrs. Merton to you before, she is certainly not formed with the "light fantastic toe,"[1] but languishes, or rather glides, down a dance in the most careless and indifferent manner you can imagine. Her partner appeared to have nearly reached his grand climacteric,[2] yet he had taken wonderful pains in trying to put himself back at least thirty years, by powdering and pomatuming his grey hairs, making his whiskers as large and as well shaped as possible, half closing his light *green* eyes, to give them an insinuating expression, though that expression was lost in the inflamed circles which surrounded their orbits; his nice cravat was well stuffed round his throat, his cloaths were of the most fashionable and jemmy make, and the well turned leg was still an object of admiration, as it had been through many a revolving season, to its owner! His determined activity, his strict attention to the figure of the dance, to the step, to his partner; the smile which was always to be seen on his countenance, so self-satisfied, so conscious of unimpaired powers of attraction,

---

1 John Milton, *L'Allegro* (1645): "Come, and trip it, as you go, / On the light fantastic toe."

2 Beginning at the age of seven and reoccurring at various years that are multiples of seven, the climacterics were considered by the ancient Greeks to be critical years in an individual's life. During these years the individual's body would undergo changes and be at greater risk of death. The last one of them—the "grand climacteric"—occurred at 63 years old.

the agility which he evidently laboured to exert, and his thin figure, were all in such direct opposition to the little fat form and composed manner of Mrs. Merton, that I carelessly turned round to the lady who stood the next couple to me, and said— "Pray, ma'am, can you tell me the name of the gentleman now going down the dance?" "He is my brother, ma'am, Colonel Singleton"—the flippant answer of the lady arrested my attention.—Surely the Colonel and Miss Singleton must have been twin children! I never saw such proximity of character and manner as in this brother and sister: they must never marry, but grow *young* (for old they can never be) together. Miss Singleton's labours must be as arduous as her brother's, though her face looks at last, more weather-beaten than does the gallant colonel's. Her natural complexion is not far removed from your Olivia's, and I thought a white satin was a bad choice for a robe; and pitied her poor shrivelled and thin neck, which, with some of her brother's wadding, would have looked to more advantage, than adorned by her superb necklace of diamonds. Feathers of the ostrich were mounted in several directions from her head, while her bared ears, and elbows, and back, and bosom, gave to her whole contour, so freezing and so forlorn an appearance, while her volatility, and frisky and girlish airs, made her person so very conspicuous, that I could not help surveying her with the utmost curiosity, as a species of animal which had never before fallen under my notice. She was dancing with a *boy*, who aped the *man*, as much as his partner threw herself back into the *girl*: and the pleased attention with which she listened to all he said; the air of maiden consciousness which she adopted, while he held her minikin[1] fan and she whispered into the youthful Adonis's ear; the tap which the *said* fan now gave him on the cheek—oh, Mrs. Milbanke, you could not have forgotten a scene so ridiculous! And then the captivating colonel holding his ungloved and white hand (so as to exhibit a ring of sparkling brilliants) at the side of his face, while Mrs. Merton spoke, as if to draw the attention of the company to something with which they must not be acquainted, and then holding his handkerchief to be perfumed from Mrs. Merton's otto of roses![2]—You cannot wonder at my thinking of the line in the

---

1 Diminutive.
2 Attar (or otto) of roses: rose oil; fragrant oil obtained from roses and used in making perfume.

song, "Sure such a pair were never seen!"[1] You will say I am very light-hearted to descant so largely on such frivolous subjects—and I should call myself so if I were sure that no splenetic feelings aided my pen; but I am disappointed in England: I expected to meet with sensible, liberal, well informed and rational people, and I have not found them; I see a compound of folly and dissimulation — but hold! let me not be harsh or hasty in my judgement, a ball-room is not the place to meet with the persons I expected, neither must I look for them within the circle of Mrs. Merton's friends. I can see that Augustus has an utter distaste to the general frivolity which reigns in these places; I suspect he will prefer my plan of a country life and retirement: but nothing has yet been said on the subject, and time steals on. Ah, my dearest friend! shall I ever more enjoy that placid happiness, that calm tranquility, which surrounded me at the Fairfield plantation? Heaven alone can tell—But in all situations, in all places, I am still, and ever shall be,

Your own affectionate and grateful
OLIVIA FAIRFIELD.

IN CONTINUATION

I HAVE not been able to write; my mind has been in too great a tumult to put pen to paper, and the time I usually employed in writing, my ever dear friend, has been spent in walking to and fro my apartment, with restless step and a perturbed heart!

The morning after I last wrote, I received a formal message from my uncle, and, according to the summons, attended him in the room, which is appropriated to his morning avocations; he rose at my entrance, met me at the door, and, with his usual formal politeness, handed me to a seat.—

"Pardon the liberty I have taken, my dear Miss Fairfield, in requesting the favour of your company; but I wished to have your approbation with regard to settlements, &c. previous to giving my lawyer necessary instructions—Augustus refers entirely to us, to make arrangements as we think proper!"

I felt uncomfortably as Mr. Merton spoke—I could not answer him.

---

1   "The New Way of the Highland Laddie," in *The Chearful Companion containing a Select Collection of Favourite Scots and English Songs, Catches &c.* (Perth: J. Gillies, 1783) CCXII, 280-81. The correct wording is "Ah! Sure a pair was never seen."

"Your late father's will," continued he—

I started from my seat—"Full well I know its contents!" cried I—"Oh, Mr. Merton, *I* cannot, *I* must not *refuse* your son the fatal interdiction of my father!—a vow—an irrevocable vow, forbids me! But, sir, your son is *not* so bound, he has still the exercise of his reason, *he* is a free agent—surely then a fear of hurting *my* feelings (for I cannot for a moment imagine Mr. Augustus Merton to be actuated by mercenary views) will not lead him to barter his liberty and his happiness, and to unite himself to a woman who is not the object of his affection!"

I believe I appeared much agitated; and that I expressed myself with great warmth and energy!

Mr. Merton looked in silence for a moment, but with extreme surprise evidently depicted on his countenance, and then said,—

"My dear young lady, if my son is so unfortunate as to be beheld by you with disapprobation, I sincerely pity him; but am sure he will readily forego all claim to your hand, rather than you should unite yourself where you cannot love!"

Ah, Mrs. Milbanke! had Mr. Merton understood the language of the looks, my emotion at this moment, my burning blushes, would have proclaimed another tale! I cast down my eyes to the ground in conscious confusion, they dared not meet his, but Mr. Merton proceeded—

"You may have seen another object prior to your introduction to Augustus, who may have gained an interest in your heart, Miss Fairfield—if so, I pity my poor boy!"

"No, indeed, sir, that is not the case!" said I, with eager warmth.—

"Then my interesting friend," said my uncle, taking my hand, "if it *be* not so, I greatly pity you—a state of *nominal* dependence (for such I trust would be the case if George Merton were your protector) would still be a severe trial to one, who has been educated as you have been.—Your father's will was singular, very singular; I make no doubt that he acted from consideration: but yet it has always struck me as not being the *kind* of will, which most men in his situation would have made—Well, let it pass, we cannot alter it, we must even act by its authority; and I repeat my fear, that a state of wardship would he *rather* disagreeable to a lady of your liberal notions?"

"Servitude, slavery, in its *worst* form, would be preferable," said I, "to finding myself the wife of a man by whom I was not beloved!"

"My dear niece"—

"My dear sir, I know what you are going to say—You would say (though you might word it in softer terms), *how* can you expect to be the selected object of the affections of Augustus Merton, when he never knew you till within a few days?—Ah, sir! I too well know the impossibility of the thing to expect it—I am aware of my own person—I know that I am little less than a disgusting object to an Englishman—I know that your son (supposing for a moment that he could get over his own prejudices as to colour) would have to encounter all the sarcastic innuendoes and jeering remarks of his companions; it would be said with confidence, and with truth, that he had sold himself for money; he would *feel* that he had done so; he would never look at me without seeing the witness of the sacrifice. I should be neglected and despised!"

"My beloved Miss Fairfield, you are voluntarily raising up bugbears to disturb your happiness; the chimeras of your own imagination affright you, and hurt your peace of mind!"

"Alas! My dear sir, it is but too true, that every feeling of my soul is wounded in my present situation—Oh, my dearest father, my misjudging father, you could not foresee the humiliating state in which you placed your child!—Suing for the hand of a man, to whom she is an object of indifference, if not aversion!"

"Again let me entreat you to calm your emotions, my dear young lady, and to see things in a different point of view."

"I see them as they are, sir," said I, shaking my head.

"Not so, believe me,—through a prejudiced medium you now look—I am confident that my son admires and esteems you—I am sure that he will devote his life to the study of your happiness, and that you will never have reason to repent the choice which your good father has made for you."

Ah, dearest friend, esteemed Mrs. Milbanke! how could I say to Mr. Merton all with which my full heart was bursting? But if Augustus had entertained a common regard, *even* an esteem, for your Olivia, would he have deputed his *father* to have entered into this conversation, which *he* seems to have avoided with the most scrupulous care? In a few days, am I to unite my fate with that of a man, who has never *said* that it is his wish, that it should be so! As well might my *fortune* only have crossed the ocean, the *nominal* wife might still have remained in Jamaica—And, oh that she was still there—oh that Mrs. Milbanke, with kind counsel and friendly advice, was yet near her

OLIVIA FAIRFIELD!

IN CONTINUATION

INDEED, my dear madam, I know not what to do; the reserve of Augustus increases rather than diminishes, I think, as time moves on—Good heavens! my dearest friend, how can I resolve to give him my hand, if he still retains this constrained manner?— A depression seems to hang on his spirits, melancholy clouds his brow. I think he strives to conceal this from his father and from *me*; but *I* cannot be blinded: and yet he is so interesting, his manners are so gentle, even his look of melancholy carries with it to me an air so touching, that I *think* to sooth his sorrows, to meliorate his afflictions, would constitute my happiness!

Do not despise me for my weakness my dear friend—to no other would I acknowledge it—and why not? Is it then a crime to love the man who is to become my husband?—Alas! it is lowering to the pride of my sex to love where I am not beloved again.

IN CONTINUATION

AUGUSTUS referred to his father all matters of settlement; I referred them to him also: so the old gentleman is prime agent in this business. I believe he understands these affairs better than the affairs of the heart. But I cannot be easy, dearest Mrs. Milbanke; I *must* come to an explanation with Augustus—and he seems to avoid a *tête-à-tête* with me, at least I fancy so.

Diamonds and pearls have been brought to me for inspection, these are not the precious *gems* I covet; the pearl of my husband's heart would be preferred by me to all the jewels of the east!— Mrs. Merton's sarcastic remarks on the gravity and the absence of Augustus, are made in my hearing, and in order to mortify and to wound me; but no *remarks* of *hers* can now have the power to add to the poignancy of my feelings.—The agitation of my mind mocks description—I have no power to retreat—and yet to advance with such a cheerless perspective in view—how can I have courage?

IN CONTINUATION

A WEEK has elapsed since I had last the resolution of addressing my beloved friend. At length, then, I have ventured beyond the limits usually prescribed to my sex. *I* have sought an interview with Augustus Merton. Indeed, my dearest Mrs. Milbanke, reason seemed to totter on her throne, while I imagined myself in danger of becoming the wife of a man, to whom I was an object of aversion. But why should I weary you with a tedious recapitulation of fears and feelings, which, knowing the sanguine temper of your poor girl, you have long ere now imagined?

I tried to argue myself into something like courage, when I formed the desperate resolution of asking to speak to Augustus alone; but it all forsook me when he entered the room, and the trembling abashed *woman* stood before him. He saw, and seemed to sympathize in, my confusion; he gently took my hand, and, leading me to a seat, placed his own near it, and seemed to wait for me to speak, with a respectful, though by no means a composed air.

"Mr. Merton," said I, at length breaking a silence painful to both, "you know the respective situations in which we are placed by the will of my ever-to-be-regretted parent?"

He bowed his head in token of assent; a word would have emboldened me, but this forbidding silence struck like a damp upon my heart. I had lost all command of myself—I rose, and, clasping my hands together in a beseeching attitude, I stood before him, saying,—

"It is not too late for *you* to recede. Oh, Mr. Merton, think how much misery will be spared to us, if *you* refuse the proffered terms. *You* have the power of doing so. A tame acquiescence to the will of my father, will secure to you the enjoyment of *his* fortune, certainly; but can it secure your happiness, if it is to unite you to an object, for whom you feel no regard. Do not fear to mortify me by such a rejection; I have the common failings of my sex, but I am fully acquainted with the numerous disadvantages under which, as a stranger, and a mulatto West Indian, I labour here. The good qualities which I possess (I hope I have some, or barren indeed would have been the soil which experienced the hand of the skilful labourer for many successive years),—I say the good qualities, which I may possess, are not to be discerned in my countenance. The *very* short time, which, by the unfortunate tenour of my father's will, is to elapse before this matter is decided, will preclude your coming to a knowledge of my temper and disposition. Indeed, indeed, I shall not be offended, I will *bless* you for saying, that you cannot accept my fortune on the terms with which it is offered you, if such terms are to be the shipwreck of your happiness!"

I paused,—Augustus looked earnestly in my face, he heaved a deep sigh.

"You surprise and painfully astonish me, my dearest Miss Fairfield!" said he; "is it possible that you can for a moment suppose, that I feel no regard for you? Are you so insensible to your own numerous and unrivalled virtues and perfections? Heaven is my witness, that I am warmly, sincerely interested for your happiness! and that the thought of your being, for *one* moment, a dependant on my. mercenary brother, and his weak and envious wife, would give me the cruellest uneasiness! But as this is the alternative to which you reduce yourself, if you are resolved on refusing my hand,"—

"I resolve to *refuse* your hand?" cried I, scarcely knowing what I said, "Oh, Mr. Merton how can you—If, indeed"—

Alas! I found out that I was betraying myself, by the eager gaze of Augustus; he held my hand in his, as he said,—

"Ingenuous, interesting Miss Fairfield! it is, at this moment, that I feel my utter unworthiness of this precious treasure.—Oh! may you never repent your goodness!"

Well! I have repeated enough of this *tête-à-tête*, to show, my dear friend, that we came to an *écclaircissement*. And yet I am neither satisfied with myself nor with Augustus. I fancy that I must have appeared forward, and perhaps, have now obtained from his principles and his pity, what he must have ever denied from a stronger feeling. I am again at my old stumbling-block you will say; and I begin to suspect, that these womanish fears will be the very bane of my happiness!

I have, at last, received a letter from Mrs. Honeywood: it is written, like herself;—but, alas! it contains sad accounts of her health, though the spirit of piety and resignation which pervades it, would leave me nothing to regret in her being removed from this painful world, except the loss of her friendship to myself, and the overthrow of her son's happiness, for his mother is the acting impulse of his life. Her physicians have ordered her from London to the sea; a "forlorn hope," she terms it; and thus I shall lose the chance of ever meeting her again. I had agreed to Mr. Merton's proposition of going to London on my marriage the more readily, as I had hoped to behold this dear friend once more. But it is not to be. The fleet sails to-morrow; I must, therefore, make up my large packet.

Adieu, my dearest Mrs. Milbanke! Continue to pray for one who must always pray for, and love you,

OLIVIA FAIRFIELD.

PACKET THE SECOND

London, —

My dear Mrs. Milbanke,
THE hasty lines which I wrote you on the morning that I quitted Clifton,* and which you received with my packet, will ere this have informed you, that your Olivia had become the wife of her cousin! In that moment of confusion, I had no time for particulars, and the hurry and bustle which has ensued, has scarcely afforded me leisure for an hour of calm reflection. Yet, believe me, my beloved friend, I am happy; and the attention and indulgence of my husband exceeds my highest expectations.—And yet, I had formed high expectations of the character of Augustus Merton (Fairfield he is now become). If I can be instrumental to *his* happiness, I shall have reason to bless my father for my happy lot.

"And why that *if*, Olivia?" methinks I hear you inquire.

Ah, madam! I doubt myself; I doubt my own abilities; I sometimes fear,—I think,—I fancy a thousand things, when I hear the deep sigh of my Augustus, when, I observe the pensive cast of his features. You will laugh at me,—you will, perhaps, do more—you will chide me for giving way to these fears, which *now* I know to be foolish, if not criminal. But what will you say of your Olivia, your pupil, when you hear that she is become the victim of superstition also, of nameless terrors, of—alas! she knows not what;—but she has been used to recount all her weaknesses to her friend, and she shall have the recital!

It was settled by Mr. Merton, that our nuptials were to take place at Clifton, and that from the church door, we were to set off for London. The old gentleman stood in the place of my father; Mrs. Merton did not particularly wish to be my attendant, and her presence could give me neither confidence nor comfort; so at breakfast I took leave of her, and she promised to follow us to town, with Mr. Merton and the retinue, in less than a week.

A neat and new post-chaise drove me to the church door, accompanied by my uncle; Augustus was there in readiness to hand me out. The morning had been fine, but as I entered the church, I felt the most sultry and overpowering heat that I ever experienced. The clergyman was ready,—we approached the altar! I leant on the arm of Mr. Merton, but I felt resolute and collected. I was obeying the will of my father. I was acting in con-

---

* This does not appear. [Author's note.]

94 ANONYMOUS

sonance with the impulse of my own heart. I believed the man to whom I was about to be united was worthy of my fondest regard, and I secretly besought the blessing of Heaven!

The ceremony began. I did not cast my eyes towards Augustus, till the priest was in the act of joining our hands, and had put to us the questions, and we had repeated the answers after him.— At the moment when I felt the hand of Augustus, a flash of vivid lightning came from the window over the altar; it was followed by a loud and tremendous peal of thunder. A cold sweat seemed to moisten the hand of Augustus,—it trembled in mine. I looked towards him, an icy paleness overspread his features—he leaned against the rails of the altar—his brow was rumpled—his hair stood erect!—a deep sigh issued from his bosom!—Yes, my friend it is too true,—for it pierced into the inmost recesses of the heart of his *wife*! The irrevocable vow was, indeed, passed; it seemed, as if the Almighty had condescended to ratify it,—it seemed—a thousand superstitious fears stole over my soul! Augustus's disorder had infected me, and it was some time ere I could recover my former tone of mind. The remembrance will *never* be erased from it,—it was something so awful, so singular.—Oh, Mrs. Milbanke, how terror-stricken must I then have stood, if I had borne about with me the weight of any unacknowledged crime, at the moment when I had united my fate with that of my unsuspecting husband!

But, I will turn over a new leaf and get to a new subject; for, if this be half as frightful to you as it has been to me, you will long since have wished me to drop it.

IN CONTINUATION

I HAVE been rattled over this vast metropolis, and have seen sights and spectacles without number. There is something very striking in this wondrous pile of novelty. I have partaken of every species of amusement with much satisfaction; for I have been accompanied by Augustus, and his kindness and indulgence, in showing "*this native*" (as Mrs. Merton would say) all the places and the curiosities, which *he* has so often been fatigued with, has given me a pretty good idea of his patience, while his readiness in answering all the questions of my inquisitive mind, has exhibited manifest proofs of his good-nature. So you find, I have had a "double debt to pay;"[1] and whilst visiting

---

1 Oliver Goldsmith's "The Deserted Village" (1770), in which he describes a cottage interior: "The chest contrived a double debt to pay, / A bed by night, a chest of drawers by day."

the London lions[1], I have been finding out the amiable qualities of my husband!

Mr. Merton's house, in which we are at present inmates, is fitted up in a style which proves the wealth of its owner. He is fond of showing off his own consequence; and the credit and high reputation of the London merchant, is his never-ending theme,— and a theme which cannot weary, while I behold, as I do in this city, their boundless liberality in providing for the distresses of their necessitous fellow-citizens!

Oh, Mrs. Milbanke, England is, sure, the favoured isle, where benevolence has taken up her abode! *Here* she dwells, here she smiles, while, towards my native island, she turns her "far surveying,"[2] her compassionate eye. She descries the sufferings of the poor negro, and promises benign assistance.—Yes! the cause of Afric's injured sons is heard in England; and soon shall the *slave* be free!

But think not that my visits have been wholly confined to places of public amusement and diversion; I have visited places of public worship also. I have been delighted and instructed, while hearing the words of inspiration explained by the lips of eloquence, combined with great ability and piety. And I have seen Westminster Abbey, with that enthusiastic awe which must ever strike a feeling mind on beholding this vast mausoleum of valour, genius, and worth!—While I read the inscriptions of heroes, and the epitaphs of poets, I could not help exclaiming, "Oh transitory state of human things!"[3] I could not help reflecting on the noth-

---

1 Probably referring to the menagerie in the Tower of London which housed a number of exotic animals. It was regularly open to the public by 1804.

2 William Wordsworth, *Descriptive Sketches. In Verse. Taken During a Pedestrian Tour in the Italian, Grison, Swiss and Savoyard Alps* (1793): "But now with other soul I stand alone / Sublime upon this far surveying cone."

3 Unknown reference. However, Olivia's ideas here are in line with those of the Roman Emperor, Marcus Aurelius, whose *Meditations* appeared in translation in 1792: "Nay, those facetious gentlemen, who, like Menippus, made a jest of the frail and transitory state of human life: consider, I say, that all these different characters are long since consigned to gloomy mansions of the dead. And, indeed, what evil are they sensible of in their tombs? Or what evil do they suffer, whose very names are buried in oblivion? In short, there is nothing here much worth our attention, but to act on all occasions with a regard to truth and justice, and to live peaceably even with those who act with fraud and injustice."

ingness of those, who were once the greatest on the earth. But, as the benefit of example is undisputed, it is right that their memories should be preserved by something more lasting than the evanescent praise of others, which is frequently carried on the fleeting breath of popular applause. Posthumous honour is coveted by all, and yet there cannot be a more uncertain distinction; we see it frequently refused to those, who, during their lives, were overwhelmed with praise. The son of genius and misfortune perishes unnoticed and unhonoured; his remains moulder at the side of one whom idleness and illiberality alone distinguished in life, but whose rich coffers, have, at his death, purchased for him the name of every virtue, which, surrounded by trophies of fame, are engraven on a monumental inscription of *brass*! How, then, can we covet these uncertain and indiscriminating *distinctions*?

Mr. George Merton is just what I had depicted him; fond of his own consequence, and anxious to increase it, by any unwearied application to the business of getting money; yet partial to the indulgencies of the table, and tenacious of his opinion. There appears none of that sympathy of disposition and sentiment between him and his wife which we look for in the connubial state. He seems gratified at beholding her pretty face, set off by every expensive adornment, at the head of his sumptuous entertainments, dispensing the luxuries of the feast to their various guests; and *she* seems perfectly indifferent who is at the *bottom* of the table, provided it is filled with a large party. Her fondness for the admiration and the attention of the other sex, is very apparent; and she is weak enough to be flattered with the silly compliments of the vainest and most shallow coxcombs. There is no reciprocity between the two brothers; they are coolly polite towards each other: but the confidence, which is usually and naturally induced from their relative affinity, is, from a total disparity of character, entirely done away.

My Augustus is, I can perceive, by no means fond of a London life; it is not at all consonant to my taste; and the sooner we can

---

(*The Meditations of the Emperor Marcus Aurelius Antonius. A New Translation from the Greek Original; with a life notes, &c.* By R. Graves). Additionally, Olivia's thoughts contrast with those of another literary black woman—Phillis Wheatley's "To The Rev. Dr. Thomas Amory, On Reading his Sermons On Daily Devotion, In Which That Duty Is Recommended And Assisted" (1773): "And when this transitory state is o'er, / When kingdoms fall, and fleeting Fame's no more, / May Amory triumph in immortal fame, / A nobler title and superior name!"

leave it, the better I shall be pleased. Perhaps the people have tainted my opinion of the place, for I am fatigued by the formal stiffness of Mr. Merton; I am sick of the affectation and vanity of Mrs. Merton, and disgusted at her selfish and mercenary husband. I long to be free from the restraints, and the dissimulation, which the common rules of good breeding impose in my behaviour towards them. My mind seems hampered, and I think I shall breathe more freely in the pure air, and amongst the sylvan scenes of the country. The plodding track of cent. per cent. and addition on addition, never suited the taste of Augustus; and, leaving his brother to accumulate thousands upon thousands, he is content to live on the fortune which my father's will bequeathed to him with his wife. The wise father, and the plodding brother, may laugh, but they cannot persuade him, that a "man's life *consisteth* in the abundance of the things which he possesseth," when the Word of God, and his own *heart*, both teach him the contrary.[1]

Yet, though I talk with pleased anticipation of the country, mistake me not, dearest Mrs. Milbanke; I by no means wish for perfect seclusion. I am not so vain as to imagine, that *my* society could form the exclusive happiness of my husband. No! I would fly as far from the extreme of solitude on the one hand, as from unrestrained dissipation on the other. Dissipation enervates the mind; it unfits it for every rational and domestic enjoyment; it deadens the feelings; in the vortex of pleasure, the heart is often corrupted, and the principles are sacrificed:—many very amiable characters have been ruined by the prevalence of fashionable example, the fear of being thought singular, and the dread of ridicule. "Who is sufficient for these things?"[2] not your doubting Olivia! and, therefore she would

> "Quit the world where strong temptations try,
> And, since 'tis hard to combat, learn to fly"[3]

Seclusion sours the temper, selfish and illiberal notions are insensibly cherished; the manners lose their polish; the warm

---

1 30 Luke 12:15: "a man's life does not consist in the abundance of his possessions."
2 A question posed by Paul in 2 Corinthians 2:16.
3 Oliver Goldsmith "The Deserted Village" (1770).

affections of the heart no longer expand in a full tide of benevolence, but return to their source, and freeze before the "genial current"[1] of social intercourse.

I have got a fine Utopian scheme of domestic happiness in my head, and the *country* must be the birth-place of it. The conversation of my husband, a contemplation of the beauties of nature, the society of rational and well-informed friends; books, music, drawing; the power of being useful to my fellow creatures,—to my poorer neighbours;— the exercise of religious duties,—and the grateful heart, pouring out its thanks to the Almighty bestower of such felicity! Say, dear madam, is such a plan likely to be realized by your
OLIVIA FAIRFIELD?

IN CONTINUATION

London.

Dido, notwithstanding her admiration of the sights with which this justly famed city abounds, is not at all displeased at hearing that we do not intend to live here; and that we shall soon have a house and an establishment of our own; and that too in the country.

"Ah, my dear Missee," says she, "we shall be there again, as if we were at the dear Fairfield plantation, only that Dido won't see the dear little creatures of her own colour running about:—but no matter, God Almighty provides for his own, and it be very, *very* hard, if poor Dido cannot find some little babies and their mammies to care after, and to doctor,[2] and to feed with goodee things, from her goodee Missee, go where she will!"

"Yes, that would be hard, indeed, Dido."

"Besides, Dido be *greater* there," said she, drawing up her head, with that air of pride which seems in some sort natural to her character, especially when she feels a sense of injury— "Besides Dido be *great* there, and housekeeper to her dear dearest lady, to Massa Fairfield's daughter: although here she be

---

1   Thomas Gray, "Elegy Written in a Country Churchyard" (1751): "And froze the genial current of the soul."
2   Dido's use of "doctor" as a verb is interesting especially in light of Mary Seacole's later understanding of herself as a "doctress." Both women implicitly reject the term "nurse."

"blacky," and "wowsky," and "squabby," and "guashy,"[1] and all because she has a skin not *quite* so white,—God Almighty help them all—me don't mind that though, do we, my dear Missee? But Mrs. Merton's maid treats me, as if me was her slave; and Dido was never slave but to her dear own Missee, and she was *proud* of that!"

But you know the honest heart of my faithful girl! Augustus treats her with that good-humoured kindness and freedom which is the sure way to win it; and she declares her new beautiful Massa is fit to bear the name of Fairfield, and to be the husband of the dearest Missee in the world.

[In the journal of Olivia, there is at this place a break of some weeks, which the editor laments; as her object in collecting the manuscript has been to portray the character and the sentiments of the Woman of Colour; and hence she has purposely excluded the letters of the other characters in this work: but as, by introducing two of them here, she will be filling a chasm, and letting the reader a little behind the scenes, she makes no apology for their insertion.]

LETTER THE FIRST.
MRS. GEORGE MERTON TO MISS DANBY.

Clifton.

You will laugh at me, and well you might, had I no other motive than the apparent one, for doing my *duty* here; and being so *pretty behaved* with my papa-in-law, in order to chaperon this copper-coloured girl, that is sent over as the wife of the romantic Augustus—No! There are wheels within wheels, believe me, Almenia? I have planned, and shall in time accomplish, a most noble scheme of revenge—I shall teach this Mr. Augustus, that

---

1 "Wowsky" is the famous Indian female in George Colman's *Inkle and Yarico* (1787). Samuel Johnson's *Dictionary of the English Language in Miniature* defines 'squab' as "thick and short." "Guashy" refers to "Quashy," a common literary name for male or female blacks in, for instance, Thomas Morris's poem "Quashy; or The Coal Black Maid" (1796), Samuel Jackson Pratt's *The New Cosmetic* (1790), John Fawcett's *Obi; or, Three Finger'd Jack* (1800), and "Quasheba" from Isaac Bickerstaffe's *Love in the City* (1767). See also "The Legend of Quashy" in Wylie Sypher's *Guinea's Captive Kings* (Chapel Hill: U of North Carolina P, 1942) 143-44.

"Hell has no fury like a woman scorn'd;"[1]

and that the thought of revenge, glorious revenge, can give a new impulse to her soul—can stimulate her character, and urge it beyond ordinary bounds! Happily, my husband's ruling passion, a desire of unbounded wealth, will come to my aid; and he will go hand in hand with me, without guessing at the secret motive by which I am actuated. There must be much time, and patience, ere the master-stroke can be struck; this *once* effected, you shall felicitate me on the accomplishment of my designs, and acknowledge that the pains I have taken deserved a splendid victory!—Pains? Yes, Almenia! for I have departed from my character—my wrongs have roused me to exertion, and you find I can even write a whole side of my paper. You ask for a description of this outlandish creature—She is very tall (I never *could* bear a tall woman), and holds herself erect; no easy lounge in her air; her eyes are, I believe, good, but black eyes are, in my opinion, so frightful;—her teeth, they say, are white, but any teeth would look white, I believe, when contrasted by such a skin! As to her manners, they are abominably disgusting; she is full of sentiment, and religion, and all that—and talks and expatiates, and is so firm and so decided—at the same moment that she would have it appear that she is all feeling and tenderness—such a compound! She has read a good deal I fancy; these bookish ladies are insufferable bores! But daddy Merton is all upon the complimentary order with her, and has made sixty thousand bows for her sixty thousand pounds!—I do not think I could hold out the probationary month if I dissembled; but by showing how much I am disgusted with Miss *Blacky*, I draw out *sensitive* Augustus, and put him on his metal; as *I* slight, *he* is doubly diligent—he will compassionate this "interesting mulatto"—he will marry her to rescue her from the "tyrannic fangs" of Mrs. George Merton! And I will— what will I not do? I have now raised your curiosity I know, for you were always one of Eve's genuine daughters—My dear friend, you may remain a long time on the tenter-hooks of expectation. So fare you well. Adieu!
LETITIA MERTON.

---

1   A phrase adapted from William Congreve's *The Mourning Bride* (1697): "Heaven has no rage like love to hatred turned, / Nor hell a fury like a woman scorned" (III.viii). The author might also have had Lieutenant General John Burgoyne's 1786 comedy *The Heiress* in mind since Letitia has the same thirst for vengeance as Burgoyne's heroine, Miss Alscrip, who closes the second act of this play with the same words as Letitia.

LETTER THE SECOND.
AUGUSTUS MERTON TO LIONEL MONKLAND,

Clifton.

UNWILLING as I was to accompany my father to this place, and averse in bestowing any portion of my thoughts towards that clause in my uncle's will which referred to myself, I yet at this moment behold things in a very different light; and though the barbed arrow of misfortune still rankles at my breast, and can never more be extracted, yet I am more interested for Olivia Fairfield, than I ever thought again to have been for any human being.

"'Tis not a set of features or complexion,
The tincture of a skin, that I admire."[1]

No, my friend, it is not; for I will confess to you, that the moment when my eyes were first cast on the person of my cousin, I started back with a momentary feeling nearly allied to disgust; for I beheld a skin approaching to the hue of a negro's, in the woman whom my father introduced to me as my intended wife! *I* that had been used to contemplate a countenance, and a transparent skin of ivory, where Suckling's expression of "even her body thought" might have aptly originated.[2] *I* that— ah! why pursue the reflection?—that such things were, I too well know; else why this weight of sorrow which has so long oppressed my weary frame? A very few hours served to convince me, that whatever might have been the transient impression made by the *colour* of Olivia, her mind and form were cast in no common mould. She has a noble and a dignified soul, which speaks in her words and actions; her person is raised above the standard of her sex, as much as her understanding and capacity. In her energy, her strength of expression, in the animation of her brilliantly black eye, there is something peculiarly interesting. At one moment, I feel for her situation and pity her,—a stranger in a strange country, where she is more likely to receive contumely than consideration; at the next, I see in her a superior being; and again I

---

1 Taken from Joseph Addison's *Cato* (1712), I.iv.
2 Augustus mistakenly attributes this quotation to Sir John Suckling, but it must come from John Donne's "A Funeral Elegy" (1610): "Her pure and eloquent blood / Spoke in her cheeks, and so distinctly wrought; / That one would almost say her body thought."

behold the child of humanity, the citizen of the world, with a heart teeming with benevolence and mercy towards every living creature!—She is accomplished and elegant; but her accomplishments are not the superficial acquirements of the day,—they are the result of application and genius in unison; her elegance is not the studied attitude of a modern belle, but the spontaneous emotion of a graceful mind: while in her conversation there is combined, with sound judgement and reflection, a *naïf* simplicity, and a characteristic turn of expression, which at once pleases and entrances the observer. The decision and promptitude with which she delivers her opinions, though accompanied by an air of modest timidity, prove that she has a spirit which will never suffer her to yield her principles or her sentiments, where her conscience tells her she is right: and that, though trampled upon, she will yet retain her native dignity of character!

You will think me raving, my friend; and so I am nearly, when I think that it is *I* alone who must rescue her from a state of miserable dependence. It is on *me* that her future happiness depends: on *me*, who, like a shipwrecked mariner, have seen my heart's only treasure snatched from my longing arms, and am become a bankrupt in all I coveted on earth!—In what a cruel predicament am I placed by my uncle's will—yet can I *refuse* Olivia, and see her eating the bitter bread of sorrow and dependence under my brother and *his* wife.—Oh, Monkland! I have *seen* the "tender mercies"[1] of *this* woman! *I* have seen her cruel, her unfeeling treatment of a meek and unoffending angel! I *know* her equal to any species of tyranny, to any plot of low malice and contrivance: she is envious of all virtue and merit, because she possesses neither herself!—She has no heart, no mind! And shall the only child of my mother's brother, shall the polished, the amiable Olivia Fairfield be reduced to such a situation?—Better had she perished on the ocean, better had the tempestuous billows overwhelmed her, ere she set her foot on this inhospitable shore! Yet, what have I to offer her? Will a widowed heart, blighted hopes, and settled melancholy, will these be fit offerings for the rich prize of her affections and her love? Can I with these hope to secure her happiness?

How if I was to disclose to her the state of my heart—how if I was to divulge to her that secret which is known alone to you and to the grave?—I know the result of such a disclosure,—the gen-

---

1 Psalm 103:4 or Luke 1:78.

erous Olivia would scorn to receive from my compassion what I could not grant from my love; her soul is too noble to bestow a thought upon selfish considerations, and she would not hesitate in preferring a dependence upon my brother, to laying an embargo on my principles, in which she would fancy my heart had no share. Yet, Heaven is my witness, inasmuch as I trust I am a lover of goodness and virtue, my heart, my soul is interested for this charming maid! My heart does not beat with the rapture of passion,—my soul is not overcome by soft emotions at her approach as heretofore.—Again am I giving way to useless retrospections. In hearing Miss Fairfield, in witnessing the chaste dignity of her manners, and the action which characterizes and enforces her expressions, I receive undissembled satisfaction; but sensible of our peculiar situation, whilst I could hang on every word she utters in company, and in her absence delight to recall them to my memory with the appropriate expression by which they were accompanied; yet, strange as it may appear, I fly from a *tête-à-tête* overcome by a weak fear almost unaccountable to myself. How can I assail her with professions of *love*, whilst conscious that my heart can never more feel that passion? How can I ask her to acknowledge herself interested for *me*, when I know that the silent tomb covers *all* for which I would have lived? and yet, how can I meet my wife, my *affianced* wife, and not enter into such conversation? My friend, you will pity me—to you, and to you alone, are my struggles and my sorrows known; with *you* I shall be acquitted of mercenary views, even though I should become the husband of Olivia—you will know that the same spirit, which *once* taught me to refuse a wealthy bride and to oppose my father's direct command, would have supported me in *this* instance also, if a stronger motive had not influenced me on the other side.— Farewell! Whatever may be my fate, to *you* I shall always lay open my heart, conscious of your friendship and fidelity towards
AUGUSTUS MERTON.

PACKET THE THIRD
OLIVIA FAIRFIELD TO MRS. MILBANKE

New Park, Devonshire.

AS I heard of no ship sailing for Jamaica, I have let my pen lie idle on my standish, my dearest madam, for the last three weeks, whilst I have been arranging my household, and making myself *quite at home*. In this, as in every thing, Mr. Fairfield has acted with the greatest indulgence. Your Olivia has only to breathe a wish, and it is accomplished; so that, in fact, I have nothing left to wish for.

This house is situated in a romantic part of Devonshire, near a bold and noble shore; the hills and dales are beautifully pictur-esque, and the diversity of wood, and lawn, and down, is very striking. It is a highly cultivated country, and a populous neigh-bourhood; and while the little town of ****, about three miles distant, supplies our table with excellent fish, it promises also to supply us with society from its summer visitants; as I understand it is a place of genteel resort in the season. The house is not too large to be comfortable; it is calculated for sociability, more than for show and gives you an idea of a contented habitation, which some of the lofty villas of Nabobs, in the neighbourhood, cannot impress on the mind with all their grandeur.

Dido is delighted; it is like the "dear Fairfield estate," and she has entered into all the mysteries of housekeeping, and bears about the insignia of her office, in the bunch of keys at her side, and the *important* expression of her face. Already she has made acquaintances with some of the peasants in the vicinity, and she bids fair to rival her mistress in the favour of the little rustics. Never did a warmer heart glow in a human bosom, than in that of this faithful creature; She considers herself as the sister of the whole human race, and loves them with a relative affection.

As yet, I have seen none of my visiting neighbours, except the clergyman of the parish; I both saw and heard him at church: and if I may form an opinion of the man, from his discourse and delivery in the pulpit, I promise myself profit and pleasure from his acquaintance; his subject was well chosen, and well handled,—his manner was devout and impressive!

IN CONTINUATION
MR. FAIRFIELD seems to enjoy himself in the country, as much as your Olivia; never did I witness a more sensible alter-ation, than that which took place in him, when we had fairly

turned our backs upon London. The insipid routine of a town life, where a man has no regular avocation, and is too far plunged into the ceremonials of the world to spend his time as he chooses, must surely be very irksome. Fairfield is of a contemplative and studious disposition; he has too much refinement and Christian benevolence in his composition to make, what is termed, a country 'squire; but he has sentiment, and a taste for the beauties of nature, to render him a *rural* though not a *modern* philosopher.

I was reading a paper this morning in one of your excellent periodical works, viz. the Tatler, when the following paragraph struck me as being applicable to my Augustus, that I will not apologize to you for transcribing it:—

"With great respect to country sports, I may say, this gentleman could pass his time agreeably, if there were not a hare, or a fox, in his county. That calm and elegant satisfaction, which the vulgar call melancholy, is the true proper delight of men of knowledge and virtue. What we take for diversion, which is a kind of forgetting ourselves, is but a mean way of entertainment, in comparison of that, which is considering, knowing, and enjoying ourselves. The pleasures of ordinary people are in their passions; but the seat of this delight is in the reason and understanding. Such a frame of mind raises that sweet enthusiasm, which warms the imagination at the sight of every work of nature, and turns all round you into picture and landscape."—*Tatler*, No. 89.[1]

Mr. Fairfield has patience with me in all my wild strolls, and sees a beautiful view of the sea, a disjointed rock, or a lofty tree, with an enthusiasm which equals mine. He is also interested and entertained with the simple and untutored urchins of the cottages; and I daily perceive, with renewed delight, that our sentiments, our opinions, and our principles coalesce. I am thankful to Heaven, for my happy, *thrice* happy lot; and humbly pray, that my Augustus's happiness may be as perfect as my own. I sometimes fancy that there has been a time, when his spirits and his gaiety must have been greater than they are at present; for I observe, the bright flashes of pleasantry, the sudden corruscations of his wit, the "scintillations of a playful mind,"[2] while they sometimes gild his conversation, with a ray, bright and dazzling as meridian day,

---

1   1709. The *Tatler* was a very influential British magazine founded in 1709 by Richard Steele, who published under the pseudonym Isaac Bickerstaffe.

2   Edward Jerningham, *Lines Written in the Album at Cossey-Hall, Norfolk, the Seat of Sir William Jerningham, Bart. Aug 4th 1786*. The correct wording is "The scintillations of her playful mind."

are instantaneously obscured, as if by a sudden recollection; and an uncontrollable feeling of sorrow imperiously absorbs every trait of hilarity. But these transitions are unfrequent, though, in general, the even tenour of his demeanor exhibits more the temper of patient resignation, than of undissembled happiness.

You will smile at my nice definitions; but be assured, that whilst he is as worthy of the best affections of my heart, as he is at present, I will not quarrel with my husband, because *his* cup of felicity does not overflow. Nay, such is the interest that he now excites in my bosom from imagining him to have felt the shaft of undeserved misfortune, that I am sure I love him the better for it. And *if* I have a wish ungratified, it is the possession of his entire confidence, not for the gratification of a low and unworthy feminine curiosity; but that I might offer him all the consolation and comfort in my power.

Adieu, for the present, my dearest madam!—to you, without reserve, I unfold all the feelings of my heart; I cannot blush to acknowledge its soft emotions; when awakened by so deserving an object. I can never forget, that when addressing you, I am writing to my most valued and tried friend!

OLIVIA FAIRFIELD.

IN CONTINUATION

New Park.

LAST week was devoted almost exclusively to the receiving and paying of visits; I am not sorry that I now find myself a little more my own mistress; perhaps I shall discover many of my neighbours to be very estimable characters on a further acquaintance; but a succession of visitors, where all are equally strangers and the mistress of the house is expected to find conversation, and to make herself agreeable, where too (as in my case) she knows that she is viewed with no common curiosity, is not only fatiguing, but awkward. Augustus endeavoured to ease me of the burden, however, and succeeded in no small degree. He has wonderful facility in general conversation, and can adapt himself to the capacities and tastes of any, whom he condescends to entertain, except they should be of that class, which we used to call, the *genteel vulgar*, meaning those important shallow-pated beings, who have but one recommendation, viz. money!— *We* saw enough of these in the West Indies, where riches are speedily amassed,—and that disgraceful traffic, which hardens the heart, and deadens the feelings, while it fills the purse, was eagerly prosecuted by such characters!

But I digress from my subject, and should not find an excuse for such a desultory way of writing as I have fallen into of late, with any other than my own Mrs. Milbanke! I must not indulge in caricaturing; and yet you will, perhaps, think I am doing so, if I merely describe things as they appear to me. Is it, that I see through a magnifying glass to discover defects?—Heaven preserve me from such an unchristian-like vision!

Within two miles of us, situated on a fine eminence, which overhangs the sea, and overlooks the beautiful little bay of ****, stands the Pagoda, the newly-raised edifice of Sir Marmaduke Ingot. Every order of architecture has been blended in this structure; and Augustus not unaptly remarked the other morning as we viewed it at a little distance, that it wanted but the bells which usually decorate the Chinese buildings, from whence its name is derived, to obtain another which would be as appropriate, viz. *the temple of folly!* The eastern nabob seemed to have harnessed his fleetest Arabian coursers to his chariot, when he came to pay his compliments to us; he really cut an appearance quite *magnifique*, as his gay equipage and dashy attendants drove through the park;—we *knew* there could be only one family so dazzling in this neighbourhood, and were therefore prepared for the guests, who made their *entrée*.

My lady is a masculine woman; very hard-favoured, and of a forbidding countenance; her voice is *nervous* (I do not mean nervously *weak*, but nervously *strong*), her utterance clear, and her conversation vastly above the common level of her sex; so much so, that I understand she is the general terror of the females in the vicinity, as she usually engrosses a great portion of the conversation, and will make herself *heard*, if not *understood*. But Sir Marmaduke, having acquired a very considerable fortune at Bengal, and liking to keep a hospitable and showy table, and to have his house filled with company; of course Lady Ingot gets a few *attentive hearers* of both sexes; and the good dinners, the turtle, and the curries at the Pagoda, obtain for her ladyship general sufferance, if not general favour. It was a very sultry morning, but Lady Ingot was wrapped in a most superb oriental shawl, while a fine lace veil descended almost to the ground, in some measure softening the asperity of her features by its partial shade. Sir Marmaduke's countenance is neither interesting nor disgusting; his cheeks are distended by a perpetual smile, and the powder on his head, seems to be laid on with no sparing hand, to cover the depredations of time. Mr. Ingot, a youth of about fifteen years of age, entered with his parents; he also was wrapped in a shawl, and his delicate fingers were warmed in a muff of the finest ermine, almost as large as himself (for he is very effeminate and diminutive in his person). His head was adorned by a hat, turned up before, with a gold button and loop, and ornamented by a plume of feathers; he is really a pretty looking stripling, if he was not made so mere a monkey of, and dressed in such a non-descript manner.

After the first compliments, her ladyship began, and, with facility of expression, and great choice of words, felicitated herself on the pleasure she anticipated in my acquaintance; assured me, that she very *rarely* met with any thing like polished or cultivated society in the uncivilized part of the world, in which Sir Marmaduke had fixed the Pagoda. The situation had some advantages,—that of air, for instance, which she allowed might be salubrious to those whose corporeal frames were formed to come in contact with it.—"But, my dear exotic," continued she, "my tender sensitive sapling Frederic, is nearly annihilated by its keenness. I assure you, Mrs. Fairfield, it requires all my maternal vigilance and precaution to guard him from the eastern blast, which beats against us!"

"And yet, ma'am, the young gentleman looks well."

"Hectic, mere hectic! pull off your shawl, and lay down your muff, my love,—recline a little on the sofa; Mrs. Fairfield will have the goodness to excuse you."

I bowed acquiescence, and her ladyship proceeded:—

"Again I must repeat the pleasing anticipations in which I fondly indulge myself, Mrs. Fairfield, on forming a confidential intercourse with you.—Alas! I have wofully felt myself thrown out of my level in this abstracted country."

"The country is a *hilly* one, assuredly, Lady Ingot," said Sir Marmaduke, who heard only what she had last said, and answered literally; and then resumed a conversation into which he had drawn Augustus, respecting a project which he had in contemplation of turning the turnpike road to put it to a greater distance from the Pagoda, as the mail-coach can now be *seen* as it passes, from the *salle à manger* windows; and some days, the guard's horn can be distinctly *heard*, when the wind is in the south.

"We have but *few* southern breezes, have we, mamma?" said Mr. Ingot, lisping, as he lay recumbent.

"I mean to get an act of Parliament," said Sir Marmaduke, "if I cannot do it in any other way. In India we manage matters more concisely; for *there*, we men in power have the law vested in our hands."

"A summary mode of proceeding, if justice be faithfully and impartially administered, has its advantages no doubt," answered

Augustus; "but in the case you are mentioning, I should imagine you will easily gain the consent of Parliament, Sir Marmaduke, as I conclude that it can be easily proved, that the alteration in question will be a convenience to you, without inconveniencing the public."

"Oh, not a jot, sir," replied the knight; "the objections that are started, are merely childish, and I can easily discern from whence they originate:—the opposing and unsuccessful candidate for the borough of ***** as he could not oust me out of my seat in Parliament, thinks proper to exert all *his* interest, to get a protest against me. But let him try his utmost, I shall not mind a few *more* thousands in *this* contest!"

"What may be his plea?" said Augustus.

"Oh, that by turning the road, I shall make it two miles further for the mail-coach, and more on the ascent; and that the post master at ***, will be obliged to sit up *half an hour* later, and burn *half an inch* more of his *farthing rushlight!*"

"Upon my honour, papa, you make me *quite* laugh," drawled out, Mr. Ingot,— "talking of the half-inch of candle!"

"This *is* an inconvenience to the *public*, surely," said Augustus.

"By no means, sir,—by no means, my good sir," said Sir Marmaduke, with warmth.—"*All* the innkeepers, from *** to **** are to a man on *my* side; and you will acknowledge them to be part of the public,—for are they not publicans?"

"Sir Marmaduke, how often have I told you that I cannot bear a pun," said lady Ingot.

"You told him so the *last* time he said it, ma'am," cried young Hopeful.

"I will allow them to be a part of the public, certainly," said Augustus, "but I fear a very interested part; and that it is *their* interest to be paid for two more miles in a stage is obvious."

The knight's answer escaped me,—not so his reddened countenance. Lady Ingot seemed to think her husband did not *shine*; and therefore she called off my attention to herself.

"Believe me, Mrs. Fairfield, there is scarcely a female besides yourself in this neighbourhood, who has ever set her foot out of England. Conceive what narrow minded, prejudiced beings they must be? Not an idea but what was planted in them at their births and has been handed down by mothers and grandmothers, and great-grandmothers, through countless generations!"

"It proves," said I, "that *those ideas* are worthy retaining? and I confess, I think our mothers and grandmothers were sensible beings. I rather lean towards old customs, and old notions, and can trace one of *my ideas* as far back as the *Old* Testament, where a lady of some note, being asked, whether she would be spoken of to the king or the captain of the boat, answered, with true feminine modesty—'I dwell amongst my own people!' It has always struck me as a most beautiful reply. Retirement seems the peculiar and appropriate station of our sex; and, the enlargement of the mind, and the conquest of prejudice, is not always achieved, perhaps, by visiting foreign climes!"

"You speak like a *perfect* English woman," said Lady Ingot; "I see you have already imbibed our air."

"I thank your ladyship for the compliment," said I: "I do consider myself as more than *half* an English woman, and, it has always been my ardent wish to prove myself worthy of the *title*!"

"Oh, you interesting enthusiast" said Lady Ingot; "with that action, that expression of countenance, so perfectly extraneous, and talking of belonging to this *yea nay* clime, where the plants indigenous to the soil, almost to a woman, sit with their hands before them, bolt upright and neither verging to the right nor to the left,—look as if they had creaked necks, and cramped *joints.*"

"I have remarked a very different deportment," said I, "and seem to have hitherto seen only those who diverge to the contrary extreme,—neither stiffened joints, nor limbs have prevented them from reclining and lounging with an air of ease, which I thought quite '*the rage*.'"

"Oh! there are some who have imitated us *East Indians*," said Lady Ingot, wrapping her shawl round her coarse limbs, in the style of drapery, and gradually inclining more towards the back of the chair on which she sat,—"*we* have had an opportunity of seeing the graceful languishment of Circassian loveliness, unrivalled for voluptuous and attractive elegance; and these degenerate imitators of that luxurious ease, which they have never *felt*, are the greatest treat to us, who see the distorted barbarism of the likeness!"

My dear Mrs. Milbanke, you have had a long specimen of the Ingots during their first visit. You have gained by it (if no entertainment) a perfect insight into their characters; therefore, I will not tell you what I *think* of them.

Augustus calls me to the evening walk. Adieu.

IN CONTINUATION

New Park.

MRS. HONEYWOOD is no more!—I have just read the account of her death in the papers. I was preparing to write you a long letter,—but, alas! I cannot. I have been recalling to my grateful memory the numberless proofs of kindness, and of maternal consideration, which I received from this regretted friend during our long voyage. She was an excellent woman, and prepared for death. But was her son prepared to lose her?—Poor Honeywood! my heart bleeds for him. I know the acuteness of his present feelings, for I witnessed the strength of his affection; and I could only compare it to that which I felt for my father: but *I* received the benign consolations of my beloved Mrs. Milbanke!

Augustus saw my emotion, at reading the death of this worthy woman,—he kissed off the tear from my cheek, and lamented, that he did not know the address of Honeywood:—"For did I," said he, "I would avail myself of the title of your husband, and invite him to a dwelling, where he would find *comfort personified* in my Olivia?"

I pressed his hand with grateful emotion.

IN CONTINUATION

New Park

THE long list of our daily-increasing acquaintance must be omitted; the characters will develop themselves, as many of them came forwards at a grand dinner of the nabob knight's, which we partook of yesterday; we wish to be on good terms with *all* our neighbours: and Augustus or myself have no partiality for what is called a *feast*, yet, being long-invited guests (or rather, I believe, this said *feast* being prepared on our account), we went. I need not describe my dress, you know I have one plain unornamented style. Augustus approves it, and of course I do not depart from it; but Dido bids me "be sure tell Mrs. Milbanke that I wore my new diamonds in my hair, which looked very pretty and *charming.*" Oriental magnificence was in full blaze at the Pagoda. Expect not a description of its splendour from the poor pen of your Olivia; she must refer you to fabled palaces of the genii, and to the gay castles of fairy princes, and *other* eastern knights. The party was a large one. Colonel and Miss Singleton were the only persons, except the inhabitants of the mansion, whose faces I recognized in the group; and with the most gallant air on the part of the colonel, and the most girlish vivacity on that of his sister, they both ran, rather than walked, up to pay their compliments. At the same moment that the hand of Augustus was seized by a lady, who, fixing her bold dark eyes full in his face, congratulated him on his marriage, and expressed her delight at this unexpected meeting. The colour faded in the countenance of my

Augustus—I thought his lips quivered—he certainly looked confused and embarrassed—he let his hand remain in hers, without
appearing to know that he did so—and the *would-be* interesting
colonel putting his hand to the side of his face, and grinning till he
showed rather more than he intended (viz. *besides all* his white teeth,
two vacancies on either side), whispered,—

"The mutual pleasure evinced by a *certain party*, is evident
enough, to call forth a disagreeable emotion on your part, if
aught disagreeable could lurk under a form so tender!"

I had not *time* to answer this complimentary whisper, had I been
prepared; for my *tender form* was at this minute presented by Augustus to Miss Danby, and I bent my *flexible joints* to her in a courtesy.
Assuredly, there was much constraint and embarrassment in Mr.
Fairfield's manner, even whilst he made this introduction; but with
the assured ease of a girl used to the world, the lady stared at me
with an expression of unbridled curiosity, which made my cheeks
glow.—What was the cause of Augustus's confusion? My dear Mrs.
Milbanke, I asked myself this question. The humbled and mortified
Olivia could answer it only thus (for neither the manners nor
person of Miss Danby could ever have been interesting to Augustus; of this I was well aware): My husband is, then, ashamed of
me—he is ashamed of my *person*—he *dreads* my being seen by any
of his former acquaintances as his *wife*;—I must then be still disgusting in his eyes—he yet has not courage to face the "world's
dread laugh!"[1] These bitter reflections passed in my mind, as I
observed that Augustus escaped from the rude survey which Miss
Danby seemed to be taking of my person, as though he could not
stand the scrutiny.—I hope it was only for a moment that I suffered
these thoughts to ruffle my tranquility!—Augustus, too, soon recovered himself; and Miss Danby offering him her hand with great
nonchalance (on seeing the nabob take mine, to lead me into the
dining-room), he gallantly lifted it to his lips as he took it.

"We used to be famous flirts, you know," said Miss Danby.
"Even *so*, believe me, Mrs. Fairfield;" said she, nodding familiarly
at me across the table.

"And we mean to resume our *old* habits, of course," said
Augustus laughing.

"And will not you retaliate?" said Colonel Singleton, who,

---

1 Olivia seems to speak half of the common phrase "the world's dread
laugh, / Which scarce the firm philosopher can scorn" quoted in texts as
diverse as James Fordyce's popular *Sermons to Young Women* (1766) and
James Thomson's *The Seasons* (1730), "Autumn."

seated at my right hand, threw his most agreeable smile into his face as he asked the question.

"I don't know how far it would be proper," said I.

"Would ladies of the present century always stop to consider of *propriety* before they venture on *this retaliation*, I think we should soon find a material improvement in manners as well as morals," said a grave-looking elderly gentleman, who sat towards the bottom of the table. "But you ladies do not give yourselves *time* for reflection." And as he said this, he turned his head towards Miss Singleton, who, arrayed in pink muslin, and adorned with pearls looked as gay and airy, as her very gay and very *airy* dress could make her.

"As to *giving* ourselves time, you ought to know that it is not at our own *command*," said she. "I protest to you, that, for my own part, from year's end to year's end, I have not a day which I can call my own."

"Oh happy *you!*" said Miss Danby; "What an enviable being!" and she, apparently spoke from her heart.

"Nay, do you really think so?" said Miss Singleton, simpering with conscious pleasure. "To be sure, society has imperious claims upon persons in a certain sphere; and I have a very large circle of acquaintance, which is continually expanding."

"The expansion of a circle: that is not badly expressed," said Lady Ingot, in a half-whisper, to Augustus.

"And a *magic circle* too!" said a young ensign, who sat on one side of the speaker.

"The colonel has also a great many friends," continued Miss Singleton.

"A charming, elegant man! I am sure, ma'am, he *must* have friends wherever he is seen!" said an elderly and highly-rouged widow, who seemed to be particularly attentive to Colonel Singleton.

"A vast acquaintance my brother has, ma'am—and people who live in the world have such *various* claims upon them; what with dinner parties, routs, concerts, plays, balls, and suppers, at Bath in the winter, London in the spring, and at the fashionable watering-places in rotation during the summer, I have not a moment, that I can call my own, of the twenty-four hours. My brother and myself seldom retire till three or four in the morning, as we can find no other period than an hour before we court repose, to talk over the *adventures* of the preceding day, and settle a plan of engagements for the next."

"Does this mode of life never weary?" asked the grave looking gentleman.

"We must never allow that *pleasure* can weary," said Miss Danby, with gaiety. "It would be a contradiction in terms.—But pray, Mr. Fairfield, do tell me, how is my friend Mrs. George Merton? Speaking of pleasure reminds me of her—she used to be a dear dissipated creature, you know."

"She is just as you remember her," said Fairfield; but again his features underwent an alteration. Miss Danby fixed her keenly-scrutinizing eyes on his face, and said,

"Pray, Mr. Fairfield, what is become of Miss Forrester?"

Here seemed the very climax of Augustus's embarrassment. Indeed, my dearest friend, I saw him start; his face was convulsed; the most deadly expression of anguish overspread his features. I was just going to put a glass of wine to my lips; I had bowed to Colonel Singleton, in return to his drinking my health; but the tremulous movement of my hand obliged me to set the glass again on the table; and, without knowing what I was doing, I sought for my smelling-bottle, and, had I not checked the first impulsive movement of my soul, I should have handed it across the table to my husband,—and should, most probably, have drawn on myself, if not on him also, the ridicule of the whole company. Miss Danby does not appear to want penetration, however destitute she may be of feeling; I am sure that she saw my emotion, and that the disorder of Augustus did not pass unobserved, for she followed up the question with—

"Poor Angelina! I should really like to know where she is. There was something *vastly* good about her; and though I used to laugh at her, yet I loved, her.—Pray, do you not know where she is Mr. Fairfield?"

"She is in *heaven!*" sighed out Augustus in a tone of voice scarcely audible, and, at the same moment, letting his fork fall on the plate he hastily averted his head from Miss Danby, and filling a bumper of wine, he eagerly swallowed it. Even Miss Danby seemed intimidated from asking him any more questions.

Lady Ingot turning towards, me—said, "A very *mal-à-propos* question that of Miss Danby's—*perfectly English!* '*How is she,*' and '*where* is she'; expecting verse after verse, like Chevy Chace.[1] Mr. Fairfield has very consisely given her the *dénouement* in *four* words: for my *own* part, I always hold it as a matter of *conscience* not to make inquiries after *absent friends*, lest I should wound the feelings of those to whom I am addressing myself. People are so

---

1 A popular traditional ballad.

very soon *married*, or *dead*, or *buried*, and gone *Heaven* knows where, that I think it quite a solecism on good-breeding; but in *India* we discriminate with great nicety on every point of sentiment and manners, and, instead of making our conversation assume the features of a Moore's almanac,[1] or a monthly obituary, raise the lively idea, and point the brilliant repartee!"

That I heard this ridiculous speech is certain, because I am able to retail it; but, my beloved friend, you would have pitied your poor Olivia, had you beheld her at this moment, as much as *she* did her agitated Augustus; evidently Miss Danby had struck the chord which jarred through his frame!—This Miss Forrester, then—this Angelina—she was the object of my husband's warmest affections—I am sure she was—his sighs—his melancholy abstractions—they are all—*all* for Angelina—and—I was going to say, that I almost envied the *shade* of Angelina—But I will try to be more rational.

When the gentlemen joined us in the drawing-room, Augustus was in high spirits, or *appeared* to be so; they were either affected, or produced by his having taken more than his usual quantity of wine. He seated himself next Miss Danby; she laughed, and chatted, and unceasingly rattled; talked of her poor Mrs. George Merton, in a pitying contemptuous tone, which intimated, that though she was her *dear friend*, she had a most hearty contempt for her. She asked, how long Mr. George Merton meant to plod on at the cent. per cent.; wondered why Augustus had thought fit to quarrel with the world, and leave it in dudgeon, when he was so formed for its enjoyment!

"I have not *quarrelled* with it, believe me," said Augustus; "I am, just now, better pleased with it, than I have been all my life before: I live according to *my* notions of happiness! (and he looked with an expression of grateful satisfaction towards your Olivia): and can I call myself out of the world, when I have, at this moment, the pleasure of sitting next to one of its gayest belles?"

"Oh nonsense, agreeable flatterer! nonsense!" said Miss Danby. "I am merely a bird of passage. Lady Ingot was obliging enough to give me an invitation to the Pagoda, and, *entre nous*, I thought I wanted a little bracing for the winter's campaign, and my father having been overwhelmed by the host of faro,[2] it was a

---

1   Francis Moore's *Almanac* (or 'Old Moore's Almanac') was first published in 1700 and was a best seller throughout the eighteenth and nineteenth centuries.

2   Faro was a popular card game (in which the players lay wagers on the top card of the dealer's pack).

scheme of *economics* for me to come here, rather than to be in hired lodgings at Weymouth, or dear delightful Brighton—But don't blab for your life.—I do assure you that I felt quite charmed to find that *you* were in the vicinity, and mean to be vastly intimate with Mrs. Fairfield. I feel a very great predilection for her already.—Upon my *honour* she is not near so *dark* as I expected to find her, and for one of *that* sort of people, she is really very well looking!"

"She is one of that *sort* of people whose *mind* is revealed in the countenance," said Augustus, warmly,—"and *hers* is the seat of every *virtue!*"

I wonder I did not get up to clasp his hand in mine; and *you* will wonder, Mrs. Milbanke, how I could overhear this conversation, without standing confessed a curious listener: but, in fact, I *appeared*, at this time, to be attending to a most florid description which Miss Singleton was giving of the plumage of a fine bird of Paradise, which had been entirely spoilt by her feather-man, to whom she had sent it to be dressed.

During the whole of the day, I had observed that the elderly gentleman whom I have previously mentioned, had been very little regarded by the major part of the company, and that by the master and mistress of the mansion, he had been wholly over-looked; while Mr. Ingot had amused himself with making faces in derision at his back, and pointing out the unfashionable cut of his coat, and his silver buckles, to any one who would attend to him. A very interesting looking young clergyman tried in vain, by looks and mild persuasions, to deter him, but finding that he was wholly unsuccessful, he seemed in despair to give up the point, and to redouble his own respectful attentions to the old gentle-man. Curiosity impelled me to inquire of her ladyship the names of these two gentlemen.

"Do you mean that antiquity?" asked she; "a relative of Sir Marmaduke's, I believe. *His* benevolence leads him to make the Pagoda almost a *public receptacle*. But as to collateral and genealogical descent, my dear Mrs. Fairfield, you will credit me that I never trouble myself about it; he may or may not be related: but I think his head is truly *Grecian*, and if it had the genuine *rust*, it would be invaluable. As *it is*, I like very well to see it at the table; it is of a *good cast*, a *classical subject* certainly."

"It bespeaks goodness as much as any countenance I ever saw," said I.

"I suspect *you* are a physiognomist," said her ladyship; "I confess that I am no *Lavaterian*:[1] my notions on the point of face-reading are deduced from the genuine Roman and Grecian antiques (of which I have some curious specimens in my cabinet of medals). As to the *sublime* and *beautiful*, and as to the *grotesque* and *singular*, I look at those for subjects of *entertainment* and *laughter* in this study."

"But there is a countenance," said I, "which, having neither a Roman nor Grecian, grotesque nor singular cast, is yet so interesting a one, that I cannot help asking your ladyship his name also?"

"His name!" repeated she, turning up her lips rather contemptuously, "he is a poor student of Salamanca, or, to speak, in a more common-place manner, he is an Oxford scholar, of the name of Waller, who is here in the capacity of tutor to Mr. Ingot; though, Heaven knows what he teaches him, for I cannot find out that Frederic is improved by his instructions. His *manners* I fashion myself Mrs. Fairfield—*that* essential part of education, I told Sir Marmaduke, I *must* have the sole management of. I have read in some obsolete author, "Train up a child in the way he should go;"[2]—now I could never bear to see the heir of Sir Marmaduke Ingot, stiffened and braced, to look as if he had been pulled out at a wire-drawer's. Ease and elegance are, in my opinion, terms nearly synonymous; hence I have made a point of letting him lounge, and loll, and curvet, in every interesting and careless attitude, from his cradle to the present period. Observe my Frederic as he now lies *serpenting* on the carpet, Mrs. Fairfield—his form is symmetry itself—no ungraceful curve, no angular asperities of attitude—there reclines the true harmony of proportion!"

At that moment the young gentleman threw out one polished limb (commonly called a leg), as the old gentleman was coming near the part of the room where he lay; I saw the movement, and by an involuntary impulse sprang forwards, and, catching him by the arm, prevented him from falling.

"You are very good, madam," said he, "thus to prop an old man, from the mischievous tricks of an urchin."

Mr. Waller (the tutor) took the hand of Mr. Ingot, "Pray rise, sir," said he; "I am ashamed to see that you tried to throw your

---

1 Johann Kasper Lavater (1741-1801) was a Swiss writer, Protestant pastor, and founder of Physiognomics.
2 Proverbs 22:6.

uncle on the carpet, and that you suffered a lady to assist him, while you continued in this lazy and disgraceful posture!"

"Uncle, indeed!" repeated he; "how often must you be told that her ladyship cannot *bear* that word, Waller? I assure you, sir, she will tell you it is the quintessence of vulgarity to use any of those appellations in good company!"

"I am not to be intimidated from speaking my sentiments, sir," said Mr. Waller; "and if the age and character of that venerable gentleman is no check on your impertinent behaviour towards him, I was in hopes that his relative claim might compel you to adopt a more decent mode of conduct!"

Mr. Ingot made a polite bow, smiled in Mr. Waller's face, and then reeled off to her ladyship, practicing the last new step; with great action he continued to whisper into her ear: she reddened and looked angrily towards poor Waller, who did not notice her I fancy; and the hopeful heir of the Ingots then fell back on the sofa, and amused himself with playing with the brilliant pendant which hung at her ladyship's ear. Mr. Bellfield (for so is the old gentleman called), turning towards me, said—

"You have here, madam, a pretty fair sample of an *only child!*— Poor fellow! I pity *him*—but I doubly pity his misguided parents—what a store of unhappiness are they not laying up for themselves?"

I had nothing to urge in extenuation of so much folly, ostentation, and self-conceit, as the Ingots had displayed, but I contrived to change the subject, and found Mr. Bellfield a very sensible and entertaining old man, somewhat cynical in his opinions, and quaint in his expressions; his manners are not modeled from the present times, but they take their tone, from his principles, which are fixed and firm, and can stand against any modern innovations and refinements.

You will think I never mean to throw my pen aside. I must for the present wave the introduction of any new characters, to talk of myself, and of my dearer self, my husband. Augustus returned home dispirited and abstracted; I avoided inquiries; for, alas! I knew that Miss Danby had recalled those thoughts which oppressed him. Unsuspicious of my being acquainted with this, he yet felt it necessary to account for his alteration of manner, and complained of a head-ache. In my turn I dissembled, and feigned sleep, when the heart-piercing sighs of my husband kept me waking at his side, during the greater part of the night; my tears flowed in silence: and thus was I an unknown participator in his sorrows. Oh, Mrs. Milbanke, how happy, how blest would be the lot of your Olivia, if her Augustus would but repose his cares in her faithful bosom! I would console him, I would listen to him while he talks of *her* whom he has lost for ever! I would throw off the weakness of my sex, I would patiently listen to his animated description of her beauties and her virtues, and I would daily strive to be more like the object of his sorrowing heart! but while he retains to himself this secret suffering, while he denies me the blessed privilege of sharing and soothing his sorrows, I feel that I *am* not half his wife—I am the partner of his bed—but not of his heart! There is so much to admire in the character of my Augustus, every day discovers so much amiability, such benevolence, such commiseration for the sufferings of others, that my regard increases with every added hour; and his dead, his lamented Angelina, could not, I am sure, have loved him with a more fervent affection. Adieu, dearest madam, I am always your own affectionate child—your own

   OLIVIA FAIRFIELD!

IN CONTINUATION

   WHEN we returned from church this morning, I found Miss Danby seated with her netting, and seeming to be very busily engaged at it, as if she had quite forgotten that six days of the week were sufficient to employ so frivolously, without trespassing on a sacred commandment.—Lady Ingot was playing at "Colonella" with Mr. Ingot, who languidly caught the shuttle-cock as he reclined on a sofa, letting his mother stoop for it when he missed, which happened more than nine times out of ten. I started at seeing the party assembled in the breakfast room, and more, at seeing how they were severally engaged—for Augustus and myself had walked to church, which is not above a quarter of a mile distant, and had entered the house by a private door.—

   "And where, in God's name, have you been these two hours?" asked Lady Ingot. "We found the mansion depopulated, we walked in at the hall door, made our way here, and have been unmolested by any human being!"

   "Not a male in the house,
   Not as much as a mouse?"[1]

---

1   Don Diego 'musing' at the beginning of Isaac Bickerstaffe's *The Padlock* (1768): "My doors shall be lock'd, / My windows be block'd, / No male in the house, / Not so much as a mouse" (I.i).

said Miss Danby.

"That is pretty true, I believe," said Augustus. "My Olivia is not content with being *good* herself, she makes *others* so likewise, and all our male servants go to church on a Sunday: we leave one female at home, to see that the house is not run away with,—if some of our *good neighbours* (smiling) do not perform that kind office for us!"

"To church! and have you, in reality, been at church?" asked Lady Ingot: "I had forgotten that it was Sunday!"

"If Mr. Bellfield and Waller had not reminded you of it, mamma, by coming in their *very best* suits to breakfast—don't you recollect"—said Mr. Ingot— "I am sure the old gentleman's square-toe'd shoes were polished as highly as his silver buckles; and I believe the well powdered locks of Waller did not escape the ken of Miss Danby, for I watched her *eyeing* him most intently during the *déjeûné*."

"What spirits you are in *mon cher* Frederic!" said Lady Ingot; "you will exhaust yourself."

"His spirits run away with him," said Miss Danby, "the idea of *my eyeing* Waller is ridiculous enough, to be sure!"

"Nay, if you come to that, *I* have been eyeing him in *church*," said I, "and am not ashamed to confess it; there is something vastly prepossessing in the countenance of that young man; and his attention to the respectable Mr. Bellfield, and their mutual devotion, is a very pleasing sight. Piety, true fervid piety, is a delightful contemplation!"

Lady Ingot writhed herself into a new Circassian attitude, and putting as much softness as she could into her voice, said,—

"Pray, were you not very cold? I never set my foot in that church but *once*, and then I was absolutely starved to death. I told Sir Marmaduke it was hazarding the very existence of our *tender one* there (looking at her son), if he ever let him enter it, unless he could portion off a large space for our separate use, and have it well stuffed and carpeted, and a chimney built, and a good register stove put in; but it seems there are great difficulties, in the way to all improvements in country parishes:—what with their rectors, parsons, their graziers and yeomanry, who talk of 'my pew,' and 'mine,' with as much tenacity, as if one wanted to deprive them of any thing *worth* retaining. Sir Marmaduke has had so many things of *consequence* to attend to since we came to the Pagoda, that he has not had leisure to settle a plan for a *little sequestration* (as I term it); for his family's accommodation at church; and for my own part, I do not much trouble about it. My *own* religion, is the religion of nature! *I* can put up my aspirations, while walking in the fields or driving on the road, just as devoutly as if I was *kneeling* on the moist and humid pavement of some time-worn, *superstitious* structure, and catching a *sudden death* at the very moment I was praying to be delivered from it,—for nothing short of a miracle *could* preserve me!"

"The *breaths* of the greasy farmers is what I chiefly dread in these *mixed meetings*," said Miss Danby.

"But you used not to dread the infinitely more *contagious* atmosphere of a crowded assembly and rout," said Augustus.

Miss Danby coloured through her rouge at this well-timed rebuke, and in some haste began to unscrew her netting machine from the table.

"And what may you call this?" asked Augustus playfully.

"Now you know very well, Mr. Fairfield, that it is a *vice*."

"Oh, I don't approve the name at all,—never bring it here again of a Sunday, I entreat you, Miss Danby. These *vicious* pursuits must not be introduced into a quiet and pastoral country."

"I do verily believe that you are become a methodist," said Miss Danby; "you are so sarcastic too in your manner that I shall begin to be afraid of you,—and shall begin to *hate* you almost as bad as my friend, poor Mrs. George, does!"

"Oh, do not say so," said Fairfield; "let me not live to be the object of your hatred, fair Almenia!"

IN CONTINUATION

I DO not know why I have dwelt on the Ingots, except that, as they are to me a new species of animal, I feel my own curiosity, as well as pity, excited in analyzing them, and imagine that you will feel similar emotions. But today we will turn to a nobler and a more delightful inspection. The rectory would be frequently haunted by Mrs. Milbanke were she with her Olivia; (oh, that *were!*) Mr. Lumley is just the clergyman which my heart depicted him. I fancy he has known great trials and struggles in bustling through life, and endeavouring to bring up a large family in respectability;—and a conscientious clergyman is, of all characters, the one which is least calculated to do this; for as much as may be, he wishes to disengage his mind from all secular pursuits ("we cannot serve God and mammon"),[1] yet this is wholly impossible, where few friends, and a scanty income, are the only

1 Matthew 6:24.

reward for a life spent in the most noble of all causes. Mr. Lumley's long residence, and zealous administration of the duties of his office, as curate of this large and scattered parish, at length moved the heart of a man of some consequence in this neighbourhood, into whose patronage the living fell on the death of a rector, to whom Mr. Lumley had been, (during a long period of twenty years) curate;—and who had *never* entered his parish except to give his flock an annual *shearing* and *sermon!*

The living was presented to Mr. Lumley, who was truly worthy to be so preferred, which is deducible from the general satisfaction exhibited by his parishioners. Easy in his circumstances, with the means of forwarding his family in the world, the good man seems to be completely happy. You would admire his whole family, Mrs. Milbanke; the father, sensible, cheerful in conversation, eloquent in the cause nearest his heart, and making it the rule of his life;—the mother, unaffected and warm-hearted, ready to apply the balm of consolation, and the drop of sympathy, to every mourner within her reach;—the girls, frank, open-hearted, and innocent;—the boys, hanging and catching his sentiments to give the tone to their own!

Caroline Lumley is a sweet girl of seventeen; her beauty does not consist so much in feature, as expression: there is a native simplicity in her manner, which I have never seen equalled—and much mistaken if the eyes of Waller have not *told* a tale, which *hers* have understood. I have asked her assistance in forwarding a little plan for establishing a School of Industry in the village; this brings her more frequently to me, than I should otherwise,—her fear of intrusion withholding her from coming unbidden. She has frequently been my companion in my morning's ramble; and she is so sweetly grateful for my notice, that your Olivia could almost fancy herself a *superior*, instead of an *inferior* being, notwithstanding her *colour!* But, thank God, I am *loved* not feared by this child of nature,—my behaviour surprises and charms her, as being contrasted with the foolish *hauteur* of other strangers who have settled here, particularly the Ingots. Mrs. Lumley called on Lady Ingot, on her first coming to the Pagoda,—Sir Marmaduke *returned* it; and in an affectedly affable manner, which proved his mushroom pride and self-sufficiency, he invited *Mr.* Lumley to dine with him, excusing himself from including the females of the family, by saying,—

"Lady Ingot had a great many claims upon her in society. She was a highly-bred woman; it was necessary to draw the line of separation *somewhere*. She was sorry to refuse the pleasure of receiving Mrs. Lumley at the Pagoda; but if she *did*, Mrs. Notary and Mrs. Bolus might expect the same honour to be extended to them likewise;—thus the very *canaille*[1] would be included in her ladyship's list of visitants, and her life would be subject to an eternal impost, from the levies of an inferior scale of beings!"

Mrs. Lumley has nothing of sarcasm in her manner, but she laughingly repeated this speech, saying,—"Verbatim, as it *came* from the courtly Sir Marmaduke; believe me, Mrs. Fairfield, though we all suspect that it was the florid composition of her ladyship, for it came off in rather too studied a manner to be *extempore*. I courtesied, and was not much mortified at coming below the prescribed standard; and the good man there, in his own placid tone, thanked the Knight for the *honour* of his invitation,—but said, he was well aware that the hours and the society at the Pagoda would ill coalesce with his humdrum mode of life and obsolete ideas, and therefore desired to be excused likewise! —This refusal on his part seemed to be vastly well taken, and Sir Marmaduke is on the best of all possible terms with us. He always bows and smiles, inquires cordially after my health, asks after my little family, *then* how many children I have, and the age of the youngest, when he meets me;—passes the children *one* day, and makes an apology for forgetting them on the *next*; and when *he*, mounted on his dashy phaeton, meets me trudging along the lanes, he invariably stops to express his fear of my getting an illness by encountering so much dirt."

IN CONTINUATION

THE amiable simplicity and good-humoured frankness of the Lumleys, are well contrasted by the assuming pride and false consequence of the Ingots, in the little trait which I gave you yesterday.—Ah, my dear Mrs. Milbanke! if the *little* great would but behold themselves as *they* are viewed by those from whom they have departed under covert of Sir Marmaduke's "*separating line*," they would surely learn to despise themselves; but those beings who court popularity are beset with a train of parasites, of Danbys and of Singletons, who flatter, who compliment, and who laugh at them in a breath!

Even Augustus,—even your Olivia, who prides herself on her ingenuousness of character, even we are silent; and we would keep on a neighbourly footing at the Pagoda, we must not always

---

1 The masses of people, rabble, riffraff.

express our real sentiments. And yet *we* purposely left the crowded haunts of the city, to escape from all the ceremonials of fashion and the tax which the arbitrary customs of the world has imposed so heavily upon reason and common sense. Yet they have followed us into retirement, and, unless we would really turn hermits, and entirely seclude ourselves from society, we must be content to pay the common levy;— for, to form a truly unvitiated and primeval neighbourhood of undisturbed truth, simplicity, and innocence, we must revert to the golden age, and to the rapt reveries of enthusiastic poets. Happy is it, when, with no overstrained fastidiousness, we can consent to take the world as we find it, when we endeavour to mend where it lies in our power, and firmly resolve not to make it worse by our own *example*. If I was to brace myself up, and with affected authority take upon me to correct the follies which I observe at the Pagoda, I should most assuredly draw down a great deal of odium on myself, and, to the other failings of her ladyship, add those of rancour and malice to her nearest neighbours.

We have heard nothing of Honeywood, or to what spot he has bent his course, in pursuit of consolation. I fear he thinks himself forgotten by your Olivia. Yet surely, he could not have appreciated her character so unjustly; rather should I suspect that he fears to obtrude on my happiness, with his grief! Yet that Power who has bestowed on me a happiness, for which I cannot be sufficiently grateful has also taught me to "feel another's woe."[1]

Adieu, my dearest friend! My heart always turns to you with a sentiment of reverential affection, which I feel but cannot express.

OLIVIA FAIRFIELD.

IN CONTINUATION

IN the plenitude of happiness, we sometimes grow childishly fastidious, and are easily put out of humour. I feel ashamed to own, that this has just been my own case: but all my weaknesses shall be confessed to my beloved Mrs. Milbanke.

I have received a letter from Mrs. Merton; she is coming to pay me a visit. You know, my dear friend, that I do not love her. I confess, that I felt a pain at my heart, wholly unaccountable even

---

1 Alexander Pope, "The Universal Prayer" (1738): "Teach me to feel another's woe, / To hide the fault I see."

to myself, as I read the intelligence. It seemed as if she were coming to disturb my halcyon felicity; it seemed,—I know not what. But you may suppose that I do not exaggerate my feelings when I tell you, that Augustus observing me, said, in a voice of affectionate inquiry,—

"No ill news, my love, I trust!"

This brought me to some sense of my weakness to call it by no harsher name. I had nothing to allege in my excuse. Indeed, I had not words to answer him, so I put the letter into his hands.— In his turn, Augustus seemed to receive a damp from the promised visit.

"Do as you like, my Olivia," said he, returning me the letter.

"We shall see Mrs. Merton, of course," said I: "you know we have no engagements."

"It *is*, of course," said he, "for *you* to forget that she invariably made you the object of her affront and insult. But *your* unparalleled sweetness and forbearance is what *I* must ever remember!"

"Oh, I am so vulnerable to praise from *you*," said I, "that I *must* receive Mrs. Merton's visit for even were I sure of experiencing similar treatment from her, I should now be doubly supported from the proud consciousness of *your* esteem!"

"No, my generous girl," said he, "*her* rudeness must never be repeated! I have now a *husband's* claim, and I will see that none injures my wife with impunity!—Yet hear me, whilst I conjure you, that from no false pride and punctilious delicacy towards *me*, you receive the visit of *my* brother's wife! God knows, that I have no relative—no affection for *her* of any kind. *She* has been my—Do not put a tax on your own feelings, to avoid wounding mine, my Olivia," said he, recollecting himself after pausing abruptly, and heaving a bitter sigh;—"for I protest that was she not the wife of my brother, I would *never* behold her more!"

"But as your brother's wife," said I, smiling.

"My Olivia will always have it her own way, and *that* way is always right," said he. "You must extend the invitation to my nephew, your little favourite."

"Most assuredly I will!"

And so ended this conversation; though I freely confess, that a gloom comes over my mind, which I cannot get rid of, when I think of entertaining Mrs. Merton as *my* guest. I do not fear her, Mrs. Milbanke; she cannot have power to harm me, blest as I am with my husband's protecting love. I do not hate her; for I trust I have attained that rule of Christian forbearance, which teaches us to "pray for those who despitefully use us."[1] But I shall feel awkward and constrained, while performing the rites of hospitality, and apparently extending the hand of friendship, where I cannot respect or esteem.

Dido is as much out of sorts as her mistress; she does not like the idea of the tonish (or rather *townish*) Abigail, and the monkey footman, who treated her with so much *sang froid*, at Clifton and in London. "But here," she says, "thanks to my good lady,—Dido be Missee below stairs, and treated by all as if me was as good as another, for all me be poor negro wench!"

Ah, my good Dido, perhaps both your "*good lady*," and yourself, may find the difference of entertaining, and being entertained! Yet Dido is determined that nothing shall be wanting on her part, towards receiving our guest *stylishly*; and she has been in a prodigious bustle ever since I made her acquainted with the contents of my letter.

Augustus bids me make up my packet for Jamaica, as he can get it conveyed to Bristol by a gentleman now setting out. May every earthly blessing attend you, my ever dear friend!—so will always pray your affectionate

OLIVIA FAIRFIELD.

END OF VOLUME THE FIRST

---

1 Matthew 5:44.

THE WOMAN OF COLOUR
VOLUME II

PACKET THE FOURTH

New Park, Devon.

SCARCELY do I send off one packet ere I begin another, so great is my satisfaction in addressing myself to my dear Mrs. Milbanke, and so well am I acquainted with the fond reception which she will always give to them. I believe I have never told you, that at the entrance of the park there is a neat little cottage, which is nearly concealed by the venerable elms which are planted in order to mark the direct approach to the house, and are continued in a fine avenue, quite in the *old* style (although the place be rather unjustly termed *New* Park). There is something formal in this straight lined road, to be sure, but venerable in their formality. I am inclined to behold them with as partial an eye as Mr. Seagrove (the gentleman of whom we rent the place), and I would not willingly lop a branch, or disturb a rook's nest. I like to walk under the shade of those trees which were planted by the hands of those who have long lain in the dust. My mind is tinged by melancholy, but it is not of an unpleasing cast. I am carried back to a remote age—I unconsciously look up to those majestic trees, which form a canopy to screen me from the fervid sun, to inquire into the manners and history of "times, long ago." The wind, whistling through their branches, seems to waft me the answer in a long-drawn sigh. I echo it responsively, and my reflections end with supposing, that the human mind, *always* the same in its feelings and emotions, its pleasures, its pains, its virtues and its vices, *life*, in every æra of existence, had nearly the same proportion of weal or woe!—So you find that my solitary meditations, like those of other illuminators, end just where they began.—But I have widely strayed from the subject with which I began; namely, the little cottage. It has been shut up till last week: its present tenant is an entire stranger. We like to know something of a person before we form an acquaintance; and yet I think it would appear very fastidious and narrow-minded in me, if I was not to visit so near a neighbour—a female too!

Full many a flower is born to blush unseen,
And waste its sweetness on the desert-air.[1]

---

1   Thomas Gray, "Elegy Written in a Country Church-Yard" (1751).

The inhabitant of that modest tenement may have a million times more innate worth than the *titled she* of a certain colonnaded Pagoda. Fairfield chimes with me in thinking it would be illiberal not to notice this stranger; yet says,

"Stay a little, my Olivia; let not the generous fervour of your feelings carry you too swiftly along; hear Mrs. Lumley's account: she, as the clergyman's wife, will most assuredly"—

"Now," said I, interrupting him, and laughing, "you must forgive me, for reminding you of the fable of the cat and the bell."[1]

"I acknowledge the propriety of the application," said he, bowing.

IN CONTINUATION

I WAS this morning walking in the park with Caroline Lumley, when we perceived four persons approaching towards us—two of either sex—each lady supported by a beau. We soon discovered them, as they came nearer, for Miss Singleton, leaning on the arm of young Ingot; Miss Danby on that of Waller. The quick retreating colour of my companion announced the latter pair to me, previous to my own observation.

"Oh, what a morning of Ossian!" said Miss Singleton, throwing out her hands with an air truly theatrical, and making a truly *Arcadian* appearance, in a gipsy hat, tied with a pink handkerchief, and ornamented by a wreath of *half*-blown roses, a mantle of the same coloured sarsnet, hung over her left shoulder, while her short and thin drapery discovered her laced stockings and delicate pink kid slipper. Miss Danby, in rather a rougher and more assured manner than the languishing shepherdess, declared the day was charmingly fine, but that there was a softness and stillness in the air, which would wholly have incapacitated her from walking with Miss Singleton without assistance.—

"So I have absolutely pulled this book-worm from his desk," said she, "to make him my walking-stick! Hav'n't I, Waller?"

"Make me any thing you please," said he, with a bow, not ungallant.

"'Pon my honour that's not so bad," said Miss Danby; "I *shall* make *something* of you yet, I believe—He'll do yet, Mrs. Fairfield, when I can cure him of 'Ma'am,' and blushing at every word," for

---

1 Aesop's fable "The Cat and the Mice" (sometimes called "Mice in Council" or "The Belling of the Cat."), in which the proverb is, it is no use having bright ideas unless we are willing to put them into practice.

the eyes of Waller had met those of Caroline, and the colour rose in *his* cheeks at the moment when it forsook *hers*.

"A stick!—Waller, a stick! That's a monstrous good one, Miss Danby—I am sure I shall make mamma laugh at that—I am sure her ladyship will enjoy the new use to which you have put my tutor, Miss Danby."

"Talking of her ladyship," said I, for I had scarcely patience to listen to the impertinence of this young puppy, "I am reminded to express my surprise at seeing that she has given you leave to walk out, Mr. Ingot, this melting day."

"He is, indeed, composed of the most *melting* materials!" said Miss Singleton, looking at him with eyes of admiration.

"Perhaps you fear that he may dissolve," said Miss Danby. "Pray, Miss Singleton, don't let your blooming Adonis slip through your fingers!"

"Lady Ingot is not afraid of the heat, 'tis the cold she dreads for me," said Ingot, lisping out every word; "and most of all, a thaw—her ladyship calls a thaw the check to every genial emotion, and to all animal circulation!"

"Oh, 'tis a most terrible feel—pray don't talk of it!" said Miss Singleton, affectedly shivering.

"Pray, Mrs. Fairfield, have you yet seen your new neighbour, the fair incognita, at the cottage?" asked Miss Danby.

"No, I have not," said I. "Is she, then, fair?"

"*That* remains to be proved," answered Miss Singleton; "but the colonel, who has a truly quixotic spirit, where a female (and, moreover, a young, and, as it appears in this case, a concealed female) is engaged, swears by *his gallantry*, that he *will* get a peep at her, and then we shall have *his* opinion; for I assure you, the colonel is allowed to be *some* judge of beauty!"

"A gallant, gay Lothario!"[1] said Ingot; "is he not, Miss Singleton?"

"Why, to be sure he *is* gay;" said Miss Singleton. "But what can be said when a man is in the zenith of life, spirits, gaiety, and fortune, and every female heart falling before him? I talk to him a little seriously now and then, when I can find time, but he is so charmingly insinuating, and such an agreeable devil, that I'm sure if he had not been my brother, I *must* have been one of his victims!"

---

1 A character in Nicholas Rowe's play *The Fair Penitent* (1703) who seduces and betrays the female lead; the name has come to mean any lecherous male.

"*Not* his victim," returned Miss Danby; "you must, you *would* have been the selected she; for I think I *never* saw two persons more alike than yourself and the colonel, both in manner, sentiment, person, and conversation."

"Now, don't flatter me," said Miss Singleton, "though I must own we have frequently been found out for brother and sister." By this time, you are tired of antiquated folly, dearest Mrs. Milbanke; believe me, I was heartily so before we got to the end of our walk, and I could see that Caroline Lumley felt awkwardly constrained before these high-flown belles, who noticed her not quite as much as they would have done a dog which they had met with me. When the *quartetto* were fairly gone, and we were seated quietly at our work, Caroline said,—

"I think, ma'am, Miss Danby has something very bold in her look and manner—do you not agree with me? She may be a very well-bred lady, for I am not acquainted with many of those—but she is not at all like *you* in her manners."

"She has seen a great deal more of the world than I have, Caroline," said I; "and is much admired in its circles, I make no doubt."

"But do *you* admire her, ma'am?"

"That is not the question," said I. "Does *Mr. Waller* admire her?"

I said this with meaning—the crimson tide covered the neck of Caroline—her *face* was bent over her work; but she answered with a vehemence, which rendered her almost breathless,—

"No; I am *sure* he does not!"

"And *I* am sure of it too," said I. "Waller has a better taste—the meretricious allurements of folly cannot draw him aside from the contemplation of virtuous simplicity!—Waller loves *you*, Caroline."

"Oh, madam!" and she covered her face with both her hands.

"Be not ashamed my love, at having raised a virtuous passion in the bosom of virtue—I speak not from motives of idle or unfeeling curiosity, but from a real wish of assisting you—deal ingenuously, then, with me, sweet girl, and tell me if my conjectures are not right?"

"They *are*, madam. Why should I conceal any thing from you? Why, indeed, when my parents are both acquainted with, and approve, the mutual passion which subsists between Waller and myself? Mr. Waller came down here a stranger, as tutor to Mr. Ingot; there was little chance of our getting acquainted with him, as the nabob's family were placed at a height so far above us, that we neither wished an intercourse with it, nor would have been allowed it if we had; but Mr. Waller's constant and zealous attendance at church—his respectful attention to Mr. Bellfield, the uncle of Sir Marmaduke (a worthy old gentleman, whose story reached my father's ear)—these circumstances first conciliated in us an interest for Mr. Waller;—and then, when my father had a long and severe fit of sickness, he stepped forwards, volunteered his services, and officiated as minister of this parish nearly three months—no persuasions of my father could induce him to accept any pecuniary reward!"

"But he had his *rich* reward in your love, Caroline?"

"Ah, madam," said she, "I felt that I could not withhold it from him—My good parents soon perceived our mutual partiality—they sought not to restrain it—but they saw the imprudence of our thinking of any thing further, till better prospects should open to Waller."

"Has he expectations, then?" asked I.

"Alas! madam, I hardly know what to call them. A dependence on the word of Sir Marmaduke Ingot is, I sometimes fear, the slightest of all probabilities. He is, you *must* see, a man who ever pays court to the 'rising sun;' who would help to lift *those* who are already exalted, if, in any way, they could conduce to his *own* exaltation, but who would be more likely to *crush* than to succour the *fallen*."

"I fear that you have drawn too just a picture of a selfish man, Caroline."

"Waller submits to the drudgery that is imposed on him at the Pagoda (and papa often compares him to Jacob serving for Rachel),[1] because he does not like to leave this neighbourhood; but there is no chance of his pupil's improvement, and this is of *itself* sufficient to depress the spirits and the exertions of a young man of talent and genius. He feels that the instructor can never derive any credit from the instructed; and though he does all in his power to give Mr. Ingot's mind a right turn, and to form it to laudable pursuits, and to plant into it just notions, yet his labours are daily subverted by the false and ridiculous theories and systems of his refined mother, and the overweening and worldly maxims of Sir Marmaduke. Mr. Ingot is any thing but a classical scholar; and, as to study, I have frequently heard Waller say, that it is impossible to fix his attention to any one subject for half an

---

1 Jacob agreed to serve Rachel's father, Laban, for seven years in order to win her love.

hour together; and when he has complained, at his first coming to the Pagoda, of the inattention of his pupil, her ladyship said,—

"'That learning was never to be thrummed into the head of any one; that *true genius* caught it at intervals, when the glow of enthusiasm stimulated the breast; that she was a decided enemy to all innovations on the liberty of the human mind; that *measuring* out the classics by the hour and the rule, might do in a large school, where there was just ten minutes for the teacher to appropriate to each boy; but that, where the exclusive attention was to be directed to *one*, it was the duty of the tutor to watch for the auspicious moment—to follow the youthful mind in all its variations—to watch it with never-ceasing vigilance, and eagerly snatch the *golden* opportunity when it panted for information and instruction!'

"The *golden* opportunity has never arrived, and Waller, in following his pupil in all his whimsical and childish vagaries, frequently compares himself to the *butterfly-hunter*."

"But Sir Marmaduke, surely, he must be a very weak man, to *suffer* his son to go on in such a manner!"

"Sir Marmaduke has not had the advantages of a liberal education himself," said Caroline, "but he does not find that he is received the worse on this account since he has *made* his fortune, and assured that his son will inherit *these* advantages, he is very easy on the subject of his mental improvement, although he would fain have it believed, that he is of a very studious turn himself, and is fond of talking of his "literary avocations," though *his* studies never extend further than the newspapers, the army list, the court calendar, and the acts of parliament concerning highways and turnpikes;—but I must put a check on my tongue," said she, "Waller would not be well pleased to hear me revealing the secrets of (his) prison house!"

"I don't think he could be *displeased*," said I, "with the artless picture which you have drawn of his disagreeable situation. But such, I fear, are frequently the trials which genius, talent, and virtue have to undergo, in a world where the trials are always proportioned to the strength!"

I cannot say how much I admire this ingenuous girl, or how deeply I am interested in the loves of this youthful pair. For the present, adieu!

IN CONTINUATION

AUGUSTUS heard my recital of Caroline's artless tale with an interest as deep as my own; his strenuous exertions will not be wanting, to render them happy as they deserve to be.—Oh! how do I glory in a husband, who thus forestalls me in every benevolent intention!

IN CONTINUATION

AUGUSTUS brought Waller home to dinner yesterday, on a more familiar footing than he has hitherto been with us. We saw him to greater advantage; he has a courage in speaking his opinions, and an independence of sentiment, which pleased us both; for it proves, that, though placed by fortune in a subordinate situation, he will not crouch nor temporize with his own principles to please his superiors. He gave us an outline of poor old Bellfield's life—

> Blow, blow, thou winter's wind!
> Thou art not so unkind
> As man's ingratitude![1]

Mr. Bellfield was a merchant of some consequence, and bore an irreproachable character both in regard to his commercial and relative connexions. His only sister married, was left a destitute widow with a small family, and it was wholly to the generosity of her brother, that she was indebted for her own and their existence. He sent the eldest boy to India, with strong recommendations; he returned Sir Marmaduke Ingot, a nabob, with an overgrown fortune: he found his uncle reduced by unmerited misfortunes, and labouring under difficulties in the decline of life, from which he had been exempt in the meridian. The hand of *protection* was most ostentatiously thrown out, not the hand which should have lifted Mr. Bellfield to his former situation, and strained every nerve to keep him there with his original credit! No! the *nephew* offered an *asylum* at the Pagoda, and the *uncle* was driven to an acceptance of it. His pride, his sense of the ingratitude he had met with, were silenced by his *necessities*;—an offer from which his spirit would have revolted, his imperious exigencies obliged him to accept!—"My poverty, but not my will, consents!"[2]

Daily getting nearer to that grave, where "the rich and the

---

1 The opening lines of a song from William Shakespeare's *As You Like It* (II.vii).

2 Spoken by the Apothecary in William Shakespeare's *Romeo and Juliet* (V.i.78).

poor meet together,"[1] in *that* contemplation Mr. Bellfield apparently looks beyond the unpleasantries which he daily encounters at the Pagoda. No tempers can be so dissimilar as Mr. Bellfield's and Sir Marmaduke's; "sanction, countenance, and favour," are the favourite words of the *great man*—while through his whole mercantile proceedings, Mr. Bellfield was invariably *sanctioning*, *countenancing*, and *favouring* in *silence*, experiencing true pleasure only, whilst benefiting his fellow-creatures. Though unhappily reduced to a dependent situation in the house of his nephew, yet he studiously maintains a freedom of opinion which does him honour, and which Sir Marmaduke finding to be impregnable, after a few useless discussions on his first coming, has ceased to attack, seldom entering into conversation with Mr. Bellfield; and thus he avoids showing him how widely different are their sentiments on most subjects. The old gentleman is suffered to pursue his own plan of amusement, and to walk over the grounds alone and unmolested, like an old horse, that "having borne the burden and heat of the day,"[2] is just suffered to exist by the master whom he formerly sustained on his back!—Lady Ingot feels an utter contempt for Mr. Bellfield, he has never been at *college* or in *India*, and hence he *can* be no companion for *her*.—She never checks Frederic in his facetious remarks on "old quiz," and "old square toes," and the duty and respect which the age, the affinity, and the worth of Mr. Bellfield ought to command from him, are thus converted into ridicule and insult! Waller is particularly attached to Mr. Bellfield; and I rejoice that there is one feeling being at the Pagoda, who will try to ameliorate his hard lot. The story of this unfortunate gentleman is interesting, my dear Mrs. Milbanke; it shows us how differently things are in reality, from their estimation in the world. By the world, Sir Marmaduke and Lady Ingot are praised and applauded for their kindness and benevolence to an unfortunate relative— *We*, who know the preceding and existing circumstances, see where their "tender mercies" tend. God bless you—so will ever pray

OLIVIA FAIRFIELD!

IN CONTINUATION

MRS. MERTON is arrived; so obliging, so amiable; her "dear sister," her "charming Mrs. Fairfield;" I really fear I shall forget myself, I am so overwhelmed by civility; the park, too, is so beau-

1 Proverbs 22:2.
2 Matthew 20:12.

tiful, "she shall be strolling in it *continually!*" (by this you are to understand she has found her legs since last I saw her): then "we look so well, so handsome, we do so much credit to the air of Devonshire; Augustus is grown quite fat. She even longs for the day when she may prevail on Mr. George Merton to follow her example, and retire to such another elysium!" This rhodomontade, convinced as we must be of its insincerity, is rather teasing—Augustus can scarcely sit it: he never *liked* Mrs. Merton, and he is of too ingenuous a disposition to conceal his marked surprise, when he hears her thus boldly avowing sentiments in direct contradiction to her practice.

IN CONTINUATION

YOU will not have much added to my packet, as I shall devote my whole time to my guest during her stay.—I must appear deficient in professions when measured by her standard; I must therefore make up, by acts of attention, for these deficiencies in words: To-morrow we are to have the party from the Pagoda to dine with us, the Singletons, &c.—Mrs. Merton may *talk* of the delights of the country, but I know she would soon weary of our domestic meals, if they were not enlivened by a few new faces,—while *I* grudge every day that is passed otherwise than in rational conversation, and a parity of sentiment. In my husband's approving looks, in listening to the ingenuous remarks of Caroline Lumley, I find my highest pleasure; and I daily pray to Heaven, that, in the midst of this abundant happiness, I may not forget that I enjoy all through its benign mercy! I pray to have my heart more and more softened towards my fellow-creatures, that I may look with an eye of compassion on their failings, as well as their wants, that I may see my own deficiencies of conduct, and not suffer myself to be so puffed up by prosperity, as to forget my God!—Adieu, my beloved friend! Remember that I must always be your affectionate
OLIVIA FAIRFIELD!

   ★ ★ ★ ★ ★
   ★ ★ ★ ★ ★

. A long, *long* chasm appears in my journal!—Ah, my dear Mrs. Milbanke! I have sometimes feared that you would never again see the hand-writing of your Olivia—I have feared that the attempt to portray my tale of sorrow would unnerve my brain—Yes, Mrs. Milbanke, *sorrow!* Your Olivia, your late *happy* Olivia, she who prayed that the Almighty would not suffer her to be puffed up by prosperity,—it is she, who, bowing, humbling herself to his chastising rod, would now fervently beseech him to enable her to struggle with adversity!

IN CONTINUATION

THE bitterness of death is past—the climax of my fate is sealed—I am separated for ever from my—Oh, Mrs. Milbanke, I must not write the word! To weeks of agony of despair, is now succeeded the calm stupor of settled grief;—the short, the transient taste of perfect happiness which I lately enjoyed, has rendered the transition doubly acute.—Oh, my dear, my misjudging father! why did you not suffer your poor child to continue in Jamaica?—there, *there* she was respected—for *your* sake, she was respected by all—while *there*, one dear, dear friend loved her for herself! Mrs. Milbanke would *always* have loved her, and cherished her, and *there* she could not have known the misery which is now her portion!—The prejudices of society which *you* feared for her there, have here operated against her with tenfold vigour; for it appears to be considered as no crime to plot against the happiness, to ruin the peace and the character of a poor girl of colour!—Ah! let me recall my words,—they are not written in that true spirit of Christianity which the benevolent Mr. Lumley would teach me. *He* is a true friend, Mrs. Milbanke—*he* feels for your Olivia; he pours *his* consolations, the consolations of religion, into her ear, and at the throne of mercy he prays that she may receiveth that support of which she stands so much in need!—"They that sow in tears, shall reap in joy!"[1] said the good man, and these words sank deep into my heart—oh, may they bring forth the fruits of piety and resignation! Crying and wringing her hands, my faithful black, my poor Dido, beseeches her "dear Missee not to write any more about it to Mrs. Milbanke, till her dear lady be better." I must take her advice; I grow faint, my hands tremble; six weeks like those which I have recently passed, must have unnerved the strongest frame!

IN CONTINUATION

IT is a long story, my dearest madam; yet you will be impatient to get it: and I must try to give you a minute relation.

What tranquil, what unalloyed happiness preceded Mrs. Merton's visit to New Park! It is only by recalling this bright

---

1 Psalm 126:5.

picture to your memory, that you can form an estimate of the soul-harrowing reverse,—it was a picture of primeval happiness, of paradisiacal bliss! In Eden, our first parents were happy till the serpent—I dread to pursue the comparison—it was necessary that *my* happiness *should* be destroyed, I had too long enjoyed that situation which—Oh, Mrs. Milbanke! my soul shudders, my heart sickens, at the recollection of those happy days which are gone by for ever!—But of what avail are useless retrospections, perhaps they are even criminal, perhaps—Alas! if I will ever let you into the melancholy history, it is necessary that I should be more *methodical*!

All civility and harmony, Mrs. Merton appeared to be the happiest of the happy, and the gayest of the gay, on becoming our guest. She was delighted at seeing Miss Danby, and seeing this, of course I pressed that lady to be with us as frequently as possible; this she acceded to: the Singletons also, drawn by the magnetic attractions of a London lady, were daily at the park. We formed constant walking parties, and Mrs. Merton's languor and *ennui* seemed have been left in London: she was more pleasant than I had ever seen her; perhaps she smiled like Judas, to destroy more surely! The incognita at the cottage, her mysterious seclusion, had frequently been the topic of conversation; in vain had Colonel Singleton essayed every means for getting a peep at her; but her impervious solitude could not be broken in upon by any method he had devised. The ladies were all anxious to know something of her, and we frequently took our evening walks near the cottage, and directed our looks to its Gothic easements, vainly trying to glimpse the object which had excited our curiosity! Mrs. Milbanke, do you remember the night of the seventeeth of—? With *you* it might have been calm; with *us* it was tremendous beyond expression! —No hurricane that I ever witnessed in the West Indies equalled it! The continued flashing of vivid lightning, the almost uninterrupted peals of thunder, the torrents of rain,—it seemed as if Heaven was pouring out its vengeance on our heads—every individual of the family arose: from my windows I saw the oaks rifted from their trunks; —I saw their branches hurled along the avenue; the whole park exhibited a scene of ruin and desolation! Mrs. Merton's shrieks rent the air, for *she* had no command over herself, while a cold damp struck at my heart, which I never felt but *once* before. *That* once,—oh, Mrs. Milbanke! it was before the marriage altar!—Yet I was soothed by the voice of my husband; I hoped, I trusted in the Almighty, and I thought of and prayed for those who were exposed to the "pelting of the pitiless storm!"[1] The morning at length broke, the sun rose with unclouded majesty, as if to smile at the devastating influence of its precursor, night. We all congratulated one another on our safety; Mrs. Merton was as much exhilarated, as she had been depressed on the preceding night; and my Augustus—*mine* did I say—oh, Mrs. Milbanke! Mr. Fairfield, ever anxious to be of service to his fellow-creatures, proposed my making a tour of the cottages, and inquiring what injuries their poor tenants had sustained, in order that he might relieve them.

"The lady at the park gate must have been dreadfully alarmed, I should think," said Mrs. Merton.

"Indeed she must," quickly returned Augustus. "Olivia, my love, you never stand on the formal punctilios of ceremony, when it is in your power to be useful; we will go by the way of the park gate, and you shall approach the house, and send in your message to its inhabitant."

An unusual animation seemed to overspread the countenance of Mrs. Merton, as she announced her intention of accompanying us in our errand of mercy.

"The park is very damp," said Augustus, who, I believe, did not much wish to have her a witness of his acts of beneficence; as he usually fulfilled the law of Revelation, and suffered not his left hand to know what his right hand had done.[2]

"Oh, you have taught me to laugh at my foolish fears concerning damp and cold!" said Mrs. Merton.

Miss Danby and Miss Singleton then walked in, and began to give a history of their affright during the storm. The cupola of the Pagoda had been carried away; Mr. Ingot ran into a dark closet, and her ladyship had been employed in trying repellent experiments to keep off the electric fluid, after stuffing her son's ears with cotton, to prevent his hearing the thunder. On hearing whither we were bound, the ladies, with one voice, declared they would be of the party; we could not refuse, but we contented ourselves with a very cursory view of the little cottages in the village, Mr. Fairfield giving private instructions for those persons to call at the house, whom he judged in most need of assistance. We at length reached the park gate by a circuitous route; for frequently

---

1 Taken from Lear's speech in William Shakespeare's *King Lear* (III.iv.29-30).
2 Matthew 6:3.

had our progress been impeded by the interposing branches of the oaks, which, rent by the storm, lay entangled under our feet, while the rain had washed off the grassy turf, as though it had been inundated by a whelming flood, and the trees were entirely divested of their verdure; the poor sheep seemed to herd together, as if not yet recovered from their affright; and the birds flew about in circles, their nests entirely destroyed. I hinted to the ladies, my companions, that I thought it better to advance to the house alone; but, impelled by curiosity, they proceeded, and only halted a few paces, whilst I applied my hand to the knocker. At the moment I did so, a violent shriek from within saluted my ears. The door was burst open—a female rushed out. She sprang by me, crying, "Save, oh save me!—Augustus, save me!"—She sank on the turf at the feet of Mr. Fairfield.— Colonel Singleton followed from the cottage. He tried, in some confusion, to account for his appearance; but I heard him not—I saw Augustus only.— Astonishment and surprise were the expressions which momentarily overspread his features,—but to these appeared to succeed, fear, apprehension, anxiety, love!—Yes, *love*, Mrs. Milbanke!—He held the inanimate form of the lady to his bosom; he conjured her to open her eyes, to awake—he called her his *wife*—his *best-beloved*, his *lamented Angelina*!—He saw, he heard *me* not, even while I franticly knelt at his feet, and conjured him to tell me the meaning of the words he uttered!

The three ladies expressed their wonder and their surprise in terms suitable to their respective characters; but I remember that both Mrs. Merton and Miss Danby seemed to recognize the lady: they called her Angelina—Miss Forrester!—Too well I remembered these names—I felt the stroke of anguish—it seemed to pierce my heart—to fire my brain!—I, too, fainted in my turn! How long I continued in this state, I know not; when I came to my recollection, I found myself in bed; Caroline Lumley and Dido sitting one on either side of me. I spoke, but I had no idea of the occurrence that had brought me there.

"Blessed be our good God!" said Dido; "I hear my dear Missee speak yet once more again!"

While Caroline kissed my hand in silence, a tear dropped on it. The traces of memory were now busily returning; they threatened to unsettle my brain!—I passed my hand before my face, and then said,—

"Oh, Caroline! was it a soul-harrowing vision that I saw? or did Augustus clasp another to his heart?"

"Do not agitate yourself, my dearest Mrs. Fairfield!" said Caroline; yet her own voice faltered, as she pronounced the *last* two words. "You must not think—every thing depends on your being tranquil!"

"*Must* not think!" said I—"Alas! I see, I feel there is some dreadful calamity fallen on my defenceless head!"

Caroline sighed—Dido fell on her knees—she clasped her hands together, and turning up her eyes, so as to show only their whites, she muttered some words with a fervency of supplication, which convinced me that her honest heart was bursting for her mistress!

"Who was that lady, whom I saw in the park?" asked I.

"Pardon me,—I must not, cannot answer you!" said the gentle Caroline.

I referred my question to Dido with my eyes.

"Oh accursed, accursed wretches!" said Dido; "they that contrived so black a plot!—Oh, my dear Missee, we will go back to our own good country!—we will pray to a good God Almighty, to teach you and me to forget that we was ever set foot on English land! My poor Missee was happy in our own dear Jamaica; there every body *knew* she was Mr. *Fairfield's* daughter—good Massa's child—and, not a blacky of them all would have touched one sacred hair of her head, but in the way of reverence and affection! But here—oh, could the poor good Massa speak out of his grave, he should cry shame and vengeance on 'em all !—Ah, my dear lady; you be too good to stay here!"

It was in vain that Caroline Lumley besought Dido to be pacified; her heart was relieved by pouring forth all the bitterness of her spirit!

"Where is Mr. Fairfield?" asked I.

Caroline spoke not; she averted her head.

"Where is your master, Dido?" asked I.

"Dido *has no* master—Dido's poor old Massee be in heaven!" said she; her lip quivering, and turning pale from passionate emotion as she spoke.

"The uncertainty under which I labour, will unsettle my returning reason," said I. "Caroline, if you expect mercy at the day of judgement, tell me who was the lady I saw at the park gate? Was she—is she—or is she not?—speak, I charge you, speak, if you will not have me die before you!"

"She is—she is"—Caroline's tears fell down her cheeks—"she is Mr. Fairfield's—"

"You shall not say it—you *dare* to say the word in Dido's hearing, before her dear Missee!" putting her hand before Caroline's mouth.

"His wife—his wife!" cried I, "is it not so? Great God! then what am I?"

"An angel, a sacrificed angel!" cried Dido, again falling on her knees.—"Ah, Missee! dear, dearest Missee! exert your own self—struggle—live—to show them all, that you be Mr. Fairfield's daughter!"

"Oh my father, my beloved, my regretted father!" cried I, "if *you* had lived, this had not been!—Yet I would not recall thee from happiness."

"Oh no, no—we must not, we cannot!" said Dido, sobbing convulsively.

"And where is Augustus?" asked I, Caroline was again silent: even Dido was so likewise. "Where is Augustus?" repeated I.

"He is at my father's," said Caroline. "Alas, Mrs.—! alas, madam! he is greatly to be pitied!"

"Oh, soften not, but steel my heart towards him, Caroline!" said I. "I must not think of *him*—of the destroyer of my peace—my fame—my happiness!"

"But hear his justification, dearest madam."

"Never, *never!*" said I; "*never* must I see him more! Better that I should *believe* him guilty, than to dwell on his virtues, to contemplate on his perfections, and to think of the felicity which *once* was mine!—Oh, Caroline, I am awakened from a dream of bliss, as short as it was delightful!"

"And my good, my dear Missee, too, who was so kind to every body—she, who was *every-body's* friend—she to be so cruelly used; they think the poor blacks have no hearts; but I believe they have more heart and soul too than some of the whites—God help them all!"

Oh, Mrs. Milbanke, I have written till my eyes are nearly blinded. As I retrace my sufferings, it seems, that to have existed under them, I must have had a *harder* heart than the white ones, as Dido calls them.

IN CONTINUATION

WHAT a day was the one I have been describing!—Towards the evening, Mr. Lumley came to visit me; he feelingly entered into my distress, and while he lamented its cause, he pointed my thoughts towards heaven, for consolation; plainly showing me that all other hope was fled. I inquired for Augustus; my soul was upon the rack to hear of him; my heart (my variable, my fluctuating, but my still doating heart) was longing to hear his exculpation, even though he could be nothing more to me!

I longed to know that he had not designedly planned my destruction; that he had not voluntarily caused my irremediable wretchedness!

"He is greatly to be pitied," said Mr. Lumley; "his distress is but little inferior to your own. To know himself the cause, though the *innocent* cause, of your ruin, is no common affliction; and his sensibility is too acute, his regard for you was too fervent, to let him bear it with firmness!"

"But *how* could he be in ignorance of the existence of his—"

"Alas! *there* is the mystery," said Mr. Lumley; "a mystery, as yet undiscovered: but I trust, that Heaven, in its own good time, will bring to light the projectors and the executors of an almost unheard-of cruelty. Mr. Fairfield has nothing to accuse himself of, except his concealed and clandestine marriage; a mode of proceeding altogether wrong, for, though existing circumstances may sometimes *appear* to acquire it, yet, in my opinion, it ought never to be adopted: disguise and concealment invariably *hide* or *lead* to something wrong; and the consequences have frequently been fatal!"

"Fatal indeed!" sighed I. "Oh, Mr. Lumley, had Augustus but confessed to me that he had once been married—had he only breathed a hint of the kind, and of his uncertainty with regard to the fate of his wife—"

"He felt *no* uncertainty," said Mr. Lumley. "To Mr. Fairfield her death appeared *certain*; and, much as he loved her—tenderly as he mourned her loss, I heard him aver (and, with what sincerity, his whole countenance testified) that he had rather, *much* rather, have had her lain for ever in the tomb, than by her sudden re-appearance and restoration to him, have thus caused the desolation of your happiness! Even Angelina, though supposing herself abandoned by a faithless seducer, even *she* would have been contented to remain in her disgraceful privacy, rather than have caused such an excess of misery by her re-union with her husband!—She seems an amiable and pitiable young creature; the faults of her husband were hers likewise; she should not have suffered her passion to overcome her principles, by yielding to a clandestine union.—Three estimable persons are thus made wretched for the *present*, though time—"

I hastily interrupted him.

"Time cannot cure a broken heart, Mr. Lumley!"

"Ah, my dear lady, I expect *great* things from you; this is an arduous struggle: but I firmly believe your strength of mind is equal to it. You must exert your courage—your fortitude—and that excellent understanding which you possess; moreover, you must lean on that Rock of support which will never fail you,— remembering, that these 'light afflictions, which continue but for a day, will work for you a far more exceeding weight of glory!'"[1] Ah! Mrs. Milbanke, if I had not felt consolation from *such* words, I had been unworthy the name of Christian!

IN CONTINUATION

AT length I begin to rouse myself from that state of inactive despair which had overwhelmed my faculties. For more than six weeks have I been confined to the house; during that period Augustus has continued the guest of Mr. Lumley, fearing to invade the delicacy of my situation by appearing *here*; and scrupulously avoiding from visiting at the cottage, lest he should hurt my feelings. To tell you the various plans which have agitated my mind, during this painful period, is impossible. I have applied to Mr. Lumley for his advice, and he has been the bearer of daily messages, of the most generous kind, from my—alas! I was going to call him—*my* Augustus. He has entreated me to continue at the Park—to consider it as my own; he has offered to remove to the utmost extremity of the kingdom, that, if possible, I may never be reminded that he continues in existence. —Alas ! I can *never* forget him, Mrs. Milbanke; I can never forget his virtues— his kindness—his attention to your poor child! Wherever I go, the remembrance of these will break in on my tranquillity, and by the strong force of contrast, blight every present prospect. I am not ambitious, my dear friend; you know, I never was. Retirement always suited my disposition, and the turn of my mind;—*now*, the obscurest nook, the most retired cot, would be my choice, where I might hide my head, and my sufferings together, and ponder over them unmolested. But yet, in privacy, I pant for independence! You, Mrs. Milbanke, are fully acquainted with the strange tenour of my father's will. By a wonderful transition of fortune, I am now, once again, likely to be dependent on the generosity of Mr. George Merton. Yes! my dear friend, it is even so;—this has been the point to which *his* wife has aimed. Heaven forgive me, if

---

1   John Wesley's "A Prayer in Time of Affliction," in *A Christian Library.*
    *Consisting of Extracts from and Abridgements of the Choicest Pieces of Practi-
    cal Divinity, which have been Published in the English Tongue.* In 50 Volumes
    (Bristol: Printed by Felix Farley, 1749-55), Vol. XXI, 231. The correct
    wording is "So these light afflictions which are but for a moment, may
    work for me a far more exceeding and eternal weight of glory."

I wrong her by my suspicions; but I fear she has played a black part in order to rob me of that fortune which I did not value! A scene of distress, like that which was exhibited here, was, I find, too overpowering for the *weak nerves* of Mrs. Merton; she left the park, at a period, when *one* victim of her machinations lay stretched, in a state of insensibility, on a sick bed;—when another was nearly wrought up to a state of phrensy by his opposing feelings;— and a third, who had long been an innocent sufferer, experienced only a variation of suffering from the recent discovery. Ah, Mrs. Milbanke! do you think that creature deserves the name of woman, who voluntarily deserted persons whom she *professed* to esteem, at *such* a period.

Eager to exculpate himself, and to convince me, that he had not been actuated by any mercenary motives, in forming an union with me, Augustus, at his first return of recollection, sent for a lawyer, and though he left himself, his wife, and his child, (yes, a *child*, a beautiful boy of two years of age), entirely destitute, he made a formal renunciation of all claim to my property. *Not* so, his brother:—by the earliest post which *could* arrive after Mrs. George Merton's return to London, her husband wrote to Augustus, and said,

"That a recent discovery having proved, that he had no claim or right to any part of the late Mr. Fairfield's fortune, *he* demanded its restoration, under the second clause of the will— and that if it was not voluntarily yielded, he should have recourse to legal means."

Stabbed to the heart at such an irrefragable proof of mercenary selfishness, feeling acutely for my situation, and disdaining that any interested motive should, for an instant, attach to his character, Augustus as hastily disclaimed all pretensions to my fortune, in a letter to his brother, as he had previously done in one to me. Mr. Lumley read me a copy of the letter—Ah! Mrs. Milbanke, what indignation at his brother's turpitude—what disdain at his false accusations—what pity—what compassion— let me say, what *affection* towards me, did it not contain?

"That God who sees my heart," said he, "knows that I married Miss Fairfield from the best, the purest intentions! It has pleased him to let our secret enemies triumph over the demolition of *her* happiness, for whom I would have yielded my life with cheerfulness. Oh, brother! let not avarice—let not any ambitious or inhuman instigations of those around you, prevail on you to rob an orphan of her dower, even though the law should make it yours. Remember, that *here*, *law* and *justice* must be at variance;

any dispassionate person *must* see the meaning of the clause annexed to my uncle's will in your favour. Your name will be held in *contempt*, and every *tear* of the forlorn and helpless Olivia, will he measured against your cruelty at the awful day of retribution! What has she now left which can reconcile her to life? Despoiled—fatally despoiled of her name and title in society, it is by benefiting her fellow-creatures, that a mind like hers can alone experience consolation: and would you deprive her of the means of exerting the benevolence of her disposition—the ever-active impulse of her pious soul? Oh, George —George! it is I, it is your brother, who has been the innocent means of ruining this angel's happiness! It is I, that on my knees entreat you, whilst scalding drops of agony blister my paper,—it is I, who beseech you to act with consideration and humanity towards this most unfortunate, and most estimable of human beings!"

Ah! Mrs. Milbanke, what a heart is this? How did I pride myself in the consciousness of possessing its tenderest regard! "Farewel, a long farewel," to all my dreams of happiness.[1]

I find I must dispatch this packet. I grieve to think how I shall be distressing your affectionate heart, by the communications which it will bring you!—but I should feel a traitor to your valued friendship, if I were to conceal my grief. From *your* advice—from *your* sympathy, it is, under Heaven that I shall draw my consolations. I feel something of comfort tranquillizing my mind, when I reflect, that my distresses are not deducible from my own misconduct; that I can meet the maternal and inquiring eye of my best friend, and fearless say, "I am still your *own*
OLIVIA FAIRFIELD."

---

1 Olivia seems to be evoking Cardinal Wolsey's lamentation of his fall in Shakespeare's *Henry VIII*: "Farewel, a long farewel to all my greatness" (III.ii).

PACKET THE FIFTH
OLIVIA FAIRFIELD TO MRS. MILBANKE

Cliff Cot, near ****, Monmouthshire.[1]

MUCH has been done within the last fortnight, and your Olivia is now addressing you from a very humble cottage in a retired part of Monmouthshire! When I found that I was considered by Mr. George Merton, as living at *his* expense, during the time I continued at New Park, it required little resolution to form the determination of quitting it as soon as possible. I made my intention known to Mr. Lumley and desired him to bring Augustus acquainted with it. Mr. Lumley attempted to dissuade me—I was not to be moved.

"Hear me, my good friend," said I, "and you will agree with me in the propriety of my resolve. To be indebted to the ostentatious generosity of the Mertons, for such a situation as this, is impossible! I believe the law might give them my fortune, and I have a spirit which disdains to enter into a litigation:—and without *him*, who, once cheered every scene to me, *this* house would be a gloomy prison!—Ah, Mr. Lumley! that cottage at the park-gate, that *little* cottage, would contain the *love* of Augustus; and that would be a *palace of content*. But I must drive such vain ideas from my mind! Am I not acting a very selfish part, Mr. Lumley, by remaining here? I am the barrier which separates Augustus from his—!" (I could not utter the word); "because misfortune and irremediable suffering have overtaken me, shall I continue to blight the prospects of all those around me? No!—I trust I have a better heart. If I cannot be happy myself, I will not retard the happiness of others!"

---

1 Monmouthshire is located in South-East Wales. Eleanor Ty writes, "The town Monmouth is located at the confluence of the Rivers Wye and Monnow. The region, roughly bordering the Usk Valley in the west, the Wye Valley in the east, and the Bristol Channel to the south, is pleasingly diversified. A portion is mountainous and rocky, but the rich land in the valleys and hills is full of woods and pastures." *The Victim of Prejudice* by Mary Hays, ed. Eleanor Ty (Broadview, 1998), p. 179, n. 9. Monmouthshire might have symbolic importance for heroines such as Hays' Mary Raymond as well as Olivia Fairfield since its ambiguous position on the border of England and Wales made its ownership and governance extremely unclear until the confusion was finally corrected in the 1960s. An eighteenth-century woman's residence in this area—on the fringes of two national borders but securely anchored to neither—seems to be a fitting location for emphasizing the liminality that both of these women embody in their respective texts.

I sighed deeply, and weak "womanish tears,"[1] almost blinded my eyes, at the moment when I made these (I trust) *virtuous* resolves. My tears were infectious; the good rector wiped his eyes.

"Oh, come here, ye prejudiced, narrow-minded beings!" said he, apostrophizing from the feelings of the moment, and entirely losing the idea of my presence in them:— "Oh come hither, ye advocates for slavery!—ye who talk of the inferiority of reason, which attends a difference of colour,—oh, come here! and see a woman,—a young—a tender woman, who, in the contemplation of her own unparalleled misfortunes, and with a heart almost broken by affliction, yet rises with unexampled pre-eminence of virtue!— See here a conquest over *self*, which ye would vainly try to imitate!"

"Ah! my good sir," said I, "I *know* what is right, and I trust the Almighty will support me in the due performance of it. I had a glorious example in my mother, Mr. Lumley.—My mother, though an *African slave*, when once she had felt the power of that holy religion which *you* preach, from *that* hour she relinquished him, who had been dearer to her than existence! And shall I then shrink from a conflict which *she* sustained? Shall I not go on, upheld by an approving conscience, and the bright hope of futurity?"

IN CONTINUATION

I HAD seen a cottage advertised to be let in Monmouthshire, which seemed to meet my wishes, with regard to the retiredness of the situation, and its size, which, from the printed description, was diminutive enough; thither I wished to bend my course, and, previous to the above conversation with Mr. Lumley, I had written to make inquiries concerning it. In the interim, I understood from him, that Augustus had received a very angry letter from his father, accusing him of the most criminal intentions in concealing his former marriage, and pointing to this as the cause of all the distressing events which had ensued. Mr. Merton ended, by disclaiming all interest or connexion with him; and he bade him seek that maintenance for his wife and child by his own exertions, of which he was justly deprived in every other way.

I also received a letter from each of the Mr. Mertons. My uncle *condoled* with me in a very *polite* and complimentary style

---

1 Olivia possibly alludes to Hubert's wavering emotions when he is faced with the duty of blinding Arthur in William Shakespeare's *King John*: "I must be brief lest resolution / Drop out of mine eyes in tender womanish tears" (IV.i.37-8).

on my "*recent* distress:"—talked of my *fortitude* and *strength of mind,* and offered me all the *service* and *advice* in his power, and subscribed himself, as usual, my *very affectionate* uncle! The professions of Mr. George were a vast deal *more* diffuse (I shall enclose both the letters); it was plain that he considered himself as the *master* of my future fate, and after bidding me not to despond, but to be reconciled to my misfortune, he ended with almost *commanding* me to come to London, and to place myself under the protection of Mrs. George Merton!

Disdaining to receive even *pretended* favours from such hands, I did not answer this letter; but replying to my uncle, I made him acquainted with my intentions in regard to my future mode of life, and voluntarily relinquished all further claim to my father's fortune, if he would secure to me, from his son, fifty pounds every three months. This, I said, would secure a maintenance for myself and Dido, and I wished for nothing further.

The earliest post brought me a fifty pound bank note, as an advanced quarter, from Mr. George Merton, with his promise of remitting the like sum every three months. The account of Cliff cottage was satisfactory; I settled to take it by letter; and ere we mentioned that we had fixed on a place of residence, Dido had privately began to pack up my wardrobe. The jewels which had been presented to me on my marriage by Mr. Merton, it was my firm resolve to give to Mrs. Augustus Merton; I had also a great curiosity to see her, and I resolved to be the bearer of them myself!

In the course of my melancholy tale, I feel that I hurry over some occurrences, while on others I am unnecessarily diffuse; but you will impute these seeming inconsistencies of style to their real cause. But as I am now sat down in one unvaried routine of solitude, and as writing *employs* my time, if it does not *amuse* it, I will endeavour to be as particular in my narrative as I can.

God bless you, my dear madam !—till to-morrow I must throw aside my pen.

OLIVIA FAIRFIELD.

IN CONTINUATION

WITH the approach of misfortune, my summer friends flew off. I imagine that Miss Danby had given out at the Pagoda, that my fortune was forfeited to Mr. George Merton,—and to trample on the fallen, is no new trait in the character of the Ingots. I received a pompous and pedantic note from her ladyship, where, after condoling with me on my *reverse* of fortune, she advised me to go out to the East Indies, where, with my accomplishments, she doubted not but my *colour* would be overlooked,—and, by a *feigned name*, I might soon form an advantageous matrimonial connexion.

I should imagine that the *crimson* was the predominant *colour* in my cheek as I perused this vile scroll, which finished with an offer of *protection*, and letters of *introduction* at Bengal, from Sir Marmaduke, if I approved the *plan*. I threw the note into the fire, and sent word to the servant who brought it, that it required no answer. The next piece of penmanship I shall transcribe verbatim:

"My dear Madam,

"NONE of your friends have more sincerely sympathized with your feelings on a recent occasion than myself, and I should not have contented myself without personally offering you compliments of condolence, had I not been informed that you were still confined by indisposition to your room; but, lest you should engage in any future plan which may prove an obstacle to my tenderest wishes, I avail myself of this method of offering you my *protection*. I have been for some time in quest of a companion who could interest my heart; fate has now propitiously blessed me with an opportunity of offering my adoration at that shrine, where my warmest admiration has been attracted, since I had first the honour of being introduced to your acquaintance. Your own terms shall be mine—our connexion shall be kept an inviolable secret from the whole world if *you* wish it, though, for myself, *I* disclaim all the prejudices of society, and should not scruple, a moment, to avow myself the *warm* admirer of a *Woman of Colour*! I remain, most unalterably,

"Your much attached, and Devoted servant,

"ROLANDO SINGLETON."

Not even to Mr. Lumley could I prevail on myself to relate this insult.—Alas! I feared not for myself; but had Augustus heard of it, his indignant spirit would have fired, and the consequences might have been dreadful. Silence, a proud silence, I have observed on this disgraceful subject, except to you. I feared even to put my resentment into *words*, in addressing the colonel, lest by any means it should transpire; and I trust this sapient hero will construe the *silence* of the *Woman of Colour* into utter contempt.—

But, oh! how slight do these insults appear from the proud and the unprincipled, when contrasted with my real source of distress! The whole world is to me as nothing; its *applause* or its *censure* would alike be disregarded by me: though I trust I shall ever retain strength and resolution to act, so as not to deserve the latter, though I may not inherit the former!

IN CONTINUATION

EVERY thing was prepared for my journey into Monmouthshire, I had not revealed my determination to a single person, save my faithful Dido. I dreaded the persuasive entreaties of Mr. Lumley; I dreaded the affectionate sorrow of Caroline and of Waller; I dreaded to hear of the distracting emotions of Augustus!

The evening preceding the day of my departure at length arrived. I resolved to walk across the park, and to visit my innocent rival; perhaps there was something of romance in this resolution, but I had determined on it; I longed to behold this (to me) most interesting of females; I wished to show her that I retained no illiberal prejudices against her; therefore putting the casket in my pocket, which contained my intended present, and flinging my shawl round my shoulders, I sallied forth. My soul seemed armed with a gloomy sort of resolution; the evening was in unison with the feelings of my mind, it was cold and stormy; the quick receding clouds as they passed above me, now illuming, now shading my way, presaged a coming storm. The park was damp, the branches of the trees lay on the ground; it seemed as if even the inanimate objects had felt the recent shock which had shattered my nerves, and were mourning the wreck of happiness: the wild thought was soothing to my soul, yet I felt that my recent convalescence prevented my walking with my usual step—now firm, now unsteady and feeble. I more than once tottered to a tree, and held by it to support me, while I recovered breath to proceed; when, turning to cast a look at the house, from a point of view where Augustus and I had always been used to admire it together, I heard a hasty and approaching step, from a copse of underwood which was near me;—the little gate fell, and Augustus stood before me!—pale, wan, his hair dishevelled, his whole form forcibly proclaiming the extent of his late sufferings!—I started on seeing him.

"Oh, best—most injured of women!" said he, clasping his hands wildly together, and flitting by me as he spoke.—

"Augustus!" said I, for my resolutions returned with the pressure of the moment; "Augustus! and do you then fly me?"

"And can *you* for a moment bear my hateful presence?" asked he, quickly returning, but his countenance evincing the agony of his mental conflict.

"Yes, I thank God that I can!" said I, "though I did not seek this interview; yet will I not shun it, but rather rejoice in the opportunity which is thus accidentally afforded me, of assuring you that I feel not the slightest spark of resentment towards you; that I will fervently beseech Heaven for your future happiness, and pray that you may forget that there exists such a being as myself!"

"And can *you* do this? Incomparable creature! can you do this?" said Augustus, as he threw himself on his knees before me, and franticly seized my hand!

"Yes," cried I; "I can do *more* than this, if you will not unnerve my resolution, by thus giving way to the excess of your feelings!— Pray, I entreat you, rise Mr. Fairfield."

"Fairfield!—alas!" said he, "I no longer bear that honoured name; I am unworthy to bear the name which belongs to *you!*"

"Whatever name you bear," said I, "I shall always consider you as friend,—you shall always be regarded in my memory with esteem."

"Kill me not by such kindness; reproach, accuse, revile me; call me base destroyer of your fame, your peace, and I will plead guilty to it all—but in mercy spare me from those words of softness, which are sharper, which cut deeper *here,*" laying his hand on his heart, "than pointed arrows!"

"Rise, pray rise!" said I; "this posture ill befits me to allow, or you to retain—Pray, Augustus, exert yourself, re-assume your self-possession; fancy you are talking to a friend from whom you are going to he separated for a long period; a friend who takes this opportunity of lamenting, that the transitions of fortune prevent her from demonstrating her regard in any stronger way than words."—

"*The transitions of fortune!*" repeated he, stamping his foot with vehemence on the ground, "say, rather, the hellish machinations, the sordid avarice of perfidious fiends of malice!—Oh, Olivia, amiable, revered Olivia! how may you regret the day when you left your native island!—better to have been landed on a savage shore of barbarians, than to have found, as you have done, your bitterest enemies, in uncle, brother, husband! *those* names which, in the *common* lot of human life, are associated with all that is affectionate and tender!"

"Oh!" said I, the tears rolling over my face, and wringing my hands in agony, "let me entreat you to leave me Augustus, if you *will* thus add to my distress. I *thought* I had acquired fortitude to sustain any trial, but, *indeed,* if you will thus give way to useless recrimination, you will make me as frantic as yourself!"

"Oh, pardon—pardon!" said he; "I know not what I do, or what I say!"

"Come with me," said I, once more reassuming some appearance of composure; "come with me."

"Whither?" asked he.

"I am going to visit your Angelina!"

Augustus staggered as he held my hand—his cheek was blanched—he *looked* at me—*never* can I forget the expression of entranced admiration and surprise, which his features underwent.

"Can you be serious, Olivia—Do I touch your hand? do I feel your throbbing pulse? or are you not a being of ethereal mold?"

"Alas! a *very* mortal!" I exclaimed; "but, anxious to behold your Angelina, to love her for *your* sake, to look at your little boy—and to tell your wife, that I will pray for her and your felicity—I have determined on going to her, and let us go together, my friend!"—The big tear rolled down his cheek.

"I have not seen—I have not been at the cottage since that day—that never-to-be-forgotten day."

"I know it," said I; "Mr. Lumley has acquainted me with your self-command and forbearance, and it is *your* example which has excited my emulation—Come, you cannot refuse to go with me—but remember, that though you have seen me overcome by the sight of your self-upbraidings, together with the sudden surprise of this interview, I am not going to overwhelm Angelina with a picture of my sufferings, and *enhance* a sacrifice to her, which I am *constrained* to make.—No! I am going to speak comfort to her, by telling her that I hope soon to regain my own tranquillity, and that it is my earnest hope that her re-union with her husband may be lasting and uninterrupted."

"Where could you acquire such heroism, such generosity of soul?" asked Augustus; "from whence do you derive such unexampled magnanimity?"

"When the mind is *thoroughly* impressed with the consciousness of a super-intending Providence," said I, "it is taught to submit patiently to all its chastisements. 'Sweet, are the uses of adversity,'[1] if it teaches us to amend our lives!"

"*Amend*!" said Augustus, "how is perfection to be amended?"

"Ah!" said I, "flatter me no longer with praise which I must never more hear—perhaps, even in this instance, I have erred—perhaps, I was too much elated by your approbation—perhaps, in the redundance of my happiness, I forgot that this was not my abiding place; and by timely chastisement I shall be brought back to a knowledge of myself!"

"If *you* can thus find any reason for self-accusation," said Augustus, "what must I *feel*, who am conscious that it was owing

---

1 A line from Duke Senior's speech in Shakespeare's *As You Like It* (II.i.12).

to my clandestine concealment of my early marriage, that my enemies plotted my ruin, and cruelly produced this desolation?"

"That your secrecy in this respect was wrong," said I, "must be allowed; but by the faults of the past take a warning with respect to the future!"

"I can hardly ask it" said he; "but if at a *future* hour, I should have resolution to write down the events which led to this sad catastrophe, will you deign to read the history with candour and lenity, for I feel that to the character of Angelina Forrester I owe this explanation!"

"I will read it with all the indulgence you can wish," said I, "for I have already acquitted you in my mind."

"Generous—generous Olivia!" said he.—

"The Lumleys will always know my residence," said I; "to them you may safely consign the packet—"

"The *Lumleys*?" returned Augustus; "and must *I* then remain in ignorance of it?— will you seclude yourself from me? shall *I* never be informed of your health, of your welfare?—shall I constantly be accusing myself as the destroyer of your peace?—shall my tortured imagination be eternally haunting me with the remembrance of your misery?"

"Pray talk more rationally," said I; "a correspondence with you must be declined for *both*—for *all* our sakes; the sooner you forget me the better; the sooner I—" I stopped, I checked the unbidden sigh, I wiped off the involuntary tear and proceeded— "Augustus, you have not *yet* learned to know me. It is part of my religious duty to endeavour to resign myself to the all-wise dispensations of the Most High. I scruple not to own to you, that, as my husband, I loved you with the warmest affection; *that* tie no longer exists, it is now become my duty to force you from my heart,—painful, difficult I acknowledge this to be, for your virtues had enthroned you there! But this world is not our abiding place. I look forwards with faith and hope to that eternally happy state where there is neither 'marrying nor giving in marriage,'[1] where there shall be no more sorrow, and where 'all tears shall be wiped away from all eyes!'"[2]

"Heavenly, heavenly Olivia!" said Augustus, "I could now reverence thee as a beatified spirit!—Oh, how weak must I appear in your eyes!"

We had now reached the cottage door—Ah, Mrs. Milbanke!

---

1 Mark 12:25.
2 Revelation 21:4.

with what different sensations had I last approached it! I involuntarily shuddered as the hollow sound of the knocker reverberated, as before, through the little dwelling—My feelings, as I entered the parlour, where sat Angelina at work, her sweet little boy playing at her side on the carpet, it would be impossible to describe; or to portray the conflicting emotions, and the animated transports, of the re-united wife and husband! While the gentle, the trembling Angelina hid her face, and poured her tears into her husband's bosom, I caught the innocent resemblance of Augustus to mine, and poured my caresses on him, that I might not appear as though I grudged them their happiness. The gratitude, the bashful timidity of Angelina, her dove-like eyes, her transparent complexion, the delicacy of her fragile form, all rendered her a most interesting object. She seems peculiarly to require the assistance and support of the lordly creature man, and to be ill-calculated for braving the difficulties of life alone. The speechless astonishment with which she received my present of the jewels, I shall never forget. I *could* have said, "'These radiant gems which banish happiness but mock misfortune, I can easily relinquish"[1]—but I contented myself with plainly desiring her to convert them to any purpose which she should deem most beneficial, and lamented that I had nothing better worth her acceptance to offer; then turning to Augustus, I said, "That your father will relent, and again receive you into his favour, I do not doubt, else should I be sorry that I had stipulated only for a maintenance for *myself* out of *my* father's fortune; but you know the delicacy of my situation, and will see that, with propriety, I could not assist you."

"I *know* that you always act with consistency, with unexampled feeling, and consideration," said Augustus.

I feared that he was again going to forget himself; I started up, I placed the little Augustus in his father's arms, then taking his tiny hand, and joining it with both his parents, I said, "May heaven protect, and bless you all! May my fervent prayers be heard for your happiness!" and before any thing reached my ear, save the sigh of Augustus, I had quitted the house, and was once more in the park! I do not take any merit to myself, my dear Mrs. Milbanke, from having made this exertion—I was in some sort actuated by a romantic and curious spirit, and I felt relieved at

---

1 William Shenstone, "Love and Honour" (1764). The correct wording is "These radiant gems which burnish happiness / But mock misfortune, to thy fav'rite's hand / With care convey."

having seen Angelina, and having beheld in her a woman who was likely to form the happiness of the husband who I must for ever relinquish!

IN CONTINUATION

A FORMAL parting with the Lumleys was not to be thought of; I wrote my adieus, my grateful thanks for their kindness. A note I wrote also to the good Mr. Bellfield, in which I lamented that my reverse of fortune prevented my exerting myself in the behalf of Waller and his Caroline; and said, "that it had been the sanguine wish of Augustus, as well as myself, to see them happy in each other." I thanked the good Bellfield for the friendly sympathy he had evinced for me, and told him, that from his example I would learn a lesson on heroism! These painful duties over, I knelt at the throne of mercy; I besought the Almighty to give me courage to bear the stroke of adversity, and to arm my mind with a portion of his divine grace!

At an early hour in the morning, a hired chaise drew up, and, followed by the weeping Dido, I entered it. All the servants stood to catch a view of me as I walked across the hall; they reverenced my sorrows: but I heard their whispered prayers and blessings as I passed. I waved my hand in token of my thanks, and hurried into the carriage: there I gave way to the oppressive feelings of my heart, while Dido wrung her hands together, and sobbed at my side. The park, the lofty trees, the little cottage, its happy inmate, every animate, every inanimate object, added to my distress. I saw the little school which I had projected—the children which I had clothed—the peasants whom I had assisted. I recollected all the plans of long years of peace and comfort which I had laid, and, shuddering at my own temerity, I felt as if the Almighty had said to me those awful words, "Thou fool! *this* night thy soul shall be required of thee!"[1] For was it not nearly so? was not my husband my heart's idol—my bosom's sovereign?—Oh, Mrs. Milbanke! perhaps I loved him too much—perhaps "it is good for me to have been thus afflicted!"[2]

You will accuse me of having formed a harsh judgement, in having condemned Mrs. George Merton, without a proof, in the beginning of this narration; but, assured of her long and irreconcilable enmity to them, Augustus and Angelina, are convinced that she has been the prime agent of this plot against us all. Dis-

---

1 Luke 12:20.
2 Psalm 119:71.

appointed vanity, and craving ambition, two powerful incentives in the mind, where they are encouraged, urged her to work their ruin. But though this is completed in her idea, and though she may revel and smile on the money she has thus unjustly gained, yet their happiness is not dependent on outward circumstances; it is seated in their minds, and in their mutual affection, which she cannot deprive them of: and when she hears of their humble content, she may make the comparison between it and her own restless grandeur.

IN CONTINUATION.

INDEED, I could be very happy in this little cottage did I not remember "such things were, and were most pleasant to me;"[1] and did not Dido constantly bewail the change in a loud and clamorous grief, which, entirely divested of *self*, on my account will not be appeased. In vain I tell her, that if two courses were before me, I should prefer our boiled mutton;—she cries and shakes her head. I assure her that my little parlour is quite large enough. She asks if I recollect the "nice large rooms at Fairfield estate, and at Kingston?" She still pines for the "flesh-pots of Egypt,"[2] but not herself, but only for "dear Missee."

"For Dido would live upon salt herrings and rice all the long year round, if she could but see *Mr. Fairfield's daughter* served any way like herself."

And the Monmouthshire girl whom we have hired as a drudge, is taught to consider me as a *princess*, at least, and must not *dare* to enter the parlour on any account, or to answer the bell, on pain of losing her place; so that, quite scared when she sees me, she drops fifty courtesies in a minute, and runs into some corner, with her back pinned against the wall, to let my *high mightiness* pass along. With the earliest dawn poor Dido leaves her pillow, in order to see my breakfast prepared for me as I have been used to have it. The various ways that she tries to allure me to eat; the various cakes and little dainties

---

1 A loose rendering of Macduff's speech in *Macbeth*: "I cannot but remember such things were, / That were most precious to me" (IV.iii.222-23).

2 Karl Marx wrote, "During the exodus of the Israelites from Egypt the hardships of the journey and hunger caused, according to the Bible, the faint-hearted among them longingly to think of the days of captivity when at least they had enough to eat. The phrase "*to long for the fleshpots of Egypt*" has become a proverb," *The Eighteenth Brumaire of Louis Napoleon* (New York: International Publishers, 1987) 142, n. 5.

which she prepares, without my knowledge, to tempt my palate, would make *you* smile, who know my *always*-temperate appetite. But how can I be angry with this well-meant and affectionate attention? The body and mind of poor Dido are, however, so unceasingly engaged, that I fear her strength will fail—and miserable in the extreme should I be, if I lost my faithful girl, and was conscious that she had been the victim of her attachment to her mistress.

IN CONTINUATION

MINE is a very snug habitation; it is a thatched cottage on the side of a hill, which commands a noble view of the Wye,[1] and the picturesque country which adorns its windings. I understand that this country is not so retired as I had imagined; many gentlemen's seats are dispersed about the neighbourhood; their owners attracted by its wild and romantic scenery. An humble inhabitant of a lowly tenement like mine, is, how-ever, likely to pass unnoticed, and a *woman* of colour will not be a courted object. I wish to be unobserved—I do not want society—for although there is no real disgrace attached to my very peculiar situation, yet there is some appearance of it. I do not conceal my name; I contemn *all* mystery: and I never can voluntarily relinquish the beloved, the honoured name of Fairfield!—Believe me, my dear Mrs. Milbanke, I do not resign myself to a state of fruitless and blameable despondency.—No! I thank God, I keep myself employed; I endeavour to *interest* myself in my pursuits; I work in my little garden; I walk where I see a retired hut of poverty, and I try to do a *little* good to my fellow beings, even in my present narrow sphere. The blessings of constant employment I take to be a secret as well worth knowing as the philosopher's stone; it is a remedy for most of the evils of life. Had I the instruction of youth, my first, my last words should be, "rational employment;"[2] for what ills, what mischiefs, daily spring from idleness!

I brought my books with me. I have scrupulously avoided opening one of a melancholy cast, while those of a cheerful and heart-inspiring turn I have selected for my parlour companions.

---

1 Forming a part of the border between England and Wales, the river Wye is the sixth longest river in the UK.

2 A common phrase used in many treatises on female education. For example, John Burton's *Lectures on Female Education and Manners* (1793) commands women to "cultivate your minds, that you may never be at a loss for rational employment, or harmless amusement; and so to improve your dispositions, by charity and candour, that the sufferings

I feel my sallow cheek glow with satisfaction, *knowing*, that in this description of myself, I am pleasing my maternal friend. It is by her precepts that her Olivia has been enabled to stem the current of adversity; and the grateful child of her forming, must always rejoice in her affectionate approbation of her conduct!

IN CONTINUATION

I HAVE had a letter from Caroline Lumley; her style is as affectionate as her heart is sincere. She tenderly reproaches me for leaving New Park without seeing her; yet acknowledges that the pain of separation was spared to them all. She slightly glances at Augustus; and tells me, he has for the present taken up his residence at the cottage: that it is rumoured that Mr. George Merton means to retain the park as a summer residence.

"I *hope* not," says the ingenuous girl; "for indeed, my dear madam, such a neighbour could give us no pleasant ideas."

With the utmost simplicity she tells me, that her walks have never extended beyond the boundaries of her father's glebe, since I have quitted the neighbourhood. I understand from this, that she has not yet lain her prejudices aside, and visited Angelina, as I desired she would. Augustus has sent regularly to the rectory, to hear if they have had any tidings of me; and they had sent him the intelligence of my safe arrival at my new residence.

I have thus given you the heads of this affectionate girl's letter. It is delightful to be esteemed by those who are worthy, and I feel much comfort in the friendship which follows me with so much kindness into this retirement!

No incident occurs, worth relating, the monotonous life which I lead at present, yet I shall not cease to scribble my dear friend.

OLIVIA FAIRFIELD

[As the journal of the ensuing month does not offer any thing which requires insertion, we shall omit it, and go on to a period more material.]

IN CONTINUATION

CAROLINE LUMLEY writes me, that Augustus has been sent for, express, to London. That it is reported that his father is

---

and failings of others may meet from you with compassion and forbearance" (Lecture XXVI, Vol. 2, 226). See also Charles Allen's *The Polite Lady: or a Course of Female Education in a Series of Letters* (London: Printed for Newbery and Carnan, 1769) 130.

dying; that he has taken Angelina and his boy with him; and that the cottage is shut up. May the Almighty soften Mr. Merton's heart—may his forgiveness reach the ear of his son, and pave the way to his own forgiveness from a heavenly Father—and may he provide for the innocent Angelina and her unoffending offspring! I shall be most anxious to hear the result of this visit. I wrote to Caroline by the return of the post, and charged her to give me the earliest intelligence which should reach her. Surely my uncle will be reconciled to Augustus—surely he will make a provision for his son!

IN CONTINUATION

DID I not tell you, some time ago, that my poor Dido looked wan and dispirited, and that I attributed it to the effects of her zealous and arduous exertions for me? To-day she is all cheerful hilarity. She walks about with her head erect, as is usual with her when labouring with any pleasing intelligence, of which she chooses to make a temporary concealment. Were you to observe her mysterious, yet consequential looks, you must be diverted; for, in spite of the solemnity which she tries to assume, I perceive that she is constantly pursing up her thick lips, to prevent their widening into a smile of satisfaction. I see a pleasing surprise is in store for her dear Missee; perhaps a fine dessert, or some favourite flowers: whatever it be, I must try to evince my gratitude by a pleased reception of her favour.

IN CONTINUATION

OH, Dido, Dido! my faithful, yet mistaken girl, into what a situation hast thou put thy mistress! and yet I cannot chide thee.— I will recount to you, dearest madam, the surprise, and the conflicting emotions which I have just experienced. Devoid of curiosity, and wishing to live unknowing as well as unknown, I had not inquired the names of my nearest neighbours; all were alike strangers to me: and consequently a mere name could afford me neither knowledge nor information. Dido, I suspect, had been more inquisitive: she had more than once spoken of a "sweet, pretty house near the cliff," and had told me there was "*one* good gentleman in Monmouthshire." I usually answered her, that I hoped there were *many* here, as well as in other parts of the world, and I never indulged her loquacity, in point of local communications; feeling a satisfaction in maintaining my *ignorance*, which was an undefinable sensation even to myself. Dido has no small portion of superstition, and has laid up carefully all those signs and omens which she has gleaned from the English servants while in Devonshire. She has several times seen a *stranger* in the *fire*, and a *friend* in my *tea-cup*; I used to smile at her simple predictions, knowing that I was expected to notice them: but little imagining that, by these predictions, she was in reality preparing me for the reception of a visitor, and one, too, of her own inviting!

Yesterday morning, Dido seemed usually officious at my toilette; she would attend it through, although I several times told her I did not need her assistance; and when I came into the parlour, I thought it looked unusually decorated with flowers. She several times remarked, that it was a very fine day, and sweet, pleasant weather; and I guessed that she wished to lure me to a walk: but not feeling inclined to go out, I seated myself at my work, and, I will freely confess, had engaged in a train of rumination which had wetted it with the tears which fell from my eyes, when I heard a treble, but soft, rap at the door of the cottage. Though an unusual sound, it did not alarm me, as the villagers do not understand the different gradations of a rap, like a London footman, till I heard the stifled whisper of Dido in the passage, and in the next minute saw her open the door of the room, and usher in Mr. Honeywood! Though much altered, paler, thinner, and in deep mourning, I could not forget him.— But, alas! I could not receive him as once I should have done; my emotions nearly over-powered me, and I sat down on the chair; my trembling limbs refused to support me; I covered, my face with my hands, and burst into tears! Honeywood's agitation seemed very little inferior to mine.

"Oh, heavens!" cried he, in a voice that was tremulous from emotion, "is it thus we meet again? Pardon my abrupt intrusion, dearest—" (he seemed at a loss for my title, and added, after a short pause,) "*Madam*! I have heard your whole history from your faithful Dido," said he: "by turns I have *rejoiced* in your happiness, *mourned* over your sorrows, and been *entranced* with admiration at your superior fortitude and resignation! Oh! why— why were you the *best* and gentlest of human beings? why were you the appointed victim of such unparalleled sufferings?"

"My friend," said I, now resuming my courage, "it is not for us, narrow-sighted beings as we are, to inquire into the dispensations of an all-wise and all-just God! Afflictions fit us for another world—for a state of enjoyment; they make us eager to quit these scenes of transient sorrow, and to go to the regions of eternal bliss!"

"And *there*," said Honeywood, with enthusiasm, "if superior reward be the allotment of superior virtue, *there*, in transcendent happiness—"

He stopped abruptly—"No," said he, "my heart refuses to complete the picture —it would still chain thee to earth! Olivia, talk not of *dying*! What! the tender maid, who lately crossed with me the world of waters,—*that* time of ever-to-be-regretted felicity,—she whose spirits, whose health, whose youth, whose genius, whose fortune, whose situation, whose connexions,—all promised long years of happiness,—she to turn already to the grave, as to her only resting place? Oh, it cannot—it *shall* not be!"

"No," said I, "I am content, even now, to wait my allotted time on earth without murmuring; but, my spirits depressed; my health weakened; youth prematurely flying away; my genius (if *any* I had) entirely damped; my fortune changed; my situation strangely singular, and isolated from my connexions; you must allow that life has not much to hold out to me."

"Oh! I know—I know it all,—I *feel* it here!" said Honeywood, laying his hand with emphatic fervour on his heart; "and, since I lost my parent, 'tis the bitterest pang I ever felt!"—and he walked round the room in wild disorder.

"Mr. Honeywood," said I, calming my emotions, "you have sought this interview; and the sympathy which you indulge for me, assures me of your friendly regard: then hear me assure you, that you see my sufferings in too strong a light. Overpowered by surprise, and the rushing remembrances which visited my heart at the moment of your entrance, I gave way to a transient weakness; but, believe me, I do not usually yield thus supinely to my feelings. I thank God, that the knowledge of my own innocence, and that of—of *him*, from whom I am separated for ever"—I sighed,—my sigh was echoed by deep-drawn one from Honeywood— "and the comforts of religion *have* supported me, and do continue to support me, in patient cheerfulness. I am not without my resources or my avocations; I can find employment, and I visit my *poor*, though I pass by on the other side of my rich neighbours. I have a sufficiency for all my wants."

"A sufficiency!" interrupted Honeywood, "the nightly depredator is not so *base* a plunderer as is George Merton; *he* steals from strangers, from aliens whom he *knows* not—whom he cares not for. But Merton, the robber of the orphan—of his nearest relative—of a young—a tender female,—curses light on his head!"

"Oh, I must not hear you talk thus," said I; "rather may repentance visit his *heart*! But you know me not, Mr. Honeywood, if you think that the mere loss of my property has given me a moment's uneasiness.—Alas! in the bankrupt of the affections, in the entire desolation of the tenderest feelings of the heart, a pecuniary thought could never gain entrance into the mind, when *he*—when *he* too suffers poverty, *I* am well contented to be *not* rich."

Honeywood looked at me, for a moment, with the utmost surprise; his whole frame seemed to experience a revulsion; his agitation was excessive; he advanced eagerly towards me; he seized my hand,

"Olivia! dearest, beloved Olivia!" and he sank at my knees, "oh, forgive the question! pity my despair,—my agony, and answer it—I *conjure* you answer me with your known candour! you loved—you loved Augustus?"

"More than my *life!*" answered I, with emphasis. "Yes, Mr. Honeywood, I glory in the acknowledgement; for he possessed every virtue and every quality to interest the heart!"

Honeywood clasped both his hands together; then he seized mine—he bathed them in tears.

"And do you try to conquer this *imperious* passion?" asked he, looking earnestly, and with a scrutinizing expression, in my face.

"Assuredly I do," replied I, "as much as is possible. I drive from my remembrance the few months of happiness—the fleeting months I passed in Devonshire; but there are times when 'busy meddling memory'[1] returns with barbarous power, to give a new edge to prevailing retrospections!"

"But with *no* reciprocation of attachment, no congeniality of sentiment, could your delicate, your sensitive mind be satisfied with a widowed heart, with—"

"That the warmest affections of Augustus were lain (as he believed) in the tomb of his lost wife, was true; but in the tender friendship of Augustus Merton, I had nothing to lament. I,—but why—why draw me into this needless recapitulation—into this strange confession? Sacred were my feelings; why—why disturb them, with unhallowed hand?"

"Why, indeed!" said Mr. Honeywood.—"Oh, Olivia! vain would I have concealed from you at this interview the purpose

---

1 Robert Blair, "The Grave" (1743): "Prone on the lowly grave of the dear man / She drops; while busy meddling memory, / In barbarous succession, musters up / The past endearments of their softer hours, / Tenacious of its theme."

with which my heart is fraught; but, forced as it is from me by the tumultuous sensations of the moment, hear me say,—that I *love* you beyond all earthly beings!—Hear me tell you, that on board the ****, while daily present with you—while listening to your melodious voice—to your noble sentiments—to the delicate purity of your conversation, I drank deep draughts of a passion which was violent as it was hopeless. Vainly did reason and reflection urge me to break my bonds; I loved my fetters, and, to contemplate on your dear idea, to turn with retrospective eye on those blissful hours of friendly intercourse was my utmost pleasure; *even* when I *knew* that you were to become the wife of another; even when I *knew* that duty and propriety bade me fly your presence! The loss of my ever-to-be-lamented mother, though it plunged me in sorrow, did not erase your image from my heart; I still remembered how you had, in the soft voice of friendship, tried to prepare me for this cruel stroke; and on retiring to this sequestered country, you were still the sylvan goddess of the shades I visited,—*you* were the benign genius of all my avocations! My fortune was greatly increased by a most unlooked-for circumstance; but of what use to me were this world's goods, isolated from *her*, who only could give them a charm? I heard of your happiness—of your felicity; I breathed fervent prayers for its continuance.—I *hope* I did not envy your husband. Think,—oh judge, then, my astonishment, my wonder, let me add, my *sorrow*, when I met your faithful black, and heard her tale of woe!—Olivia, Heaven is my witness, that in sympathizing in your afflictions, not a thought of *self* intruded at *that* hour. But *now*, oh dearest, amiable Olivia! if a *life* devoted to your happiness; if a fortune devoted to your service; if a love, a reverence, an admiration, unbounded as they are sincere, can move you to pity, oh, hear my suit!—deign, oh deign to pity me! forgive the seeming impetuosity of this declaration! feelings such as mine are not to he controlled! You are free, you are unfettered;—I may now, with pride; with glory, avow, that I doat on you to distraction; that your recent trials in the hard school of adversity have heightened (oh, how highly heightened!) you in my esteem; and that the pity of Olivia Fairfield would be more precious to me, than the love of any other woman!"

This rapid address, so unexpected, delivered with such enthusiasm, such fervour, bewildered and astonished me. I seemed to gasp for breath, and could only find strength to interpose at this moment.

"My *pity*, believe me, you have: sensible as you appear of the indelicacy of your present avowal, I will forbear to make any comments upon it. You have frequently told me, that mine is a decided character—"

"Oh stop, look not so determined, have mercy, gentlest, sweetest Olivia!" cried he, almost distractedly seizing my hand.

"The skilful surgeon," said I, "probes deep, the more speedily to heal the wound. I *now*, and to the *last* moment of my existence, *shall* consider myself the widowed wife of Augustus Merton!"

Honeywood let go my hand; he let his head rest on the table, hiding his face.

"My good friend," said I, "exert your resolution, nor let a *woman* be your superior in this quality. I have suffered, Mr. Honeywood, but I have struggled to sustain my sufferings with fortitude, and with consistency of character. Consider my situation, impartially and coolly, and see if I should not suffer in your opinion, were I to act in any way but the one I have fixed on; *that one* which my judgement approves, and which my heart must ever ratify!"

"Cruel, inexorable Olivia!"

"Not cruel," said I; "more cruel would it be to give you hopes which I could never realize."

"But surely, then," said Honeywood, after a silence of some minutes, "you will allow me your friendship—you will let me try to be instrumental to your happiness—you will let me renew our former delightful intercourse? Here, in this sequestered nook, let me try to cheer your solitary hours, to guide your steps in the evening ramble, to follow your benevolent impulse in your charitable visits to the neighbouring cottages!"

"Surely, Mr. Honeywood, you forget what you were asking me;—your regard for me is, I am sure, of a disinterested nature!"

"If I know my own heart!" said he, laying his hand upon it.

"*Then*," said I, "you will rather deny yourself a trifling gratification than injure my character. Consider the appearance that it would have, if I were to admit your visits, secluded as I am from all other society."

"The *appearance*!—and does Olivia regard appearances? She whose conduct could stand proclaimed before men and angels—shall she become the victim of a name—a nothing—shall she—?"

"Pray stop, Mr. Honeywood; in your eager warmth, you forget that you are arguing only from the disappointment of your own feelings; for, believe me, my ease and comfort would depend on my not being subjected (or rather in my not subjecting myself) to the malevolent sarcasms of the world!"

"If you so *lightly* hold my friendship —if you can so *coolly* forbid my visits," said he—"Oh, Olivia! could I but make you sensible of what I suffer at this moment, when I hear you refuse every thing that I propose—when you will not let me be of service to you—when I have not the power of evincing the sincerity of my professions!"

"I believe them all," said I; "and they make exactly *that* impression which they *should* on a woman, who has plighted vows of eternal fealty to another!—Honeywood, farewel! Take with you my thanks—my gratitude—my sincere esteem!"

"You *drive* me from you?" said he.—"Oh, Olivia! who can resist your commands?—May heaven bless and preserve you! May peace revisit your bosom! May *your* heart never experience those pangs, which now are piercing mine!"

Then, suddenly lifting my hand to his heart—to his lips—and to his forehead, he let it fall on my lap, and rushed out of the house.

IN CONTINUATION

FOR a few moments I gave way to all the weakness of my soul. Compassion for Honeywood, gratitude for his warm regard, were, you may believe, blended with other conflicting emotions. I even regretted that the punctilious decorum of the world prevented me from enjoying his society, till I recollected, that, by such an intercourse, I should be tacitly giving encouragement to hopes which I could never realize. Tears still stood on my cheeks, when Dido bolted in; a wise grin on her face, her black orbs sparkling like diamonds—

"What! my dear Missee crying? Ah! how glad me be to see dearest Mr. Honeywood once again! Dido did always like Massa Honeywood; and me be so glad he lives but just here, for now my dear Missee can see him every day—every day—and he be living in so nice grand house!—Oh dear, dear! what fine gardens there be, Missee, at Massa Honeywood's!—But ah, Missee, Missee!" tapping my cheek with her hand, "it be your own house, if you do like it;—me do know it be—me do know it be!" and she clapped her hands together, and danced around the room with marks of the greatest delight, in her manner.

"Dido," said I. It was of no use to speak; Dido heard me not.

"Iss, iss, me think it be very pretty house, indeed,—it be like the dear Fairfield plantation! Iss, iss, and me shall be housekeeper again, and have my bunch of keys at my own side! for here, God help Dido, there be nothing to lock. Now, be then good Missee, my own Massa's daughter!"

"Dido!" said I again, in rather a louder key. Dido turned round. "Dido, do you love your mistress?"

"You *know* Dido loves her Massa's own daughter, better than she loves her own self."

"And *you* can be happy where your mistress is?"

"Oh iss, iss!—Where Missee be happy, Dido be so too,"

"Then we shall *both* be very comfortable here."

"Not *here!*" said Dido, and her arms fell lumpishly down at her sides.

"And *why* not here?"

"Massa Honeywood's be very fine house!"

"Very likely I shall never go to see it."

"Never!—Oh, my dearee Missee!"

"*Never,* Dido!"

"Oh, my good God almighty! me thought—Dido did think—but 'tis all of one—me know nothing in this England town, but disappointments—me will never believe any thing that me sees again,—no, that me won't; for me cou'd have well sworn, that when Massa Honeywood comed here, this very morning, that he wou'd have asked my dear Missee to come and live to his house; for me was sure—me *thought*—that my Missee was his own very sweetheart!"

"But, Dido, were you as certain that your mistress would go and live with Mr. Honeywood, if he had asked her? Did you think your mistress could so soon change the object of her affections? Do you think she has already forgotten her husband?"

"Husband! he be no husband of my dear Missee's."

"Dido, I consider myself, I always *shall* consider myself, as his *wife!* Talk no longer to me on this subject—you pain—you grieve me to the heart!"

"Me would not grieve dear Missee for all the world—me would not!"

"I believe you, my good girl; I know you are my friend—I look upon you as such—I talk to you as one—I will confide to you, Dido, that Mr. Honeywood *did* come on the errand you imagined!"

"He did, he did!" cried she; "me thought he did, me thought so all along!" and she kissed my hand in delight.

"That I *could* not listen to him, I have told you," said I. "Ah! what sentiments could so ill accord with my feelings? Generous and candid, he was convinced by my reasoning—and I shall see him no more!"

"No *more!*" said Dido, "see him no more! and this little bit of a nut-shell of a house for my own dear Massa's daughter?"—

"Dido, how often must I tell you, that happiness is independent of situation, and that in a palace I should be more unhappy than I am in this little cottage, because I should not have *him* to share it with me?"

Ah, my dearest friend! why tire you with a longer recapitulation of this conversation? why recapitulate the conflicts which this visit from Honeywood has occasioned me?—I will resume my pen when I feel more fit to be your correspondent.

IN CONTINUATION

"MR. MERTON is no more: Augustus is still in London."

So says Caroline Lumley, in a letter just received: It is reported that he has died without a will; if so, his immense property will be equally divided between his sons. Pray heaven that it may be so! and pray Heaven that Augustus may know many, *many* years of peace and happiness with his Angelina!

IN CONTINUATION

HONEYWOOD continues to absent himself from the cottage, but by a thousand delicate and different attentions I am reminded of his proximity. I know not how to act: by affecting not to discover, I am tacitly approving his attention, whilst, in refusing them I shall wound his already bruised heart. A fine bouquet of flowers on my mantle-piece; an aromatic heath on my window; a newspaper, or new pamphlet, on my breakfast-table; a pine-apple, brought in by Dido, as a dessert!—oh, Mrs. Milbanke, what can I say to Honeywood for such well-meant kindnesses? Why should I put a construction on his behaviour which should hurt his feelings? And yet the consciousness of what these really are, the knowledge of his contiguity, operates as a check upon all my actions; and I am absolutely as if *spell-bound*, a prisoner in this little cot, and my *smaller* garden, when, because I would range free and uncontrolled, a tenant of the air, I chose this situation! Dido too, poor, affectionate, and simple-hearted girl, loving Mr. Honeywood for his attention to a mistress on whom she doats, though she puts a check upon her tongue, and never names the *name* of Honeywood, yet has it always in her thoughts; and her looks convey that sort of tender reproof which I cannot express, not unaccompanied by exultation, either when she sees me notice any thing which is just arrived from Elm Wood (for this I find is the name of Honeywood's place)—.

IN CONTINUATION

CAROLINE LUMLEY gives me one piece of information, which you will rejoice to learn, as much as I did; for, thank God, in the desolation of my heart, it yet can glow with satisfaction to hear of another's happiness.—A great nephew of Mr. Bellfield's has lately discovered him: a very young man; liberal in principle, and of much goodness of heart. He has heard of his dependent and unworthy situation at the Pagoda; and, contemning the treatment of Sir Marmaduke, he has written to make a proffer of any part of his fortune to his uncle; and has done it in the most noble and handsome manner: at the same time that he refuses to introduce himself to Sir Marmaduke Ingot, his *own* uncle, by whom he would be certain of a welcome reception, as his recently acquired fortune would be a certain passport to the Pagoda.

Caroline says, that tears coursed each other down the rugged cheeks of the good old man, as he made this generous offer known to Waller, but that he steadfastly refuses to accept any pecuniary gift from his relation; though he is going to pay him a visit immediately, with a determination of residing with him during the remainder of his days. His sorrow at leaving his young friend, Waller, he expresses in a manner very flattering to the worthy young clergyman, "Who would find his own situation insupportable, *he says* (Caroline prettily and modestly inserts), if it were not for his being in our vicinity."

IN CONTINUATION

AT length, my dear Mrs. Milbanke, your Olivia has received the long anticipated acquittal of Augustus Merton. Conscience has pricked the heart of Mrs. George Merton. She was seized by a violent and alarming illness, a few days previous to the decease of her father-in-law, and, while contemplating the near approach of death, the world, its pleasures, and its riches, faded from her view, and the whole weight of her unacknowledged crimes lay at her heart, she sent for Augustus, who, luckily, was come to town, and, in the presence of her husband, made a full confession of all the malicious plans by which she had contrived to circumvent his happiness. She produced proofs of her guilt, in letters to and from the agents of her machinations, which made the truth of her relation but too apparent. These letters Augustus has transmitted to me for perusal. I cannot transcribe so black a scene of guilt!— Neither can I transcribe Augustus's letter to myself: and, let me own the weakness of my heart, neither can I part with it.—Ah! Mrs. Milbanke, such a heart as is there laid open—such nobleness of sentiment—such respect—such consideration—let me add, such tenderness towards your Olivia, who but would be proud of keeping such a memorial of his esteem!

I will try to form a little narrative of these letters, and the confession of Mrs. Merton; and give to you, my beloved friend, the necessary information under that form. There will you see the fatal effects of female vanity, and of disappointed pride. There will you see—but I must not forestal myself.—All that can now be done in the way of reparation has been effected. Mr. Merton made a will, and has divided his fortune equally between his sons, on Mr. George Merton's foregoing all claim to, or interest in, my fortune; and this has been formally relinquished to me by him, in the same packet that brought me this very pleasing and unlooked-for intelligence.—Yes! my friend, Augustus received the embrace, the affectionate blessing of his dying parent! He is now enabled to provide for his Angelina and his child, and your Olivia, is now contented!—She is more—she is grateful to that God who has melted the heart of the poor sinner; and, from the bottom of her own, she can forgive Mrs. George Merton; and, in full confidence of the undiminished regard of Mrs. Milbanke, continues to sign herself,

Her affectionate and grateful child,
OLIVIA FAIRFIELD.

THE NARRATIVE

You are not to be informed, that Mrs. George Merton was the only daughter of Mr. Manby, who, from a very obscure and plodding tradesman, through industry and good luck (as it is called), rose to be a wealthy merchant in the city of London. Without the advantages of a liberal education, and rising from the very dregs of the people, his notions were illiberal, his principles sordid and confined. The *poor* man, if he possessed every *virtue*, and a *title*, was an object of contempt and opprobrium; the *rich*, if the most *worthless* being in creation, and a *chimney-sweeper*, would, from him, have received attention and consideration. His wife, whose ideas were nearly as confined as his own, was yet assailable to the great tempter of her sex, vanity; and while Mr. Manby talked of thousands and ten thousands, she would enumerate on the thousand and ten thousands of *fine things* which could be purchased by them. The mere hoarding of guinea upon guinea was the first pursuit of the one; the desire of making a show with their riches, was the first wish of the other: but nothing could persuade Mr. Manby to diverge from the beaten track. The front of his large premises in **** Lane was taken up in warehouses; and the small back parlour, to which he retired every evening, could not, with all Mrs. Manby's *attempts*, be converted into any thing of a fashionable or dashy appearance. She was obliged, therefore, to content herself with showing her riches on her large and portly person; and when she sallied out on the Sunday's walk, to the park, attired in all the colours of a rainbow, with her real lace *weil*, she was frequently gratified by hearing some of her *quondam* friends in **** Lane, whisper, as she sailed along, "streaming, in the wind,"[1]

"Look there! that is the rich Mr. Manby's wife."

An only child smiled on the union of this couple; she soon became the idol of both her parents: and, while the father carefully instilled into his offspring the *value* and the *consequence* of money, and taught her to distinguish a guinea from a shilling, before she could articulate; the mother, equally in character, dazzled her infantine eyes with finery, and laboured earnestly to decorate her little person in the costliest garb, and in the most becoming manner.

At an early age Letitia Manby was placed at a boarding-school a few miles from the metropolis, where the conductress of the seminary knew how to fall in with the dispositions of her employers. She had penetration to discover the ruling passion of the parents who committed their children to her care; and *that* discernment, which, if it had been applied to the discovery of the different traits in the characters of her pupils (to the encouragement of their virtuous, and to the correction of their vicious propensities), would have qualified her for the discharge of the office she had undertaken, being wholly turned towards the failings of their parents, and to making them subservient to her own interest; it may be presumed that those young ladies, who were ushered into the world, formed under her auspices, were likely to come forth with all the follies inherent to their sex, and to their different dispositions.

Miss Manby was by nature vain; she was also jealous of her own consequence, and frequently vaunted of the great wealth to which she was sole heiress! Her father could not be prevailed on, even when she returned from school—"mistress of every polite

---

1 Perhaps a reference to John Milton's *Paradise Lost* (1667): "Th' imperial ensign, which, full high advanc'd, / Shone like a meteor, streaming to the wind" (I.536-7).

accomplishment," and "her education *complete*,"—as the subtle governess notified to Mrs. Manby,—not even for the sake of this darling child could he be prevailed on to relinquish his old habits, and his accustomed mode of life. The back parlour in **** Lane could not be forsaken for a house with a veranda (or *weranda*, as Mrs. Manby termed it), in one of the squares at the west end of the town—but every thing else that his dear *Letty* liked, she should have: and when Miss Manby declared, that she could not live without a *friend*, that she *must* have a friend, for that she had always been used to an *intimate* friend at school, but that not one amongst *all* of her very *particular* friends would visit her now she was come back to odious **** Lane, Mr. Manby told her she should have a friend—and the only sister of Mr. Manby, who had married a clergyman (whose whole subsistence had been derived from a curacy in Northumberland) being about this period carried off by malignant fever, which reigned in the neighbourhood, and to which her husband had previously fallen a victim, *Mrs.* Manby thought there would be something very *benevolent* in taking her orphan daughter for Letty's *friend*.

Mrs. Forrester had been a different woman to her sister; she had naturally good understanding, and a rightly turned heart: and marrying Mr. Forrester, a man of probity and worth, she had, in the retirement of Northumberland, cultivated those talents, which had hitherto lain dormant in her mind; and, with the assistance of her husband, had become an accomplished, as well as an amiable, character. They had one child, and to the little Angelina had been transmitted all the beauty and the softness of her mother; all the intelligence and magnanimity of her father. This amiable girl knew neither sorrow nor care, till, by the fatal event which has been previously mentioned, she lost both her parents, and was restored, from the very brink of the grave, to behold herself alone and friendless, thrown on the wide world, a destitute orphan at the early age of seventeen! When, therefore, her aunt wrote her a letter of condolence; and offered her an asylum in **** Lane, to become the "friend and company-*keeper* of *her* Letty," the gratitude of this child of nature was unbounded, and she eagerly accepted the invitation, and lost no time in going to her kind relatives!

The transition from the pure air of Northumberland to **** Lane, from wide heaths expanded lawns; from mountains and vales, where nature in her "wildest works is seen,"[1] to the close

---

1 Untraced reference.

atmosphere of the most combined part of the metropolis, was very striking to poor Angelina. The manners, too, of her new friends,—Mr. Manby so short, so quaint, so odd in his expressions—Mrs. Manby so fond of dress and finery, her whole conversation turning on the *riches* of her husband, and on her daughter's *beauty*—the vanity and self-consequence of *Letty*, the air of authority and imposing command which she assumed towards *her friend*, was so perfectly novel to Angelina, that she would have felt her situation beyond endurance, if her recent and irreparable afflictions had not paralysed her feelings, and rendered her almost impervious to any thing which might succeed to them. Religion had been firmly planted in the mind of Angelina Forrester, and to "bear and forbear,"[1] which is, perhaps, the hardest duty which the Christian fulfils (especially if endowed with great sensibility of disposition), in that palsy of the mind which she experienced at her first introduction to London, she practised without much difficulty; and when her feelings resumed their wonted station, her reason returned also, and she did not deviate from a conduct, which she found was the only one she could adopt, with a probability of comfort, in her present situation.

Miss Manby considered Angelina, "Lina" (as she abbreviated the name) as an inferior being; Mrs. Manby thought she had done a noble action in receiving her niece in **** Lane, and in making her the "company keeper" of Letty; and Mr. Manby would not have increased his family circle for a useless member, and one who brought him no profit, except to please "his girl!"— The *pleasure* which Miss Manby derived from the society of Angelina would be rather difficult to define. She seemed to take a delight in showing her finery, in pointing out the difference of their situations—"But *I* am so different from you, Lina"—"that gown is well enough for *you*, *I* could not be seen in such a one." Angelina was made the companion of the young lady when she could get no other, but when a more dashy girl appeared, "I do not want you now, Lina," was said with all the air of an arbitrary and supercilious mistress. Of a dull day, when Miss Manby had the vapours, Lina was to read full six hours at a stretch in the most silly novel which could be procured from the next circulating library; for, unless there was a *great deal* of love, and a long

---

1 As a living example of stoicism during the period of the Roman Empire, the Roman slave Epictetus built his life and teachings around the Greek maxim "anexou kai apexou": "bear and forebear."

account of the hero and the heroine's person, Miss Manby usually pronounced it a "stupid, dull thing;" and Lina was dispatched eight or nine times in a morning till she could hit on a book, glowing with the description of beauty, and warm with the declaration of passion. Mrs. Manby usually sat by to hear the novel, and if the heroine was fair, with blue eyes, the description always was the exact resemblance of her dearest Letty.

Mr. Merton and Mr. Manby had some dealings together with regard to commercial business; in which, added to the great riches of the father, Mr. Manby discovered such readiness in, and application to *his* one thing needful, in George Merton, that he came home delighted with the young merchant; and, after calculating Mr. Merton's fortune over his bowl of punch in the evening, he suddenly seized the ladle, and filling a bumper, said, "Here's George Merton to you, little Letty, and may God send you such a husband!" This roused the curiosity of Mrs. Manby; she knew that the Mertons were considered as the very first people in the mercantile world, and "Law! Mr. Manby, then you must make an entertainment, and introduce him to our Letty," quickly followed Mr. Manby's toast.

"I don't want a husband—I couldn't *abide* a husband of pa's choosing—I know he can't be handsome or genteel," said Mis Manby, affectedly turning up her lip!

"Now I can tell you Letty, he is both one and the other," replied the father; "I never saw a likelier young fellow in my whole life: and as to calculations, why he is fit to meet the prime minister for the loan!"

An invitation was given and accepted, and Mr. Merton, accompanied by his two sons, dined in **** Lane. George Merton, tutored by his father (who liked the idea of getting old Manby's fortune into his family), was all politeness and attention to the young heiress, while Augustus, perfectly undesigning and unconscious, sat near the modest and innocent Angelina; and perceiving the disregard of the rest of the party, he was the more respectful and attentive, pitying her situation; as, at the first view, he perceived that she was a superior being to those with whom she was placed. George Merton might have been called a handsome young man, but the redundancy of youth, the animation, the brilliancy which at this time played on the countenance, and sparkled in the eyes of Augustus, made him an object of greater attraction than his brother to Miss Manby. She could scarcely conceal her vexation when she saw him bestowing that attention on Lina, which she would fain have engrossed to herself. More than once, with a commanding air and an authoritative voice, she ordered Lina to fetch her handkerchief and her smelling-bottle, in order to send her out of the way; but the malicious expression which sat on her features, effectually disgusted Augustus; he saw through her contemptible jealousy, and, on the fair orphan's return to the company, he beheld her with that commiseration which her situation inspired. Augustus Merton was the very personified hero of Miss Manby's fruitful and impassioned imagination; she immediately fell *violently in love* with him, and told pa and ma, that she liked Mr. George Merton well enough, but he was not to compare with Augustus—Augustus too, *sounded* so well—so novel-like—'Augustus and Letitia, a novel, founded on facts,' would be delightful! Mr. Manby had none of his daughter's reasons for preferring Augustus Merton to his brother; *he* had never read a novel in his life; and with regard to beauty, "handsome he, that handsome does," was his maxim. Augustus had thrown out one or two severe innuendos, in contempt of that spirit of *hoarding* which Mr. Manby had displayed, and he plainly saw that George was his father's favourite—but swayed by his wife, who assured him, that, "Letty would pine herself into a consumption if *crossed* in her *first love*," he at length consented to break the matter to Mr. Merton.

Mr. Merton had long seen that Augustus did not follow up his schemes of business with true mercantile avidity; there was an open-heartedness, a manly generosity in his character, which could only have been derived from the Fairfield family, and which had rendered him the idol of his mother, while it had had the contrary effect on his other parent. The prospect of settling Augustus so advantageously was very satisfactory to Mr. Merton; and, sending for his youngest son, he told him, that, seeing he had no wish of pursuing the commercial speculations, in which his family were embarked, with any portion of spirit, he could now put him into a way of making his fortune at a single stroke. The whole soul of Augustus recoiled when he heard the proposition of his father—What! marry Miss Manby? marry the haughty, the cruel, the unfeeling Letitia Manby? she, who tyrannized over a helpless orphan, to whom she apparently extended her protection!—*that* gentle being, whose patient forbearance, whose modest sweetness, had gained her an interest in his heart, which was scarcely known to himself!—No, never could he unite himself to Miss Manby!

In the firmest and the most decided manner Augustus expressed his dislike of Miss Manby, and his repugnance to the connexion. Mr. Merton was enraged with his son, and told him, as he valued his favour, if he expected from henceforth to be beheld as a son, he expected an implicit compliance with his wishes in this instance. Augustus temporized with his father—for the first time in his life, the treacherous emotions of his heart inclined him to play a double part—he promised to visit in ★★★★ Lane; he did so, but while the young heiress absolutely doated on him, while she exposed her preference to every common observer, Augustus could scarcely conceal the disgust with which he suffered her civilities, nor how deeply he quaffed the delicious draughts of love as they fell from the honied lips, the chastened smiles, of the unconscious Angelina! Wholly unexperienced and new to the world as Angelina was, there was something in the respectful regard, in the tender manner which Augustus Merton displayed in his behaviour towards her, which seemed to give life a new charm in her eyes. Yet these floating and delightful ideas had never been discussed in her mind; for she beheld Mr. Augustus Merton as the elected husband of her cousin, and frequently whispered to herself that Letitia was a most fortunate creature.

Miss Manby kept Angelina, as much as was possible, at a distance, while Miss Danby (a *ci-devant*[1] friend, who had at length got over her scruples concerning ★★★★ Lane, in the prospect of Miss Manby's approaching union with the son of Mr. Merton, a man of great fortune and consequence) was her intimate companion and confidante!—Poor Angelina, confined in a close apartment up three pair of stairs, brooding over her past sorrows, and her present difficulties, would have become the victim of melancholy despondence, if the thought of Augustus Merton had not sometimes lulled her griefs, with airy and gay dreams of happiness.

The insulting and contumelious treatment which she met with from *the friends* in the parlour, and which were invariably backed by Mrs. Manby, could not have been sustained, if the benevolent friendliness of Mr. Merton had not frequently been exerted in her behalf; and on one of those instances of illiberal and vaunting superiority, when poor Angelina had given way to the bitterest emotions of her soul, Augustus Merton had accidentally found her;—prudence, duty, reflection, fled at the sight of her distress! and he abruptly made an impassioned avowal of love, as sincere as it was fervent. Surprise of the most delightful kind rendered

---

1 Former, or ex.

Angelina dumb; whilst Augustus hastily assured her, that nothing but his affection for her, and his compassion for her situation, could have induced him to bear the society at **** Lane for one half hour! He lamented that the prejudices of his father forbade him to offer her his hand in a public manner, but with vows of constancy he besought her to hear him. He conjured her to consent to his proposal of a private marriage, that she might be his beyond the reach of fate or fortune!—The fond, the confiding, the grateful Angelina, was ill-calculated to carry on a contest against her own heart;—she met Augustus Merton one morning in **** church, where they were formally and legally united in marriage bonds; after which, the bride retired to private lodgings, which her husband had taken for her reception. To save appearances, and to avoid a discovery, Augustus consented to continue to visit, for a time, in **** Lane. But the suspicions of Letitia Manby were awake, though she contrived to conceal them from the object of them. In conjunction with her mother, she set every inquiry on foot to discover the retreat of Angelina, and when this had been accomplished, a train of revenge was laid as black as it proved successful. With all the apprehensive fears of a friend zealous for the honour of his family, Mrs. Manby sought the elder Mr. Merton, and under a strict charge of inviolable secrecy, confided to him her fears, that Mr. Augustus Merton had an intention of disgracing himself by marrying a low creature whom she had protected *merely* from *benevolent* and charitable motives.

Mr. Merton was greatly shocked at the intelligence of Mrs. Manby: but, eager to snatch his son from (what he termed) ruin, he ordered him to embark immediately for Ireland to transact some commercial business of an urgent nature which would necessarily detain him some time; and, during his absence, Mrs. Manby took upon herself the charge of putting the young lady out of his reach. Poor Augustus, in this instance, dared not disobey his father—no time had been given him for reflection; he just snatched a hasty farewel of his darling Angelina, in an agony of mind little short of distraction. He left her all the money he had, and promising to write to her frequently, he tore himself away, and got on board the vessel, which was already under weigh.

And now it was, that in all the affected distress of insulted honour and maternal affection, Mrs. Manby sought out her niece. Breaking violently, and unushered, into her apartment, she assured her, that she had been trepanned and ruined by a villain, under the stale pretext of a false marriage. At first, the indignant Angelina thought it doubting Heaven, to doubt the faith and honour of Augusus Merton; but proofs, behind proofs, were produced by Mrs. Manby, of a false clergyman being hired by Augustus, for the performance of the marriage ceremony, for which there had been prepared a fictitious licence, and that the whole business had been formal and illegal—that she could no longer hope!—

The agony of the innocent orphan is not to be described; more especially when she found that she was likely to become the mother of a witness of her own shame and the guilt of her seducer. To her aunt she now turned herself, as to her only friend; and on her knees conjured her to bestow pity and forgiveness! Mrs. Manby evinced more feeling than Angelina had ever experienced from her before. She said, she could not take her back to **** Lane;—she must never tell her Letty what she had done for her, but she would not let the only child of her own sister perish; and she would send her into some retired part of Wales; and she would pay for her maintenance there, if Angelina would consent to go by a feigned name, and never attempt to see or hear from her vile seducer! Alas! Angelina could easily promise this, convinced of *his* falsehood, whose heart she had hitherto believed the seat of truth.—She only wished to hide her shame and sorrow in obscurity! She was quickly transported into Wales, and the small-pox soon after carrying off the woman with whom she had lodged in London, and also a young woman, who had immediately tenanted Angelina's vacated apartments on her quitting them, Mrs. Manby managed this (to *her*) lucky circumstance very adroitly; and the death of poor Angelina was credited even by Mr. Merton. Miss Manby was the malicious suggester of all the schemes which her parent had so promptly executed; and being convinced, that Augustus Merton would never accede to her tender wishes, even if he were to outlive his affection for Angelina Forrester, she determined, that during his absence, she would marry his brother; the more effectually to revenge herself on Augustus, by thus securing the favour of Mr. Merton towards his eldest son.

Mr. George Merton easily fell in with the views of this crafty young lady. Mr. Merton was delighted to find that the Manby wealth would still be centred in his family, and within a very few weeks after the marriage of Miss Manby and Mr. George Merton —Mr. Manby was deprived of life, by a sudden stroke of apoplexy; and thus, nearly fifty thousand pounds fell into the eager grasp of the *lucky* George Merton! Mrs. Manby outlived her husband but a few months. The place of Angelina's conceal-ment was perfectly well known to Mrs. George Merton; and, through her mother's former agent in this business, she contrived that her stipend should be continued regularly.

We will pass over the agonizing feelings of Augustus Merton, on being informed of the untimely fate of his beloved Angelina. The idea of her falling a victim to a direful malady;—alone, and unprotected—her only friend—her *husband*, at a distance, was dreadful! He pondered over her virtues; he delighted in retracing her mild and gentle attractions; the modest excellencies of her mind; and he gave way to all the oppressive grief which pierced his soul; while the very sight of Mrs. George Merton—of *his brother's wife*, was torture! The look of exultation and triumph which sat on her countenance gave him a sensation of abhorrence and disgust; and he fled from her presence as he would have has-tened from a venomous reptile!

Time elapsed; yet still the wounds of Augustus's heart were unclosed. He still sighed over lost happiness; and the death of Mr. Fairfield, in Jamaica, with the tenour of his last will, were at length made known to his relatives in England! Strange as the tenour of this will appeared; miserable as must be the future fate of Olivia Fairfield, if dependent on *his* brother; yet Augustus declared to his father, that the affections of his heart were for ever lain in the tomb of Angelina Forrester (he had not thought it nec-essary to avow his private marriage since the fatal event of her death had taken place) and that he could never marry his cousin! But, consenting to meet Olivia at Clifton,—the natural benevo-lence and philanthropy of his heart got the better of this resolu-tion, and he made the virtuous sacrifice of his own feelings to Olivia Fairfield's happiness!

It would be incredible that there could have existed such a character as Mrs. George Merton, if the melancholy fact were not made too apparent—and that by her own confession. The happi-ness which ensued to the union of Augustus and Olivia, the fortune which Augustus enjoyed, once more excited all the malice of her heart; and, burning with revenge at beholding the tranquil serenity of their countenances, she thought to put the death-stroke to all future comfort by restoring Angelina to the sight of her husband—returning them both to poverty, and over-whelming the hapless Olivia with complicated misery!

Angelina, in her sequestered nook, had (soon after her retreat to it) become the mother of a fine little boy; and in rearing her off-spring with maternal tenderness, she had received all the comfort of which her existence seemed capable. She had a half-yearly remittance from town, sufficient for her decent maintenance; it was continued to be paid by Mrs. Manby's agent, *after* that lady's death, and Angelina was given to understand, that this was done in consequence of the secret and dying injunctions of that lady; and that Angelina was desired implicitly, to follow his directions in every step of her future life. The marriage of Augustus Merton to Miss Fairfield had been carefully communicated to Angelina through this channel; and if a doubt had still hung on her mind with regard to this falsehood, and the turpitude of his conduct towards her, the knowledge of this event entirely decided it. She became inured and resigned to her lot: she deeply lamented her inexperienced weakness, and that credulity which had induced her to consent to a private marriage; but her conscience was eased of the weight of intentional guilt, and her faith in the promises of God, firmly planted in her mind, she looked forwards to a happy futurity with chastened hope!

From this torpid tranquillity, Angelina was once more roused by a letter from the agent, informing her, that the house in which she resided was advertised for sale, and that he had in consequence taken a cottage for her in Devonshire, to which she was required to move without loss of time; that the situation was more eligible, and that she would remain as secluded, and as much unknown, as in Wales.

These orders Angelina dared not disobey; but the thought of removing to such a distance was very unpleasant. She had associated ideas of comfort and quiet with the cottage which had been her asylum in trouble, which had sheltered her defenceless head from the cruel taunts of a malicious world, and which had been the birthplace of her child; and she set out on her journey with a heavy and a foreboding heart. To her great surprise and mortification, she found that her new habitation was attached to a gentleman's park, and near a bathing place of general resort; she feared to stir abroad, lest she should attract the prying eye of curiosity. She had from time to time observed a gentleman walking near her cottage, and, fearing a discovery and recognition of her person by some of her former acquaintance, she secluded herself with double vigilance, till surprised, whilst sitting in her parlour, by the abrupt entrance of Colonel Singleton, who addressing her in a strain of gallantry, as fulsome as it was ill-timed, she lost her presence of mind in the indignant sense of the insult, and rushing from the house was caught in the arms of her still-doating husband!

END OF THE NARRATIVE

OLIVIA FAIRFIELD—IN CONTINUATION

THUS, my dear Mrs. Milbanke, have I given you the simple statement of *facts*. In the full acquittal of Augustus Merton, believe me, I do not feel my own hard fate. Mine was a disinterested attachment, my dearest friend; and I glory in saying, that I prefer his happiness to my own. I have just received a note of congratulation from Honeywood. I suspect that Dido has been the means of so speedily conveying this intelligence to Elm Wood. Poor girl, she was nearly frantic with joy when she heard of it. How grateful am I for her faithful attachment! Mrs. George Merton is recovered from her illness. Her mind disburdened of its load, became tranquil, and her health mended in consequence. Ah! if the inward feelings of the guilty were made apparent, I believe we should find, that, even in this world, they experienced no light punishment.

IN CONTINUATION

MORE wonders!—More events to communicate to my dear friend. I have just parted with another visitor—with the uncle of Mr. Honeywood! He introduced himself to me uncalled for—unexpected: but I received him with a cordial welcome, for I beheld the good Mr. Bellfield!—Yes, Honeywood is the generous, the noble-minded nephew, who has sought out his worthy and unfortunate relative, and who has caused the tears of delighted gratitude to rush to the eyes of this respectable old man!

"Ah!" said the venerable Bellfield, as he pressed my hand in his, "I glory in this nephew, my dear madam; there is only one man, whom I know, that is his equal—" He stopped. The long-absent crimson visited his time-worn cheek; his confusion convinced me that he alluded to Augustus. He proceeded—"There is only one woman worthy of him—and *she*—ah! madam—much esteemed and respected young lady—suffer an old man to speak—suffer him to ask you, whether it be charity, whether it be humanity, to let this excellent youth pine away the flower of his days? to be exiled from that society which he prizes beyond every other? to be ever within the hearing of her manifold virtues, of her extraordinary endowments, and still to experience the punishment of Tantalus,[1] in not

---

1 As his punishment in Tartarus, the deepest portion of the Underworld, Greek hero Tantalus stood chin-deep in water with fruits above his head. Whenever he tried to drink or eat, the water receded and the fruit moved out of reach. It was from the eternal torture of temptation without satisfaction that Tantalus' punishment became associated with the English word "tantalize."

daring to enter her presence? Let not my plain speaking offend you, dearest lady," seeing that I rose from my seat—"I ask these questions from the sincerity of my heart. You have it in your power to raise my nephew to the highest state of happiness which he is capable of enjoying in this state of being.—You acknowledge his worth—you are not blind to his virtues—then why—"

"Mr. Bellfield," said I, interrupting him, "little did I think that I could ever regret receiving a visit from you—and are you, too, joined in a party against the unfortunate Olivia? Is it the venerable, the good Mr. Bellfield that seeks to persuade this beating heart to become an apostate to its first love?"

"Is it Miss Fairfield," asked Mr. Bellfield, looking at me with some severity of expression in his countenance,—"is it Miss Fairfield who talks of a passion which she ought never to *name?*— which she ought to exert all her fortitude, all her resolution, to extirpate for ever from her heart?"

"Heaven is my witness!" cried I, "that I consider Augustus Merton as the husband of Angelina, that for the 'wealth of worlds'[1] I would not interrupt their happiness. To define my feelings, exactly, I cannot; yet I feel a consolation—a romantic satisfaction, in imagining myself as the widow of my love! Had death taken from me the object of my affections, this bosom never could have known another lord. Think then, my dear sir, how much more acute was my misfortune, when, by a single stroke, an instance almost unparalleled—duty—religion—even honour, bade me instantly resign my living husband!"

"You are an extraordinary creature!" said Mr. Bellfield, wiping his eyes; "and to say the truth, I do not wonder at Honeywood, when you have the power to make all old fellow, like myself, play the child and blubber before you!—But, ah! my poor Honeywood, my good boy!"—and snatching up his hat and, stick he walked out of the house.

I will not say any thing of this new exercise of my feelings, for I must, ever sympathize with those whom I love; and that her Olivia, loves both Honeywood and his good old relative, Mrs. Milbanke will readily believe.

---

1   Olivia may be evoking these lines from Mark Akenside's *The Pleasures of Imagination. A Poem. In Three Books* (1774): "O! he will tell thee, that the wealth of worlds / Should ne'er seduce his bosom to forego / That sacred hour" (II, 688-90).

IN CONTINUATION

MR. BELLFIELD visits me daily. Never since our first interview has he dropped a syllable concerning his nephew's attachment, though his virtues are the never-varying topic of his discourse; and they form so striking a contrast to the pride, the arrogance, and the supercilious importance of Sir Marmaduke Ingot, that I cannot wonder at his garrulity. He has given me a brief sketch of Mrs. Honeywood's life. I will weave it into a little narrative for your perusal.

THE HISTORY OF MRS. HONEYWOOD

It has been said, that Mr. Bellfield took the orphan and destitute children of an only sister into his house, resolving to become their protector—and this he was in the fullest sense of the word. From that hour he discarded all thoughts of matrimony, although his temper and his inclination would have led him to seek for connubial happiness; and his heart had long felt a secret preference in favour of a lady, whose character and connexions were very suitable to his own, but from the moment when he voluntarily resolved to be the father of the fatherless, he steadily applied himself to the conquest of every tender sentiment for this lady, and his endeavors were so far crowned with success, that through a long term of years, during which he maintained an undiminished intercourse with her, she had never imagined that his regard for her had ever risen beyond the bounds of friendship!

Mrs. Moreton had left three children; the eldest was Marmaduke, whom his uncle soon perceived to have very ambitious notions joined to an imperious and irascible disposition. His views of gain were too ardent and sanguine to bear the plodding means of patient industry and perseverance, by which an independence must be acquired in England; and his young heart burned to go to a climate where a fortune would be speedily acquired, and every luxury of life be within his reach, ere time should have impaired his powers of enjoyment:—a country, where the following maxim has too frequently been adopted by the youth who have set out on the career of gain—"Get money,—honestly, if you can;—but, whatever you do, get money."

Mr. Bellfield was an easy man,—he was indulgent to all with whom he was concerned; and perceiving that the whole thoughts of Marmaduke were turned towards the East, exerted all his interest (which was, at that period, very great, as his mercantile connexions were very extensive), and fitted out his nephew for

Bengal. The second son continued with his uncle, and died of a decline, when he was just starting in manhood.—This was a sore affliction to Sophia Moreton; she had loved her brother Charles with fond affection: he had always been her favourite brother, and constant associate and companion, during the last three years that she had returned from school to keep her uncle's house. Mr. Bellfield dried the tears of his lovely niece—the good man doated on this amiable girl, whose manners and whose person were particularly calculated to conciliate regard; while the virtues of her heart gave a rich promise of future worth. Bereft of her brother, Sophia redoubled her attentions towards her kind uncle; and it might be said that she lived only to evince her duty and her gratitude towards him: and Mr. Bellfield has frequently been heard to say, that this was by far the happiest period of his life.

Sophia Moreton was a blooming girl of eighteen, when a young West Indian was consigned to the care of Mr. Bellfield, in order to acquire a local knowledge of England by a few months residence in it, as a finish to commercial education. The house of Honeywood had for some years maintained a correspondence with that of Bellfield, in the mutual transaction of business; and always ready to do a good natured action, the good Bellfield welcomed the youth most cordially, and he became an inmate of his house. Delighted with the charms of the gay metropolis, full of health, with spirits and unsubdued gaiety in all the flush of effervescent youth, Honeywood enlivened every party, and gilded every hour by his unceasing vivacity. He was soon attracted by the beautiful simplicity of Sophia Moreton, and, hasty and impassioned, with all that fervour of disposition which so peculiarly characterizes his countrymen—he declared that health, that happiness, that *life* itself depended on his taking back the lovely Sophia to the West Indies as his wife. Sophia thought Mr. Honeywood handsome and agreeable, but she had seen very little of him; she could not be said to know his character. She felt her heart shrink within her, at the idea of leaving her uncle, and venturing herself with him on "untried seas and unknown shores;"[1] but Honeywood, the ardent Honeywood, was not to be dissuaded from his purpose: he swore that he would never return again to his father, unless she would accede to his wishes; and on his knees he frantically besought Mr. Bellfield not to withhold his

---

1 Perhaps a loose rendition of lines from Alexander Pope's translation of Homer's *The Odyssey* (1725-26): "With heavy hearts we labour through the tide, / To coasts unknown, and oceans yet untried" (Book IX).

consent, not to condemn him to everlasting ruin! Mr. Bellfield made some allowance for the sanguine temperament of this young and hot-headed West Indian; he felt that it would be a bitter trial to him to part with his beloved Sophia; but self-denial had long been the good man's practice: and the known wealth and established respectability of Honeywood's father, the pleasing qualities of the young man, and his (apparently) warm regard for his niece, made him think that he should probably be opposing the advancement of Sophia, and her future happiness in life, by not furthering the union. He sounded his niece on the subject—poor Sophia was not deeply in love, but she hesitated not to acknowledge, that she certainly felt a preference, a sort of interest for Mr. Honeywood; and in reality this *was* the *true* state of her heart. But this open avowal from one of her modest disposition, Mr. Bellfield construed into something of a warmer kind, and became in consequence more eager to forward the union of the young couple, while Sophia imagining she was pleasing her uncle by a *compliance* with his wishes—an uncle to whom she owed every thing—no longer hesitated to become the wife of Honeywood; and Mr. Bellfield remitted with her ten thousand pounds as her wedding portion.

On their first arrival in the island, all was delighted fondness on the part of Honeywood; proud of the beauty of his bride, and of the fortune which she had brought him, he introduced her to all his acquaintance, and they existed in one continued swirl of hilarity and amusement. The elder Mr. Honeywood received his daughter-in-law with much satisfaction, and Sophia had nothing to complain of: and yet there was a vacuity in her mind, a want of relish for all the gratifications which waited her, which she ingenuously attributed to the absence of her respected uncle; that good man, in whose society and conversation she had always found her highest enjoyment; whose approbation of her conduct had always been the stimulus of her exertions.

Sophia too soon perceived that there was no stability in the character of her husband; his principles were not fixed, but veered with every impulsive movement of his feelings, and the rapid and changeable turns of these, in his impetuous constitution, were constantly engaging him in some plan, which interested him only, as long as any difficulty appeared in the pursuit. Nothing could dissuade him from any design which he took in hand; and his various and chimerical speculations (after the death of his father, which happened in a few years after his return to Jamaica) becoming more extensive in their aim, were consequently more serious in their failure, which occurred but too frequently. It was in vain that Sophia, by gentle persuasions, would have induced him to pursue one undeviating and steady track; immediately on the defeat of one wild scheme, his whole soul was rapt on the projection of another, and his large fortune, in consequence, became much impoverished, and his affairs in great confusion. The consignments of Mr. Bellfield were not attended to, and poor Sophia, amidst the pressure of domestic disappointment and maternal solicitude, for the future fate of her little boy, felt a greater weight at her heart, from the fear that her good uncle would suffer from her husband's imprudences. A prey to unceasing disquiet and anxiety, daily witnessing acts of the most unlicensed extravagance, with no power or influence in checking its career, her health was on the decline, and she eagerly accepted her husband's offer of revisiting England for its restoration; but in fact to see her beloved uncle, towards whom her heart yearned with fond affection: and to ask his advice relative to the education of her son, who was now of an age to be put to school, and for whose morals she dreaded the tainted atmosphere of Jamaica.

Sophia found her uncle depressed in spirits and circumstances. Time had imprinted its passing hand on his head, but his heart was still the same, and he folded his beloved niece to it with unsubdued tenderness. Sophia at this moment lifted up the anguished sigh, and sincerely wished she had never quitted those paternal arms which now sheltered her in their fond embrace!

Charles Honeywood was placed at an eligible school, Sophia resumed her duties in her uncle's family, and the old man smiled once again. Sophia's health might have mended from the genial air of her native clime, from the kind indulgence of her protector, if the fear, the anxiety, which she suffered on the account of Honeywood, if the evident embarrassment of her uncle's affairs—embarrassed by the negligence of her husband—had not imbittered every moment!

Months and years passed on, and Sophia's presence was not re-demanded in Jamaica. The inconstancy, the neglect of her husband, the entire loss of his affections, had been but too apparent previous to her quitting him, though her conduct had been irreproachable; and by patient suffering, and undiminished attempts to please on her part, she had mildly essayed to win him back to the path of duty.

The involvement of Mr. Bellfield's affairs became truly alarming, when the failure of Mr. Honeywood's house in Jamaica, by reducing her kind, her generous uncle to the verge of ruin, almost broke the heart of the affectionate Sophia. It was soon after that the news of Honeywood's death determined her to revisit a place which had lain the foundation of all her sorrows, in order to gather up a maintenance for her son (that son, whose education completed, was now all that a fond mother's most sanguine wishes had depicted), if from the wreck of a once-noble patrimony she could but snatch a little pittance, something to assist her uncle—to support her Charles—she should be content!

The struggles which Mrs. Honeywood underwent during three years of anxious inspection into the intricate and perplexed affairs of her late husband, effectually undermined her health; and she returned to England with a competency snatched from the ruin of his fortune, to resign her life in the arms of her disconsolate son, and to be in utter ignorance respecting the fate of her honoured uncle;—(for, of the title of her brother Marmaduke,—of his return to England, and his large fortune, she was wholly unacquainted).

On losing his mother, Honeywood had nearly resigned himself to despair, when he was roused from his agonizing emotions to attend the death-bed of an old gentleman who was distantly related to his grandfather, Mr. Moreton, and who resided at Elm Wood in Monmouthshire. This gentleman having no near relative, made a will bequeathing Honeywood the bulk of his fortune, in estates and money, to the value of three thousand per annum. The heart of Honeywood experienced no exhilaration at this acquisition of property, while yet a stranger to the fate of his uncle Bellfield, while yet mourning the loss of his beloved mother. He continued at Elm Wood, after the demise of the old gentleman, and in one of his accidental conversations with Dido, she gave him, in her simple manner, the history of the neighbourhood of New Park; and happened to mention the name of "good old Mr. Bellfield, as one of her dear Missee's best friends." Honeywood did not notice the discovery to her, but instantly wrote to the venerable gentleman as has been mentioned.

THE END OF THE NARRATIVE

OLIVIA FAIRFIELD TO MRS. MILBANKE
IN CONTINUATION

DEAREST Mrs. Milbanke! I am foiled in my best designs. Augustus has forestalled me—he has presented the amiable Waller with a living in the adjoining parish to Mr. Lumley. It was one which we had both set our eyes upon, as a desirable situation for our young friends.—Ah! how am I daily constrained to bear added testimony to the worth of Augustus Merton!

IN CONTINUATION

YES! My beloved friend, I am coming to you. I waited but for you to suggest a scheme which my heart has long anticipated. Your letter is arrived, and Dido is already packing up with avidity. We will revisit Jamaica. I shall come back to the scenes of my infantine happiness—of my youthful tranquillity. I shall again zealously engage myself in ameliorating the situation, in instructing the minds—in mending the morals of our poor blacks. I shall again enjoy the society of my dear Mrs. Milbanke—I shall forget the lapse of time which has occurred since I parted from her, and shall again be happy! Eager to be with you once more, I almost count the tardy minutes as they move along.

IN CONTINUATION

MY passage is taken in the ****; and to-morrow I set out for Bristol. England, favoured Isle!—Happy country, where the laws are duly administered—where the arts—the sciences flourish, and where religion is to be found in all its beautiful purity. Farewel!—a long farewel!—Fain would I have taken up my abode in this charming clime,—but Heaven forbade it. Yet, England, I shall carry with me over the world of waters a veneration for thy name, a veneration for that soil which produced a Lumley—a Bellfield—and an Augustus Merton!

DIALOGUE BETWEEN
THE EDITOR AND A FRIEND.

Friend.—What do you propose from the publication of the foregoing tale? If your *Woman of Colour* be an imaginary character, I do not see the drift of your labours, as undoubtedly there is no moral to the work!

Editor.—How so?

Friend.—You have not rewarded Olivia even with the usual meed of virtue—*a husband*!

Editor.—Virtue, like Olivia Fairfield's, may truly be said to be its *own reward*—the *moral* I would deduce from her story is, that there is no situation in which the mind (which is strongly imbued with the truths of our most *holy faith,* and the consciousness of a divine *Disposer of Events*) may not resist itself against misfortune, and become resigned to its fate. And *if* these pages should teach one child of calamity to seek *Him* in the hour of distress who is always to be found, if they teach one *skeptical European* to look with a compassionate eye towards the *despised native of Africa*—then, whether Olivia Fairfield's be a *real* or an *imaginary* character, I shall not regret that I have edited the Letters of a *Woman of Colour*!

FINIS

Appendix A: Lucy Peacock, "The Creole" from The Rambles of Fancy; or, Moral and Interesting Tales. Containing The Laplander etc., *Vol. II* (London: T. Bensley, 1786) 110-77

[Lucy Peacock's long prose fiction about a Creole heiress who may or may not be of color (but is definitely aligned with Negro slaves) has many thematic similarities with *The Woman of Colour* including a cultured but vulnerable Caribbean heroine who triumphs without resorting to marriage, a bigamy plot, and attention to the issues of prejudice, slavery, and emancipation. It is included here as another example of the way in which a dark-skinned Caribbean woman was used as a didactic figure in a "moral tale."]

A series of years had propitiously revolved, since the bands of hymen united George Sedley to the most amiable and beauteous of women: the web of their destiny seemed formed of the fairest and most delicate texture, and fortune had scattered their path with her richest treasures.

Their residence was at a beautiful villa, detached from the tumult of cities, where they enjoyed the pleasures of rational society and rural retirement.

At the close of a delightful summer, as Mrs. Sedley was one day sitting at a window which commanded an extensive view of the adjacent meadows, her feelings were sensibly affected by beholding a woman extended on the ground, apparently in the agonies of death. Her head was supported by a youth about eighteen years of age, whose countenance expressed the most poignant grief. The compassionate Harriot Sedley immediately ordered the unfortunate woman to be conveyed into the house, and a physician to be sent for; though she appeared to be reduced more through want and sorrow than by pain or disease. By the timely care and attention of her benefactress, her health in a few days became perfectly re-established; and the youth, who was her son, endeavoured to assume an aspect of more composure; for, till now, he had remained at her bed-side, a prey to all the horrors of despair.

Mrs. Sedley found the unfortunate stranger to be a woman of talents and high accomplishments. She was about the age of forty; tall and elegant in her person; her complexion was dark; and her face, though it could not be called handsome, possessed such sweetness and sensibility, that rendered it more captivating than beauty itself.

Mrs. Sedley felt an earnest desire to know what singular calamity had thus reduced one whom address and education seemed to have designed for the most elevated sphere of life: she was cautious, however, of expressing her curiosity, fearing she might heighten the wretchedness of her friend, by any apparent distrust of her character or conduct.

At length the stranger, as they were sitting one day together, thus addressed her.

★ ★ ★

AFTER the unspeakable obligations, Madam, I have received, it is a justice I owe to your kindness, and my own character; to convince you, by relating my wretched story, that my misfortunes have not originated from vice or misconduct: the world may, indeed, accuse me of the latter; but it is an ill judging one, which censures alike the innocent and the guilty.

I was born (said she) in one of the West India islands: my father was an English merchant, who having married the daughter of an opulent planter there, settled in the island. I was an infant when my mother died; and, being the only child my father had, enjoyed his affection undiminished; but, though his fondness was to such excess that he could not endure the thought of parting with me, this extravagant partiality was by no means injurious to my education, as the liberality of his fortune enabled him to invite over men of eminent abilities, to cultivate and improve my talents.

I acquired a perfect knowledge, not only of the French and Italian, but also of the Latin language, besides making some progress in moral and natural philosophy.

Being sole heir to my father's wealth, which, I before said, was considerable, I was not destitute of admirers: but I beheld all mankind with equality; nor had yet seen the man with whom I thought I could be content to unite my fate, for my disposition being naturally contemplative, and having dedicated a large portion of my time to the Muses, my mind became insensibly tinctured with that generous enthusiasm they ever inspire. To render marriage that permanent state of bliss, which my fond imagination had pictured it, I believed more was requisite than wealth, titles, or external accomplishments. I looked for sympathy of soul, and perfect union of ideas. Like Clarissa, I wished, 'to pass my life in rational tranquility, with a friend whose virtues I could respect, whose talents I could admire. And who would make my esteem the basis of my affection.'[1]

I had just entered into my twentieth year, when it pleased heaven to deprive me of the best of parents. By his death I became possessed of a fortune surpassing my most ambitious desires: but this acquisition, I can with sincerity affirm, was far, very far from compensating the loss I sustained in him. I performed the last sad melancholy office to his ever-honoured remains, and cried over him the unfeigned tear of filial sorrow. As my father, during his life, was naturally fond of those amusements which enliven the fashionable circle, I had mingled much more in it than was agreeable to my tranquil turn of mind. Now, being entire mistress of my actions, I resolved to indulge myself in a manner of living more suited to my disposition. Having, therefore, retired to an elegant villa, which my father had fitted up in a remote part of the island, I reduced my numerous acquaintance to a few select friends and there found myself in possession of the greatest sweeteners of human life;

Friendship, retirement, rural quiet, books,
An elegant sufficiency, content.[2]

A stranger to love, envy, or ambition, my days were crowned with joy, and my nights with undisturbed repose.—Delightful hours! why so soon did you spread your airy pinions, and leave me to weep for that peace which can return no more.

I had been but a few months settled in my tranquil abode, when a young man arrived in the island with letters of recommendation to my father, from a friend of his in America. I

---

1 The quotation comes not from Samuel Richardson's famous heroine but that of Isaac Bickerstaffe in his comic opera *Lionel and Clarissa* (II.xi).

2 James Thomson, *The Seasons*, "Spring": "An elegant sufficiency, content, / Retirement, rural quiet, friendship, books, / Ease and alternate labour, useful life, / Progressive virtue, and approving Heaven!" Compare with the "fine Utopian scheme of domestic happiness" in Olivia's mind at the end of her last letter in packet two.

acquainted the stranger with the loss I had experienced in the best of parents; at the same time assuring him, that any services it was in my power to render him he might command.

From that hour he had free access to me. His stature was of the middle height, graceful and well proportioned; his education was liberal; his judgment correct, and his manners gentle and engaging: but his countenance! Oh, why did nature form it so ingenuous? why was not perfidity and ingratitude stamped on every feature? These attractions too easily subdued my unguarded heart; my joys became all centered in the agreeable stranger.

In a few weeks after his arrival, he took advantage of that partiality which I am fearful, he was too sensible I entertained for him; and professed a passion for me, so sincere and disinterested, that I easily gave credit to that which I so ardently wished. Wealth is surely not enviable! happy is the village maid whose innocence and beauty are her only dower: no riches, no titles, to allure, she enjoys the affections of her faithful shepherd, unbiassed by sordid interest or ambition.

But to resume a story which, would to Heaven, I could for ever blot from my remembrance! I did not long endeavour to conceal that passion which was my greatest pride. It is true, the object of it was undistinguished by wealth or station; but these I viewed with contempt, when set in competition with those virtues and accomplishments my fond imagination ascribed to my beloved Groveby. He continued to urge his love; and with such success, that in six months after we were married.

This step drew on me the censure of all my acquaintance, who thought it madness in me to lavish so large a fortune on a young man possessed of no other recommendation than that of a good person and education.

Their reflections, however, gave me little concern: I had found a man who seemed formed to render my life permanently happy; and rejoiced that heaven had enabled me to exalt him to that sphere to which, I flattered myself, his worth and talents would become an ornament.

Perfect harmony subsisted betwixt us two years; but, alas! at the end of that period I perceived with grief, that indifference gradually succeeded the ardour of affection which had till then influenced the conduct of my husband. To a heart less tender, perhaps less fond, than mine, this change might have been imperceptible; but my love was of that delicate nature, as to startle even at the shadow of unkindness. Oh, that it had been but a shadow!

He spent whole days from me; my endearments were irksome to him; and if I inquired into the cause of his dejection or displeasure, he answered me with such coolness and reserve, as cut me to the soul.

Oh, Madam; may you never experience the pangs of unreturned affection; may you never feel the tortures I then endured! for I still loved the dear, ungrateful youth, with undiminished ardour; and time, which had weakened and destroyed his passion, seemed only to have added strength to mine.

At length, one day, he told me that, being weary of a climate which he found by no means agreed with his constitution, he was resolved to return to America; and ordered me to prepare immediately for our departure, as he had settled for our passage in a vessel which sailed in a few weeks.

I was rather surprised at this information, as he had never before intimated his intention: I did not, however, oppose his design; but instantly made preparations for our voyage. Most of our effects being conveyed on board, and the time having arrived, within a few days, for our departure, my husband went one day to dine on board with the captain of the vessel. I awaited his return till late in the evening, when I began to grow alarmed at his delay, fearing that some accident might have befallen him: but oh, Madam! how shall I describe my agony, when, on sending a messenger to enquire for him, I discovered that the vessel had been under sail some hours, and that my perfidious husband had embarked in it.

A cold sweat bedewed my limbs, a mist of darkness seemed to gather round me, and I sunk motionless to the ground: oh! that I had remained for ever insensible, that death had for ever freed my wearied spirit from this scene of wretchedness!

I remained almost in a state of insanity several days, when a nervous fever ensuing, reduced me so low that my life was despaired of: youth, however, and the natural strength of my constitution, baffled the disease; and health returned, though my peace of mind was for ever fled.

I now saw myself deprived of that affluence to which, from my infancy, I had been accustomed; for my unkind Groveby had, some months before, unknown to me, converted our estates into cash; all which he had taken with him, leaving me only one small plantation, which I was likewise under a necessity of disposing of, to supply my immediate exigencies.

This sudden reverse of fortune gave me an opportunity of discovering a similar alteration in the conduct of my acquaintance:

the warmth of friendship was now changed into cool indifference; and those few who still continued to wear the appearance of cordiality, rendered my visits irksome, by satirical remarks, or mortifying reflections.

From my honest negroes alone I received consolation; their affection remained unshaken, and glowed with more fervour amidst the clouds of sorrow, and misfortune that surrounded me. I could, indeed, have raised a considerable sum by disposing of them; but, though born in a clime which authorizes the inhuman custom of bartering our fellow-creatures for gold, I ever loathed and detested the horrid practice.

Surely, my dear Madam, we have no right to tyrannize over, and treat as brutes, those who will doubtless one day be made partakers with us of an immortality. Have they not the same faculties, the same passions, and the same innate sense of good and evil? Should we, then, who are enlightened by the holy precepts of Christianity, refuse to stretch forth the friendly hand, to point these human affections to the most laudable purposes, the glory of God, and the real advantage of society.

Let us not mislike them for their complexion,
The shadow'd livery of the burnish'd sun.[1]

It is the charming variety with which nature has adorned her works, that so much raises our admiration and delight. The lily would bloom less fair, uncontrasted by the rose and the splendor of day become less welcome, was it not for the pleasing vicissitude of night. Is it then reasonable to despise a part of the creation, for contributing towards the beauty of the whole?

You will, I hope, Madam, excuse this unnecessary digression; but I have experienced such unshaken affection from these poor creatures, and have at the same time been so frequently witness to the cruelty and oppression which are daily exercised on them, that I could not refrain from entering with warmth on a subject in which my feelings have been so often wounded.

Many of the negroes had grown old in my father's service; and though their lives had passed with labour, gentleness and kind treatment had rendered the toil light. I could not endure the

---

1 A reworking of Morocco's speech to Portia in *The Merchant of Venice*: "Mislike me not for my complexion, / The shadow'd livery of the burnish'd sun," (II.i.1-2).

thought, therefore, of dooming their age to the iron hand of tyranny, to whatsoever poverty I might myself be reduced.

Thus resolved, I assembled them together; and, to the best of my remembrance, spoke to them in the following manner.

'MY HONEST FRIENDS,

'You see it has pleased heaven to deprive me of that affluence of which I was formerly possessed: you have all been faithful and affectionate; and many of you have spent your youth up in my own or my father's service. Assure yourselves, then, that I do not consider it the least of my sorrows, that fortune has not left it in my power to render your age peaceful and independent, as your youth has been faithful and industrious. But that God, whom you have been taught to adore, will befriend you, if you continue to serve him with humility, with patience, and with resignation. Do not however imagine, I conjure you, that I mean to doom you to foreign slavery; no, my friends, you are from this moment free. Liberty is all your poor mistress has to bestow on you; all she has now left to recompense you for your faithful services.'

It is impossible to describe the effect this address produced on the negroes; not a dry eye was seen among them: so far from being elated with the freedom offered them, they seemed desirous of rushing again into slavery, that I might reap the benefit arising from the sale of them.

This striking instance of their gratitude served only to confirm me in my resolution; so that, after bedewing my hand with their tears, they all departed, except one negro girl, who threw herself at my feet, with the most lively expression of grief, entreating me to kill her rather than discard her; declaring, that she preferred death to that of being separated from me. I could not withstand this mark of her affection, more particularly as my Theodore, whom, you now see the companion of my misfortunes, was then an infant, and my weak state of health rendered me incapable of paying him that unremitted attention his tender years required. With this girl I retired to a small abode, in a distant part of the island, and resigned myself wholly to the care of Providence; the money I had raised on the plantation before-mentioned, being now very nigh exhausted.

On the evening of the second day after my arrival, I perceived the negroes I had discharged advancing towards my new habitation. They had been at work on some plantations, and were approaching, to share with me the fruits of their honest industry.

At first I absolutely rejected their generous offer; but, finding that my refusal sensibly afflicted them, I consented to accept a third part of the money they offered.

From this day they constantly persisted in devoting to me the above portion of their wages, accompanied with such evident marks of satisfaction, that my acceptance of their services seemed to afford them the highest pleasure they were capable of enjoying.

In this solitude I remained twelve years; during which time I made frequent inquiries after my husband, writing repeatedly to several of my father's correspondents in America; but could not gain the least intelligence concerning him. I continued, therefore, entirely supported by the affectionate negroes, by whose assistance I was supplied, not only with the necessaries, but, I may add, even with the comforts of life. This state of dependence was, however, to an ingenuous mind, painful and humiliating; but I had, alas! no other resource!

My chief employment and delight was that of cultivating and improving those talents and virtues with which heaven had endued my beloved son: for his sake, I once more courted the sciences and the Muses, from whom sorrow had long estranged me.

My days were thus gliding on, when I became acquainted with a gentleman, named Seamore: he had formerly been a captain in the navy, and had spent his youth in the service of his country; but finding that the upstarts of an hour too frequently bore off the well-earned prize from the hardy veteran, he resolved no more to hazard the dangers of the deep, but to forget the toils of war in the serene joys of domestic life. With this intention, and the hopes of improving a moderate fortune, he purchased a large plantation in the island; to which he retired with his daughter, the fair Juliana. This gentleman was acquainted with my unhappy story by one of my negroes, employed on his plantation: he expressed an earnest desire to see me; which being related to me, the negro with my permission conducted him one evening, accompanied with his daughter, to our obscure retreat.

Juliana appeared to be about sixteen years of age. Her stature was below the middle height, but finely proportioned; her features were delicate; and, as the poet beautifully says of Lavinia, "The modest virtues mingled in her eyes."[1]

On their entrance she entreated me, with an air of peculiar

---

1   James Thomson, *The Seasons*, "Autumn."

sweetness, to pardon that curiosity, excited by my superior virtues and unmerited misfortunes.

I found little difficulty in returning this compliment; for there was something so engaging in her aspect, that I uttered only the sentiments of my heart, when I assured her that, to whatever cause I was indebted for this visit, I should consider it with pleasure, since it introduced me to one so truly amiable.

From that time scarce a day passed in which we did not see each other. The captain discovered a striking partiality for my dear boy, and generously offered to be the patron of his future fortunes.

Not long after this, I perceived an alarming change in my Theodore; his vivacity forsook him, he grew thoughtful and melancholy, and a total decline of health seemed gradually to have taken place.

One day, when I had been for some time endeavouring to discover if any secret grief was the occasion of this unhappy alteration in him, he said, 'Alas! my mother, it is an hopeless, guilty passion, that is thus consuming my youth. It is love, to which honour, gratitude, and every tie of friendship, forbids me to aspire.—And yet who could behold thee, Juliana, and resist thy soft attractions? Thy innocence, thy beauty, and thy heavenly goodness!—Oh, fortune! till now, I was insensible of thy unkindness! Possessed of health and content, I sighed not for affluence I never knew. But love has taught me to be ambitious! Why was the curse of poverty entailed on me? Why am I doomed to languish in sight of that bliss I must never enjoy?'

He then told me that chance had discovered the situation of his heart to Juliana, and that they had exchanged vows of eternal truth. 'But, alas!' continued he, 'can I, to gratify my own passion, thus impose on the unsuspecting openness of my generous patron? Can I return his friendship by seducing his lovely daughter from the path of duty; by seducing her into the arms of one who, by that action, will dispossess himself of his only inheritance, his honour and integrity? No, my mother, rather let me lose her for ever, than, by baseness and ingratitude, cease to deserve her!' I embraced him with transport, and looked up with gratitude to heaven for blessing me with a son whose virtues so highly adorned human nature. Yet this excess of joy was damped by the miserable reflection, that I might perhaps in a short time lose him forever. I tried every effort to divert the deep melancholy to which, with sorrow, I beheld him daily made the prey; but finding all my attempts ineffectual, I resolved to remove to a more distant part of the island; hoping that absence and change of objects might restore to my beloved son his wonted serenity.

With this resolution, I went one morning to our friend, and disclosed to him the means I proposed taking, to extinguish a passion, which promised to be fatal, not only to my Theodore, but, if suffered to take too deep root, highly injurious to the peace of his charming daughter.

When I had concluded, the captain, to my surprise, instead of betraying the least chagrin or displeasure at the discovery of the reciprocal attachment between his daughter and Theodore, told me, that he could not discern the least reason why it should be injurious to either: 'If they love each other, why, my dear friend,' said he, 'should we prevent their happiness? The virtues and accomplishments of your son will, I am persuaded, more than counterbalance the trifling advantage which fortune has given to Juliana.'

I was astonished at this uncommon instance of generosity. 'These,' said I to myself, 'are the warm effusions of an heart uncorrupted by the sordid maxims of the world!' I flew immediately to communicate the joyful tidings to my beloved Theodore; but will not attempt to describe his transports. The happiness of his amiable mistress was not less complete; her lips, now with pride, confessed the passion her heart had long cherished.

The hours were revolving in this uninterrupted course of tranquility, when the generous Seamore was called to England by the death of a friend, who had appointed him sole guardian to an only child. He had, indeed, for some time before meditated a return to the place of his nativity; but this event hastened his resolution. We were to accompany him; and, at the request of Juliana, her nuptials with Theodore were to be deferred till our arrival in England.

In a short period we began our voyage; and sailed for some weeks without interruption; when a storm arising, we were in great danger of falling victims to its rage: our vessel continued two days at the mercy of the tremendous hurricane; but at the close of the second, when the loud billows began to sink in peace, and serenity again to smile on the agitated deep, we perceived that a part of the ship had taken fire.

It is impossible to describe the horror, the consternation, and unspeakable anguish, which was variously pictured in the countenances of the wretched crew. Our only resource was that of the long boat which was immediately hoisted and filled. Our noble friend, with the commander of the vessel, had been for some time endeavouring to extinguish the flames; but finding every effort fruitless, he turned his whole thoughts on his daughter, and was approaching to convey her into the boat, when the flames, which had communicated themselves to that part of the ship on which he stood, compelled him to seek instant protection in the waves. Juliana, who had till now supported herself with fortitude, superior to her age or sex; on beholding the dire fate of her father, fainted in her lover's arms. I perceived the contending passions which agitated the soul of my Theodore: duty and love at once divided his affections. I entreated him to waste no time on me, but instantly to convey the afflicted maid into the boat. This request he complied with, thinking, when he had placed her in safety, to return and provide for mine and his own: but, alas! he was no sooner in it, than the sailors pushed off from the ship, declaring that if more were suffered to enter, the boat must inevitably be overset.

My Theodore, in the most pathetic manner, endeavoured to prevail upon them. To take me with them, offering to trust his own life to the mercy of the waves: our friend likewise, whom we had before the happiness of seeing preserved, by the timely interposition of the sailors, urged this request in vain; and thus every hope for my escape seemed cut off.

The grief which spoke in the countenance of my Theodore, on perceiving the boat row from the ship, is inexpressible. But what was my astonishment when I beheld the affectionate youth plunge into the waves, and swim back towards the vessel! I lost all thought of my own situation, wholly absorbed in the fate of one dearer to me than life. I conjured him, in accents incoherent, to return to the boat, and not let me die a death more painful than that which awaited me, by seeing him perish. He was, however, deaf to my remonstrances; and when he had swam within a few yards of the vessel, at his request I threw myself from the deck: as I fell, with one hand he caught a part of my garment, by which he for some time supported me amidst the surrounding waves. But his strength being at length exhausted, we were on the point of sinking, when providentially we were discovered and taken up by some fishermen in a small skiff.

As soon as we were set on shore, our care was to make the strictest inquiry after our friend and his lovely daughter, whom we flattered ourselves had escaped in safety to some part of the coast. Our hopes were alas! disappointed; our endeavors to discover them proved fruitless; and at length we heard, with unutterable grief, that a boat full of passengers, which appeared to be escaping from some wreck, was seen to overset; by which means the unfortunate crew must inevitably have perished. This, it is too probable, was that in which our lamented friends took refuge. Theodore's grief was severe beyond conception. We resolved, however, to sail for England; for which place we were certain, should our fears prove groundless, they would likewise embark.

Fortunately, I had presence of mind, before we left the ship, to secure twenty guineas in a handkerchief; with the assistance of which we procured our passage, and arrived at Portsmouth: but this, at the conclusion of our voyage, was reduced to two guineas; with which we resolved to travel by short stages to London, where we might, from some of their connections, either gain intelligence of our unfortunate friends, or, what was more probable, be ourselves the messengers of their sad catastrophe.

We began our journey; but at the end of three days, notwithstanding the most rigid economy, our cash was entirely exhausted. I leave you, Madam, whose heart wealth cannot steel against the sympathetic feelings of woe, to imagine the horrors of our situation, destitute of friends or money, in a land of strangers, and deprived even of a sheltering habitation, in which we might unmolested breathe our last sigh.

In this forlorn state we continued our way, till I became so weak that I found it impossible to proceed further: I doubted not but my last hour was at hand; death seemed to promise a speedy oblivion to all my cares; but it required more than human fortitude to support the stroke which severed me from my Theodore, whom filial tenderness had rendered dearer to me than the tie of nature.

The thought of leaving him friendless, exposed to want and sorrow, filled my soul with those tortures which the most agonizing dissolution could not have caused. I swooned in his arms; and was conveyed, by the distracted youth, into that field in which our miseries first excited your generous compassion.

"Alas!" said Mrs. Sedley, as the narrative concluded, "how unequal are the distributions of Providence! Surely, my dear unfortunate friend, a larger portion of human ills than usual, have imbittered thy life. Whence is it, that the heart, warmed and expanded by the social virtues, should be thus suffered to shrink at the touch of poverty? Methinks it militates against the laws of justice; and nothing but the certainty of a future state can reconcile us to it."

"It ill becomes us," replied the Creole, "to arraign the dispensations of the most High: adversity is the lot of man, designed by

Heaven to wean him from these transient scenes, and fix his hopes on bliss more permanent; without it the virtues of patience and resignation would have no existence."

"How amiable, how forcible, is your philosophy!" said Mrs. Sedly "if you, my friend, encompassed by sorrows and misfortune, can repress the sigh of accusation, how ought my heart to dilate with gratitude for the happiness I enjoy, possessed of an affluent fortune, and blessed in the affections of a man whose virtues render him the delight and admiration of all around him! Oh, Mrs. Groveby! were you but acquainted with his amiable qualities, how would your tongue, like mine, grow lavish in his praise!" Mr. Sedley had been for some weeks on a party of pleasure; the strangers, therefore, had not yet had an opportunity of seeing him; but, from the lively picture which his fond wife drew, they already viewed him with the highest admiration.

His return was now expected daily; and the impatient Harriot began affectionately to count the moments of his delay.

At length she had the joy of seeing the chaise approach. Mrs. Groveby and her son, conscious of the delicacy of their situation, retired to another part of the house, while their generous benefactress flew on the wings of love to welcome her husband. How, alas! were her joys blasted, when she perceived him borne into the hall, pale and fainting. Severe as this shock was, she endeavoured to support it with fortitude, lest any tender attention to her unfortunate husband, who had been wounded in a duel, should be omitted. She attended him to his chamber, and hung over him with unutterable grief. When a surgeon had examined the wound, he pronounced it to be mortal; and advised him, if he had any temporal affairs to settle, to lose no time in adjusting them. Mrs. Sedley was no sooner acquainted with this melancholy sentence, than she fainted; and was conveyed by her attendants into another apartment, where the amiable Creole, by participating her sorrows, endeavouring to alleviate them.

Her anxiety, however, did not suffer her to remain long absent from her husband, from whom she feared death would in a short period divide her for ever. When Sedley perceived her again enter the chamber, he made signs for the servants to leave the room; and, pressing her hand, spoke to her in the following manner.

I find, my dear Harriot, (said he) that I am hastening to eternity; "cut off even with the blossoms of my sins:"[1] I have,

---

1 A line from the Ghost's speech in *Hamlet*, I.v.75.

perhaps, but a few short hours to live; let me therefore employ them, by atoning, in some measure, for my past offences, by vindicating the innocent, and making what reparation is yet in my power to those I have injured.

I had not been many hours at Dover, at which place we proposed staying some days, before the packet-boat arrived from France: I, with many others, flocked to the beach, in order to view the passengers; (fatal curiousity!) among whom was a young woman of exquisite beauty: she walked from the boat with a melancholy, dejected air, leaning on the arm of an old man, whom I imagined to be her father.

I will frankly confess, that from the first moment of beholding her, I was captivated by her charms; and resolved, contrary to all laws of honour and humanity, to gratify my base desires.

I found little difficulty in introducing myself to their acquaintance, as they slept in the same inn at which I lodged; and discovered, that they were on their way to London, but that they did not intend to pursue their journey till they received letters, which they were hourly in expectation of. I was rejoiced at this information, as I thought it would give me time to ingratiate myself with my fair enslaver with whom I became more and more enamoured. In a few days they received letters they expected and prepared to renew their journey. Unwilling so soon to relinquish the object of my pursuit, I pretended business, and accompanied them to London. There I took every opportunity of pleading my passion to my fair mistress; but she continued inflexible and unmoved.

I as obstinately continued to pursue her; till, after repeated remonstrances, she was constrained to free herself from my importunities, by discovering my base designs to her father.

The unsuspecting captain, who imagined the hearts of all men as generous and unpolluted as his own, was fired with indignation at the treachery and dissimulation of my conduct. He reproached me in the most bitter language his honest resentment could dictate; which I retorted with equal if not superior asperity, till a challenge seemed the only alternative to appease the injured pride and honour of both.

We went immediately to a retired part of the town, and drew upon each other; but were soon interrupted by some people, who overheard the dispute, and suspected our design: they did not, however, arrive before I had received the wound, which will in a short time terminate my existence.

My antagonist was taken into custody; and I was conveyed to

an adjacent tavern, where a surgeon being arrived, pronounced my wounds to be dangerous.

I was no sooner acquainted with his opinion, than I determined, contrary to the humane persuasions of those around me, to be instantly conveyed home, for, alas! I had wounds of the soul, which wanted the hand of conjugal fidelity to heal.

Oh! Harriot, bear witness, when I am no more, that with my latest breath I acknowledge myself the aggressor, and from my soul acquit my noble friend.

Into what an abyss of grief has not my folly plunged him! What pangs does not his amiable daughter suffer from reflecting, that the merciless hand of justice will, perhaps, tear from her the tenderest of parents!

Suffer them not to languish under the cruel thought; send them instant intelligence, that I confess the justice of my doom, and pronounce the innocence of my friend.

Mrs. Sedley lost no time in executing the desires of her husband; she immediately dispatched Theodore to the unfortunate captain and likewise letters to some powerful friends, requesting their interest to procure his speedy enlargement.

After this, she returned overwhelmed with sorrow to the chamber of her husband, whom she endeavoured to console with the hopes of returning health.

'No,' said he, 'my hour is at hand'; I shall soon appear at that grand tribunal, where our actions are weighed in the balance of impartial justice; where guilt is seen in its native deformity, and where virtue brightens into perfection. Oh! that I had reflected on this e'er it had been too late; but, intoxicated with success, I forgot that I was mortal, and darkened those hours with vice, which heaven deigned that virtue should illumine.

Oh! Harriot, listen, while I unfold a tale, at which your gentle nature will recoil.

It was the will of heaven not to increase the native pride and vanity which I possessed, by giving me an illustrious birth; my father, being distinguished only by honesty of heart, and simplicity of manners.

He resided many years in the family of a man of high rank, who intrusted him with the management of his estates, in which he acquitted himself with unblemished integrity. Being frequently with my father, I was early introduced to the notice of his noble patron; who was so pleased with the vivacity and pliability of my temper, that he offered to educate me with his own son. This proposal was too advantageous to be rejected, and I was immediately taken under his protection. A few months after he had adopted me, our generous friend accepted a lucrative post in America, to which place we accompanied him. There I made a rapid progress in my studies, and arrived at my nineteenth year. My kind patron then began to think of procuring me some employment suitable to the education he had liberally bestowed on me; and was on the point of purchasing for me a commission in the army, when a paralytic stroke in a few weeks put an end to his existence.

All my shining prospects now vanished; for I had but faint hopes of protection from the son of my benefactor, who by no means inherited his father's virtues.

My patron was no sooner dead, than his heir threw off the guise of friendship, which he had till then worn, and gave me to understand, that I must no longer expect countenance or protection from him, but instantly seek another residence.

I was much hurt and chagrined at this treatment from one whom I was conscious I had never deliberately injured. I had, indeed, always suspected that he entertained no real esteem for me and was sensible that he viewed my acquirements with an invidious and malignant eye; but did not imagine him capable, so soon, of violating the laws of hospitality. Fortunately for me, my father, who expired a few months before, had left me possessed of one hundred pounds, with which I resolved to embark for the West Indies, where I flattered myself I might obtain some advantageous employment, as I knew I could be well recommended to persons of rank there.

I immediately proceeded to put this scheme into execution, and agreed for my passage in a vessel, which was to sail in a few weeks.

During this fatal period, the ship arrived from England which conveyed you, my Harriot, supreme in youthful beauty, to the American shore. I gazed—I loved! my whole soul was lost in speechless admiration! With faltering accents I inquired into your name and family; and, oh! with torture, heard that fortune had placed you far, far beyond the reach of my romantic hopes.

I frequented all places of public resort, where I had the least opportunity of seeing you; and frequently attempted to converse with you; but, as you were constantly attended by your father or some friend, my endeavours were frustrated.

The time of my departure at length drew nigh: I was on the brink of exiling myself for ever from the woman on whom my soul doated with the most extravagant fondness: and yet, to what purpose would have been further delay?

Could an obscure youth, undistinguished by birth or fortune, dare to aspire to the heiress of Sir Charles Saville? What madness! what presumption!

In this agitated frame of mind, I embarked for the West Indies; but, on my arrival there, understood that a generous and wealthy planter, to whom I had letters of recommendation, was lately deceased.

I introduced myself, however, to his daughter, who received me politely; and, with an air of amiable frankness, gave me free access to her elegant mansion. She was a young woman who possessed one of the largest fortunes in the island; but, unlike the generality of her sex, she secluded herself from the excess and folly to which wealth too frequently gives birth.

I had not been her guest long, before I observed that she grew thoughtful; and after some time discovered, that her heart was impressed by the most tender passion, of which I believed myself to be the object: her looks, her actions, her sighs betrayed that which her modesty strove in vain to conceal.

This was, at first, far from affording me satisfaction; for my whole soul being engaged by the charming image of my Harriot, I viewed all other women with contempt and indifference. Conscious, however, of the extravagance of my passion, and not wholly insensible to the advantages arising from an alliance with the amiable Creole, I endeavoured to oppose the cool arguments of reason and interest to the impetuosity of love; and, at length, acquired so far an ascendancy over my passion, that I resolved to take advantage of the partiality which Zemira entertained for me. I easily persuaded her that our affection was mutual; so eagerly do we grasp at the illusion we ardently wish to be real! and in a few months led her to the altar, and made her mine by the most solemn ties.

In the society of my amiable wife, I now endeavoured to forget those fatal charms, the remembrance of which had so long embittered my hours; for oh! to my confusion, I must acknowledge she possessed sweetness of temper, understanding, and accomplishments, sufficient to have made even the most capricious of our sex completely happy. We spent two years together in one tranquil scene of domestic quiet, when I accidentally received information that you, my Harriot, still continued single and disengaged.

Trivial as this circumstance may appear, it revived that fatal passion, which time had almost extinguished; and those charms, on which I had gazed before with admiration, were now rendered more resistless by the powerful magic of fancy. The society of my Zemira grew every hour less pleasing; my existence became insufferable, and at length I formed and executed the most villainous design that ever disgraced the heart of man.

My fond wife had, on the day of our marriage, generously presented me with deeds and writings, which invested me with unlimited power over that wealth which she abundantly possessed: with these, dead to every feeling of justice, honour, or humanity, I embarked secretly for America; leaving my unsuspecting Zemira, with her infant son, exposed to all the horrors of indigence and despair. What agonizing pangs do not the reflection now cost me! What worlds would I not give to consign that one base action to the depths of oblivion!

At America, to elude all inquiries which might be made after me, I changed my name from Groveby to that of Sedley.

"Groveby!" exclaimed Mrs. Sedley; "then indeed my conjectures were, but too well founded!"

From America, (continued the expiring man) I sailed for England; where I heard that you, my Harriot, resided: and soon after my arrival, by the power of that wealth I so unjustly possessed, obtained the permission of your guardian to address you. What followed I need not add: my passion was not unsuccessful; and in a few months I was happy in making you mine by the strongest of all human engagements.

"How will it surprise you," replied Mrs. Sedley, "to find that I am no stranger to the unfortunate Zemira! though I little imagined myself so nearly interested in her sorrows." She then related, in a few words, the melancholy circumstances in which she discovered the amiable Creole and concluded with assuring him that she was at that moment in the house.

Sedley raised his eyes to heaven with astonishment and admiration; and, having remained silent a few minutes, said that he would endeavour to summon fortitude to support an interview with his much-injured wife.

The gentle Harriot then left the apartment of her husband, and went into her own dressing-room, to communicate the discovery to her friend. She found her so deeply engaged in the contemplation of a gold chain which she had taken from the table, that she did not at first perceive the entrance of her benefactress; and when she looked up, her countenance was so visibly discomposed, that, agitated as her own mind was, Mrs. Sedley could not forbear observing it, and inquiring into the cause.

"Alas, Madam!" replied she, "it is not now a time to intrude my sorrows on you. Only tell me, I conjure you, by what means you became possessed of this chain? for, oh! it is the same which, on our nuptial day, I gave to my perfidious Groveby!"

"Prepare, yourself," said Mrs. Sedley embracing her tenderly, "for tidings the most distressing and severe; for a scene of woe in which we are mutually involved! Oh! my friend, I am the wretched, though innocent cause of your sufferings! How shall I utter it; how will your generous nature bear the thought, that, Groveby and Sedley are but one! The story is long; and but an hour past I was blessed with ignorance. But let us not waste the precious moments; the expiring Groveby waits for you with impatience, to receive his last repentant sigh!"

The Creole, who to the softest sensibility united a dignity of mind, which enabled her to meet with fortitude the severest shocks of fortune, followed her friend into the chamber of her expiring husband.

On her entrance, notwithstanding he had endeavoured to prepare himself for the melancholy interview, it was with the utmost difficulty he was prevented from fainting; while his injured and compassionate wife, kneeling at his bedside, bedewed his hand with tears of pity and forgiveness. Having gazed on her for some time, "Justice," said he, "has at length overtaken me!— Thy wrongs, Zemira, will be revenged: death approaches, armed with the keen arrows of guilt, to sink my despairing soul into everlasting anguish!"

Zemira could interrupt him but with tears.

"Oh, thou injured saint!" continued he, "this goodness over-powers me. How much better could I have borne the keenest reproaches! they could not thus have pierced my soul! Canst thou indeed forgive? Canst thou forget?"

Here the agitation of his spirits became so violent that he was unable for some minutes to proceed. He then resumed: "I find that life is ebbing apace: adieu, my much-injured Zemira! You will find I have made you what reparation was in my power, by restoring that wealth of which I so unjustly deprived you. Farewell, my Harriot! I am on the verge of eternity. How dreadful is the prospect! And yet a ray of hope illumines the dreary path: unbounded is the mercy of heaven!—Tell Theodore—" Death closed the period: he fell back in a swoon; and in a few minutes after expired.

Mrs. Sedley gave way to all the extravagance of unrestrained grief; but the Creole, familiarized to sorrow, beheld the corpse of her repentant husband with an uncommon firmness of mind:

"When I look back," said she,

When I look back on all my former days,
The only comfort the review affords,
Is that they're past.
For thro' their course I cannot recollect
One free from sorrow, guilt, or disappointment.[1]

Theodore, who was, at the request of Sedley, dispatched to his unfortunate antagonist, arrived in a short time at the place of his confinement. But here let me drop my pen, nor attempt to describe emotions: on his entrance he discovered Seamore, and his beloved Juliana!

Overpowered by surprise and joy beholding the dear youth whom she imagined death had for ever torn from her embraces, she fainted in the arms of her lover: his caresses, however, soon recalled her fleeting spirits; and her happiness was rendered complete by the assurance he gave her of her father's safety, and likewise that of his amiable mother. In return, Seamore informed him, that the boat in which they escaped was driven by adverse winds on the coast of France; and recited their adventure with Sedley, at Dover; of which Theodore had before but imperfectly heard. The duteous youth did not long indulge himself in the society of his Juliana; impatient for his mother to participate in his joy, he lost no time in bearing to her the happy tidings; and with astonishment was made acquainted with the reverse of fortune which had taken place during his absence.

The generous Creole, who rejoiced that it was now in her power to recompense the filial piety of her beloved son, instantly put into his possession that wealth which his repentant father had resigned, reserving only to herself a moderate income. Seamore was in a few weeks honourably acquitted; and increased their happiness by his presence, at Sedley Hall; where the nuptials of the enraptured Theodore with his Juliana were celebrated.

The amiable Creole spent the evening of her days in peace; and, in an uninterrupted scene of tranquility, lost the remembrance of those sorrows which had discolored the former part of her life. She preserved the most inviolate friendship for Mrs. Sedley; who at her death, having no relations, bequeathed to her

---

1   Elizabeth Singer Rowe, *Friendship in Death in Twenty Letters from the Dead to the Living*. Letter VI, To Clorinda.

friend the whole of her fortune; which being considerable, enabled the generous Zemira to exercise, in a more extensive degree, that benevolence of soul for which the was so eminently characterized.

FINIS

Appendix B: Anonymous Poem "written by a Mulatto Woman" (1794)

[If *The Woman of Colour was* written by a Caribbean woman of color, she would not have been the first to have published in England. This poem, "written by a Mulatto Woman," predates the novel by twelve years; however, there is nothing within the body of the poem that suggests the race of either the 'brother' or the speaker. Without the clarifying note at the beginning, contemporary readers would have assumed that the protagonists are both educated, pious, and white. The race neutral approach taken by this "Mulatto Woman" poet presents the startling possibility that educated women of color like her and Olivia could have published many such anonymous poems, articles, etc. in eighteenth-century British texts. Furthermore, the decision to market the poet's race and gender in the introductory note reinforces an idea that *The Woman of Colour* makes evident on a much larger scale: it is entirely acceptable, even desirable, to use a woman of color's own voice to promote personal religious crusades such as missionary work as well as political ones like the abolitions of prejudice and slavery.]

The Evangelical Magazine for 1796. The Profits arising from the sale of this Magazine are applied to Charitable purposes. Volume IV (London: Printed by and for T. Chapman, 1796) 559

The following Lines were written by a Mulatto Woman, in the Island of Grenada, and sent to a Missionary on his removal from that Island to Jamaica, in the year 1794— [The information provided to contextualize the poem here as well as in the subsequent footnote could have been supplied either by the author or a source familiar with her.]

BROTHER, adieu! may heav'n your steps attend,
And ever from all ill your soul defend;
Shadow you as a cooling cloud by day,
A cheering fire by night, to guide your way!
Should sore disease afflict your feeble frame,
May you have power to trust in Jesu's name!

May pious friendly S—* her aid afford,
And in the dear disciple, serve her Lord!
O! may you find in her a hand and heart,
That will in all your sorrows bear a part!
Such as poor WEASIL found t'assuage his grief,
When angel-like she minister'd relief.
I trust your way is sanctioned from above,
That God hath pointed out your quick remove:
Obedient, rise at his command and go,
And by his grace sit loose to all below.
Bind on your armour, stand in his great might,
Go scatter all around the Gospel light:
O! fix on Christ a single steady eye,
And on his cross let self and nature die.
Be ev'ry wish resign'd to him alone,
And daily cry, O Lord! thy will be done!
So may your soul be fill'd with faith and love,
Your mind replete with wisdom from above;
The Spirit's unction on the word attend,
And by its energy hell's kingdom rend.
I fain would humbly drop a word or two,
Far from intending to dictate to you:
Believe, your good its only aim and end,
And say, let God, by whom he chuses, send.
Has it pleas'd Providence to cast your lot,
Among the unenlighten'd and untaught?
Behold them truly precious in his sight,
Who sinners calls from darkness into light;
And never, never with the world, despise
The soul Christ purchas'd when he clos'd his eyes.
Ever abhor the smiles of worldly fame;
Among the poor diffuse the Saviour's name;
Keep in your mind a gracious filial fear,
Lest the ungodly's food become a snare;
Be on your guard against the subtle arts,
Which steal from God unwary youthful hearts;
Let not entanglement from female charms

---

* A Lady who attended Mr. Weasil, a Minister of the Gospel in Jamaica, during his sickness and death. [Author's note.]

Bereave you of your locks, and bind your arms;
Guard your affections from a vain delight,
In those shut up in sin and error's night,
Lest the unequal yoke you should put on,
And you, (tho' twain) will have to walk alone.
O! may you daily antedate that rest,
Which, seeking, you shall find among the blest.
Rejoicing, trust the promise of his word,
And humbly wait the coming of your Lord.

Appendix C: Minor Heiresses of Color in British Long Prose Fiction

[Minor heiresses of color appear with other Britons in these selections from late-eighteenth and early-nineteenth century long prose fictions. The mere suspicion of being 'a girl of colour' could jeopardize a female student's standing at school, as Musgrave's Alicia Sleigh finds out; that is, unless a school was built around a girl of color, as it is with Austen's Miss Lambe and Marshall's Alicia Seldon. For marriageable women of color, Negroes, like Bissett's Mrs. Dulman, are disparaged for over-stepping societal boundaries, as when Mrs. Dulman marries a white man and aspires to ascend into a 'white,' cultured society; Britons are more enamored of emotionally unsophisticated ingénues such as Mrs. Mathews' mulatto, Miranda Vanderparcke, whose desire to marry emerges from pure love rather than racial, social, cultural, or material aspiration. With the exception of Alicia Sleigh, (who is, technically, not colored), the theme of 'improvement' affects each of these women of color, making them a stark contrast to the figure of perfection that Olivia makes in *The Woman of Colour*.]

1. From Agnes Musgrave, *Solemn Injunction*, vol. I (London: Minerva Press, 1798), Chap. XI, 182-87

As our heroine is again at school, again subjected to the insults of a few illiberal minded girls, I think it is needful to explain to my readers from whence arose the cruel and unmerited treatment she received.

When Mrs. Dalrymple consigned her lovely charge to the care of Mrs. Selden, she had informed her, Miss Sleigh was an orphan, both her parents having died in Jamaica. This soon was known in the school, where there were a number of West Indian girls, on which account it was a rule, strictly adhered to, that no child of colour, (that is no child of mixed blood whose ancestors within the fourth degree of descent were negroes) were admitted there, however exalted her fortune, or future rank in life might be; conscious a girl so situated would, from the creole young ladies, meet with many slights, and that it would prove a certain source of trouble, as in the West Indies the distinction is kept up by the women with so scrupulous an exactness, as never to mix, on equal terms, with people so descended.

The abilities of Alicia excited envy in the hearts of some of the young ladies at Mrs. Selden's, whose junior she was, yet excelled them in every thing she was taught; and sorry am I to add, the amiable dispositions of our youthful heroine served but to add fuel to the fire her talents had kindled.

At the head of the party was Miss Aislabie, a creole of Jamaica, whose father possessed large estates in that island. This girl, finding it out of her power to render Alicia disliked, or to make her the object of ridicule to her companions, after making various efforts, at length insinuated she was a girl of colour. As none of the young ladies belonging to Jamaica could remember any person of consequence whose name was Sleigh, therefore, "it might be, as Miss Aislabie said, she might be a girl of colour; and what a strange thing it was of Mrs. Selden to take such a girl into the school; they all agreed their papas and mammas would be highly offended."

Yet, notwithstanding Miss Aislabie's arts, our heroine had a powerful party who espoused her cause, consisting chiefly of the younger and middle classes of girls, whose hearts felt the full force of her numberless amiable and engaging qualities; by these was she considered as deeply injured, and the spirit of party ran as high in the youthful society of Edgecumbe house, as it can do in a more august assembly; or, as it can do in electing the members of that honorable house.

Sometimes, in the bitterness of her soul, Alicia meditated applying to Mr. Meynell for a removal from her present situation.—But no; she thought, by quitting Mrs. Selden's, where, from its owner, she had received repeated proofs of regard, she would but give cause of triumph to the malicious Miss Aislabie, and her party.—Shrink not, had Mr. Kirby said, from danger or difficulty; it is but by such trials I shall obtain that fortitude I have been told is so needful I should acquire; it is but by exercising them the faculties of the mind attain strength.

Such were the reasons Alicia confessed to herself, as actuating her conduct; but a latent, though perhaps not altogether improper pride, urged her stay, checked all complains, and taught her to overlook, with an air of conscious superiority, the indignities her adversaries meanly stooped to practice: destitute of all studied revenge, tho' unyielding, she steered a course, which in a more extended circle might serve as a model for prudent conduct. Vainly the little party who looked up to her, as the model of all perfection, entreated leave to speak of the persecution raised against their favorite, and oft had she to restrain their ardour in her cause.

Returned to school, noticed by Lady Bertram, protected by Mr. Meynell, laden with presents of various elegant trifles, Alicia no longer appeared the same being. Miss Aislabie's party decreased, every day was some one of Alicia's persecutors begging to be received into her favour, so that at the commencement of the midsummer holidays scarce a girl in the school, except Miss Aislabie and her sister, but what believed and declared Miss Sleigh had an equal right with themselves to the very brilliant complexion she possessed.

2. From Jane Austen, *Fragment of a Novel January-March 1817. Now first published from the Manuscript*, ed. R.W. Chapman (Oxford: Clarendon Press, 1925) Chap. 11, 151-55

Mrs. G. was a very well-behaved, genteel kind of Woman, who supported herself by receiving such great girls & young Ladies, as wanted either Masters for finishing their Education, or a home for beginning their Displays.—She had several more under her care than the three who were now come to Sanditon, but the others all happened to be absent.—Of these three, & indeed of all, Miss Lambe was beyond comparison the most important & precious, as she had paid in proportion to her fortune.—She was about 17, half Mulatto, chilly and tender, had a maid of her own, was to have the best room in the Lodgings, & was always of the first consequence in every plan of Mrs. G.—The other Girls, two Miss Beauforts were just such young Ladies as may be met with, in at least one family out of three, throughout the Kingdom; they had tolerable complexions, shewey figures, an upright decided carriage & an assured Look;—they were very accomplished & very Ignorant, their time being divided between such pursuits as might attract admiration, & those Labours & Expedients of dexterous Ingenuity, by which they could dress in a stile much beyond what they *ought* to have afforded; they were some of the first in every change of fashion—& the object of all, was to captivate some Man of much better fortune than their own.—Mrs. G. had preferred a small, retired place like Sanditon, on Miss Lambe's account—and the Miss Bs—, though naturally preferring any thing to Smallness & Retirement, yet having in the course of the Spring been involved in the inevitable expence of six new Dresses each for a three days visit, were constrained to be satisfied with Sanditon also, till their circumstances were retrieved ... The particular introduction of Mrs G. to Miss Diana Parker, secured them immediately an acquaintance with the Trafalgar house family, & with the Denhams;—and the Miss Beauforts were soon satisfied with "the Circle in which they moved in Sanditon" to use a proper phrase, for every body must now "move in a Circle,"—to the prevalence of which rototory Motion, is perhaps to be attributed the Giddiness & false steps of many. Lady Denham had other motives for calling on Mrs G. besides attention to the Parkers.—In Miss Lambe, here was the very young Lady, sickly and rich, whom she had been asking for; & she made the acquaintance for Sir Edward's sake, & the sake of her Milch asses. How it might answer with regard to the Baronet, remained to be proved, but as to the Animals, she soon found that all her calculations of Profit wd be vain. Mrs. G. would not allow Miss L. to have the smallest symptom of a Decline, or any complain which Asses milk cd possibly relieve. "Miss L. was under the constant care of a physician;—and his prescriptions must be their rule"—and except in favour of some Tonic Pills, which a Cousin of her own had a Property in, Mrs. G did never deviate from the strict Medecinal page.

3. **From Edmund Marshall, *Edmund and Eleonora: or Memoirs of the Houses of Summerfield and Gretton. A Novel, in Two Volumes*, vol. I (London: John Stockdale, 1797) 93-103, 108-10, 144-48**

CHAPTER XV

The summer of the year 17—had been passed by the worthy baronet and his family in the most delightful, and in the most benevolent and useful manner imaginable; Sir Gregory employed very many labourers and workmen in his improvements at the Dale; his own and the benignity of Lady Gretton went hand in hand with that of their excellent neighbours, the doctor and Mrs. Summerfield, and as the baronet had taken out his dedimus,[1] he acted in the commission of the peace, and gave the same unusual satisfaction in his magisterial capacity, that he so firmly exhibited in his private character, closely imitating the example of his

---

1 A writ to commission private persons to do some act in place of a judge; for instance, to examine a witness.

worthy predecessor, and the practice of his surviving brother, the respectable rector of the two parishes of Summerfield and Hawthorn-Dale.

The summer had now, for some time, given place to autumn; the year was in its decline, and the days were shortening a pace: it was towards the latter end of the month of October, when the doctor, whose custom it was alternately to officiate at his church of Hawthorn-Dale, when it was Mr. Adamson's turn of duty at Summerfield, was returning home in the evening after the service of the day; he had been detained rather longer than usual by a vestry and some justice business which had been the consequence of it; the moon was already risen; his postchaise was slowly passing through a watery lane; when his nephew, the young Edmund, who accompanied him, suddenly exclaimed—"Look, look, uncle! what is that white figure reclining against that old willow tree upon the right hand of the road? It is something alive, and it has surely much the appearance of a young woman dressed all in white." The doctor called to the postillion to stop, and he desired William his groom, who was on horseback, to ride up to the tree, and inform himself what the object was which had so forcibly attracted the notice of his nephew. William presently returned, leading in his hand a tall, slender young girl, who appeared almost fainting through fatigue and the want of necessary refreshment. The doctor and Edmund instantly alighted from their carriage; they could then perceive by the light of the moon, which shone out remarkably clear and brilliant, that the young creature whom William was supporting, was a tall, elegant Mulatto girl, dressed in a white muslin jacket and petticoat; she was so nearly exhausted, that had it not been for the recovering assistance of a cordial, which, for benevolent purposes, the doctor generally carried in one of the pockets of the chaise, she would, probably, have sunk lifeless by its side.—She was recovered by its application, and the doctor and his nephew, with great gentleness, placed her with them in the carriage.

She was now able to relate her story:—She told them she was a native of the island of Jamaica—that her name was Alicia Seldon—that her father was a wealthy planter in the parish of Westmoreland, and that some months since she had been entrusted to the care of the captain of a West Indiaman, who, together with his wife, were returning to England—that her father had, as she was informed, placed a considerable sum of money in the hands of the captain for her use, and to pay the expences of her passage and her education at an English boarding school—that she had been attended by a maid-servant, in whom her father placed great confidence—that on their passage the captain's wife had died of a violent fever, after which, she said, his behaviour to her grew extremely offensive—that he had made no scruple to make love to her, and she could perceive he had found means to bribe her servant to assist him in his vile designs upon her honour. She added, that when they arrived at Portsmouth, the captain obliged her to go ashore with him, under the pretence of making a visit to a lady of his acquaintance: in this house she was no sooner arrived, than he renewed his attempts—the doors were locked upon her—her maid-servant had been left on board, and she had now every thing to apprehend from the wretched woman whom the captain had called his friend: she had thought her fate to be inevitable, when, owing to the kind assistance of the young woman of the house, who pitied her situation, she had been enabled to make her escape through a window, and had wandered, how far she could not tell, till she had been thus fortunately met with, and relieved by the doctor and his nephew.

Alicia had told her tale with so artless a simplicity, as to entitle it to full credence; there was a bare possibility that she might be an impostor, but it was scarcely probable that so young a creature could possess so wicked a spirit of invention. The doctor desired her to be comforted, and to be assured he would give her protection; "you have escaped," said he, "my poor child, from very bad hands, and you shall find a refuge in very good ones; my wife shall be your protectress, I will myself write to your father, and I will instantly see the vile captain properly taken care of."

The carriage now stopped at the parsonage; the doctor handed out of it, his young female traveler, and to the no small surprize of Mrs. Summerfield and the baronet's family, who had just taken their tea at the doctor's, introduced to them the young beautiful Mulatto girl. Her story was again recited; it was believed, and the baronet readily consented to join his signature to that of the doctor's, in a warrant to be backed by the Lord Mayor of London, for the apprehension of the West India captain, upon the double charge of an assault and a robbery.

The warrant was duly executed upon this base betrayer of a friendly confidence, on his arrival at the port of London; Alicia recovered all her clothes, and the greatest part of her property, and the vile wretch, the captain, gave bail to answer the heavy charges against him, in a court of justice.

CHAPTER XVI

The houses of Summerfield and Gretton were now amply convinced by the apprehension of the villainous captain, his surrender of Alicia's effects, and the elopement of the infamous accomplice of his crimes, that the story told by the young beautiful Mulatto girl, was, in all its circumstances, strictly true. It only now remained, to make Mr. Seldon, her father, acquainted with the providential escape of his child, and to put in execution his design in sending her to England for the completion of her education.—The doctor and his lady had great and reasonable objections to the placing of a young lady of Alicia's age at any of the fashionable boarding-schools; it was, therefore, proposed to her, to reside at the parsonage, under Mrs. Summerfield's protection, and to receive lessons in dancing, drawing, and music, from Mr. Adderley, and that Mr. Walter Rosemary should instruct her in geography and arithmetic.

Mr. Adamson undertook to give her lectures in Lowth's English Grammar[1] and Mrs. Tomlyn offered herself to be her instructor in the French Language, if the doctor thought the acquisition of another language necessary to this their amiable *protégée*.

It was with the utmost gratitude that Miss Seldon consented to this arrangement; she kissed the hands of Mrs. Summerfield again and again for her extreme goodness to her, declaring, with an effusion of joyful tears, which evinced the gentleness and sensibility of her heart, that, to have left her present situation, would have so utterly depressed her spirits, as to have rendered her unfit for any tuition; but that she now felt herself so relieved by the good Mrs. Summerfield's resolution in her favour, that she would apply herself with such diligence, in acquiring whatever it might be thought proper to teach her, as to convince her protectors that she was not entirely unworthy of their favour.

The amiableness of this young creature's manners and disposition, had so engaged the affections of the ladies of both families, that it was difficult to say, whether Alicia was a greater favourite with Mrs. Summerfield, Lady Gretton, the venerable Mrs. Williamson, or the worthy governess of Eleonora, Mrs.

---

1 Robert Lowth (1710-87) was a bishop of the Church of England and a professor of poetry at Oxford University. His textbooks on English Grammar were incredibly influential.

Tomlyn; as to the little Eleonora, she was so devotedly fond of her dear Brunette, as she called her, that, by her own choice, she never would have been a moment absent from her;—but Alicia not only stood high in the good graces of the heads of the two houses, but she had so recommended herself to every domestic, both at the castle and the parsonage, by her affability, condescension, and generosity, that it was with the most cheerful alacrity she was waited upon by the men and women-servants, both at the castle and the parsonage; indeed, she gave the least trouble possible, and had modestly declined accepting any particular servant on her own account, which the doctor, who now had a considerable sum appropriated to her use, in his hands, had offered her, Saying, whenever it was proposed, "that, the doctor's and Lady Gretton's maid-servants were all so good to her, that she had no sort of occasion for any such distinction."

Mr. Adderley now visited the parsonage three days in the week, instead of two, which had been his customary allotment; the philosopher of Hawthorn-Dale did the same, and such was Alicia's diligence and application to the several branches of her education, that the former gentleman declared, she had the greatest genius for music, drawing, and dancing, that he had ever met with; and Mr. Walter Rosemary would profess, rubbing his hands together, as was his custom when he was pleased, that the young Jamaica lady would, he believed, soon become a very complete geographer and arithmetician, and that with the doctor's and Mrs. Summerfield's consent, he had no doubt of making her an adept in astronomy and electricity; the doctor and Mr. Adamson were no less satisfied with their pupil in the progress she made in a grammatical knowledge of her own language —Alicia and our young Edmund wrote their exercises together, and she was soon capable of composing with great correctness and propriety of expression....

CHAPTER XVIII

"And pray Sir,"—said Humphrey Claggett, who was attending Dr. Summerfield upon certain parish business, the next day after the ball at the parsonage—"Pray Sir," said honest Humphrey, "if I may be so bold, is it usual for these Tawney-moor young ladies to dance so well, as I saw the young Jamaica lady dance last night? I declare she danced as well, if not better, than the best Christian dancer of them all; I could not have believed, unless my own eyes had beheld it, that any young creature, who had never been baptized, could foot it so nimbly and so genteely; for I am told, in Miss Seldon's country, they never christen your Tawney-moors and your Black-amoors, but I dare say, if I may be so bold, you intend to have Miss christened before she is much older."

"Friend Humphrey," replied the worthy doctor, "you are totally mistaken concerning Alicia; she was baptized long since in her own country; her father pays a clergyman very handsomely, who resides upon his estate, not only for christening and reading prayers in his own, that is Mr. Seldon's immediate family, but every negro upon his plantation, both the men and the women, have received baptism from the chaplain, Mr. Devayne, and every child is christened as soon as it is born; and, to the very great honour of this humane planter, he has liberally given freedom to every slave upon the plantation. These poor blacks are become as free, Humphrey, as you, or I; and to remove your surprize at Miss Seldon's dancing, you are to understand, that she had learned to dance before she left Jamaica, though her master was by no means equal in skill to Mr. Adderley, under whose superior instruction she has been very greatly improved."

It was no easy matter to stop the tongue of honest Humphrey, when it was once set a going; he proceeded, as the doctor had not ordered him silence—"And God bless him, (Mr. Seldon) say I, for his goodness to these poor creatures, who, for ought I know, may have as good souls as ourselves, though the cases which contain them are of a different colour....

CHAPTER XXIII.
Though the hunting season was now pretty far advanced, yet did the baronet's beagles continue to meet twice a week at the Summerfield Arms. They had recently had an extra, or volunteer dinner, at honest Humphrey Claggett's; at which it was agreed, in honour of Lady Gretton, who had more than once graced the field with her presence, to adopt an uniform of her ladyship's selection—it was a garter blue frock with a buff velvet cape, a kerseymere waistcoat striped buff and blue, a jockey cap, and the gold buttons of the coat, in compliment to the lady of the castle, had the letters L.G.H. inferred upon them, intimating that the hunt wished to have the title of Lady Gretton's Hunt.

Alicia, from almost the first month of her residence at the parsonage, had been indulged in riding a very gentle bay galloway which had long been in the habit of carrying the doctor in his rides about his two parishes; he had now resigned it to Alicia, who was the frequent companion of Edmund when he rode out with Mr. Adamson. Mr. Adderley had been sometimes of the party, and, as he was almost as good a horseman as he was a fencer and musician, he had so well instructed the beautiful young Mulatto in the art of riding, that she by this time rode very gracefully; and under the peculiar escort of the young Edmund and Mr. Adderley, Lady Gretton had permitted Alicia to accompany them to the field; and with the consent of Mrs. Summerfield she assumed the uniform, and was allowed, to her very great joy, to consider herself as a member of Lady Gretton's Hunt.

Nothing could exceed the joy of our good baronet at his Eleonora's growing attachment to the country; it gave him the most sincere pleasure that as he took delight in a little gentle hare-hunting; his French-horns always attended her ladyship, and in compliment to the baronet and his lady, no less than for their own gratification, there was generally a very respectable field.

The month of March was already commenced; it was the last day of hunting for the present season; they had had a remarkable good day's sport, and Sir Gregory had invited the company, which had that day included besides the family at the parsonage and the constant members of the hunt, several of the neighbouring gentlemen to dine with him at the castle when the sport of the day should be over.

The horns and clarionets had, as usual, given their firm flourish; they had sounded the preparation for dinner, when a servant announced that a post-chaise and four had driven into the courtyard of the castle, and that it contained a black gentleman in a very singular dress—In an instant it occurred to Sir Gregory that the stranger could be no other than the uncle of Alicia, and he immediately was at the door of the chaise to receive him.

The fact was, that he had arrived at Summerfield some hours before the letter he had written to acquaint Dr. Summerfield with his arrival in England, and the postillions had, by mistake, conducted him to the castle instead of the parsonage.

The Maraboo of Senegal (for such he was) was attended by one black servant who rode with him in the carriage, and one other on horseback: he was himself a remarkable fine figure—in height upwards of six feet, of a very placid countenance, and formed very differently from the Africans that we have usually seen, for he was most exactly proportioned: his dress was a turban, a quilted robe of spotted gold muslin, and a caftan, or vest, of purple satin richly embroidered with silver flowers—his whole appearance and demeanour was calculated to inspire respect.

Sir Gregory Gretton received the African Prince with great cordiality; he conducted him to his library, and having given orders for suspending the dinner for half an hour, Dr. Summerfield, his Lady, and his niece Alicia, were introduced to the Maraboo by Lady Gretton herself; he embraced his niece, and he made acknowledgments in good English, and in very handsome terms to the families of the castle and the parsonage, for the protection they had given Alicia—"The gratitude," he said, "of his brother and sister Seldon, as well as his own, was more than he could express; that Mr. and Mrs. Seldon had deferred their intended visit to England till the sailing of one of their own ships, but that they had intrusted to his care (a vessel from Senegal, freighted on his account, having arrived at Jamaica in order to convey himself to England) their two sons and their tutor, who would present themselves at Summerfield in a few days—That he had thus preceded them being desirous, as quickly as possible, to embrace his niece, and to pay his respects to her protectors."

It was submitted to the worthy Maraboo, whether he would have a separate dinner served to himself and Alicia in the library? the doctor and Mrs. Summerfield offering themselves to attend him, or would join the rest of the company, who were by this time assembled in the dining-parlour?—he chose the latter.

4. From Robert Bissett, *Douglas; or, The Highlander. A Novel. In Four Volumes*, vol. I (London: Anti-Jacobin Press, 1800) Chap. X, 311-12

Our hero being asked now, by his aunt, to take a turn round the room, they were presently joined by the Doctors and other gentlemen. Mrs. Lighthorse observing our hero cast his eyes on a very vulgar couple, bedizened out with a most profuse finery, asked him, "Well Charles, what do you think of that lady with the mutton fist?"

"What," said he, "the vulgar dowdy, with the broad shoulders, large face, thick lips, pug nose, and wide nostrils?"

"The same."

"I suppose she is some rich tradesman's wife, from Shoreditch."

"Your conjecture is natural, I allow," said she, "but not just. Her maiden name was Dutchsquab, *she is a negro-driver's frow, fresh from Demarara*; she had married Monsieur Heureux, but he dying, and leaving her very rich, she married the person with her, John Dulman, Esquire, as he now styles himself, who wanted

dame Heureux's money, in order to pay debts he had incurred
to a very expensive mistress, and to be able to indulge her
extravagance. John Dulman and his *dame* taking a fine house in
London, tried to become people of fashion; gave concerts,
parties, routes. The *dame* endeavoured to learn drawing, music,
and all fine accomplishments, but nothing could *whitewash the
negro.* Negro driving itself has no great tendency to liberalize
the mind, and Dutch minds are not the most easily liberalized
any more than the Dutch manners are the most easily refined.
She is a strange compound of French vanity and ostentation,
with Dutch vulgarity and avarice. Dulman himself is a poor,
mean, pliant creature, one of those trifling characters that defy
analysis. He has, now and then, tried to be a rogue, but the stupidity and confusion of his head prevented success. Whoever
gives sumptuous entertainments will not want visitants. They
have a numerous set of acquaintance, some of them very low,
who fancy the Dulmans elegant people, while the genteel part
laugh at them."

5. From Mrs. Charles Mathews, *Memoirs of a Scots Heiress*, vol. II (London: T. Hookham, 1791) 182-97

The next morning while we were at breakfast, our society was
increased by an abrupt visitor. On hearing a rap at the street
door, Mrs. Semhurst smiled, and said, "Oh, here's Miranda:
some new distress, I suppose": she then began to warn me not to
be surprised at the sight of the lady who she imagined was
coming in: "she is our next door neighbour," said she, "and a very
extraordinary foreigner."

She had proceeded no farther, when a young female, genteel
and elegant in her look and manner, hastily introduced herself.
Seeing a stranger, she paused; but a word of encouragement from
Mrs. Semhurst brought her forward: she had in her hand an open
letter, and I presently discovered that she knew but little English,
and came to have its contents explained.

While this was doing I could not detach my eyes from the
young lady. I remarked great symmetry in her features, and the
most pleasing expression in her countenance; she had fine
eyes, fine teeth, and long glossy black hair, which without any
assistance, or any decoration but a simple ribbon, covered her
shoulders in a profusion of ringlets. Her person was exquisitely formed, and her motions highly graceful; but she was
almost a negro. The hue of her skin perhaps wanted some

shades of the deep African dye; but it had passed the degree of copper colour.

When her queries were answered, and I had been introduced to her, she returned home; and Mrs. Semhurst gratified the curiosity my countenance must have proclaimed, by giving me a brief account of this charming mulatto. She said, she was the niece of a Dutch gentleman who occupied the next house, and who had been originally bred up to the study of physic. His name was Vanderparcke, and this young woman was the daughter of his brother who had settled in Batavia, and married a negro woman there. Miranda had been left an orphan when very young: her riches were immense, and this uncle was her faithful guardian, and only relation in England. She had been here only a year; and Dutch being her native language, she was frequently at a loss to express herself, though she had already made a wonderful progress; but the attainment of our language was impeded by Dr. Vanderparcke's ignorance of it, and therefore it was that she applied on all occasions to Mrs. Semhurst who had known her from her first arrival. —To this account she added great encomiums on Miranda, who, though but eighteen years of age appeared to have reached an uncommon pitch of excellence.

A few days made this ebon-beauty as familiar with me as with her better-known friend; and such was my situation that my only anxiety was lest it should be too blissful to last. I received an immediate return from lady Donachmuir, not only congratulating me on my new acquisition, and saying whatever could recommend me; but inclosing bills to the amount of fifty pounds. I availed myself of Mrs. Semhurst's permission by renewing my acquaintance with such of lady Cadwicke's and Mrs. Dibart's friends as I thought would be acceptable visitors to my patroness; and I blest lady Jane Alderway's cruelty.

Mrs. Semhurst in a few days after I came to her, mentioned Mrs. Agthorpe as her daughter; but made no mention of her son. It did not become me to be inquisitive where I supposed there was a reason for concealment; but a letter being brought to her one morning when Miranda and I were with her, she could not forbear crying out as she looked at the direction, "Thank Heaven, it is from my son."—"From Mr. Cyril?" said Miranda.—I started involuntarily—Mrs. Semhurst changed colour, and looked at me, while Miranda eagerly glancing at the writing, kissed the seal with the utmost affection and respect, and returned it to Mrs. Semhurst, who opened and read it in silence, I all the while tormented with fears of I knew not what.

I had never from any one heard Mr. Cyril's name, and I now, made suspicious by deceit, feared it had been secreted for some purpose which would be fatal to my present enjoyments. But Mrs. Semhurst, as soon as she had perused the letter, and pointed out to Miranda a paragraph intended for her decyphering, relieved my torturing anxiety by saying I was perhaps surprised at hearing she had a son.—"I did not intend," said she, "to have told you of him till you had lived with me long enough to be satisfied of my prudent regard for you, lest at the first notice of a young man here you should have taken wing. You have no cause of alarm," she added, "for Cyril is very sober and well inclined: his letter says I may expect him in a few weeks as he leaves Rome this day; but I assure you, Miss Hamilton, that though he comes sooner than I supposed he would think of returning, I will not expose you to the malice of the world by suffering him to live at home. He will be very happy in your society when he visits here; but I must remember I have a ward's interests to consult now."

Grateful as I felt for such extraordinary attention and kindness, I could not but represent to Mrs. Semhurst the propriety of my rather withdrawing from her house. This she opposed strenuously; and I 'nothing loth,' submitted to her decision. At that moment I wanted nothing but the absence of Miss Vanderparcke to have courageously closed to Mrs. Semhurst my peculiar situation, but this spark of bravery was soon extinguished—I dreaded the resentment of the lady in Audley square, who was often with us, and when Miranda was gone I employed the opportunity only in learning that this Mr. Cyril was the identical person who had expressed so much concern for me at my bankers'. His mother accounted for the visits he had designed me, by his wish to assist me in recovering a part of my property, and said it was his report of my distress that had induced her to call on me while at Richmond, and had informed her of my connection with captain Dibart's family.

Two months of the three to which my invitation extended, had slid away in a manner that sunk all past evils in present enjoyment. Mrs. Semhurst was lady Cadwicke to me, Miranda was a sister; and in forwarding her in her various and eager pursuit of improvement, I found a constant source of entertainment and delight. Knowing the period, for which I was engaged, she obtained from Mrs. Semhurst and myself, a promise that if we at its expiration chose to separate, I should fix myself permanently at Dr. Vanderparcke's, who, good old man! was almost as desirous as his niece that I should live with her: Mrs. Semhurst, whenever this was mentioned, put it off with an arch smile; and 'Yes, yes, as soon as ever I wish to part with Miss Hamilton, you shall have her.'

Miranda's character of mind was as foreign as her hue. Her spirits were indeed 'finely touched:' the least circumstance affected them: joy would transport her to delightful frenzy, and the gaiety of her heart would operate on every joint and every muscle; but she had feelings so exquisitely tender, that did the distress even of a stranger but intrude with half a step on her most vivid pleasures, the exulting bosom beat no more with rapture; her joys were in an instant annihilated, and sorrow occupied her dusky countenance: tears of sympathy would start from her eyes, nor would she rest or attend to aught else while an effort to relieve the sufferer remained unexerted.

Soon after the time I am speaking of, we were for a while deprived of this amiable girl's company: her fine nerves required the sea-air, and she left us to go to the Kentish coast. Her letters now amused us: the jargon she wrote in was diverting, though not always intelligible, and her observations were acute and just. In this interval Mr. Cyril returned: he had been informed of the addition I had made to his mother's family, and received me with the utmost cordiality.

We staid but a short time in town after this. Mrs. Semhurst renewed her engagement with me for another three months; she offered me at the same time a twenty-pound note which I declined accepting, as I really did not want money; and I went with her to her house in Sussex. Mr. Cyril went into Hampshire to make a short visit to his sister, and in about a fortnight after our removal, he, Mr. and Mrs. Agthorpe, Dr. Vanderparcke and Miranda, joined us.

Of Mrs. Semhurst's daughter, Mrs. Agthorpe and her husband, it is unnecessary and unfair to give portraits. I knew them never intimately; and as they are now no more, it is fitter that their actions should be their biographers than that I should attempt to design their characters.

Miranda's health when she returned to us was apparently re-established: the sports and graces attended the charming moor, and she attracted the utmost notice. But a few weeks made a lamentable alteration in her; she grew emaciated, weak, and hectic. We were all seriously apprehensive for her: she expressed a wish to return home: her uncle went with her: Mr. and Mrs. Agthorpe left us; and Miranda's increasing illness soon after drew Mrs. Semhurst again to town, whither Mr. Cyril and I accompanied her. He took up his abode in the Temple, and as it was a season of the year when London is emptying, our leisure was wholly at liberty to attend Miranda.

Soon after she began to droop, an idea had entered my mind, which all my subsequent observation tended to strengthen, that Miranda's malady was love, and Mr. Cyril the object of it. The playful girl had precluded common suspicion by the artlessness of her conduct and her characteristic simplicity. At her first meeting Mr. Cyril after his return home, I witnessed the ecstasy of her joy. Wild as her native woods, and free as the gale that agitated them, she was ignorant of the cold reserves fashion enjoins, and all the hypocrisies of cities. What she felt she expressed in all the force of nature; and those to whose tuition she had been committed, saw too clearly the beauty of her mind to spoil it by imposing shackles on it. Miranda could do nothing reprehensible while Reason was her judge; for she was purity itself, darkly as she was arrayed; but Miranda sinned every hour against arbitrary fashion and servile custom.

She greeted Mr. Cyril in her first interview with all the love of a sister for a sister: she hung about him: she kissed his hands and lips with rapture; and when Mrs. Semhurst laughed at her extravagance she, totally ignorant of the cause of her merriment, replied archly, "Never mind: colour won't come off." She tried, by repeating English words, to convince him of her industry in his absence; and closed her account with inexpressible pathos, by saying, while she looked at him with extreme tenderness, and the tears gushed from her eyes—"No praise—what could I do but learn when you away?"

On the part of Mr. Cyril I perceived less emotion, but his fondness seemed equal: he call her his dear Orra-moor, his good girl, and heard with evident interest of her endeavours and progress; but I saw nothing in him that looked like that species of attachment which the dissimilarity of their complexions might have been thought to secure them from. He seemed to love her, but as a daughter; and as he had ten years advantage of her in age, the idea was not absurd.

On our return to town she again mended, and though weak, was able to visit us frequently. I now saw clearly into her heart: she had felt her uneasiness increase while in the house with Mr. Cyril: she had fled him to get rid of it: her flight was inefficacious, and absence still more pernicious to her quiet. His presence again cheared her; and that she might not again be compelled to fly, she was struggling against her internal enemy.

Attention to this amiable girl had called my thought from myself, and till she was out of all danger prevented my perceiving that Mr. Cyril's behaviour to me was not such as common intimacy, and our comparatively short acquaintance would account for. As his friends were for the most part out of London at this time, he was perpetually in Harley street, would stay late in the evening, and then, as if out of mere laziness, prefer sleeping there. He seemed to have no suspicion about Miranda, or, if he had, he endeavoured to damp her hopes by a mode of conduct that should lead her to imagine him attached to me.

Appendix D: Historical and Social Accounts of People of Color in Jamaica

[These contemporary accounts of people of color are excerpted from popular historical and social commentaries. In tone, the prejudice in Moreton's flippant, chatty anecdotes describing his interactions and sexual escapades with Creole and 'Mongrel' women of color even exceeds the vitriol present in Long's discussions of Jamaican people of color. Of the three observers, Edwards offers the most balanced, sympathetic consideration of these people, probably because his committee work on behalf of the Jamaican Assembly (see Appendix G1) brought him firsthand knowledge of the injustices they faced. Altogether, these 'histories' embody most if not all of the bilious stereotypes that long prose fictions like "The Creole" and *The Woman of Colour* are clearly written in opposition to.]

1. **From Bryan Edwards, *The History, Civil and Commercial, of the British Colonies in the West Indies Abridged from the History written by Bryan Edwards esq.* (London: Mundell & Son, Edinburgh, & J. Mundell, Glasgow, 1799) Book IV, Chap. 1, 130-35**

Of the people of mixed complexion, who are called people of colour, there are various degrees. A sambo is the offspring of a black woman by a mulatto man, or of a mulatto woman by a black man. The mulatto is the offspring of a black woman by a white man; the quadroon is the child of a mulatto woman by a white man, and the mustee of a quadroon woman by a white man. The Spaniards introduced nicer distinctions, which it is needless here to enumerate.

I believe, over all our sugar islands, the descendants of negroes by whites, whom the law entitles to the full privileges of freedom, are such as are three degrees removed from the negro venter.[1] All below this go by the general term of Mulatto.

In Jamaica there was anciently a distinction between those born of freed mothers and such as had been immediately released by the will of their owners. This arose from a maxim of law which

---

1 Womb.

originated from the mother country, and was established over the colonies, that the property of what is born accrues to the possessor of the mother. Until the year 1748, persons born under the latter circumstances, that is, whose mothers had been manumitted by their masters after their birth, were denied the trial by jury, and held unworthy of giving judicial evidence. These hardships have been in part mitigated; but much yet remains to be done. In most of the British islands, their evidence is only received in those cases where no particular act is passed in favour of the white person accused. The negro has a master to protect him from gross abuse; but the mulatto, by this partial institution, has no security against hardship and oppression. They are likewise debarred from being appointed to the lowest offices of public trust: They cannot hold the King's commission even in a black corps; nor can they vote for representatives at elections.

It is to be acknowledged, that their degraded situation is in some degree mitigated by the generosity which the members of West Indian assemblies are ready to grant to people of colour, whose education and baptism entitles them to respect even in contradiction to express statutes on the subject.

Still, however, partial instances of generosity do not justify the humiliating state of subjection to which this unfortunate people are reduced. The lowest and most worthless white will behave with insolence to the best educated free man of colour; and as contempt always degrades a character, they are unprofitable members of the community.

Whatever may be said upon the propriety or impropriety of equalizing these people with those of a different complexion, can it be denied that wisdom and humanity demand the immediate redress of one intolerable grievance? The injury I allude to is their incapability to appear as witnesses, even in cases where they complain of personal injustice. What attachment to his soil; what gratitude to the protection of laws; what motive to benefit the society to which he belongs; or, in fine, what dignity or independence of mind can that man possess, who is conscious that every miscreant of a paler complexion may insult him with impunity?

Not only from the sphere above him has the free mulatto reason to expect ill usage: Situated, as he is, in an insulated and intermediate state between the black and the white, he is despised by the one, and enviously hated by the other. The black may consider his subjection to a white man as in some measure tolerable, but the idea of being the slave of a slave he utterly abhors.

In their behaviour to whites the mulattoes are modest and

implicit. They are accused, however, (I am afraid with justice) of abusing their power over the blacks. Indeed, a different line of conduct cannot be possibly expected. The slave who is made a master is ever the most unfeeling tyrant, as the meanest parasite of prosperity is the most insolent insulter of misfortune.

There is one charge brought against the mulattoes, which, though it cannot be denied, confederation of circumstances will enable us to palliate: I mean the incontinency of their women. These are over all the West India islands maintained as kept mistresses to white men. But if we examine the situation of these unfortunate women, we shall find much more reason to blame the cruelty of their keepers, in inviting them to this disgraceful life, than of their imprudence in accepting the offer. Uninstructed in maxims of morality, untaught even in the simplest parts of education, unable to procure husbands either from among the whites or the young men of their own complexion, (the former regarding such an union as base and degrading, the latter, too degraded themselves to form such a settled connection); under such circumstances, they have a strong apology to plead for their conduct.

Besides, this connection between the keeper and the mistress, if not in the light of wedlock, is considered at least as equally innocent. They call their keeper by the endearing appellation of husband; they are faithful and affectionate to his interests; and to the rest of mankind they behave with decency and distance. Few, very few indeed, abandon themselves to that infamous species of prostitution which is openly avowed in the populous cities of Europe.

The injustice of retaining so many beautiful, and in all respects amiable women, in the disgraceful state of concubinage, demands immediate redress. But by whom shall the example be set? By the victims of this injustice it *cannot*, and by the seducers I am afraid it *will* not, be effected. To the humane dispositions of these people of colour, the most agreeable testimony is given by a respectable author, Don Antonio de Ulloa, when speaking of the forlorn and friendless circumstances to which many poor Europeans are reduced (who, emigrating to the Spanish West Indies in hopes of better fortune, can find no means of subsistence). Many of these (says the Spaniard) traverse the streets till they have nothing left to purchase food or lodgings. Wearied with going in quest of employment, affected by the disappointment of their hopes, and the unfavourable change of climate, they retire, sick and melancholy, to lie down in the squares of churches and porticoes. The people of colour here display their generosity, when the rich and selfish merchant refuses his mite to relieve their miseries. The mulatto and the negro pitying their afflictions, carry them home to their houses; they nourish comfort, and restore the poor sufferer, and if they die, say prayers for their souls. Such is the pleasing account of the generosity of the mulattoes of Carthagena, and any one acquainted with those of the other West Indies will not hesitate to ascribe the same character to them which we have here aligned to the former.

In treating of the Creoles or natives of the West Indies, and of the mulattoes or those of mixed blood, we have confined ourselves to those who are either partially or entirely white. We should now treat of the free blacks in a distinct chapter, were there any striking dissimilarity between these and the blacks in a state of slavery. Our next chapter, therefore, is appropriated to the confederation of the negro character in general.

2. **From Edward Long, *The History of Jamaica. Or, General Survey of the Antient and Modern State of That Island: with Reflections on its Situation, Settlements, Inhabitant, Climate, Products, Commerce, Laws and Government. In Three Volumes*, vol. II (London: T. Lowndes, 1774) Chap. XIII, Sec. III, 328-36**

... of all the vices reigning here; none are so flagrant as this of concubinage with white women, or cohabiting with Negresses and Mulattas, free or slaves. In consequence of this practice we have not only more spinsters in comparison to the number of women among the natives (whose brothers or male relations possess the greatest part of their father's patrimony) in this small community, than in most other parts of his majesty's dominions, proportionably inhabited; but also, a vast addition of spurious offsprings of different complexions: in a place where, by custom, so little restraint is laid on the passions, the Europeans, who at home have always been used to greater purity and strictness of manners, are too easily led aside to give a loose to every kind of sensual delight: on this account some black or yellow *quasheba* is sought for, by whom a tawney breed is produced. Many are the men, of every rank, quality, and degree here, who would much rather riot in these goatish embraces, than share the pure and lawful bliss derived from matrimonial, mutual love. Modesty, in this respect, has but very little footing here. He who should presume to shew any displeasure against such a thing as simple fornication, would for his pains be accounted a simple blockhead; since not one in twenty can be persuaded that there is either sin or shame in cohabiting with his slave. Of these men, by far the greatest part never marry after they have acquired a fortune; but usher into the world a tarnished train of beings, among whom, at their decease, they generally divide their substance. It is not a little curious, to consider the strange manner in which some of them are educated. Instead of being taught any mechanic art, whereby they might become useful to the island, and enabled to support themselves; young *Fuscus*, in whom the father fondly imagines he sees the reflected dawn of paternal genius, and Miss *Fulvia*, who mamma protests has a most delicate ear for music and French, are both of them sent early to England, to cultivate and improve the valuable talents which nature is supported to have so wantonly bestowed, and the parents, blind with folly, think they have discovered. To accomplish this end, no expence nor pains are spared; the indulgent father, big with expectation of the future *éclat* of his hopeful progeny,

> "disdains
> The vulgar tutor, and the runic school,
> To which the dull cit' sends his low-born fool.
> By our wise fire to London are they brought,
> To learn those arts that high-bred youths are taught;
> Attended, drest, and train'd, with cost and care,
> Just like some wealthy duke's apparent-heir."

Master is sent to Westminster, or Eton, to be instructed in the elements of learning, among students of the first rank that wealth and family can give: whilst Miss is placed at Chelsea,[1] or some other famed seminary; where she learns music, dancing, French, and the whole circle of female *bon ton*, proper for the accom-

---

1 Westminster and Eton are elite private schools. Located near to West-minster Abbey, Westminster School's history dates back to the 12th century; Eton secondary school was founded in 1440 by Henry VI and is still extremely popular with British royalty. Rather than referring to a particular school, Long's reference to 'Chelsea' seems to suggest the area known for its great number of fashionable and successful private schools, especially for girls. For a solid account of these Chelsea schools, see "Social history: Education: private schools," *A History of the County of Middlesex: Volume 12: Chelsea*, ed. Patricia E.C. Croot (2004) 190-95.

plishment of fine women. After much time and money bestowed on their education, and great encomiums, year after year, transmitted (by those whose interest it is to make them) on their very uncommon genius and proficiency, at length they return to visit their relations. From this period, much of their future misery may be dated. Miss faints at the sight of her relations, especially when papa tells her that black *Quasheba* is her own mother. The young gentleman too, after his introduction, begins to discover that the knowledge he has gained has only contributed to make him more susceptible of keen reflections, arising from his unfortunate birth. He is soon, perhaps, left to herd among his black kindred, and converse with *Quashe* and *Mingo*, instead of his school-fellows, *Sir George*, or *My Lord*; while mademoiselle, instead of modish French, must learn to prattle gibberish with her cousins *Mimba* and *Chloe*: for, however well this yellow brood may be received in England, yet here so great is the distinction kept up between white and mixed complexions, that very seldom are they seen together in a familiar way, though every advantage of dress or fortune should centre with the latter. Under this distinction, it is impossible but that a well-educated Mulatta must lead a very unpleasant kind of a life here; and justly may apply to her reputed father what Iphicrates said of his, "After all your pains, you have made me no better than a slave; on the other hand, my mother did every thing in her power to render me free." On first arriving here, a civilized European may be apt to think it impudent and shameful, that even bachelors should publickly avow their keeping Negroe or Mulatto mistresses; but they are still more shocked at seeing a group of white legitimate, and Mulatto illegitimate, children, all claimed by the same married father, and all bred up together under the same roof ... Habit, however, and the prevailing fashion, reconcile such scenes, and lessen the abhorrence excited by their first impression.

To allure men from these illicit connexions, we ought to remove the principal obstacles which deter them from marriage. This will be chiefly effected by rendering women of their own complexion more agreeable companions, more frugal, trusty, and faithful friends, than can be met with among the African ladies. Of some probable measures to effect this desireable purpose, and make the fair natives of this island more amiable in the eyes of the men, and more eligible partners in the nuptial state, I have already ventured my sentiments. A proper education is the first great point. A modest demeanour, a mind divested of false pride, a very moderate zeal for expensive pleasures, a skill in oeconomy, and a conduct which indicates plain tokens of good humour, fidelity, and discretion, can never fail of making converts. Much, indeed, depends on the ladies themselves to rescue this truly honourable union from that fashionable detestation in which it seems to be held; and one would suppose it no very arduous task to make themselves more companionable, useful, and esteemable, as wives, than the Negresses and Mulattas are as mistresses: they might, I am well persuaded, prove much honester friends. It is true, that, if it should be a man's misfortune to be coupled with a very profligate and extravagant wife, the difference, in respect to his fortune, is not great, whether plundered by a black or by a white woman. But such examples, I may hope, are unfrequent without the husband's concurrence; yet, whenever they do happen, the mischief they occasion is very extensive, from the apprehensions with which they strike multitudes of single men, the viler part of whom endeavour to increase the number of unhappy marriages by every base art of seduction; while others rejoice to find any such, because they seem to justify their preference of celibacy, or concubinage. In regard to the African mistress, I shall exhibit the following, as no unsuitable portrait. All her kindred, and most commonly her very paramours, are fastened upon her keeper like so many leeches; while she, the chief leech, conspires to bleed him *usque ad deliquium.*[1] In well-dissembled affection, in her tricks, cajolements, and infidelities, she is far more perfectly versed, than any adept of the hundreds of Drury. She rarely wants cunning to dupe the fool that confides in her; for who "shall teach the wily African deceit?"[2] The quintessence of her dexterity consists in persuading the man she detests to believe she is most violently smitten with the beauty of his person; in short, over head and ears in love with him. To establish this opinion, which vanity seldom fails to embrace, she now and then affects to be jealous, laments his ungrateful return for so sincere a passion; and, by this stratagem, she is better able to hide her private intrigues with her real favourites. I have seen a dear companion of this stamp deploring the loss of her deceased cull with all the seeming fervency of an honest affection, or rather of

---

1 *Usque ad deliquium* literally means "all the way to a spontaneous loss of consciousness caused by insufficient blood to the brain." Long implies that his African mistress is a 'chief leech' who bleeds her cull until he faints or swoons.

2 Joseph Addison's *Cato* (1712): "In troth, thou'rt able to instruct gray hairs, / And teach the wily African deceit!" (I.iii)

outrageous sorrow; beating her head; stamping with her feet; tears pouring down in torrents; her exclamations as wild, and gestures as emphatic, as those of an antient Roman orator in all the phrensy of a publick harangue. Unluckily, it soon appeared, that, at this very time, she had rummaged his pockets and escrutoire; and concealed his watch, ring, and money, in the featherbed upon which the poor wretch had just breathed his last. And such is the mirror of almost all these conjunctions of white and black two tinctures which nature has dissociated, like oil and vinegar. But, as if some good was generally to arise out of evil, so we find, that these connexions have been applauded upon a principle of policy; as if, by forming such alliances with the slaves, they might become more attached to the white people. Perhaps, the fruit of these unions may, by their consanguinity with a certain number of the Blacks, support some degree of influence, so far as that line of kindred extends: yet one would scarcely suppose it to have any remote effect; because they, for their own parts, despise the Blacks, and aspire to mend their complexion still more by intermixture with the Whites. The children of a White and Quateron are called English, and consider themselves as free from all taint of the Negroe race. To call them by a degree inferior to what they really are, would be the highest affront. This pride of amended blood is universal, and becomes the more confirmed, if they have received any smattering of education; for then they look down with the more supercilious contempt upon those who have had none. Such, whose mind has been a little purged from the grossest ignorance, may wish and endeavour to improve it still more; but no freed or unfreed Mulatto ever wished to relapse into the Negro. The fact is, that the opulent among them withdraw to England; where their influence, if they ever possessed any, ceases to be of any use. The middle class are not much liked by the Negroes, because the latter abhor the idea of being slaves to the descendants of slaves. And as for the lower rank, the issue of casual fruition, they, for the most part, remain in the same slavish condition as their mother; they are fellow-labourers with the Blacks and are not regarded in the least as their superiors. As for the first mentioned, it would probably be no disservice to the island, to regain all those who have abandoned it. But, to state the comparison fairly, if their fathers had married, the difference would have been this: their white offspring might have remained in the colony, to strengthen and enrich it: the Mulatto offspring desert and impoverish it. The lower class of these mixtures, who remain in the island, are a hardy race, capable of undergoing equal fatigue with the Black, above whom (in point of due policy) they ought to hold some degree of distinction. They would then form the centre of connexion between the two extremes, producing a regular establishment of three ranks of men, dependent on each other, and rising in a proper climax of subordination, in which the Whites would hold the highest place. I can foresee no mischief that can arise from the enfranchisernent of every Mulatto child. If it be objected, that such a plan may tend to encourage the illicit commerce of which I have been complaining; I reply, that it will be more likely to repress it, because, although the planters are at present very indifferent about the birth of such children upon their estates, knowing that they will either labour for them like their other slaves, or produce a good price, if their fathers should incline to purchase them; yet they will discountenance such intercourses as much as lies in their power (when it shall no longer be for their interest to connive at them), and use their endeavours to multiply the unmixed breed of their Blacks. Besides, to expect that men will wholly abstain from this commerce, if it was even liable to the severest penalties of law, would be absurd; for, so long as some men have passions to gratify, they will seek the indulgence of them by means the most agreeable, and least inconvenient, to themselves. It will be of some advantage, as things are circumstanced, to turn unavoidable evils to the benefit of society, as the best reparation that can be made for this breach of its moral and political institutions. A wise physician will strive to change an acute distemper into one less malignant; and his patient compounds for a slight chronic indisposition, so he may get relief from a violent and mortal one. I do not judge so lightly of the present state of fornication in the island, as to suppose that it can ever be more flourishing, or that the emancipation of every Mulatto child will prove a means of augmenting the annual number. The retrieving them from profound ignorance, affording them instruction in Christian morals, and obliging them to serve a regular apprenticeship to artificers and tradesmen would make them orderly subjects, and faithful defenders of the country...

In general only I may suppose, that for every such child, on its attaining the age of three years, a reasonable allowance be paid to the owner: from that period it becomes the care of the public, and might be provided for, at a cheap rate, until of an age fit for school; then be instructed in religion; and at the age of twelve apprenticed for the term of four years; after this, be regimented in his respective district, perhaps settled near a township; and, when on militia or other public duty, paid the same subsistence *per* day, or week, that is now allowed to the Marons. The expediency must be seen of having (as in the French islands) such a corps of active men, ready to scour the woods upon all occasions; a service, in which the regulars are by no means equal to them. They would likewise form a proper counter-balance to the Maron Negroes; whose insolence during formidable insurrections, has been most insufferable. The best way of securing the allegiance of these irregular people must be by preserving the treaty with them inviolate: and, at the same time, awing them into the conservation of it on their part by such a powerful equipoise, composed of men dissimilar from them in complexion and manners but equal in hardiness and vigour.

The Mulattos are, in general, well shaped, and the women well-featured. They seem to partake more of the white than the black. Their hair has a natural curl; in some it resembles the Negroe fleece; but, in general, it is of a tolerable length. The girls arrive very early at the age of puberty; and from the time of their being about twenty-five, they decline very fast, till at length they grow horribly ugly. They are lascivious; yet, considering their want of instruction, their behaviour in public is remarkably decent; and they affect a modesty that they do not feel. They are lively and sensible, and pay religious attention to the cleanliness of their persons: at the same time, they are ridiculously vain, haughty and irascible. They possess, for the most part, a tenderness of disposition, which leads them to do many charitable actions, especially to poor white persons, and makes them excellent nurses to the sick. They are fond of finery, and lavish all the money they get in ornaments, and the most expensive sorts of linen. Some few of them have intermarried here with those of their own complexion; but such matches have generally been defective and barren. They seem in this respect to be actually of the mule-kind, and not so capable of producing from one another as from a commerce with a distinct White or Black. Monsieur Buffon[1] observes that it is nothing strange that two individuals should not be able to propagate their species, because nothing more is required than some slight opposition in their temperaments, or some accidental fault in the genital organs of either of these two individuals, of different species, should produce other

---

1 Georges-Louis Leclerc, Comte de Buffon (1707-88), French naturalist, mathematician, and biologist whose work influenced Charles Darwin.

individuals, which, being unlike either of their progenitors bear no resemblance to anything fixed, and consequently cannot produce anything resembling themselves, because all that is requisite in this production is a certain degree of conformity between the form of the body and the genital organ of these different animals. Yet it seems extraordinary that two Mulattoes, having intercourse together, should be unable to continue their species, the woman either proving barren, or their offspring, if they have any, not attaining to maturity; when the same man and woman, having commerce with a White of Black, would generate a numerous issue. Some examples may possibly have occurred, where, upon the intermarriage of two Mulattos, the woman has borne children; which children have grown to maturity: but I never heard of such an instance; and may we not suspect the lady, in those cases, to have privately intrigued with another man, a White perhaps? The suspicion is not unwarrantable, if we consider how little their passions are under the restraint of morality; and that is the major part, nay almost the whole number, with very few exceptions, have been *filles de joye*[1] before they became wives. As for those in Jamaica, whom I have particularly alluded to, they married young, had received some sort of education, and lived with great repute for their chaste and orderly conduct; and with them the experiment is tried with a great degree of certainty: they produce no offspring, though in appearance under no natural incapacity of so doing with a different connexion.

3. **From J.B. Moreton, *West India Customs and Manners: Containing the Strictures on the Soil, Cultivation, Produce, Trade Officers, and Inhabitants; with the method of establishing and conducting a sugar plantation. To which is added the practice of training new slaves* (London: J Parson, 1793), 108-27**

Young ladies who have been confined to the narrow limits of Jamaica from their infancy, are soft, innocent, ambitious, flirting play-things and in a more particular manner, those who are retired in the country; when they dress, they decorate themselves elegantly: abroad they appear as neat as if they came out of bandboxes, lovely and engaging—at home, diametrically the reverse. If you surprise them, as I have often done, you will be convinced of the truth of this assertion, that Ovid, with all his metamor-

---

1 Girls of pleasure, euphemism for prostitutes. (French.)

phoses,[1] could not match such transformations: instead of the well-shaped, mild, angelic looking creature you beheld abroad, you will find, perhaps, a clumsy, greasy tomboy, or a paper-faced skeleton, romping, or stretching and lolling, from sofa to sofa, in a dirty confused hail, or piazza, with a parcel of black wenches, learning and singing obscene and filthy songs, and dancing to the tunes.

"Creole misses, when scarcely ten,
Cock their eyes and long for men."

But still as they arrive to riper age, they delight more and more in the tender passions: when they take a liking to men, though entire strangers to them, they seldom fail to shake off all manner of modesty and shame to gratify their extravagant desires:— though guarded and cooped up in their chambers by their parents, or friends, they will find ways and means to get to men,—their eyes, their looks, and fondling actions, all betray wantonness and love: their little hearts are a sort of tinder, that catch fire from every spark who flatters their vanity, and whispers them soft nonsense:—they are pliable as wax, and melt like butter; and though naturally delicate in their texture, they are fondest of strong, stout-backed men...

Notwithstanding the little foibles of Creole women, they have many good qualifications, and are vastly better than the men, and much cleanlier in some respects than British or Irish women. It is often the case for the little innocent country misses to make love to men, though strangers, by billetdoux or messages: I have been sometimes honoured with importunities of this kind, and did not reject their offers; as much as I could learn, the summit of their wishes was only to "please their inclinations," (as they say in their songs). Their ideas of marriage and the solemn engagement of the connubial tye, are rather superficial: and that may be well accounted for from what I have already said, as they seldom or never go to church; and though taught a smattering of reading and writing, are obligated to negroe and mungrel wenches for the principal part of their education, amongst whom they see nothing from their infancy but

---

1 The Roman poet Ovid wrote a fifteen-book poem, *Metamorphoses*, to explain the creation and history of the world in terms of Greek and Roman mythology. Transformation is the unifying theme which Ovid uses to bring together this vast collection of narratives.

jilting, intrigues, and scenes of obscenity. Says the little wanton miss with Rochester,

"Marriage! O hell and furies, name it not."[1]

Or, with Pope,

"Not Caesar's empress would I deign to prove,
No—make me mistress of the man I love."[2]

A man who enters into the marriage bond with a Creole lady who has poor relations or friends, though he gets some property with her, will repent his bargain, and will find himself disagreeably circumstanced in various respects; for it will not be his wife and little progeny alone he will have to provide for, but all the poor brothers and sisters, uncles and aunts, cousins and half-cousins of his good-natured spouse; nor can he without offending her prevent their hanging on; nor will they endeavour to provide for themselves, or descend to honest industry, whilst they are supported by him in idleness:—his better half tells him, "My dear, if you love me, you should love my relations and friends also; my dear, if you wish to support me and my little ones, you should support them also:" hence it would be, "As you married me, you should marry them also;" the equations are all equal—fine Algebra!

When a little miss makes a slip, it is soon over-looked by her indulgent parents or fond friends; she will love a man dearly for making her a mother, till which time she is a maid; and the dear little pledge of their stolen bliss will be tenderly nursed; but it commonly happens when they wish to conceal their tricks, that they are sent to Europe for their education; one of them seldom remains any time in England, till fame sounds "a rich West Indian heiress." She soon gets a number of admirers, and at last some English sharper, Irish fortune-hunter, or Scotch gentleman worth nothing, makes her an honest woman.

After Creole masters and misses have been some years in England, and introduced into all the fashionable pleasures and

---

1 John Wilmot, Earl of Rochester (1647-80) "A Satyr Against Marriage" (1680) (21).
2 Alexander Pope (1688-1744) "Eloisa to Abelard": "Not Caesar's Empress would I deign to prove; / No, make me mistress to the man I love;" (87-88).

vices of London, Bath, Bristol, &c, and return to their native regions, everything seems flat and insipid to them: they cannot bear to live peaceably and quiet on their plantations—no, they must have superb houses and grand retinues in town, far beyond their abilities; and there again their restless passions are at war: Miss Jenny Gauva, nor master Billy Pompion, cannot endure the sultry heat of the climate, nor the vulgar insipid conversation and disagreeable company of Miss Marice Firefly, Miss Kitty Bare-bones, Tommy Caliloo, or Jacky Salamander, their once favourite companions; no, dear London for ever. Ranelagh, Vauxhall, Sadler's Wells,[1] and the theatres, are their themes; nay, even their poor faithful slaves though once their youthful companions, whose calibashes they often assisted to drain when full of high-seasoned pepperpot, are become filthy brutes or hottentots to them:—no, dear England's white-headed, white-legged, swing-ingly polite and obliging footmen and waiters for ever. But this great and affected nicety soon wears off, till they return to their original creolism.

"Send a goose to Dover,
And a goose it will come over."[2]

...I once lived contiguous to a few families of these soft authors of delight, and spent many, happy vacant hours among them: their rural habitations were to me terrestrial paradises—but one was an elysium: when the scorching toils of the day were over, I often escorted them along lime or cane intervals, and sometimes through thickets of Guinea grass six or seven feet high, to pluck star apples, neeseberries, oranges, &c. &c. at the neighbouring

---

1 All fashionable places of pleasure. Ranelagh was a public pleasure garden in Chelsea. It was considered much more fashionable than its older rival, the Vauxhall Gardens in Kennington. Founded in 1683 by Richard Sadler as a place of entertainment, and briefly popular for the medicinal wells that were subsequently found on his property, Sadler's Wells put on pantomimes, variety acts and light opera in London during the summer months when the Theatres Royal (Covent Garden and Drury Lane) were on hiatus.

2 Moreton is paraphrasing the first verse of the song "The Pink of Maca-ronies" sung in John O'Keeffe's *Agreeable Surprise* (1781): "In Jacky Bull, when bound for France, / The gosling you discover; / But taught to ride, to fence, to dance, / A finish'd goose comes over. / With his tierce and carte,—fa! fa! / And his cotillion so smart—ha! ha! / He charms each female heart—oh! la! / As Jacky returns from Dover."

gardens and orangeries; and when the starry mantled night over-spread her sable canopy, and luna only guided our steps, we frequently went to a river, where we all bathed naked together, without restraint or formality.

"In murmuring Mina oft and oft again,
We brac'd our limbs and gambol'd in the stream."[1]

I was well acquainted with a widow lady and her two daughters, who lived in a lonely retired part of the country surrounded by hills and woods, where they had a plantation and about one hundred and forty slaves; the old lady, well knowing from her own youthful experience how brittle female ware was, anxiously wished to dispose of her daughters to advantage, and was remarkably attentive to every gentleman who frequented her house; at a certain time she invited a number of gentlemen to a dinner, in hopes that some of them would be smitten; for five or six days preceding this great and grand entertainment, every thing was hurry, bustle, and confusion: the house was washed inside and outside, the floors and piazzas of fine cedar were rubbed with wax, and shone like polished mahogany; the young ladies chamber was cleared of all nasty trumpery, and exposed to view. At last the day appointed came ... At length the gentlemen crouded, and the tables were quickly overspread with an amazing number of dishes, five times more than ever I have seen at an Irish wedding.

Presently Miss Louisa and Miss Laura (as I shall call them) made their appearance; they were gaudy and elegantly dressed, and extremely tight laced; their cheeks had been artfully scorched with red peppers, which gave them beautiful blushes: they seemed all lovely, all divine; nor did their female sable attendants, which were dressed in white, as emblems of innocence, cut a despicable figure.

During dinner the gentlemen were as polite as possible to the young ladies, each endeavouring with all his might to insinuate himself into their good graces, by the eloquence of his eyes and tongue. "Pray, Miss Louisa, will you permit me to help you to a

1 Moreton might be evoking the spirit of these lines from Mark Akenside's *The Pleasures of the Imagination* (1744): "When joined at eve, / Soft-murmuring streams and gales of gentlest breath / Melodious Philomela's wakeful strain / Attemper, could not man's discerning ear / Through all its tones the sympathy pursue" (471-75).

bit of the turkey; it is very fine!" "Tank you, sir, wid all my haut." "Pray miss, what part do you like best?" "Sir, Ise don't love turkey rump—Ise love turkey bubby." Miss Laura was taken notice of for having no appetite; though she was pressed by the different gentlemen, she could eat nothing—at length a military gentleman who sat next to her, asked her if she was indisposed, what could it be that affected her, that it made him very unhappy: Little miss replied, "O sir, Ise can't tell." Her mother then peremptorily demanded to know what was the matter with her?— and Laura replied, "Me quite sorry mamma, Ise went in a bush today to do my —, and Yellow Legs come, and he knaum my—, and him puke; O I'm quite sorry for poor Yellow Legs!" At which uncouth expression some of the company smiled, and I was in pain for poor Laura, for she was my favourite. The fact appeared to be this: she had been that forenoon, as usual, in the cook-room, where she ate a calabash full of substantial pepperpot; it had a purgative effect on her, she had a necessary call backwards, and her favourite lap dog, Yellow Legs, followed her; you may guess the rest...

After the gentlemen were all departed, miss Louisa and miss Laura took off their stays, and put on their romping frocks, and asked me to take a walk with them, as usual; during the excursion through a spacious and delightful garden, imbowered with shaddock, cushue, cocoa-nut, orange, and other fruit trees, we at length seated ourselves in a lonely and lovely arbour of grape and granadillo vines, where delicious fruit were pendant all round, whilst the mocking birds were warbling their melodious strains; miss Louisa and miss Laura sung most charming catches, which inspired me with ideas different from what I before entertained; on our return through a plantain walk, we went intentionally astray...

From what I have said you will, I suppose, conclude that I have been a vile profligate, and that it is ungenerous in me to expose the foibles in young ladies, by whom I was so much favoured. In answer thereto, I only write to you as a friend; and was you now in Jamaica, you might never find out the families I allude to, for I have concealed their names and places of abode: and I still regard the young ladies, though I abhor their manners and customs; I think it is to be lamented that in such a flourishing island as Jamaica, there are not proper seminaries for the instruction of both sexes, of those whose parents cannot afford them an European education; those seminaries should be well supplied with English masters and mistresses whose abilities and morals would bear strict scrutiny; also, with men and maid servants from England. The children should be put to school at an early age; nor should they have any intercourse, if possible, with any of the black or tawny race, to corrupt their dialect and morals.

I think it is very necessary that every man should study the nature and dispositions of different women, as well as of men; and he cannot get a proper knowledge of the former without some sinful experience, disease and expence: I would recommend it, even to my son, to get introduced into a bawdy house at times, but to be particular in his choice of the company who introduced him, as to their friendship and integrity; and if he got a few comfortable kickings, with two or three smart touches of a fashionable disease, so that he got properly cured again, to make a long and lasting impression on his mind, and after trying the tempers and dispositions of other women, their strength and weakness, &c. he would be cool as ice to the ogling incitations of jilting coquets, and the vile allurements of distempered harlots, who with fictitious smiles and aching hearts procure their existances: he would shun their dens of infamy, and detest their horrid keepers, wicked hags of hell; and if his constitution was not too far impaired, he might make a prudent loving husband, a good father, and a good master; he would know the value of a truly virtuous woman better than the bashful youth who never went astray. "Who can find a virtuous woman? For her price is far above rubies."[1]

Do not imagine from what I have said, that every Creole lady is so soft and ignorant as Miss Louisa and Miss Laura. I have mentioned before, that those who are educated properly from their infancy are as chaste and well bred women as any in the world; I only point particularly at those who receive their education amongst negroe wenches, and imbibe great part of their dialect, principles, manners and customs ...

Having thus far endeavoured to give you some idea of Creole men and women, I shall next treat of Mongrels; a Mongrel is any thing that is engendered or begotten between different kinds, and resembles neither in nothing but form; such as a mule that is begot between an ass and a mare; or in the human species, a Sambo, that is begot by a Mulatto and a black: a Mulatto, that is begot by a white and a black: a Mestee, that is begot between a white and a Mulatto: a Quadroon, that is begot between a white

1 Proverbs 31:10.

and a Mestee, &c. &c. A Sambo is of a sooty dark brown colour, with hair or coarse wool, like that of a negroe, but rather longer; a Mulatto is of a yellow sickly colour, without the least tincture of rosy bloom; a Mestee is much fairer than a Mulatto, but of a sickly hue; a Quadroon is as fair as some whites, but rather delicate and sickly inclined. When Mongrels of different kinds copulate together, they beget Mongrels differing from themselves, of which there may be innumerable gradations; for in my opinion, Mongrels, though thirty generations distant from blacks blood, cannot be real whites.

All Mongrels, male and female, have a vast share of pride and vanity, baseness and ingratitude in their compositions: their delicacy and ignorance being such, that they despise and degrade their parents and relations inclining to the sable race; the men, if born to estates or properties (as many are), are much of the same nature of the illiterate white Creole men; not much inferior, but of course more negrofied; and when they are not kept at a proper distance and under due subjection, are often very insolent and impudent. When those spurious cubs, having no trades, squander what their infatuated parents bequeathed them, they turn out the most thieving pilfering vagrants; for never having practised any industry, but beggared themselves by their profligacy and dissipation, Creole fashion, they are quite ignorant ever after of the ways and means to earn their livelihoods industriously and honestly. If a gentleman wished his Mongrel son to do well, he should do nothing more for him than to give him a smattering of reading, writing and arithmetic, to procure his freedom, and bind him at an early age to a trade, during which time to stint him in both money and cloaths, and to convince him that he might never expect any other favours; in such case, he might labour for a livelihood, and come to some good. I knew a Mulatto man in Spanish-Town, whose father did little more for him than to procure his manumission, and bind him to a millwright; and this very man in the year 1784, when I was in Jamaica, was attorney for thirty or forty plantations, and supposed to be worth 4 or 500*l*. sterling.

As for Mongrel women, though the daughters of rich men, and though possessed of slaves and estates they never think of marriage; their delicacy is such, for they are extremely proud, vain and ignorant, that they despise men of their own colour; and though they have their amorous desires abundantly gratified by them and black men secretly, they will not avow these connections. It would be considered an indeniable stain in the character of a white man to enter into a matrimonial bondage with one of them; he would be despised in the community, and excluded from all society on that account.

"All men shou'd wed with their similitude;
Like shou'd with like in love and years engage,"

When one of them gets a child as brown or browner than herself, it is considered a very great blemish in her character; on the contrary, if it chances to be fairer, it is her greatest pride and glory: her friends and relations rejoice—the bantling is handled and dandled—the father is flattered and praised—"a man, for true"—the mother is caressed—a joyful mother! On which account females use every art to set themselves off to the best advantage, to make themselves pleasing and engaging companions for white men; and when one of them is disbanded by the man who had her in keeping, (or as they say, she had in keeping) she plumps up her breasts like an innocent virgin, or wanton bashful bride, visits balls and plays, and stroles about until she is picked up by somebody else. They are very artful, and dispose of their ware to the greatest advantage; maidenheads are very inticing; and though their arms have been as common as the chairs of barbers for years, they will impose themselves for maids; for in these cases they are more knowing than whites. I have often met many fine looking Mongrel girls, young and innocent to appearance, as deceptious as any Covent Garden country miss.

Some men are so weak and silly as to think that black girls will not suit their purposes, and bargain with the parents of Mongrels to hire their daughters for the use of prostitution. Nay, even Creole ladies, as I have said before, will hire their negroe wenches to white men for that use. If you wish to get a fine young Mongrel, you must solicit the favour of the mistress, or give five pounds to the black mother as well as to the tawny daughter.— They say in their song,

"Come, carry me in a room;
Come, carry me in a room;
And give them five pound piece.

Come, carry me in a room;
Come, carry me in a room;
And lay me on the bed."

The black women use every means to draw young men to their rookeries, in order to prostitute their daughters; I have been often compelled by the mother to spend a whole night with her gingerbread daughter.—Those gypsies have a wonderful ascendancy over men, and have injured many, both powerful and subordinate; the poor slaves on a plantation are obliged to pay them as much adoration as the Portuguese do the Hostess or Virgin Mary;[1] for the government of the cow-skin depends in a great measure on their smiles or frowns; therefore I beg, whatever department of life may be your lot, that you will keep your employer's bosom-gipsy modestly at a distance; that is, not to be free or familiar with her, and not to be respectful or impudent to her, whereby you will loose your consequence, and she will insult you; and do not quarrel with her if possible.

Never strive to seduce your friend or employer's kept-mistress, for it is mean, and will injure you with batchelors in general; but if she haunts you, so that you cannot well avoid her, do not be a Joseph: I was once plagued by a letcherous tawny whore, who followed me in every private room, singing bawdy catches, with wanton gestures, and luring and lascivious invitations; and because that I acted through principle, and had nothing to do with her, the deceitful Mrs. Potipher,[2] the vile incendiary, the damnable daemon of iniquity, artfully insinuated all the base stratagems which her malicious heart could devise against me; by which means my employer treated me so ill, that I was obliged to discharge myself.

---

1 By "Hostess," Moreton is probably referring to St. Martha, the sister of Mary and Lazarus, who was known for the illustrious hospitality she gave to Jesus when he stayed in Bethany.

2 Moreton is evoking the story in Genesis 39 in which Joseph rises to become overseer in the house of Potiphar, an Egyptian captain. In this exalted position, Joseph is sexually propositioned a number of times by Potiphar's wife, whom he continually refuses to "lie" with. During one such occasion, Joseph runs away from Mrs. Potiphar's advances only to find that she has managed to grab his clothing off his back as he leaves. In a fit of pique at his continued rejection, she uses this clothing as evidence to accuse Joseph of attempted rape. Potiphar immediately throws him into prison. But in prison, Joseph is vindicated "because the Lord was with him." By illustrating his experiences as a principled yet persecuted 'Joseph,' Moreton gives his male readers carte blanche to act upon their sexual appetites with mulatto women since his own life illustrates that there is nothing for them to gain (and everything to lose) from maintaining a sexually principled stance.

Appendix E: People of Color in British Epistolary Narratives

[Taken from real and fictional epistolary narratives, these selections highlight two of the ways that people of color influenced British society. In three of these letters, people of color are called "prints," "shadows," and 'Mongrels'—pejoratives that, collectively, embody their marginal status as negative reproductions— inferior byproducts of unions between original black and white people. These letter writers depend on such 'negative reproductions' for developing and refining British standards of beauty, class, and culture. Wesley, on the other hand, is decidedly more positive in his consideration of the "poor African" even though his letter was written at a time when reports of a slave rebellion in Dominica were alarming Britons and turning them against the idea of abolition. Wesley would die a mere eight days after he wrote to Wilberforce. But his letter is a potent reminder to the statesman of the religious, national and human villainy that slavery engenders—an image that surely stayed with Wilberforce even after he unsuccessfully argued for the abolition of the slave trade in Parliament in April 1791. Altogether, the people of color represented on the margins of British epistolary narratives certainly play a central role in establishing the criteria by which eighteenth-century Britons came to understand their own national identifications with 'Britishness,' morality, and 'whiteness.']

1. **From Richard Griffith, *The Gordian Knot: or, Dignus Vindice Nodus. A Novel. In Letters* (Dublin: P. Wilson, J. Exshaw, H. Saunders, W. Sleater, D. Chaberline, J. Potts, J. Hoey, and J. Williams, 1769) Vol. IV, Part II, Letter LXXIX, 44**

Sir Thomas Medway, To Mr. Sutton.
Windsor.
I have returned hither, because I would be at home, and now there is no other spot in England, where I feel I have any manner of connection...

But to return to Windsor.—Philosophers say, falsely, that beauty is arbitrary; that use, custom, or habit, alone, establishes its empire. I shall leave them to argue it, in architecture, or all the rest of the arts and sciences; but with regard, to the *human face divine*, the Europeans must certainly bear the *belle*, against all the negro nations, *under the sun*.

For, not to insist on the preference of a white skin, before a black one, which may be but an arbitrary idea, yet surely the difference of colours, in the blueness of the veins, the suffusion of the cheeks, with the contrast of the hair, must afford a more pleasing variety to the eye, than mere black and white can possibly do. We are *pictures*, they but *prints*.

2. From Hester Thrale, "Letter To Mrs. Pennington," No. 5 George St., Manchester Square, *Saturday, June 19, 1802*, in *The Letters of Mrs. Thrale*, selected with an introduction by R. Brimley Johnson (London: John Lane the Bodley Head Ltd., 1926) 143

Well! I am really haunted by *black shadows*. Men of colour in the rank of gentlemen; a black Lady cover'd with finery, in the Pit at the Opera, and tawny children playing in the squares,—the gardens of the Squares I mean,—with their Nurses, afford ample proofs of Hannah More and Mr. Wilberforce's[1] success towards breaking down the *wall of separation*. Oh! how it falls on every side! and spreads its tumbling ruins on the world! Leaving all ranks, all customs, all colours, all religions *jumbled together*, till like the old craters of an exhausted volcano, Time closes and covers with fallacious green each ancient breach of distinction; preparing us for the moment when we shall be made *one fold under one Shepherd*,[2] fulfilling the voice of prophecy.

---

1 Hannah More (1745-1833) poet, dramatist, member of Samuel Johnson's literary circle, philanthropist, and moral and religious writer. William Wilberforce (1759-1833) was an outstanding English parliamentarian and one of the main advocates responsible for bringing about the abolition of the slave trade in 1807.

2 From John 10:14-16: "I am the Good Shepherd; I know My sheep, and My sheep know Me—just as the Father knows Me and I know the Father—and I lay down My Life for the sheep. I have other sheep which are not of this fold. I must bring them also. They will hear My Voice, and there will be One Flock, and One Shepherd."

3. From Clara Reeve, *Plans of Education with remarks on the system of other writers. In a series of Letters between Mrs. Darnford and her friends* (London: T. Hookham and J. Carpenter, 1792) 89-93, 96

LETTER XI.
LADY A—TO MRS. DARNFORD.

Do not be angry with me, my dear Mrs. Darnford!—It is so natural to communicate our pleasures to those we love best, that I could not forbear shewing your letters to Lord A—. He was surprised to find you so deep in knowledge of a national kind, and pleased to see you entering so warmly into the best interests of mankind. He is pleased that you have defended a due subordination of rank, and that you do not wish the boundaries thrown down, and all men put upon a level; because he thinks, that in their different degrees and occupations men are most useful to each other, and that the result is the harmony of the whole.

My lord says, he can strengthen your arguments against the emancipation of the negroes, by two considerations; the first is, the present consequences; the second, the future. The first seems to be already coming forward; namely, that the negroes, being apprized of the steps that have been taken here in their favour, are preparing to rise against their masters, and to cut their throats. We have heard of very late rebellions, that have, with difficulty, been crushed, and we may expect to hear of more daily.

The second consequence to be expected is, that when the great point shall be carried for them, they will flock hither from all parts, mix with the natives, and spoil the breed of the common people. There cannot be a greater degradation than this, of which there are too many proofs already in many towns and villages.

The gradations from a negro to a white are many: first, a black and a white produce a mulatto; secondly, a mulatto with a white produce a mestee; thirdly, a mestee and a white produce a quadroon, a dark yellow; the quadroon and a white, a sallow kind of white, with the negro shade, and sometimes the features. All these together produce a vile mongrel race of people, such as no friend to Britain can ever wish to inhabit it.

These considerations should be recommended to the patrons

of the Black Bill of Rights;[1] perhaps they may not have reflected upon these points, and the mischiefs they contain.

The king of the French, when he was king of France, banished all the negroes from his country;[2] it would be wise to do so in Britain, while it is yet in our power.

You are to understand this reasoning to proceed from my lord; who says farther, that he has no doubt to call the negroes an inferior race of men, but still a link of the universal chain, and, as men, entitled to humanity, to kindness, and to protection; and he thinks, their masters ought to be amenable to the laws, if they overwork, or otherwise ill-treat them.

If we have known an Ignatius Sancho, and a Phillis Wheatly,[3] they are exceptions to the general rules of judgment, and may be compared with a Bacon and a Milton,[4] among the most civilised and refined of the race of Europeans.

Thus much is for my lord, and as a return for your thoughts, which you have communicated to us. For myself, I have travelled

---

1 Probably a reference to the abolition bill that William Wilberforce introduced into parliament in 1791. It was soundly defeated by a 75 vote margin (163/88).

2 Perhaps an oblique (and, if so, incorrect) reference to either of two declarations (1738 and 1777 [*Déclaration du roi pour la police des noirs*]) both of which re-articulated the conditions under which colonists could bring slaves to France without losing them. Both declarations were amendments to the Edict of 1716 that originally allowed slave importations to France. These declarations were aimed at reducing the number of free blacks in France by policing their introduction to French society and limiting their ability to stay if manumitted. The 1777 law also prohibited the entry of all blacks, mulattoes and other people of color into France.

3 Ignatius Sancho (c. 1729-80) was a friend of David Garrick, correspondent of Laurence Sterne, and mentor to Julius Soubise. His own collection of letters was published posthumously in 1782 to great public acclaim as a testimony of the intellectual capabilities of the African. A contemporary of Sancho's and celebrated by him in one of his letters, Phillis Wheatley (1753-84) was an African child-prodigy poet from Massachusetts whose poems were published to great public acclaim in England in 1773.

4 Sir Francis Bacon (1561-1626), statesman, celebrated philosopher, and poet best known for his work as defender of the scientific revolution. John Milton (1608-74), well known for *Paradise Lost* (1667) and many other poetic classics.

with you through all your gradations to the bottom of the valley; and shall be happy to climb up again with you; for I perceive you mean to ascend by the same gradation, and to give us your Plan of Education for each, as you go along...

LETTER XII
Mrs. Darnford to Lady A—.
Indeed, madam, I owe you no thanks for shewing my letters to my Lord A—. You expect me to be sincere; I did not intend them for his inspection: but his remarks are very just, and his arguments strengthen mine....

4. John Wesley, "Letter to William Wilberforce," Balam, February 24, 1791

Dear Sir:

Unless the divine power has raised you up to be as *Athanasius contra mundum*,[1] I see not how you can go through your glorious enterprise in opposing that execrable villainy which is the scandal of religion, of England, and of human nature. Unless God has raised you up for this very thing, you will be worn out by the opposition of men and devils. But if God be fore you, who can be against you? Are all of them together stronger than God? O be not weary of well doing! Go on, in the name of God and in the power of his might, till even American slavery (the vilest that ever saw the sun) shall vanish away before it.

Reading this morning a tract wrote by a poor African,[2] I was particularly struck by that circumstance that a man who has a black skin, being wronged or outraged by a white man, can have no redress; it being a "law" in our colonies that the oath of a black against a white goes for nothing. What villainy is this?

That he who has guided you from youth up may continue to strengthen you in this and all things, is the prayer of, dear sir,
Your affectionate servant,
John Wesley

---

1 "Athanasius arrayed against the world." Dubbed the "Father of Orthodoxy," Athanansius (c. 296-373) was one of the greatest champions and defenders of Catholic beliefs.
2 Perhaps referring to Olaudah Equiano's *Interesting Narrative*, which was published in 1789.

Appendix F: The Woman of Colour: Contemporary Reviews

[Advertisements in the *Morning Chronicle* newspaper on Tuesday 25th and Monday 31st October, 1808, refer to *The Woman of Colour* under "books published this day"; however, as indicated below, reviews do not start appearing until 1810.]

1. *The British Critic* (March 1810): 299

The writer tells us in his title page, that he is the author also of "Light and Shade," "The Aunt and Niece," "Edersfield Abbey," &c. &c. What can be the fate of all these books? How soon must they return from whence they came, filthy rags? Yet it must be confessed that this Woman of Colour is by no means illiterate or without ingenuity of contrivance; the moral also is excellent. It is, that there is no situation in which the mind may not resist misfortune by proper resignation to the will of heaven. It is very hard after all, that the poor heroine does not get a husband, for she is made very much to deserve one.

2. *The Critical Review* (May 1810): 108–09

The author of this work tells us, that the moral he would deduce from the story of the Woman of Colour is 'that there is no situation, in which the mind, which is strongly imbued with the truths of our *most holy faith*, and the consciousness of a divine *Disposer* of *events* may not *resist itself* against misfortune, and become resigned to its fate.' All this may be very true but we have our doubts of the morality of this tale. We do not see what good is to accrue from reading a story, in which an amiable female is despoiled of her name and station in society, through the machinations of a rejected and jealous woman, and three worthy characters made wretched for no one reason in the world. Olivia Fairfield, the Woman of Colour, comes over to England with a fine fortune to marry her cousin, by the desire of her late father; if she does not do this, her fortune is forfeited. This cousin is represented as amiable and handsome. They are united; and the good and superior qualities of Olivia engage the esteem of her husband in spite of her colour. She is happy in possessing this esteem and displays much good sense and feeling. It however turns out that her husband had two years before clandestinely married a beautiful girl, who was dependant on his brother's wife; and as this wife wished to have married Augustus Merton, instead of the brother, she determined to wreck her vengeance on her rival. She accordingly makes her believe, that she was seduced by a false marriage; and, in the absence of her husband, sends her into a remote country, and on his return propagates a report of her death which is believed, and he afterwards marries his cousin of colour. She then removes the former wife and contrives to throw her in the way of her husband; her re-appearance makes all the confusion that can be wished; and of course the Woman of Colour's marriage is null and void. The author has endeavoured to throw into the character of Olivia, a wonderful quantity of magnanimity, fortitude, and religion, and has, in some measure, succeeded. But Olivia is rather too methodistical; *providence* is for ever in her mouth; she indulges a little too liberal in her use of the *Most High*, and plumes herself too much on her religious duties, and her quotations from Scripture. The character of her black servant Dido, is the most natural of any. Mrs. George Merton evinces a malignity, which we trust is unnatural; and the East Indian Nabobs family present nothing new.

3. *The Monthly Review* (June 1810): 212

On our first perusal of this tale, we wished for a greater display of retributive justice in the events, until the fair author reminded us that the best rewards of virtue and the severest penalties of vice are not dependent on external circumstances.—She is too apt to 'express the jests' in italics, though some of them perhaps would never be 'smoked' without that illustration: but her style is easy and unaffected, and her story is interesting; while the useful aim and good principles of the novel are deserving of commendation.

Appendix G: Jamaican Petitions, Votes of the Assembly, and an Englishman's Will

[Jamaicans, like James Craggs, often petitioned the Jamaican Assembly to allow their illegitimate, mixed-race children access to rights and privileges routinely enjoyed by all classes of whites. These records indicate that heiresses of color also did so on behalf of their children. The petitions of Patience Hermitt and Susannah Young were "assented to" and became 'Acts' after three favorable readings of their bills before the Jamaican Assembly. Such Acts entitled Hermitt, Young, and their respective offspring "the same rights and privileges with English subjects born of white parents, under certain restrictions." Alternately, Andrew Wright's will, notarized under English law, presents another way that a white father could secure significant property and monies to his 'reputed' children and get around the 1761 Jamaican Act designed 'to restrain and limit ... exorbitant grants and devises made by white persons to negroes and the issue of negroes' (passed 19th December 1761, Act 28).]

1. **From *Votes of the Honourable House of Assembly of Jamaica, ... Begun the 25th October, ... 1791 ... And ended the 15th of March, 1792 Being the Third, Fourth and Fifth Sessions of the Present Assembly* (Saint Jago de la Vega: Printed by Alexander Aikman, 1792)**

Page 83

A petition of James Craggs, of the parish of Vere, esquire, was presented to the house, and read, setting forth,

"That, by an act of the legislature of this island, made and passed in the year of our Lord 1761, entitled, 'An act to prevent the inconveniences arising from exorbitant grants and devises made by white persons to negroes, and the issue of negroes; and to restrain and limit such grants and devises,' the petitioner is prevented from making such disposition of his estate and fortune as he is inclined to do, unto his reputed son and daughters, named John Craggs, Elizabeth Craggs, and Susanna Craggs, free quadroons, the children of Ann Summers, of the parish of Vere, a free mulatto woman, and which said children have been severally baptized and instructed in the principles of the Christian religion, and have been educated in a decent and reputable manner:

"And praying, that the house will give leave for a bill to be brought in, for enabling the petitioner to settle and dispose of his estate, real and personal, by deed or will, in such manner as he shall think proper, notwithstanding the said act:"

Ordered, That the above petition be referred to Mr. Osborn, Mr. Anderson, and Mr. Turner; that they enquire into the allegations therein set forth, and report the facts, with their opinion thereon, to the house.

Page 76

A petition of Patience Hermitt, of the parish of St. Catherine, a free mulatto woman, on behalf of herself and of Mary Hermitt, Benjamin Hume-Hermitt, William Hermitt, Catherine Hermitt, and Ann Hermitt, free quadroons, the children of the said Patience Hermitt, was presented to the House and read, setting forth,

"That the petitioner hath been baptized, educated, and instructed in the principles of the Christian Religion, and in the Communion of the Church of England, as by law established, and hath been decently brought up; and hath caused her said several children to be baptized, and, as they arrived at a proper age, hath brought them up in the same principles, and given them such an education as will enable them to earn their livelihood in an honest and industrious manner, and put them on a more respectable footing than people of colour are in general; but, from the unfortunate circumstance of their births, they are subject and liable to the same pains and penalties with persons of that complexion who have been brought up in ignorance an idleness:

"And praying that the House will give leave for a bill to be brought in for granting to her and her said children, and their issue, the like privileges as have heretofore been granted to persons in the same circumstances."

Ordered, That the above petition be referred to Mr. Bryan Edwards, Mr. Shirley, and Mr. Rodon, that they enquire into the allegations therein set forth, and report the facts, with their opinion thereon, to the House.

Pages 91-92

Mr. Bryan Edwards, from the committee to whom the petition of Patience Hermitt, of the parish of St. Catherine, a free mulatto woman, on behalf of herself, and of her several children, Mary Hermitt, Benjamin Hume-Hermitt, William Hermitt, Catherine Hermitt, and Anne Hermitt, free quadroons, was referred, reported, that the committee had enquired into the allegations set forth in the said petition, and do find they are true, and are of opinion that a committee should be appointed to bring in a bill agreeably to the prayer of the said petition.

Resolved, That the House do agree to the report.

Ordered, That Mr. Bryan Edwards, Mr. Shirley, and Mr. Rodon, be a committee for that purpose.

Page 96

A petition of Susannah Young, of the parish of St Elizabeth, a free mulatto woman, on behalf of herself and of her several children, William Salmon, John Salmon. Charles Salmon, Edward Salmon, Sarah Salmon, Ann Salmon, and Susannah Young Salmon, free quadroons, was presented to the House and read, setting forth,

"That the petitioner has been baptized, educated, and instructed, in the principles of the Christian Religion, and in the communion of the Church of England, as by law established, and hath caused her said children, William Salmon, John Salmon, Charles Salmon, Edward Salmon, Sarah Salmon, Ann Salmon, and Susannah Young Salmon, to be baptized, all of whom, except the youngest, are sent to England, there to be brought up and educated in the same religious principles:

"That the petitioner begs leave to represent, that she is possessed of property, real and personal in this island, sufficient to maintain herself and her children and to place them in situations much more respectable than that of free people of colour in general, but, from the unfortunate circumstances of their births, the petitioner and her children are subject to the same pains and penalties to which free-people are liable who have no property:

"And praying that the House will give leave to bring in a bill granting to the petitioner and her children, and their future issue, such privileges as have been heretofore granted to persons under the like circumstances."

Ordered, That the above petition be referred to Mr. Vanheelen, Mr. Lewis, and Mr. Bryan Edwards, that they enquire into the allegations therein set forth, and report the facts, vita their opinion thereon, to the House.

Page 106

Mr. Vanheelen, from the committee to whom the petition of Susannah Young, of the parish of St Elizabeth, a free mulatto woman, on behalf of herself and of her several children, named William Salmon, John Salmon, Charles Salmon, Edward Salmon, Sarah Salmon, Ann Salmon, and Elizabeth Young Salmon, free quadroons, was referred, reported that the committee had enquired into the allegations set forth in the said petition, and do find they are true, and are of opinion that a committee should be appointed to prepare and bring in a bill agreeably to the prayer of the said petition.

Resolved, That the House do agree, to the report.

Ordered, That Mr. Vanheelen, Mr. Lewis, and Mr. Bryan Edwards, be a committee for that purpose.

Pages 120-21

Mr. Bryan Edwards, according to order, presented to the House a bill to entitle Patience Hermitt, of the parish of St. Catherine, a free mulatto woman, and Mary Hermitt, Benjamin Hume-Hermitt, William Hermitt, Catherine Hermitt, and Ann Hermitt, free quadroons, the children of the said Patience Hermitt to the same rights and privileges with English subjects born of white parents, under certain restrictions; which was received and read the first time.

Ordered, That the said bill be read a second time on Monday next...

Mr. Vanheelen, according to order, presented to the House a bill to entitle Susannah Young, of the parish of St. Elizabeth, a free mulatto woman, and William Salmon, John Salmon; Charles Salmon, Edward Salmon, Sarah Salmon, Ann Salmon, and Elizabeth Young Salmon free quadroons, the children of the said Susannah Young, to the same rights and privileges with English subjects born of white parents, under certain restrictions, which was received and read the first time.

Ordered, That the said bill be read a second, time on Monday next.

2. From Andrew Wright's "Last Will and Testament" (1806)

I Andrew Wright of the Parish of Saint Elizabeth in the County of Cornwall in the Island of Jamaica Esquire but now residing in

Great Tower Street in London do make publish and declare this to be my last will and testament in manner and form following...

...in trust to pay and apply a competent part of the residue of the ... monies to arise from the sale of the said produce and consignments aforesaid for the ... education and benefit of my reputed daughters Ann Wright and Rebecca Wright born of the body of Ruth Sinclair until such of my said daughters as shall be last living under the age of twenty one years and unmarried shall attain that age or be married or die which ever of the said last mentioned events shall first happen...

...half part thereof the whole into two equal parts to be divided in Trust for the said Ann Wright and her assigns and during the term of her natural life and to the intent that she and they may hold and enjoy the same without impeachment of waste and from and after her decease in trust for all and every child and children of the said Ann Wright lawfully to be begotten to be divided between or amongst them...

...and I do hereby also direct and declare that in case the said Ann Wright and Rebecca Wright or either of them shall at any time or times after my decease without the previous consent in writing of the trustees or trustee being of this my will return or come into the said island of Jamaica single and without having been married then and in such case ... of them or her so returning single and without having been married or without such previous consent in writing of the trustees or trustee for the time being of this my will of and in my said real and personal estate hereinbefore devised and bequeathed respectively for their benefit as aforesaid shall be in trust for and shall go over to such person or persons as would by virtue of the trusts and limitations hereinbefore contained be entitled to such shares of my said real and personal estate respectively in case they the said Ann Wright and Rebecca Wright or such of them as shall so return as aforesaid were they virtually dead without issue of their or her bodies or body as aforesaid...

I hereby nominate and appoint the said John Chambers, John Pusey Wint, Jeremiah Snow and James Cross and the survivors and survivor of them and the Guardian and Guardians of the persons and person of the said Ann Wright and Rebecca Wright until they respectively attain the age of twenty one years or be married which shall first happen...

...And I direct my said executors to devise to the said Ann Wright and Rebecca Wright respectively as soon as conveniently may be after my decease true copies of this my last will and tes-

tament to the intent that they may be fully acquainted with the contents thereof and particularly the clause prohibiting their return to Jamaica under the circumstances aforesaid and I do hereby revoke all my former wills in witness thereof... To this my last will and testament contained in nine sheets of paper set my hand to the first eight sheets and to this ninth and last sheet thereof my hand and seal this twenty first day of February in the year of our Lord one thousand eight hundred and six.
Andrew Wright.

Select Bibliography

Arrizón, Alicia. "Race-ing Performativity through Transcultura-tion, Taste and the Mulata Body." *Theatre Research International* 27:2 (2002): 136-52.

Armstrong, Nancy. *Desire and Domestic Fiction: A Political History of the Novel.* Oxford: Oxford UP, 1995.

Bhabha, Homi. "Of mimicry and man: The ambivalence of colonial discourse" and "Signs taken for wonders: Questions of ambivalence and authority under a tree outside Delhi, May 1817." *The Location of Culture.* London and New York: Routledge, 1994.

Bost, Suzanne. *Mulattas and Mestizas: Representing Mixed Identities in the Americas, 1850-2000.* Athens, GA: U of Georgia P, 2003.

Braithwaite, Kamau. *The Development of Creole Society in Jamaica, 1770-1820.* Oxford: Clarendon P, 1971.

Campbell, Mavis Christine. *The Dynamics of Change in a Slave Society: A Sociopolitical History of the Free Coloreds of Jamaica, 1800-1865.* Rutherford, NJ: Fairleigh Dickinson UP, 1976.

Carey, Brycchan, Markman Ellis and Sara Salih, eds. *Discourses of Slavery and Abolition: Britain and its Colonies, 1760-1838.* Hampshire, NY: Palgrave Macmillan, 2004.

Coleman, Deirdre. "Janet Schaw and the Complexion of Empire." *Eighteenth-Century Studies* 36:2 (2003): 169-93.

Craton, Michael and James Walvin eds. *A Jamaican Plantation: The History of Worthy Park, 1670-1970.* London and New York: W.H. Allen, 1970.

Dabydeen, David. *Hogarth's Blacks: Images of Blacks in Eighteenth Century English Art.* Athens: U of Georgia P, 1987.

Ferguson, Moira. ed. *The Hart Sisters: Early African Caribbean Writers, Evangelicals, and Radicals.* Lincoln and London: U of Nebraska P, 1993.

Gallego, Mar. "On Which Side of the Colored Line? Multiple Liminality in 'Tragic Mulatto' and 'Passing' Novels." *Betwixt-and-Between: Essays in Liminal Geography.* Ed. Philip C. Sutton. Madrid, Spain: Gateway, 2002.

Gaspar, David Barry and Darlene Clark Hine, eds. *Beyond Bondage: Free Women of Color in the Americas.* Urbana: U of Illinois P, 2004.

Gordon, Shirley C. *God Almighty, Make Me Free: Christianity in Pre-Emancipation Jamaica.* Bloomington: Indiana UP, 1996.

Grégoire, Henri. *On the Cultural Achievements of Negroes.* Trans. Thomas Cassirer and Jean-François Brière. Amherst: U of Massachusetts P, 1996.

Hall, Douglass. *In Miserable Slavery: Thomas Thistlewood in Jamaica, 1750-86.* London: Macmillan, 1989.

Hartman, Saidiya V. *Scenes of Subjection: Terror, Slavery, and Self-Making in Nineteenth-Century America.* Oxford and New York: Oxford UP, 1997.

Henriques, Fernando. *Family and Colour in Jamaica.* Bristol, UK: Macgibbon and Kee, 1968.

Hill, Errol. *The Jamaican Stage 1655-1900: Profile of a Colonial Theatre.* Amherst: U of Massachusetts P, 1992.

Holgersson-Shorter, Helena. "Illegible Bodies and Illegitimate Texts: Paradigms of Mulatta Literature." Diss. U of California, Berkeley, 2001.

Imtiaz, Habib. "'Hel's Perfect Character' or The Blackamoor Maid in Early Modern English Drama: The Postcolonial Cultural History of a Dramatic Type." *LIT: Literature Interpretation Theory* 11:3 (2000): 277-304.

Jordan, Elaine. "Jane Austen Goes to the Seaside: *Sanditon*, English Identity and the 'West Indian' Schoolgirl." *The Postcolonial Jane Austen.* Eds. You-me Park and Rajeswari Sunder Rajan. London, England: Routledge, 2000.

Kriz, Kay Dian. "Marketing Mulatresses in the Paintings and Prints of Agostino Brunias." *The Global Eighteenth Century.* Ed. Felicity Nussbaum. Baltimore: Johns Hopkins UP, 2003.

Leslie, Kent Anderson. *Woman of Color, Daughter of Privilege: Amanda America Dickson 1849-1893.* Athens: U of Georgia P, 1996.

Midgley, Clare. *Women Against Slavery: The British Campaigns, 1780-1870.* London and New York: Routledge, 1992.

Monteith, Kathleen E.A. and Glen Richards, eds. *Jamaica in Slavery and Freedom: History, Heritage and Culture.* Kingston, Jamaica: U of the West Indies P, 2002.

Morrison, Toni. *Playing in the Dark: Whiteness and the Literary Imagination.* New York: Vintage, 1992.

Paton, Diana. *No bond but the law: Punishment, Race, and Gender in Jamaican State Formation, 1780-1870.* Durham: Duke UP, 2004.

Paton, Diana and Pamela Scully, eds. *Gender and Slave Emancipation in the Atlantic World.* Durham: Duke UP, 2005.

Pratt, Mary Louise. *Imperial Eyes: Travel Writing and Transculturation.* London and New York: Routledge, 1992.

Prince, Nancy. *A Black Woman's Odyssey Through Russia and Jamaica: The Narratives of Nancy Prince*. Intro. by Ronald G. Walter. New York: M. Wiener, 1990.

Raimon, Eve Allegra. *The "Tragic Mulatta" Revisited: Race and Nationalism in Nineteenth-Century Antislavery Fiction*. Rutgers: Rutgers UP, 2004.

Ramchand, Kenneth. *The West Indian Novel and its Background*. Second ed. London; Kingston; Port of Spain: Heinemann, 1983.

Roach, Joseph. *Cities of the Dead*. New York: Columbia UP, 1996.

Sansay, Leonora Mary Hassal. *Secret History, or, The Horrors of St. Domingo*. Philadelphia: Bradford & Inskeep; R. Carr, Printer, 1808. Reprinted 1971.

Seacole, Mary. *Wonderful Adventures of Mrs. Seacole in Many Lands*. Ed. Sara Salih. London: Penguin, 2005.

Sharpe, Jenny. *Ghosts of Slavery: A Literary Archaeology of Black Women's Lives*. Minneapolis and London: U of Minnesota P, 2003.

——. *Allegories of Empire: The Figure of Woman in the Colonial Text*. Minneapolis and London: U of Minnesota P, 1993.

Shepherd, T.B. *Methodism and the Literature of the Eighteenth Century*. New York: Haskell House, 1966.

Shepherd, Verene A., ed. *Women in Caribbean History*. Jamaica: Ian Randle, 1999.

Sollors, Werner. *Neither Black Nor White Yet Both: Thematic Exploration of Interracial Literature*. Cambridge: Harvard UP, 1999.

Stallybrass, Peter and Allon White. *The Politics and Poetics of Transgression*. Ithaca: Cornell UP, 1986.

Sutherland, Wendy-Lou Hilary. "Staging Blackness: Race, Aesthetics and the Black Female in Two Eighteenth-Century German Dramas: Ernst Lorenz Rathlef's 'Die Mohrinn zu Hamburg' (1775) and Karl Friedrich Wilhelm Ziegler's 'Die Mohrinn' (1801)." Diss. U of Pennsylvania, 2002.

——. "Black Skin, White Skin and the Aesthetics of the Female Body in Karl Friedrich Wilhelm Ziegler's *Die Mohrinn*." *Colors 1800/1900/2000: Signs of Ethnic Difference*. Ed. Birgit Tautz. Amsterdam: Rodopi, 2004.

Tobin, Beth Fowkes. *Picturing Imperial Power: Colonial Subjects in Eighteenth-Century British Painting*. Durham and London: Duke UP, 1999.

Wesley, John. *Thoughts Upon Slavery*. London: printed by R. Hawes, 1774.

Winer, Lise. (Ed.) *Adolphus, A Tale (Anonymous) & The Slave Son (Mrs. William Noy Wilkins)*. Kingston, Jamaica: U of the West Indies P. With Introduction and annotations by Bridget Brereton, Rhonda Cobham, Mary Rimmer, Karen Sanchez-Eppler, and Lise Winer, 2003.

Woodard, Helena. *African-British Writings in the Eighteenth Century: The Politics of Race and Reason*. Greenwood P, 1999.

Young, Robert. *Colonial Desire: Hybridity in Theory, Culture and Race*. London and New York: Routledge, 1995.

Zackodnik, Teresa C. *The Mulatta and the Politics of Race*. Jackson, MS: UP of Mississippi, 2004.